ADVANCE PRAISE FOR *THE BLACKWOODS*

"Brandy Colbert delivers yet again with a whip-smart look at gender, Blackness, aspiration, and what the Hollywood machine has historically given and taken from performers of color. *The Blackwoods* is a story about the messiness of family and the burdens and triumphs of carrying the legacy of Black excellence. As a family, the Blackwoods are so tenderly drawn and beautifully human, I found myself wishing I could spend even longer with them well after I'd turned the final page."

—**Christina Hammonds Reed**, *New York Times*
bestselling author of *The Black Kids*

"A gorgeously layered, expansive, and emotionally generous page-turner, *The Blackwoods* made me think about fame and family and legacy in ways I never had before. To put it simply, it swept me off my feet."

—**Nina LaCour**, author of the Michael L. Printz
Award winner *We Are Okay*

"Wholly absorbing and meticulously researched. I was captivated from page one by this multigenerational story of Black Hollywood royalty. You will fall in love with Blossom Blackwood, her ambitions, and her entire family."

—**Malinda Lo**, National Book Award–winning and *New York Times* bestselling author of *Last Night at the Telegraph Club*

"Bingeable as the best movies, this epic, beautifully written tale of one famous Hollywood family is Brandy Colbert at the top of her game. Full of secrets and lies, loss and love, history and destiny, *The Blackwoods* shines."

—**Laura Ruby**, National Book Award finalist and author
of *Thirteen Doorways, Wolves Behind Them All*

THE
BLACKWOODS

Also By
BRANDY COLBERT

Black Birds in the Sky:
The Story and Legacy of the 1921 Tulsa Race Massacre

The Voting Booth

The Revolution of Birdie Randolph

Finding Yvonne

Little & Lion

Pointe

THE
BLACKWOODS

BRANDY COLBERT

Balzer + Bray
An Imprint of HarperCollins*Publishers*

Balzer + Bray is an imprint of HarperCollins Publishers.

The Blackwoods
Copyright © 2023 by Brandy Colbert

Library of Congress Cataloging-in-Publication Data

Names: Colbert, Brandy, author.
Title: The Blackwoods / Brandy Colbert.
Description: First edition. | New York : Balzer + Bray, an imprint of
    HarperCollins Publishers, [2023] | Audience: Ages 14 up. | Audience: Grades
    10-12. | Summary: Told from multiple points of view, Ardith and Hollis
    Blackwood's lives are upended when their great-grandmother, legendary
    actress Blossom Blackwood, passes away, and family secrets emerge.
Identifiers: LCCN 2023000095 | ISBN 978-0-06-309159-7 (hardcover)
Subjects: CYAC: Families—Fiction. | Secrets—Fiction. | Fame—Fiction.
    | Actors and actresses—Fiction. | African Americans—Fiction.
Classification: LCC PZ7.C66998 Bl 2023 | DDC [Fic]—dc23
LC record available at https://lccn.loc.gov/2023000095

Typography by Corina Lupp
23 24 25 26 27 LBC 5 4 3 2 1
First Edition

For Black Hollywood:
those who were beloved, those who were forgotten,
and those who paved the way, no matter how small the role

THE BLACKWOOD FAMILY TREE

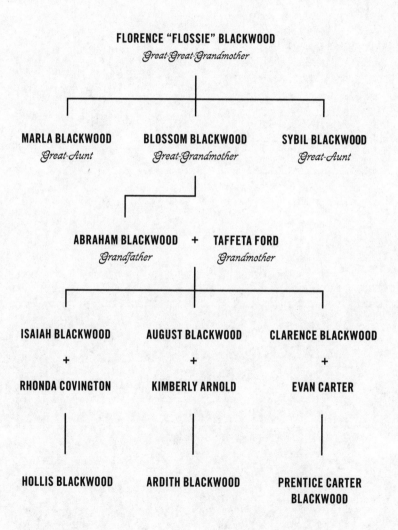

FLORENCE "FLOSSIE" BLACKWOOD
Great-Great-Grandmother

MARLA BLACKWOOD
Great-Aunt

BLOSSOM BLACKWOOD
Great-Grandmother

SYBIL BLACKWOOD
Great-Aunt

ABRAHAM BLACKWOOD + **TAFFETA FORD**
Grandfather   *Grandmother*

ISAIAH BLACKWOOD
+
RHONDA COVINGTON

AUGUST BLACKWOOD
+
KIMBERLY ARNOLD

CLARENCE BLACKWOOD
+
EVAN CARTER

HOLLIS BLACKWOOD

ARDITH BLACKWOOD

PRENTICE CARTER BLACKWOOD

A Celebration of Life

The memorial service could only be held at the home in Hancock Park.

There were several places in the city that had meant a lot to Blossom Blackwood—certain pockets of South Los Angeles, film studio lots in Hollywood and Burbank, her Baptist church in Inglewood. But the house in Hancock Park was symbolic—not only of her hard work and ability to persevere in a neighborhood that was never supposed to accept her, but of her family, who considered it a second home. And the only thing she'd loved more than the house was that family, now gathered under its roof and missing her desperately.

A week before, they had all come together—Blossom's son, her grandchildren, her great-grandchildren—for the cremation service at Forest Lawn, where their beloved Bebe's ashes were now entombed in a mausoleum. She'd made arrangements long ago to be laid to rest in the same place as some of the people she'd most admired: Dorothy Dandridge, Sam Cooke, Elizabeth Taylor, Spencer Tracy. And Nat King Cole, who'd integrated Hancock Park back in the 1940s, helping Blossom gain the courage to buy a home there decades later.

If Blossom hadn't reached the same heights of fame as those acting titans of her youth, she had certainly earned her spot among them. She was the sort of actor who had been widely known in the business as one of the most talented of her generation, though not the most celebrated. As recognizable for her acting as she was for her activism later in life, her career had spanned decades, encompassing dance, theater, film, and television work, and was marked by nominations for some of the most prestigious industry awards, including the Emmy statue she'd insisted on keeping next to the sugar bowl on her kitchen counter.

Now Blossom's daughter-in-law, Taffy, stood in that same kitchen, micromanaging the catering staff in her vintage violet-hued Chanel suit. Abraham Blackwood, her husband and Blossom's only child, sat upstairs on the edge of his mother's bed. He'd excused himself by saying he was simply staying out of Taffy's way; in truth, he wanted a moment of quiet, a bit of peace before the small group of people they'd invited came by to pay their respects. Abe picked up one of the pillows, squeezed it to his chest, and inhaled long and deep, knowing that soon the scents he'd always associated with his mother—lavender and rose water—would fade forever from her things.

Across the hallway, his adult son August was holed up in the guest room, furiously typing away on his phone. He knew better than anyone that he shouldn't be answering emails on this day of all days, but work didn't stop just because there had been a death in the family—even if the internationally known star who had passed on was the reason August, an entertainment lawyer, had emails to answer at all. But August's younger brother, Clarence, was nobody's fool; he didn't bother knocking before turning the knob of the door, poking his head in as August hit send on the first email. August looked up with surprise and then shame as Clarence pointedly stared at the phone and told him the guests would be arriving in a few minutes.

Their eldest brother, Isaiah, was in his favorite hiding place, behind the shed in the backyard, with a joint he'd rolled that morning. This spot wasn't exactly a secret; everyone, including his wife, teenage daughter, and even Bebe, knew he liked to smoke weed there, usually before meals and often afterward, too. He knew he wasn't fooling anyone—especially not his mother, Taffy, who always made a big show of sniffing the air loudly when he entered the house, reeking of pot—but he'd been doing it too long to stop now. Besides, Bebe might not have encouraged it, but she didn't mind it, either, and it was still her house, as far as Isaiah was concerned.

Isaiah's wife and Clarence's husband had just left together for one last run to the store to pick up ice and toilet paper, slipping through the trio of teenagers who sat on the front porch: Bebe's great-grandchildren. This wasn't the first time they'd experienced a death in the family, but it was the first one the cousins would be old enough to process as it was happening, from the phone calls informing them Bebe had passed in her sleep to the private funeral in Glendale last week to this moment, finally saying goodbye.

Prentice leaned back on his elbows, eyes lasered to his phone screen. Ardith sat in the middle, head hanging low, brushing tears from her eyes before they could drop to her lap. On the other side of her, Hollis squeezed Ardith's shoulder, then drew her cousin into her arms as Ardith's sniffles deepened into sobs. Hollis glared over Ardith's head until Prentice felt the heat of her gaze and slowly set his phone down. He wasn't all that great at comforting people, but he patted his hand up and down Ardith's arm anyway. Everyone knew Ardith and Bebe had been the best of friends.

Memories of Blossom would linger for each of the Blackwoods in the coming days, weeks, months. Some of them would be expected—thoughts of her cooking, of course, or the warmth with which she greeted everyone who stepped across the threshold of her home. Some would sneak up on them, such as the fact that there was no longer anyone to put Taffy in her place, or how it felt like there was an anchor missing when they gathered at the house in Hancock Park, unmooring everyone, everything.

Her soul may have been at rest, but Blossom Blackwood would continue to live with the family long after she was gone, in ways they never could have imagined. And, once exposed, the secret she'd kept for nearly seventy years would stir up drama worthy of a Hollywood star who'd never quite gotten her due.

PART ONE

*Waiting in
the Wings*

Hollis

Hollis Blackwood hadn't understood the meaning of fame when she was a little girl—not truly. She'd noticed that, sometimes, people she didn't know would do a double take when they pulled up next to her family's car at a stoplight, or start whispering to each other when her father was picking up a prescription from the pharmacy or choosing steaks at the Gelson's meat counter. The fifth time a stranger had approached their table at a restaurant, asking for a picture as they were digging into their entrees, she remembered wondering why people were so interested in her family in particular. Even at six years old, Hollis suspected that not *everyone* could know Isaiah Blackwood made the best chocolate chip pancakes on the planet. She'd been sitting in her car seat in the back, on their way home from dinner, when she'd blurted, "Why do people care so much about Dad?" Her parents loved to tell the story to anyone who would listen. The punch line was that they were driving past a billboard for one of her father's new movies, his supersize face grinning out over West Hollywood.

By the time she was in fourth grade, though, Hollis had completely understood what fame meant. It meant that when people walked up to her father in public, even when he was having a bad day, he would still give them a big smile and pose for a selfie. It meant that, when the release of one of her father's movies was approaching, her parents would begin leaving her with Grandpa Abe and Taffy when they went out, so they could shield her from the ever-lurking paparazzi. It meant that, despite her parents' best efforts, Hollis herself was considered interesting enough for the gossip blogs to post the occasional photo or quick write-up, simply by virtue of being a Blackwood.

Today, however, was not about her or her parents—it was all about her great-grandmother. And as she observed all the people who had come together to remember Bebe, Hollis was overwhelmed, just as she had been when she was a little girl, by what fame meant. At ninety-six years old, Bebe had lived longer than many people in her generation, including her Hollywood peers, so there weren't many of her contemporaries in attendance. Even the sisters she'd so deeply loved had each passed on before her: Marla from natural causes twelve years before, and Sybil eight years ago, from a stroke. But Blossom Blackwood had made such an impact on just about everyone she'd met—and so many she hadn't—that her family had been forced to trim the memorial's guest list down to only a couple dozen people, for both privacy and security concerns. They were there because they all loved her, each in their own way, and it was clearly a celebration of life, just as Grandpa Abe had promised. The speakers he'd had installed throughout Bebe's home a few years ago were playing jazz, the big, brassy kind that his mother had so loved.

Hollis walked down from the second floor, trying not to draw too much attention to herself as she looked for her cousins. She passed a group of movie producers gathered at the base of the stairs in the foyer, holding glasses of dark liquor; Hollis, like most people, might not have even known their names—or the power they held in Hollywood—except for the fact that they were old friends of Bebe's. They were a stark contrast to the guests she spotted through the doorway on the other side of them, a line of people Bebe had gone to church with. Dressed in their Sunday finery for the occasion, they were gathered in front of the warming trays placed on the dining room table, their eyes darting around as they took in their lavish surroundings. Grandpa Abe was standing by the front door, greeting two people she recognized as the stars of *The Incumbent*, the HBO political drama Bebe had guest-starred on for a couple of seasons back in the early 2000s. Hollis smiled when anyone made eye contact, but she didn't stop to speak with them. She wasn't in the mood to make small talk with strangers on most days, but especially not today. As nice as it was to see so many people celebrating Bebe, she couldn't help wondering how many of them were actually there for her great-grandmother and how many were more interested in being seen.

She attempted to glide through the living room unnoticed, but before she could make it to the other side, Taffy called out to her from the fireplace. Hollis stifled a sigh and made a detour to her grandmother, whose sharp brown eyes were already roaming up and down Hollis's knee-length lavender dress. They'd all been asked to wear something purple, which had been Bebe's favorite color, but from the way Taffy was looking at her, you'd think she had come in sweatpants.

"Yes, Taffy?"

Even when Taffy wasn't posing, she looked as if she was ready for a photograph, her posture perfectly straight and angled—an instinct left over from her modeling days.

"How are you doing?" Taffy asked, her gaze lingering on Hollis's chest.

Hollis glanced down, wondering if she'd chosen the wrong dress. It looked okay to her, but maybe her perspective was off so soon after her surgery. She was still getting used to how she looked and felt after the breast reduction.

"I'm fine, Taffy," she said, her neck feeling hot. "How are you?"

"I'm managing. Have you seen your cousin?"

It was clear to Hollis, from the exasperation in Taffy's voice, that she was talking about Ardith. She would never dare speak of her beloved Prentice that way. Hollis wondered if Taffy even cared at this point that her grandchildren noticed the way she played favorites. "No, I was actually just going to look for her."

"She should be in here, mingling."

Hollis took a deep breath so she wouldn't roll her eyes instead and said, "This is a memorial, not a film premiere."

"It's a celebration of Bebe's life," Taffy said, holding up the glass of white wine in her hand. "And she's the one carrying Bebe's legacy into the future. What does it look like if she spends the whole time hiding out with you?"

"It probably looks like she's grieving, Taffy," Hollis said evenly. "Which she is. Why would she need to mingle?"

Taffy leaned in closer and lowered her voice. "Because in case you haven't noticed, there are some important industry people here. It's an *opportunity*. I'm looking out for her."

Hollis blinked. Never mind that Ardith was currently a series regular on a hit show that had just been renewed for its second *and* third seasons. Taffy was always this hard on Ardith—especially when Ardith's career was in a place where her choices reflected on the family.

When Hollis didn't respond, Taffy pursed her lips and said, "Please send her my way when you find her."

Hollis turned away and finally allowed herself to roll her eyes. She would do nothing of the sort. Taffy was the last thing Ardith needed to worry about today.

Hollis nodded at one of the staff watching the side door that led to the back patio—which, mercifully, was not part of the gathering—and slipped outside, relishing the quiet that followed. She stopped to close her eyes and take a deep breath. If she was still this shaken by the fact that Bebe was nowhere to be found in the house that had been like a second home to them all, there was no way Ardith was taking this well.

Hollis found her cousins sitting at a wrought-iron table not far from the pool. Prentice's chin was in his hands, shirtsleeves rolled up and elbows planted on the table. Ardith was curled back into her seat, looking as if she wished she could disappear.

"I thought it had finally sunk in when we were at Forest Lawn, but I woke up feeling even worse today," she said, toying with the crumpled tissue in her hand. "Like, this is the *real* goodbye, you know?"

Those were the most words she'd said all day, and Hollis noticed how her voice sounded uncharacteristically croaky. "Yeah, I know," she responded, and her cousin gave her a small, sad smile.

Though Ardith's career meant that Hollis didn't see her as much as she used to, her cousin was still her closest confidant in the family. The two of them were born less than a year apart, and they'd been spending time together at least once a week since they were babies, thanks to Bebe's No-Excuses Saturday Breakfasts. Hollis was used to being part of a Hollywood family by the time Ardith's acting career had begun to take off, but it was still strange to see her cousin's red carpet photos in her news feed, or read a *Variety* article naming Ardith one of the most talented teen actors of the moment. She'd landed the role of Tinsley on *You Can Say That Again* when she was only eight years old, catapulting her to early fame. While there had been a brief lull in her career when that sitcom finally came to an end, the Blackwood name meant that she continued to book auditions—and, though that name would get her into any casting room in Hollywood, her talent was what ensured her star would only continue to rise.

At times like this, though, when Ardith's dress was wrinkled from sweat, her face wasn't made up for television, and her naturally reddish-brown hair was pulled into a simple Afro puff, Hollis thought she looked like any seventeen-year-old you might pass on the street.

"If I hear one more person from Swanson Avenue tell me Bebe's in heaven watching over us now, I'm gonna lose my shit," Prentice grumbled.

At fifteen, he was the youngest cousin and yet, somehow, the most jaded. "It's so clichéd."

"It's not clichéd if it's what people believe," Ardith countered. She and Bebe were the only religious members of the family, their regular attendance at Swanson Avenue Baptist Church bonding them in a way that no one else understood. Hollis couldn't decide how she felt about the concept of religion, switching from agnostic to atheist and back again. She and Prentice had visited Swanson Avenue a handful of times, but it had been six years since they'd sat in one of those church pews, for Ardith's baptism. Though their views on religion all differed, Ardith had never seemed to judge their beliefs—or lack thereof.

"Oh. Right. Sorry." Prentice bit his lip and began scrolling on his phone.

Ardith didn't look annoyed. "No, I get it," she said. "Some of the congregation can be pretty intense. You should see some of the cards they've given me today." When Prentice didn't respond, she frowned at him. "For real, though, could you stay off your phone for, like, one minute?"

"Could you stop acting forty-five for, like, a second?" he muttered. But then his eyes widened, and he held the phone away from his face, then close again, as if he couldn't quite believe what he was seeing. "You have got to be fucking kidding me."

"What?" Hollis asked, the low level of dread she'd felt all day beginning to rise up in her chest. Things had gone a little too smoothly. So far, there had been no paparazzi outside of the house, which was a minor miracle, as far as she was concerned. No matter how private an event was kept, someone outside the family always managed to leak the location. She hadn't missed the blurry photos of them at Forest Lawn printed on the front page of the tabloids just days earlier, one with the headline BLACKWOODS SAY BYE-BYE TO BLOSSOM. Her stomach turned over again just thinking about it.

"Some asshole is talking about Bebe."

"What are they saying?" Ardith asked. But Prentice ignored her, eyes glued to his screen.

When he didn't answer after another moment, Hollis grumbled, then swiped the phone from him.

"Hey!" he protested, trying to grab it back, but Hollis was too quick. She jumped up and walked a couple of feet away, looking at the gossip blog pulled up on her cousin's phone.

It was an especially cheap-looking website she'd never heard of, and, as Prentice had said, the article was all about Bebe's death and the rumor that there was a private memorial gathering today to honor her. But it was what she read a few lines down that must have caught Prentice's attention.

The site had decided to dig up the subject of who Grandpa Abe's father was—something Bebe had never revealed to the public or her family. Not even to Grandpa Abe himself. The question was nothing new; hardly a year went by that one of the Blackwoods wasn't asked about it in an interview, or an article that mentioned Bebe decided to speculate on the subject. But Hollis's hands squeezed tight around the phone as she looked at the way this blog was writing about her great-grandmother's choice:

Looks like the identity of Abraham Blackwood's father will remain an unsolved Hollywood mystery. Whatever it was that Blossom Blackwood was so determined to hide, the Oscar-nominated actress took it straight to her grave.

Whatever Blossom Blackwood was so determined to hide—what was that supposed to mean? Hollis had seen enough tasteless headlines and articles about her family that it wasn't surprising someone would write this about Bebe. But to imply her great-grandmother was trying to keep some deep, dark secret instead of simply protecting her privacy, and to do so on the day they were celebrating her life—well, it was low even for a blog like this.

Hollis had drifted so far into her thoughts that she didn't notice Prentice had crept up behind her until he snatched the phone back. He returned to his seat with a smirk.

"What is it?" asked Ardith again, now clearly frustrated with both of them.

"They're just talking about Grandpa Abe's dad," Hollis said, pushing a stray loc behind her ear. No need for her cousin to get upset about this, too.

Ardith shook her head. "Ah."

"It's fucking gross, but . . ." Hollis spread her arms wide as if to say, *Comes with the territory.* She glanced at Prentice, hoping he would take her cue to drop it.

But when Prentice spoke, it was clear that same line in the article was bugging him, as well. "Why do you think Bebe never told anyone about Grandpa Abe's dad?"

Ardith groaned. "Not you, too."

"Maybe because it's not anyone's business?" Hollis said. "Besides hers? And maybe Grandpa Abe's? Come on, Prentice."

"Yeah, but Grandpa Abe was born, like, a million years ago," he pressed. "If it wasn't a big deal, she could have just told someone, and then everyone would stop asking about it all the time."

"That's not how it works," Ardith said quietly.

"Yeah," Hollis agreed, trying once more to end the conversation. "And maybe it was just something Bebe didn't want to talk about, for whatever reason. I don't know, maybe he was abusive, or an addict, or—" She stopped abruptly, looking at Ardith again. "Sorry. Not that being an addict is bad, I just meant—"

"Hollis, it's fine," Ardith said. "I know what you meant."

And her cousin didn't look upset, but Hollis felt her cheeks heat with embarrassment. All these years after Ardith's mom's death, and Hollis still didn't quite know how to navigate that topic.

"Okay, but for real," Prentice said, leaning toward Ardith. "You were closer with Bebe than anyone. She really never told you anything about this guy, whoever he was?"

Hollis's mouth dropped open. "Prentice, I swear to god—"

"No, she didn't," Ardith said firmly, and her cousins fell silent. "But she did always tell me that it doesn't matter how much of yourself you give, it's never going to be enough for some people. And that if you don't give them what they want, they'll probably just make up something anyway. She told me we have to go on living our lives the best we can even when that happens, because there's nothing we can do about it." She paused, then softly repeated, "Nothing."

No one spoke for a moment. Prentice shifted awkwardly in his chair.

"I'd better go inside," Ardith said, wiping underneath her eyelids with the edge of her pinkie to catch the smeared mascara.

Hollis took a breath, wondering what it must be like to not have to discuss public musings about your family's private life anytime something important happened. "Careful. Taffy is looking for you. She thinks you should be *mingling*."

"That's why I'm going inside."

"Seriously? To 'network'?"

"Of course not." Ardith pushed her chair back from the table with a loud scrape. "I'm going to talk to all the people from church instead. Just like Bebe would."

Hollis grinned. Taffy may have been hardest on her, but Ardith knew better than anyone exactly how to piss her off.

When the food had all been picked over and the last few stragglers had made their way out the door, Hollis's parents invited the family back to their home to keep the celebration going. Her father, Isaiah, wanted them all to watch one of Bebe's films to close out the day. He said this with heavy-lidded eyes after polishing off his second piece of one of the church ladies' pies.

"Couldn't we just watch it here?" Uncle Clarence asked. "We haven't packed up her things yet."

"Come on, man. You know it'll be better at our place."

Hollis closed her eyes just as her uncle rolled his. Her father was obnoxious about their home theater. He always referred to it as his *screening room*, and he refused to watch movies on a regular TV or laptop like a normal person.

"Darling, that's a lovely idea, but your father and I are going to head home," Taffy said, resting a manicured hand on Isaiah's shoulder. "Perhaps we can do it again soon."

Grandpa Abe nodded from across the room. He was sitting in the flowered armchair, looking exhausted. "Sorry, son. It's been a long few weeks."

"Of course, you guys. I get it." Hollis's dad reached up to squeeze his mother's hand as he looked around the rest of the room. His eyes landed on August. "How about it?"

Uncle August shook his head. "I'm out, too. I have to put in some serious hours before Monday on this contract."

"Looked to me like you already put in some serious hours today," Clarence murmured. His husband, Evan, nudged him in the ribs.

"August, is that true?" Taffy asked with a frown.

His silence was her answer. He at least had the good sense to look guilty.

Taffy sighed. "How could you do that? Look at your father, how important today was to him. You—"

"I'm sorry," Uncle August said, throwing his hands in the air. "I didn't mean to disrespect anyone. But maybe some of you have forgotten, I actually go into an office every day."

"Oh, now I don't work because I don't sit behind a desk and push contracts around?" Isaiah said, even though his brother hadn't been looking at him as he spoke.

"I didn't say that, Isaiah. What I'm saying is, I don't have the luxury of making my own hours. I took time off last week for the funeral, I took time off today. I guess you've also forgotten I'm working out Bebe's estate? I'm sorry my schedule doesn't fit into your artist's lifestyle."

"You selfish—" Hollis's father began, but he was interrupted by Grandpa Abe, who stood up and commanded in a loud, booming voice, "That's enough!"

The room went completely silent. Hollis, Ardith, and Prentice exchanged looks from the love seat they had all crammed onto. Grandpa Abe rarely raised his voice.

"This day is about Mama," he continued. "Shame on you for fighting. Shame on you for being anything other than kind to each other on a day when we're celebrating what she meant to us." Grandpa Abe made eye contact with each of his children before he began walking toward the foyer. "Taffy, I'm ready."

Isaiah and his brothers went after their father, apologizing over one another as they followed him to the front door. Taffy stood in the center of the room with her hands on her hips and blew air from the side of her mouth. "I swear, sometimes they're more immature than their own children."

Hollis wasn't sure if Taffy had meant for them to hear her, and she was too tired to point out that they had. She felt Ardith bristle next to her.

"Want to ride over with us?" Hollis whispered to her cousin, hoping she hadn't changed her mind about coming now, too.

"Yes, please," Ardith whispered back, her eyes grateful.

The ride back to Pasadena was, thankfully, uneventful. Hollis's mother drove while her father spent the ride staring out the passenger window, the cool evening breeze gliding over his face. Hollis was glad to have Ardith next to her, though her cousin seemed even sadder than before.

When they were home, the two went straight upstairs to Hollis's room, where Hollis pulled out her favorite yoga pants and hoodie, and let Ardith grab something for herself. It felt good to change out of their dresses; lighter somehow, as if they were shedding the weight of the past few weeks. Ardith went to the bathroom, and Hollis lingered in front of the full-length mirror, staring at herself. She'd been afraid to look too long in the days immediately after her surgery. Her chest had been all bandaged up, and she was worried she'd made a huge mistake going through with the breast reduction. But now the bandages were off and she was almost completely healed, just in time for the first day of her senior year on Monday. And looking at her new self, she was glad she'd had the surgery. Her surgeon had promised it would help with the back pain she had noticed increasing over the years, and for the first time since she was twelve, she'd be able to wear clothes that hugged her body without covering her chest in shame.

The bathroom door opened, and Ardith emerged wearing Hollis's mother's old Spelman T-shirt. Being up here with her cousin reminded Hollis of the sleepovers they used to have when they were younger, when Ardith would often spend a weekend—or, sometimes, longer than that—with them. Aunt Kimberly had been in and out of rehab back then, so Hollis's parents had offered to let Ardith stay with them whenever they'd needed it. They'd needed it a lot during Aunt Kimberly's last few years, but Hollis wouldn't have wanted it any other way. It felt like having a sister, and even though Ardith had been working on *You Can Say That Again*, she was still very much a little kid who loved ballet class and playing video games and debating the merits of her American Girl doll versus Hollis's. They didn't get to see each other as much now that they were older and Ardith was working more, but when they did spend time together, Hollis was relieved that Ardith was still the same cousin and friend she'd always been.

"You go back to school on Monday, right?" Ardith asked, her folded dress tucked under her arm.

"Yeah." Hollis paused, leaning against the doorway of her walk-in closet. "I'm nervous people are going to notice, but is it weird that I'm also worried they *won't* notice?"

Ardith perched on the edge of the bed. "Are you still glad you did it?"

"For sure. It's different, but not in a bad way. Just, like, a new and improved me, I guess."

Ardith smiled. "Definitely. And are you and Dwayne . . . ?"

"I don't . . . I don't know." Hollis swallowed, her mouth suddenly dry. Every time she thought of what had happened with her and Dwayne, she felt like it had all been a dream. She'd wondered if things would just go back to normal after that night. But when he'd stopped by to check on her a few days after her surgery, she'd been surprised to feel a persistent flutter low in her belly. Nothing about Dwayne had changed, but she couldn't deny the new energy that pulsed between them. "We've been texting, and everything seems like it's the same, but it's obviously not."

"Do you want it to be the same?"

"Maybe?"

"Well, I like Dwayne," Ardith said. "And you guys could be a total power couple."

Hollis raised an eyebrow. "What do you mean?"

"Uh, a Lipscomb dating a Blackwood? People would eat that up."

"No way. Who am I? The only thing people know me for is my name."

"Um, yeah? That's, like, most famous people these days."

"Well, Dwayne is more than his name. He's going to be pro in two years, no doubt."

Hollis's best friend was the son of Kenley Lipscomb, a two-time NBA

19

All-Star whose decades-long career had finally come to a close last year when he retired from the Clippers. But Dwayne had only ever known his father as someone who showed up on ESPN more often than he did at the dinner table. Dwayne knew what it meant to be part of a family like theirs, to be someone people already had opinions about before they'd even met you, but he was also an all-American basketball player whom colleges had been scouting since he was in middle school. Hollis didn't have any aspirations to go into the industry—not even an industry-adjacent role like Uncle August, who was an entertainment attorney—but Dwayne had been preparing to go into the family business since they were in elementary school.

"You're more than your name, too, Holl. All I'm saying is you would be cute together. And you're lucky you get to be around people our age all the time." Ardith sighed, tracing her finger along the pink linen duvet. "I spend about ninety percent of my life with adults."

"You could always take a break and go back to acting in a few years."

"What's the point? I know my set teacher better than any of the teachers at my actual school."

"Yeah, and you have another whole two years of high school to change that if you want. And then college. Actors do that all the time. You can go to Yale or Harvard or wherever and then come back."

Ardith looked as if she were pondering this idea, but she shook her head. "I'm already signed on to the next couple of seasons of the show, and . . . I guess I don't really want to leave acting, you know? Not even for a little while. Sometimes it sounds amazing to just go be a regular person who'll get a regular job someday, but I feel sick if I think about it too long."

"So you were born to do it. You just need to make more actor friends your age."

Ardith stared at her.

"Okaaaay. Church friends?"

"Maybe. There aren't that many people there our age, either. Not who I want to be around." Ardith shrugged. "I guess I don't mind spending so much time with people older than me because I always love being at work so much. Like father, like daughter."

"God, that whole thing with our dads was pretty intense." Hollis bent to pick up her dress from the floor. "I can't believe after all that, he still didn't come."

"I can. That would mean actually caring about something besides the law firm." Ardith leaned back on her elbows. "I'm pretty sure his last day off was for my mom's funeral. Eight years ago."

"Wait, what about that time Grandpa Abe made him come to Hawaii with everyone?"

"Okay, yeah, but not since then. And that was still, like, six years ago. And you shouldn't have to be forced to hang out with your family. We're all busy, and we still make time."

Hollis remembered sometimes Ardith would have her bag all packed up after the weekend, ready to go home, only for Uncle August to call and ask if she could stay another night or two or three. Hollis had always been happy to have her cousin around, but she also knew that Uncle August throwing himself completely into work after Aunt Kimberly died had hurt Ardith, even if she acted like it didn't.

"Can you talk to him about it?"

"It's not worth it. You saw him tonight. He just freaks out and shuts down. Says he's trying to provide a good life for us. But that doesn't really mean as much when I've been working since I was a baby. I could support both of us if I had to."

"Maybe Grandpa Abe can talk to him when he cools down a little?"

"Eh, it's okay. If he didn't want to work so much, he wouldn't. How much more money do we need?" Ardith paused. "Besides, I'll probably get my own place next year, anyway. Then we'll really never see each other." She cracked a smile, but it disappeared so quickly, Hollis almost missed it.

Once everyone was settled into the leather recliners and plush couches of the screening room, Hollis's dad rose and turned to face them, holding up the *Love, Gertie* Blu-ray case, Bebe's face staring back at them, radiant. Ardith came to stand by his side, hands clasped behind her back.

"Thanks for ending the day with us," Isaiah began, looking out at Hollis, her mother, and Prentice and his dads. The room felt cozy, but Hollis could tell he wished the whole family were there. "I talked to Dad, and he agreed that *Love, Gertie* was the best choice for tonight. This was Bebe's very first leading role. She was in her mid-thirties when she filmed it back in 1961, but she didn't look a day over twenty."

"She always said how proud she was of this film in particular," Ardith continued, making eye contact with each person in the room. "She said she had almost given up on ever making it in the movies, and then this role came along. Now, without further ado, we present to you *Love, Gertie.*" Ardith spread her arms wide as if her uncle were about to perform a magic trick. Then she took her seat at the back of the room next to Hollis, and a few seconds later, the movie began.

Tears sprang to Hollis's eyes when the opening credits started and Bebe's name flashed across the screen. Blossom Blackwood was a name that seemed made for the movies. The film had been shot in black and white, and Hollis sometimes felt that it dampened Bebe's beauty, muting the richness of her deep brown skin and coffee-colored eyes. But tonight, all she could think about was how stunning Bebe looked, even in shades of gray.

When her favorite scene in the film started, Hollis leaned forward, elbows on her knees. Perched on the steps of a fire escape, Bebe launched into a sentimental ballad called "Freddie Gone Overseas," about the love of her life, who was stationed abroad in France during World War I. Her voice was clear and powerful and filled with longing. Hollis closed her eyes to get the full effect. When she opened them, Bebe was singing the final notes, a single tear traveling down her perfectly angled cheek.

Hollis sat back in her seat with a small sigh. She looked to her right, where Prentice was staring at their great-grandmother, completely engrossed, and then to Ardith on her left, who was wiping fresh tears from her own eyes. In that moment, they had all realized just how special it was that they could still spend as much time with Bebe as they wanted, even if it was only through a screen.

Big Ideas

1942

By the time Blossom Blackwood was fifteen years old, she knew she wanted to be a performer.

Of course, she had already considered it for quite a while. Her big sister, Marla, would never let her forget the time she'd declared, at the age of six, that she was going to be "an actress in the pictures" someday. But nine years later, she knew for certain that she was going to do whatever it took to become a real entertainer. In whichever form it came.

Blossom remembered, years ago, her mother taking her and her sisters to see *Imitation of Life* at the Lincoln Theatre near their home in Los Angeles, how even though she'd been young, she hadn't been able to tear her gaze away from the heartfelt performances of Louise Beavers and Fredi Washington. She hadn't completely understood the story, and a part of her knew they were playing other people, that she wasn't actually getting a peek into the lives of real families. But she loved the drama of it all, the reality the actors created out of nothing—the impassioned dialogue, the tears that glistened in the actresses' eyes, the emotion that jumped right off the screen and into Blossom's soul. For nearly two hours, she sat mesmerized in the dark theater, forgetting about her real life with Mama and Marla and Sybil.

After that, she would practice monologues in the mirror, trying to imitate the theatrics she'd watched onscreen. Eventually, when Sybil was old enough to join in, Blossom began writing plays for the three of them, always assigning herself the lead and her sisters the supporting roles. This often meant giving up her share of the candy they were allowed to buy at the drugstore, but she didn't mind; the thrill of putting on a show in their tiny front yard was worth it. When spring arrived, they would gather the orange poppies that bloomed on a nearby hill and spread the petals in the outline of a makeshift stage. Their mother, Flossie, would dutifully watch every performance from the porch, a cigarette perched between her lips, and sometimes they'd even round up enough neighborhood kids to have a proper audience.

Once Blossom reached junior high, she began auditioning for the school plays, and each year, she earned a spot in the cast, grateful for even the tiniest role. Anytime she found herself in front of an audience, no matter how small, Blossom returned to that feeling she'd had in the theater, watching *Imitation of Life*: that performing was a temporary escape from the monotony of her everyday existence, a chance to experience what it was like to be someone else, even for a little while. And that was the closest thing she'd ever felt to magic.

Blossom knew better than to tell anyone about her dream. Mama had been a vaudeville performer when she was younger, before the girls were born. She'd gained a small amount of fame traveling the Black vaudeville circuit with an act called the Feldman Sisters, though she was neither a Feldman nor related to the two sisters she'd performed with. But whenever Mama spoke of those days, she never failed to mention how difficult they were, and Blossom knew her mother wouldn't like hearing she planned to enter a business that remained so unwelcoming to Negroes.

So, Blossom kept her hopes to herself, but she spent as much time as she could daydreaming about her future. Especially during her freshman year classes at Jefferson High. One day, her mind would send her traveling overseas to entertain the troops, like Pearl Bailey. The next afternoon, she would picture herself singing in nightclubs on the Sunset Strip, like Lena Horne.

"Psst, Blossom!"

She shook herself out of her current reverie, in which she'd somehow gone back in time to perform with the Dandridge Sisters at the Cotton Club, and looked up to find Pretty Michael staring at her from the next desk over.

Her cheeks grew warm. His nickname certainly fit him, with his rich brown skin and hazel eyes, even if he hadn't so much earned it as lucked into it, as Marla always said.

Blossom looked quickly to the front of the room; Miss Pearson was facing the blackboard, writing out algebraic equations with a thick piece of chalk.

"What?" she whispered back to Pretty Michael, leaning over just a little bit into the aisle.

"Whatcha thinking about?"

She frowned slightly. "What do you mean?"

"You totally staring off into space, girl. Like you ain't even on this planet."

Blossom sat up straight in her chair, as if that would convince him she'd been paying perfect attention to the lesson the entire period.

"Nothing important," she said with a small shrug.

"Sure." Pretty Michael winked at her, but before she could argue, he resumed copying down the equations from the board, intermittently twirling his pencil between his fingers.

A moment later, Blossom felt a sharp pinch on the back of her arm, and she turned to see Helen blinking meaningfully at her from behind her Harlequin eyeglasses. Helen's eyes traveled to Michael and then back to Blossom, and when she wiggled her eyebrows, Blossom shook her head and turned right back around.

Blossom was no fool. She had noticed how Pretty Michael had been looking at her since the beginning of the school year. As if she was different somehow. It was the same way all the girls had started looking at him in junior high the year before. Blossom was still short, or "tiny and small-boned," her mother said proudly, as if her size were something to be celebrated instead of simply taken as fact. But when it had become apparent she wasn't going to grow or transform in any evident way the summer before senior high school, Blossom decided to take matters into her own hands. She began wearing her hair in victory rolls, an intricate style that took her an extraordinarily long time to perfect. First, she had to wait for the hot comb to heat up on the stove, anxious as she thought of how close it would soon be to her skin. Then, she would sit perfectly still at the kitchen table while Mama or Marla took special care not to burn her neck or ears as the comb hissed and steamed its way through her thick locks, the smell of heat and hair grease filling their home. As Blossom worked on her freshly pressed hair, she let her imagination run wild, pretending she had finally made it as a famous actress in the pictures, like Fredi Washington, the glamorous colored woman who played Peola in *Imitation of Life*. She would twist and turn in the mirror, admiring herself from every possible angle, until her mother or Marla or Sybil fussed at her for spending so long staring at herself. But apparently, she wasn't the only one who liked what she saw.

When Blossom stepped out the front doors after the final bell, Pretty Michael was there, watching. He was alone today, which was unusual; he was always surrounded by friends, all of the boys who would flock to him, try to be the first one to make him laugh. Blossom nodded at him and began to make her way past, but he caught her elbow as she strode by.

She whirled around, looking down at where he was touching her and then up at him. "Yes?"

At her look, he let go of her arm. "Erm, I was wondering if I could walk you home today, Blossom?"

Though it had only been there for a couple of seconds, Blossom could still feel the warmth of his hand on her skin. She tried not to think about it as she said, "I can make it there by myself, thank you."

Michael laughed a bit, shifting his books to one arm. "Well, of course you can. But wouldn't you like some company?"

Blossom took a deep breath. Michael wasn't a stranger. They'd grown up around the corner from each other; their families had known one another since before she could remember. Perhaps no one would even think twice about them walking home next to each other. But something hung heavy in the air between them; something that told Blossom this wasn't just her old friend Michael asking to walk his old friend home.

"That would be fine," she said in her most demure voice, with a look she might have practiced in front of the mirror once or twice.

"'That would be fine,'" he teased her. She immediately flushed, but before she could tell him what she thought of him in that moment, he had scooped her books up with the armful of his own and they were on their way.

Michael wasn't just a pretty face. She'd almost forgotten how funny he could be. He told her a story from his English class, and when he widened his eyes and did a perfect impression of Mr. Johnson—*"If you didn't bother to open your book last night, I'll thank you to not to open your mouth today"*—Blossom fell into laughter. And not the polite giggle she used to sound more ladylike, but her *real* laugh, the one that came deep from her belly.

"So, you really weren't thinking about nothing earlier today?" Michael asked after she had caught her breath. "'Cause you was smiling real big."

"Aren't I allowed to be happy?"

"Not in the middle of an algebra lesson, you're not."

That made Blossom smile once again. "I was thinking of what I'm going to be doing when Jeff is just a distant memory," she said, cocking her head back in the direction of their school.

"But we got three more years there."

"Then I have plenty of time to plan," Blossom replied, and before she knew it, she'd said something to him that she hadn't said aloud since she was a little girl: "I'm going to be an entertainer."

Then it was his turn to burst into laughter—but Blossom's look quickly silenced it. "You serious?"

"Course I am. Why wouldn't I be?"

"I guess . . . Well, you were pretty good in *Our Town*—"

"Pretty good?" She'd only played one of the secondary characters, the town busybody, but she'd heard the audience reaction, felt their eyes on her every second of her time onstage.

"You were great," he said quickly, "but—"

"But what?" Blossom stopped, placing her hands on her hips.

Pretty Michael stopped, too. He slowly shrugged. "But do you really think you're the kind of girl who goes into that business, Blossom?"

"The business of making people happy?"

"No, it's just . . . Those people are different."

"Different from who?" The longer he spoke, the more Blossom could feel her pulse beginning to pound loud and heavy in her ears.

"You know. The people who be singing for white folks in clubs we couldn't even afford to go in. Wearing them skimpy little costumes, in front of all those strangers." He shook his head. "You ain't that kind of girl."

"First of all, Michael, you sound like your mother. Those costumes are part of the act. Dancers have to be able to move—you can't do that in some heavy skirt that goes down to your ankles. And performing isn't about who I am—it's about getting to be someone else entirely. Stepping into the shoes of a person I might never meet in real life, imagining what it's like to be them. Don't you know how exciting that is?" She squeezed her hands together. "Besides, some of the most talented Negroes in the whole world come to perform right here on Central Avenue. We're in the middle of it all—the Harlem of the West Coast."

Michael was still looking pensively at the ground. "I just don't know if you should start getting big ideas. My uncle says it ain't natural for women to be out in clubs like that. Or working on movie sets when they got babies at home."

"Well, my mama says I should think for myself, and that's exactly what I intend to do," Blossom said, leaning down to catch his eye. "Remember my mama? The one who used to work in that business you don't think I'm fit for? Those are real people up there performing. And they're doing real work. *Hard* work." She began walking again; Michael started up after her. "And we're only fifteen. I'm not worried about children who don't exist."

"Aw, don't be cross with me. I was just—"

"I can make it home from here. Alone." She held out her arms for her books.

Pretty Michael sighed. "Blossom . . ." he pleaded, his light eyes resting on her. Blossom couldn't tell from his expression whether he was frustrated or amused. And in that moment, she didn't care.

When she didn't respond or budge, he reluctantly slid the books back into her arms. And though they were headed in the same direction for most of the way home, Blossom marched several steps in front of him the entire time, never once turning around.

Michael gave Blossom a wide berth for the next few days—though, if he'd tried to talk to her, he wouldn't have succeeded. She refused to look at him in any of the three classes they had together; even in algebra, where they sat just a few feet apart, she kept her gaze focused directly on the blackboard. When she needed to hand a quiz to Helen, she made sure to pass it back over her left shoulder instead of her right. And when she accidentally knocked her pencil to the aisle one day, only for it to be hastily retrieved by Michael, she briskly thanked him without turning her head.

Blossom knew that perhaps she was being too hard on him. But he'd hurt her feelings, the way he'd laughed away her dreams and then tried to convince her there was something *immoral* about them. And, truth be told, she was annoyed with herself for being so foolish as to share them in the first place. Pretty Michael was a lot of things, but a dreamer he was not.

Once, back in fifth grade, the class had done an exercise where they wrote a one-page short story about the life they envisioned for themselves. Blossom had most enjoyed singing at the time, so she'd said she wanted to be a Broadway star, like the great Ethel Waters. Back then, she hadn't been so embarrassed. It felt like it was still acceptable at that age to dream, even if you were a girl, of a life that wasn't focused on finding a spouse and having children. Blossom didn't feel so odd when some of her classmates said they wanted to be doctors or fighter pilots, goals that weren't any less ambitious than singing and dancing across a New York City stage. Michael, however, had proudly stood and shared that he was going to procure a good job with the city, marry the prettiest girl in school, and have four or five children. Blossom remembered wrinkling her nose at how dull his dreams sounded—if you could even call them dreams.

A week after she'd stormed away from him on their walk home, Michael was waiting for her again on the front steps. But this time, he was standing directly in the center, hands clasped behind his back, so she couldn't miss him.

She attempted to ignore him and walk right by, but Michael stepped quickly to the side, blocking her path. When she tried to move the other way, he moved with her, and so they were doing a little dance for a moment, which made Michael laugh and Blossom groan with frustration.

Finally, she stopped and turned her glare on him, the first time she'd looked in his eyes since last week. "What do you want?"

"To apologize. For making you so cross at me that day. I didn't mean it, Blossom." And then, from behind his back, he pulled a single brilliant orange poppy. "For you."

Blossom looked from the flower to the hangdog expression on Michael's face, his eyes big and contrite. "Where did you find this?" She hadn't seen a poppy yet this season.

He didn't answer her question; when he spoke, his voice was so soft she had to lean in to hear him. "Say you'll forgive me."

Blossom ran her finger along the delicate edges of the petals, struck as ever by how such a vibrant hue could grow in nature, right there in Los Angeles. A boy had never given her anything before, and she never would have expected a romantic gesture like flowers from the ever-practical Michael. *A* flower, but even that made it more special, somehow.

Perhaps she was feeling generous, but she couldn't deny that it was harder to be upset with Michael than it was to get along with him. Perhaps the sun had something to do with it as well, the way the light shone down on him, making his skin glow golden-brown against the white of his shirt. Or, perhaps it was the beseeching way he'd asked her to forgive him, how it had made her knees go weak, just the tiniest bit.

"You can walk me home if you'd like," she said, and started off without him. Blossom smiled to herself at the sound of Michael's eager footsteps hurrying to catch up to her once he realized what she'd said.

And so Pretty Michael walked Blossom home every day for the rest of the school year. There wasn't a discussion about it, just as they never again discussed her aspirations. After all, it hadn't escaped Blossom that Michael never said he understood or supported what she'd said she wanted to do, just that he was sorry he'd upset her. But that was fine with Blossom. She and Michael had plenty to talk about on their walks—school, the war in Europe, their families.

One day, their conversation found its way to Blossom's father. "He ever come around?" Michael asked.

Blossom shook her head. "We've never known him."

"Not even when you were little?"

"Either he didn't want to come around or Mama didn't allow it. We don't know him."

Michael's thick eyebrows rose. "Not even Marla?"

"Not even Marla."

"You miss him?"

"It's a bit difficult to miss someone you haven't met." Blossom smoothed her palms down the front of her skirt as they walked. She was never quite sure what to do with her hands when Michael carried her books. She didn't always let him, but he always offered. "Do you miss yours?"

"Nah. My pops ain't treat my mama right. Better off without him."

"Oh." Blossom had known Michael and his mother lived alone in their house, and that his uncle had stepped in to help raise him, but she hadn't known anything about his father. "I suppose sometimes . . ."

He looked at her expectantly, as Blossom gathered the courage to say what she'd been thinking.

"I suppose sometimes I think maybe my sisters and I are lucky our daddy's not around. We get Mama all to ourselves. And it's so easy with the four of us, I can't imagine anyone else living in our house, complicating things."

"The Blackwood girls," Michael said, shaking his head with a smile.

"What about us?" Blossom hadn't meant for it to come out so sharply, but she got the feeling he was poking fun at them, and she wasn't sure why. Blackwood was her mother's family's name, the Blackwoods from Mississippi. Flossie had always been proud to pass her name down to her daughters; did Michael have a problem with that?

"Aw, nothing. Just never met anyone like y'all."

"Oh."

He cleared his throat and kept his gaze on the path ahead as he said,

"Especially you. You're . . ."

Blossom held her breath, near desperate for the words that lay on the tip of his tongue.

"You're one of a kind."

Blossom knew the power of speech; she felt it every time she watched a film and saw how the actors spoke with one another, how just the right word or phrasing could bring tears to their eyes or coax out a coquettish smile. But no one had ever spoken to her quite like that, until this afternoon. Blossom felt heat rising from the tips of her toes to the crown of her head. Those five words, simple as they were, made her happier than if Michael had presented her with an entire bouquet of orange poppies.

On their last day as freshmen, Blossom's friend Gladys hosted a small end-of-year party. The gathering was right after their last class, and both Blossom and Michael had been invited, so it only made sense for them to walk to Gladys's house together. Blossom had grown used to walking and talking with Michael, but today she felt different. For one, they were no longer freshmen. She didn't know about him, but she already felt more grown-up than when she'd walked in the front doors of Jeff that morning.

"My uncle says *sophomore* just means 'wise fool,'" Michael said as they strolled down a street lined with small, neat houses. "It's Greek."

"Your uncle seems to know a lot," Blossom said. Today, both their hands were free of books, and their arms dangled inches away from each other as they walked.

"He says it's important for colored folks to be educated. Even if we have to do it ourselves."

Blossom nodded. "Mama is always talking about our education. I suppose because she didn't get a proper one growing up."

Her mother liked that she and Marla went to Jefferson High, which had a large colored student body but was also populated with white, Asian, and Mexican kids. Flossie also appreciated that the school had a strong music program and celebrated the artistic and athletic talents of its students. Just a few years ago, Mr. Browne, the music teacher who'd graduated from Jeff himself, had been hired as the school's first Black educator, integrating the all-white faculty.

"Miss Flossie didn't go to school down South?"

"Her mama and daddy were sharecroppers in the Mississippi Delta, and she had to miss school to work the fields for most of the year."

"How'd she end up leaving?"

"Same as lots of other colored people who don't want to live under Jim Crow. She saved some money and took a train up North."

Michael looked at Blossom from the corner of his eye. "And that's when she started doing vaudeville?"

"Mm-hmm. When she left home, she joined an act with these two sisters, and they traveled all over the country. She thought maybe she'd be able to make it in Hollywood, so she eventually came out here." Blossom paused. "She played a maid in a movie once, but she couldn't find acting work after that. Then she had us."

"My mama said . . ." Michael paused for a moment, as if he wasn't sure he wanted to continue on. But he did. "My mama said Miss Flossie is real strong. Raising you and your sisters by herself."

"But Miss Rose is raising *you* by herself."

"There's only one of me, though. She says she'd have more to worry about if I were a girl. Let alone three girls."

Blossom didn't know if she agreed with that, and normally, she would have challenged him on it. But what Miss Rose had said about Blossom's mother—that she was strong—kept repeating over and over in her head. She was used to people having opinions about how her mother had chosen to raise her family, and they weren't usually full of praise. "Your mama said that about mine?"

Michael nodded. "She did. And she's right. Because . . . you're strong, too, Blossom. I like how you speak your mind to me, even when we're disagreeing. You have your own thoughts and opinions, and you're real smart, too."

The words came out in a rush, as if he had to say them as quickly as possible. They filled Blossom with pride, that Michael liked her for her. When she peeked at him, he was looking back at her. They smiled softly. She wasn't just imagining that something felt different between them. And now they were heading to a party and it was almost as if he were escorting her. Courting her. She quickly looked down at her saddle shoes, hoping he couldn't read her thoughts on her face.

Gladys lived in a little mint-green bungalow with a roof the color of terra-cotta. She greeted them at the door when they arrived, having changed into a different dress than the one she'd worn to school. The soft pink of the cotton frock was pretty against her deep brown skin.

"Hi, Blossom. Hi, Michael. Nice to see the two of you."

Blossom rolled her eyes, reading the smile that was plastered across Gladys's face.

"Hi, Gladys," Michael said, oblivious, as she held the door open wide. "Thanks for having us."

Once they were inside, where the party had already begun, Michael spotted some of his friends. "I'm going to say hi to William and Thomas," he said. Blossom nodded.

Gladys leaned in close as soon as Michael was out of earshot. "Is it true? Are you going steady with Pretty Michael?"

"I am not," Blossom responded. "We're just friends."

"You've been spending an awful lot of time together. Walking home from school every day?" Gladys's voice lowered to a whisper. "He carries your books!"

"Not all the time. And isn't that what friends do, Gladys? Spend time together?" Blossom looped her arm through her classmate's and said, "Now, show me that collection of race records you're always going on about."

Gladys's mother was home, but she didn't bother them. She stayed in her bedroom, where Gladys said she'd been spending the majority of her time ever since Gladys's brother, Charles, had been drafted and sent to Great Britain. Like most Negroes, he wasn't trusted to be a combat soldier—he did service work, such as unloading the many supplies that came in on trucks each day—but knowing how close he was to the fighting had nearly incapacitated their mother. Still, Gladys had evidently persuaded her to help with the food for the party, as there was a whole spread on the dining room table: deviled eggs, fried chicken, orange Jell-O salad, and even a cake with pink frosting.

"This looks so nice, Gladys," Blossom said, admiring the food.

Gladys looked at her shyly. "Mama did what she could to make it special."

The government had begun imposing rations that year, probably with more to come. Each family had received their first ration books just last month, to be used for sugar. Blossom had heard Mama complaining about how meager they were, so she knew Gladys's mother was generous to use her rations for a party that wasn't even feeding her family.

The boys and girls mostly gathered in separate groups, but Blossom flitted throughout the room. She and Gladys weren't best friends, but they were in the same larger circle of colored kids who saw one another outside of school, so she knew everyone there. Michael caught up with her at the food table, where he placed two deviled eggs on a napkin. He offered her one, and she took it, though she instantly regretted it. There was no delicate way to eat a deviled egg in front of a boy like Pretty Michael. She angled herself away from him and ate the egg in two quick bites, dabbing her mouth with the corner of a napkin.

"Blossom, do you have a minute?"

"Sure," she said.

Then, to her surprise, Michael gently took her by the hand and led her out of the dining room, through the kitchen, and into a little nook by the back door. Blossom's heart thumped fast and heavy. She had never even touched a boy for this long, let alone held one's hand. Michael's fingers wrapped confidently around hers, his palm warm and dry.

In the nook, he took her other hand in his, gazing softly at her. She swallowed, waiting for him to speak.

"I've wanted to ask you this for weeks, but I didn't . . . I couldn't . . . I wasn't sure how to ask."

"What is it, Michael?"

He licked his lips, then briefly closed his eyes before he replied, "I . . . Well, you know how much I like walking with you every day and talking to you, and I . . . I want you to be my girl. Would you go steady with me, Blossom?"

She felt as if her heart was going to leap out of her chest. How could this be so surprising, yet feel like something she knew would happen all along? She exhaled as she thought about how to answer him. Her first instinct was to say yes, of course she would, but—

"Mama doesn't allow us to go steady. Not until we finish high school. She wants us to concentrate on our studies."

"Oh." Michael's mouth turned down.

"No, I mean, I want to." She hesitated. "I can be your girl, but it has to be in secret. Maybe Mama will come around, but Marla wasn't allowed to all this time, so I don't know why it would be different for me."

Michael rubbed his thumb lazily across her palm, and Blossom had to inhale deeply to continue standing solidly on her feet. "That's fine, Blossom. We'll keep it a secret if we have to. I'm . . ."

"You're what?"

"I'm just happy." In one swift movement, he cupped his hands around her face, lifted her chin, and brought his soft lips down on hers. It was Blossom's first kiss, and Michael's, too, she suspected, as they awkwardly adjusted to their height difference and the surprise of being so close to each other. But then they became more comfortable, and Blossom shivered with pleasure at the weight of Michael's hands as he moved them down to rest on her waist.

She was breathless when they pulled away, and it was a couple of moments before Blossom found the courage to look directly into his eyes again. "I'm happy, too."

He pressed his lips to each of her cheeks and the back of her hand. Then she smoothed down her skirt, he straightened his collar, and they walked back out to the party as if nothing had changed at all.

Ardith

The day after her great-grandmother's celebration of life, Ardith found herself at Swanson Avenue Baptist Church for the first time in nearly a month—the first time since Bebe's passing. As she pulled into the parking lot alone, she felt like a stranger, attending services in an unfamiliar space.

And yet, as soon as she entered the vestibule, she was right back at home. Ardith stopped for a moment to breathe in the slight mustiness—a combination of the velvet cushions on the church pews, well-worn after decades of use, and the old-book smell from the hymnals that lined the wooden pockets on the backs of the benches. When she'd first stepped into Swanson Avenue Baptist eleven years ago, she'd been awed. The church was medium in size; not tiny, but nowhere near the megachurches spread around the city. At six years old, though, it had seemed huge, with all the unexplored rooms and corners, and the new faces that greeted her and Bebe as they'd walked down the aisle, looking for empty seats among the pews that first day. She'd been nervous, but once Bebe had leaned down and whispered that it was no different from introducing herself to all the new people she met at auditions and on set, the unease began to melt away.

Like Bebe's, so much of Ardith's life had been lived on camera in character, but some of the best parts of her real life had been spent right there at Swanson Avenue. At church, she wasn't Ardith Blackwood, star of *You Can Say That Again*, great-granddaughter of Blossom Blackwood, daughter of Kimberly Arnold—she was Sister Ardith, just another kid singing along with the choir and praying with the congregation. Bebe had made it clear long ago that she did not want attention because of who their family was, and she stayed because the members of Swanson Avenue didn't treat her and Ardith any differently from the other families who worshipped there. Ardith was forever grateful for that. Occasionally, someone who was attending services for the first time might rush up to her or Bebe, asking for photos and autographs, but Sister Robinson, the pastor's wife, was always quick to take them aside and explain how things worked, and Ardith had grown to expect a certain type of refuge when she walked into the church.

From her first service, Swanson Avenue had felt like part of her DNA, which was funny, since her parents had never regularly attended that church or any other—something her mother had almost seemed proud of. "I spent most of my twenties thinking I was going to get struck down whenever I went to a wedding," she used to joke. Even Bebe hadn't become a member until after Grandpa Abe was grown, but the precedent had been set by the time Ardith was born. So, on Sundays, for so many years, it was just the two of them, driving across town to Inglewood, listening to Mahalia Jackson and Shirley Caesar and the Staple Singers on the way.

Today, Ardith kept her head down as she walked into the sanctuary and took a seat near the back of the church. She found comfort in the sameness of it all: the same maroon-and-gold robes in the choir stand; the deacons sitting up front in their pressed suits and shiny shoes; the array of ornate, brightly colored hats sprinkled throughout the pews. Ardith had just slid her Bible from her bag when she felt a body park itself next to her in the pew.

"Morning," Lexie Arrington said with a tentative smile.

Ardith and Lexie were the same age, but Ardith didn't know her very well. Lexie's mother had always been a little too eager to talk to Bebe, something that Lexie had clearly been embarrassed by. When they were little, Lexie would tug on her mother's wrist, trying to pull her away when she'd been talking too long, but Sister Arrington would raise her eyebrow and say, "Sweetie, can't you see I'm speaking with Sister Blossom? Don't be rude." As they'd gotten older, Lexie had stopped trying to intervene and usually just stood a few feet back, rolling her eyes apologetically to Ardith.

"Morning," Ardith said, returning her smile.

"I'm . . . I'm really sorry about your great-grandma." Lexie's eyes darted around nervously as she spoke. "She seemed pretty cool."

"Thanks. She was."

As if on cue, Lexie's mother plunked down onto the pew, leaned over her daughter, and said, "Did you get the flowers we sent?"

"Oh, I'm—" Ardith began, but Sister Arrington kept right on going.

"We sent them to Sister Blossom's house, thinking someone would be there to get them. We would've sent them to you and your father, but I didn't have your address, and Lexie said she didn't have your number, for some reason." She glanced at her daughter just long enough to convey her skepticism, then her bright eyes were back on Ardith. "We got the biggest bouquet we could find. Sister Blossom deserved the very best."

"I'm sure we got them, Sister Arrington. I know they were beautiful. Thank you." Ardith's tone, polite but detached, was the one she reserved for people who insisted on being overfamiliar. Her therapist said that as a well-known actor, Ardith was the focus of parasocial relationships, one-sided situations where people she'd never even met were so invested in her life that they believed they actually knew her. But knowing why people acted that way didn't make it any easier when she was confronting it head-on. Ardith turned and let out a sigh of relief when Donnie, the church pianist, began cueing up the choir.

Pastor Robinson strode into the sanctuary, holding his Bible tight to his chest as he sang, one arm raised to the sky. As soon as he was situated behind the pulpit, he exclaimed, "The Lord sure did see fit to grant us another blessed day, he *surely* did. Can I get an amen?"

Ardith called, "Amen!" along with the rest of the congregation, and for the next couple of hours, she tried as hard she could to tune out everything around her. It was impossible not to notice the people who kept peeking at her during the service, clearly noticing the empty spot on the pew beside her. The gospel didn't course through her veins with the same intensity as most Sundays. It was still there—it was always there—but so was the dull ache that lingered in her heart. No matter how hard she tried, she couldn't turn off the part of her brain that reminded her Bebe wasn't just absent because she was under the weather, like she'd been the last few weeks of her life. She was really and truly gone.

During the break in the service when they were supposed to greet their neighbors, Ardith remained in the same spot, hopeful no one would notice her if she sat still as a statue on the pew. But then Sister Singer approached. She pressed a sturdy card into Ardith's hands, a big pink Hallmark envelope with Ardith's name written across the front in shaky blue cursive. "We're all praying for you, Sister Ardith," she said in her slow, honeyed voice. "We sure do miss Sister Blossom."

Ardith felt the tears gathering in the corners of her eyes, and then, as she tried to thank her, they overflowed. "Let it out," Sister Singer said, patting Ardith's hand. She unearthed a purse-size package of tissues from the bag that hung off her arm; Ardith took them, grateful, and pressed tissue after tissue against her cheeks and eyes, willing her tear ducts to dry up on command, like they did whenever she had to cry on set. But this was real, and the love radiating from Sister Singer reminded her of how lucky she was to have a safe space like Swanson Avenue, a place where people had known her for most of her life and treated her like family.

Her breathing finally returned to normal by the end of the service, as Pastor Robinson mopped his forehead with a handkerchief. He was spent from his fiery sermon about the selfishness of the world, during which he'd challenged each one of the Swanson Avenue Baptist congregation members to question what they were doing to help. Ardith glanced up as a woman about the age of her grandmother Taffy rose from the front row and stepped up to the microphone in front of the pulpit: Sister Robinson, the first lady of the church. She smoothed her hands down the front of her fitted forest green suit and opened her mouth, her eyes finding Ardith's immediately.

"As most of you know, we lost a devoted and beloved member of the congregation a few weeks ago," she began, her voice so strong and clear she didn't even need the microphone. "Every member of Swanson Avenue is special, but I think we can all agree that Sister Blossom's light shined just a little brighter than most."

Murmurs of agreement echoed around the sanctuary, with some *mm-hmm*s and *amen*s sprinkled in, and a few hands waving their affirmation.

"While most of us have paid our respects to Sister Blossom, it is also important to acknowledge her family during this difficult time," Sister Robinson continued. "I'd like to lead the congregation in a prayer for Sister Ardith, who lost the matriarch of her family. Please join hands and bow your heads with me."

Ardith shifted on the pew. A person didn't have to be present for prayers to be sent up, and she had hoped they might have done this on one of the Sundays she hadn't been here. But as Lexie slipped her hand into Ardith's, she let herself close her eyes. It would be over in a moment.

"Heavenly Father," Sister Robinson said, "we call on you to bless Sister Ardith, who has lost one of the most important people in her life. A person who was kind, loving, and selfless, and endlessly spread her joy around this congregation. We don't question why you called her home, dear Lord. We just ask that with her help, you keep watch over Sister Ardith. Continue to lead her down the right path, help her avoid temptation, and impress upon her the strength of your word. In Jesus's name . . ."

"Amen," the congregation said in unison. Ardith said it as well, though it felt a bit odd to affirm a prayer for herself. Still, she knew that out of all those people in church that day, someone must have one eye open, watching her. She didn't want anyone to think she was ungrateful for the support.

And sure enough, when Ardith looked up, Sister Robinson's gentle gaze was focused directly on her.

Ardith darted to the bathroom immediately after the service so she wouldn't get caught in another conversation with Lexie's mother—or, worse, have to turn down an inevitable invitation to brunch. It may have been the Lord's day, but she didn't have to test herself further by sitting through a meal with Sister Arrington. Bebe had always been her shield; now that she was gone, Ardith didn't quite know how to handle those types of situations.

The door to the bathroom opened just as she stepped out from the stall to the sinks, and Ardith prayed the woman hadn't followed her in. But it was the first lady she found standing in the doorway instead.

"Sister Robinson!" Ardith said. "Hello."

The pastor's wife was usually stationed at the front doors with her husband after services, thanking the congregation for coming and wishing them a blessed week. A blush crept into Ardith's tawny-colored skin as she remembered the prayer for her. She knew she should say thank you, but she felt awkward bringing it up. She'd appreciated the sentiment, but she also didn't like the attention it had brought on her.

"Sister Ardith, you're just the person I wanted to see," the first lady said with a kind smile. "The pastor and I would like to invite you to have brunch with us this afternoon. We'll just be at Stella Mae's with Deacon and Sister Miller. Nothing fancy," she said with a laugh. "But we would be so happy if you could join us."

She and Bebe had eaten brunch with the pastor and first lady several times in the past, but she hadn't known what to expect now that Bebe was gone. She should have realized they wouldn't have forgotten about her. Ardith pumped soap from the dispenser into her palm, turning on the water with her other hand. "That's so nice of you and the pastor to think of me."

"Then join us. If not for the company, then for the pancakes. You know they're the best in all of Inglewood."

Ardith was exhausted; after the day celebrating Bebe, she'd ended up spending the night at Hollis's house, just like she used to when they were little, but she hadn't slept well. She'd started out in the guest room, but after tossing and turning for hours, she'd slipped into bed next to Hollis. And, just like when they were younger, listening to the rise and fall of her cousin's breathing had eventually soothed her enough that she'd drifted off to sleep herself, getting a couple hours of rest before she had to go home to get ready for church.

As much as she wanted to head straight to bed again for a nap, Ardith knew Bebe would be disappointed in her for declining a personal invitation from the pastor and his wife. So she cleared her throat and said, "I'd love to come to Stella Mae's. Thank you."

The entryway of Stella Mae's was packed, as always, with members of Swanson Avenue and other nearby churches waiting for their tables and booths. When Bebe was alive, sometimes she and Ardith had been part of the crowd. Ardith had liked it better when they were able to snag a table by themselves, but there had always been someone willing to make room for the two of them, and Bebe had rarely refused their offers. She'd felt it was an extension of the church service, a continuation of their fellowship, and Ardith could tell she'd genuinely enjoyed communing with the other churchgoers.

Now Ardith felt even more conspicuous than she had during the prayer. Not only was she with Pastor and Sister Robinson, but they breezed right by the people standing in front, to a big booth waiting just for them. Ardith kept her head down the whole time, just like when she'd walked into the church hours ago, but she felt the eyes searing into her, heard the murmured whispers as she squeezed through the crowd. She assumed the pastor would sit in the middle of the booth, a prime position where he could hold court, but she ended up there herself, in between Sister Robinson and Sister Miller, the head deacon's wife.

Their server appeared quickly, a young Black guy who looked about Ardith's age. She smiled at him when they made eye contact, but his eyebrows furrowed in response. He looked away as he dug an order pad out of his pocket and slid a pen from behind his ear.

"Welcome to Stella Mae's. I'm Orlando, and I'll be taking care of your table today. How y'all doing?"

"Just fine, young man," Pastor Robinson boomed, and Ardith wondered if he had trouble turning off his church voice after the sermon. "What's the special today?"

"We got a fried catfish plate. Comes with coleslaw, hush puppies, and your choice of mac and cheese or potato salad. It's real good."

"That sounds—" the pastor began, but his wife cut him off.

"He'll have the baked chicken with greens and cornbread."

Ardith held back a laugh as the pastor tried to negotiate with his wife, who was going on about the steak he'd just eaten the night before.

When it was her turn to order, she took one final look at the menu before glancing up at the server. This time she knew she didn't imagine it—he was giving her a sour look.

"Questions about the menu?" His face was back to normal, but his voice was flat.

Ardith knew what this was. He recognized her, and for some reason, he was going to do whatever it took to make sure she knew she wasn't anyone special. It used to bother her when strangers had already decided they didn't like her without having met her, but she'd gotten over it pretty quickly. "Child," Bebe had once told her, "some people just aren't going to like you. Maybe they don't like the shape of your nose, or the way you pronounce a word, or what your character did on the show last week. Maybe they just don't like you because you're in the business. It don't matter. You don't know them. And you don't *want* to know someone who would judge you before you've ever spoken a word to them."

Ardith tried to remember this as she politely said she'd have the shrimp and grits. Once the server left to take their orders to the kitchen, Sister Miller turned to Ardith.

"I hope you won't take this the wrong way, dear," she began, and Ardith immediately tensed. Nothing good ever started out that way. "But we were wondering if you'd even return to Swanson after Sister Blossom's homegoing."

Sister Robinson smiled tightly. "What Sister Miller means is that we knew you were grieving, and sometimes grief brings on big changes in a person's life. With your busy schedule and your great-grandmother no longer here, God rest her soul, we weren't sure Swanson Avenue would remain a priority for you."

Ardith slid her water glass closer. "I've been coming to Swanson Avenue since I was six years old. It's like home for me."

"Yes, but, well," Sister Miller continued. "Not all young folks in your position would make the same choice. We've seen the things temptation can do to people in your business. Take your poor mother, for example—"

"Sister Miller." The first lady's voice was soft, but the admonishment behind it was clear.

"It's okay," Ardith said. "Sister Miller is only saying what a lot of people wonder, I think. And no, I don't find myself confronting temptation as an actor. No more than the average person, anyway. My mother was sick. She suffered from addiction. That would have been a challenge for her no matter what her job was. She just happened to be famous."

Sister Robinson briefly laid her hand on top of Ardith's shoulder and squeezed. "God rest your mother's soul, as well. She would be so proud of you, Sister Ardith."

Ardith was relieved when Deacon Miller began telling stories as he always did, this time from his days of dating Sister Miller—or "courting," as he called it. Ardith didn't think they were as funny as the rest of the table seemed to believe; in fact, some of the stories made her cringe, but she was glad the attention had moved away from her. And, despite the uncomfortable moment with Sister Miller, she was happy to be there, with people who had known and appreciated Bebe like she had. She knew, at any rate, that it was better than being alone. Ardith usually returned home on Sunday afternoons to an empty house, her father always having some reason to be in the office. Or, if he'd decided to work from home, she would spend the day wondering how it was possible to feel so lonely when another person was just a couple of rooms away.

As they walked out to the parking lot afterward, bellies full, Sister Robinson took Ardith's arm and stopped her a few feet back from everyone. "I'm sorry for what Sister Miller said earlier. Please understand we have nothing but sympathy for what you're going through—what you've already been through."

Ardith nodded, unsure what to say. Over the years, people had told her how strong she was, having lost her mother, but what was the alternative?

Sister Robinson smiled. "I know that you have your big, beautiful family, but we are your church family. Your other home. If you need anything, please don't hesitate to ask. I'll be praying for you. We may not always say the right thing at the right time, but you are in all of our thoughts."

Ardith felt the tears from earlier threatening to re-emerge, and she swallowed quickly a few times to tamp them down. She was happy. That she'd come today, that Sister Robinson was looking out for her, that she was still supported even though Bebe was no longer there. She was surprised by how much she'd needed today, this assurance that she'd placed her faith exactly where it should be.

That evening, Ardith and her father ate a quiet dinner together, which they usually managed to do about once a week. Most of the time, they both arrived home too exhausted to eat, or her father had ordered takeout at the office, or if she was on a late shoot, she ate at craft services.

"Is everything all right at work, Daddy? I know you've been busy," Ardith said as they stood next to each other at the kitchen sinks. She rinsed a smear of pasta sauce from a plate and handed it to her father to load into the dishwasher. She felt him tense up a bit next to her, and she wondered if he was still bothered by the argument with his brothers yesterday. She wasn't asking because of that; the truth was, she didn't have a whole lot to talk to her father about. Work was the easiest thing, most of the time.

"It's fine, Ardie. Thanks for asking. How about you? Good day at church?"

"It was." She paused, then added, "The pastor and his wife asked me to brunch today."

"Ooh," her father said in an affected voice. "Sounds fancy."

Ardith laughed. "We just went to Stella Mae's."

"What did they want?" he asked, wedging a water glass into the top rack.

"Daddy, don't say it like that. They wanted to spend time with me. The first lady said a special prayer during the service, and . . . I think they're worried about me now that Bebe's gone."

"Ah. Well, it's good they're looking out for you. I know you've always loved going there." Then he cleared his throat and said, "There is something I wanted to talk to you about. Someone called me last week. A director who used to work with your mother. Do you remember Barton Lerner?"

Ardith nodded, even though his name was only vaguely familiar.

"He hasn't directed in a while, but he's still producing. He says there's been a renewed interest in your mom's old films. People are downloading and streaming more than they ever have. He thinks it's a whole new generation discovering her. And interest in her movies means there's interest in who she was as a person—internet searches for her are up, too."

Ardith's hands froze under the running water. It was the second time today someone had brought up her mother. "Interest in Mommy's life?" she asked. "Or in how it ended?"

Kimberly Arnold had been Hollywood's favorite—until she wasn't. She'd been a true It Girl, a star of romantic comedies and Oscar-nominated dramas alike. She regularly lit up movie screens and was a staple on red carpets. But Ardith's earliest memories were of how she lit up their home. Her mother had been full of love: for Ardith, for the Blackwoods, for Ardith's dad. She'd met August at an after-party for the premiere of a movie in which she'd had a supporting role opposite Hollis's dad. "Your father was so serious," Mommy had once told her. "He looked so uncomfortable at that party, and all I wanted to do was make him laugh." They were complete opposites, but they had loved each other fiercely, and that was all that mattered. Ardith could still remember the way Daddy had looked at Mommy when he didn't think anyone was watching; it had made her think, even at a young age, that she should never settle for anything less than that when it came to love.

In those early years, the only thing Mommy had loved as much as her family was acting. Her parents had died in a car accident weeks before her eighteenth birthday; acting, she said, was a way for her to deal with her devastation, to escape her life when it became too much. And, for a while, it was perfect. The work had come easily to her—not only acting, but the business of being an actor. Commercial work led to small roles on television, which turned into guest star roles; soon after, she moved into supporting work in film, which eventually led to leading roles, again and again. And every minute she wasn't acting or spending time with their family, she was enjoying her fame—attending parties and film premieres where every outfit she wore would show up hours later on a best-dressed list. In those moments, she was dazzling.

Ardith didn't know exactly when her mother had started using. Her father knew she would sometimes drink too much or do harder drugs when work was particularly busy, something she had admitted to having done since she was a teenager. She always said she was in control of it, and Daddy said she drank and used less in the years after Ardith was born. But Ardith was old enough to remember when Mommy, who had always been so present in her life, driving her to auditions and rehearsals and set whenever she wasn't working herself, had begun to disappear, leaving Daddy or Bebe or Hollis's parents to fill in. She'd stayed in bed a lot when she was home, and when Ardith would peek in on her or bring a glass of water to her room, her mother's words would sometimes come out slurred or jumbled, like her tongue was too thick for her mouth. Then she began disappearing for days or weeks at a time. Sometimes Daddy was distraught—this, Ardith would later learn, had been when no one knew where she was, or when she'd call to say she was all right and needed some time away, but her father knew she was on a bender. Other times, he seemed relieved that she was gone; this was when she'd checked into a rehab facility.

But within a few years, despite the Blackwoods' best efforts, Mommy's addiction was no longer a secret they could keep. And it seemed to Ardith that the only thing the media was more excited about than her mother's wins were her failures. She had gotten into a car accident while she was high; no one had been hurt, but the fact that she was under the influence soon became public, after she went into rehab. The internet was relentless; whereas before she had been an "inspiration," she soon became a tragic example of typical Hollywood excess—a promising young actor with the world in front of her; a marriage into a legendary Hollywood family; and, in her final chapter, mistakes that burned down everything she'd built. The studios stopped offering her roles, or even auditions, and while the public generally seemed sympathetic to her struggles, no one wanted their movie or television show to be mired in the drama of Kimberly Arnold's fall from grace.

Soon, no one—not Bebe, not Daddy, not even Ardith—could reach her. "She was an addict," Daddy had said years later, in that matter-of-fact lawyer way of his. "No matter what I did, she was going to find a way to do what she wanted, Ardie."

Kimberly was found in a hotel room the day after the Emmys, dead from an overdose. She was thirty-five years old.

Afterward, many people compared her to Dorothy Dandridge. Ardith understood why; Dorothy Dandridge had also OD'd, though whether it was accidental or intentional had never been confirmed. And she, like Ardith's mother, had been going through a difficult time, having trouble finding work, among other personal issues.

Ardith always wished Kimberly could have just been remembered for who she was: loving mother and wife, beautiful human, and an ambitious, charming actor who never stopped dreaming for herself and the people in her life. But the older she got, the more she accepted that her wish was likely impossible. What she had said to Sister Miller at Stella Mae's this afternoon had been the answer she'd given many times before, whenever someone asked about Mommy. But it wasn't the whole truth. Ardith didn't let on to anyone that she, too, sometimes wondered if her mother would still be alive if she hadn't been an actor, if she hadn't had to confront her struggles while the world was watching. Maybe she would have been able to manage her addiction if she hadn't lived a life that demanded so much of her, even when it was apparent she had so little to give at the end. When her addiction had been made public, it seemed as if everyone in the world felt entitled to decide what her story was, something Ardith could remind herself of with a simple internet search. Was there anything her mother could have done to reclaim her story?

And was there anything Ardith could do now? Maybe Bebe was right—sometimes your story isn't up to you and there isn't anything you can do about it.

Ardith pushed those thoughts back down where they belonged, and turned off the water. She looked at her father, who continued.

"He says the interest is positive—so much so that he's going to create an exhibition at the Academy Museum commemorating your mother and her work," August said. "How do you feel about that?"

"I . . . I don't know. I'd like to think it will be a good thing, but . . ."

"I know." He slowly shook his head. "Revisiting what happened . . . I'm worried this will undo all the work we've done to put it behind us."

You mean all the work we've done to avoid dealing *with it?* Ardith thought but didn't say. Just as she wondered if her mother would have been a different person if she'd never become an actor, she often asked herself whether her father would have thrown himself into his work so completely if her mother were still alive. She didn't remember him working so much when she was younger, and he'd never complained about how hard it was when her mother was still sick and the tabloids were preying and he was trying to work his way up to senior associate at the law firm. But he'd also never been to therapy. Ardith had been going since she was nine, the year her mother died, and sometimes she thought her father used work as his form of therapy—though, more often than not, it seemed like he just wanted to forget everything that had happened. She tried to squash the thought down whenever it arose, but sometimes it felt as if she'd lost both her parents when her mother died.

"But," her father went on, "he doesn't need our permission to go forward with the exhibition. He believes the interest is strong enough that the response will be big. And he wanted to see if we'd like to be involved."

"How?"

"We could contribute some of her things, of course. And he'd like you to speak at the opening, if you feel comfortable with that."

"Oh." Ardith's breath caught in her throat at the idea of speaking about her mother after so many years of doing whatever she could not to publicly address her or what had happened. "When would the event be?"

"Sometime after the new year. He mentioned maybe February, to align with the twentieth anniversary of *Riviera Sunset*'s release."

Ardith loved *Riviera Sunset*. It was her favorite of all of Mommy's performances, a romantic dramedy about an American au pair who falls in love while working in the South of France. Still, what if the celebration encouraged the media to start back up again, digging into her mother's past and rehashing old headlines, just as they'd done after Bebe died? Ardith had already dealt with multiple journalists who tried to connect her and her mother, lobbing interview questions that suggested she might someday be on the same path—and they hadn't been as subtle as Sister Miller's attempt at brunch. Though her publicists had put a stop to it, the thought of having to answer those types of questions again made her feel numb. All it would take was one reporter who really wanted to tell that sort of story and make those connections, and it wouldn't matter how hard she'd tried not to become a child star cliché.

"When does he need to know if we'll be involved, Daddy?"

"Soon, so he can start building out the exhibit and the opening night program. But we have some time to think about it."

Ardith nodded. "Can you tell him we'll get back to him in a couple of weeks?"

"Sure, Ardie. That sounds good to me, too." August folded the dish towel, patted Ardith's shoulder, and said, "I'm going to finish up some work before bed. I'll call Barton tomorrow and tell him we need some time."

Hollis

Hollis's father was obsessed with high school movies. She'd grown up on a steady diet of the classics: *Cooley High. Rebel Without a Cause. Fast Times at Ridgemont High. Dazed and Confused. Clueless*. Pretty much anything by John Hughes. But somehow, despite watching nearly every movie ever made about high school—even the terrible ones her father refused to acknowledge—none of them had prepared her for Dupree Academy.

On paper, it didn't appear all that different from other private prep schools in Los Angeles. Small class sizes, from grades seven through twelve. The parents were involved, the faculty was engaged, and the students were academically challenged, with plenty of extracurriculars to keep their college applications well-rounded. Dupree's alumni included people of rare accomplishment: Emmy, Grammy, Oscar, and Tony winners (including one EGOT); multiple MacArthur Fellows, recognized for their achievements in science, writing, dance, and filmmaking; models and comedians; and several current and former US senators, representatives, and federal judges. And by the time Hollis had begun attending, it was also a who's who of the children of such people, who hoped that whatever Dupree had contributed to all of those successes might be passed along to their kids.

Sometimes she wondered how their small campus managed to fit all of the egos.

If she was being fair, some of that ego had been earned. There were kids who were famous in their own right, such as several child-turned-teen actors, like her cousin Ardith (though Ardith went to an all-girls' school in Brentwood when she wasn't working). A few of them were seen in class only a few weeks at a time, and others were so successful that they never returned to Dupree after their careers took off.

But there were enough celebrity kids, like Hollis, to make distinctions among them. Kids who had also showed up in tabloids and on gossip blogs simply because of who their parents were, kids whose baby photos had fetched millions of dollars from magazines for exclusive rights. And many of them wouldn't let you forget their parents were tech billionaires, owned professional sports teams, or had walked the runway in each of the Big Four Fashion Weeks.

Hollis found it tacky to talk about fame, especially when it wasn't something you had chosen for yourself. Yes, she was part of a family whose name could automatically score the best restaurant reservations and hotel suites in just about any city, but she didn't need to remind people of it every second of the day. She didn't want to be famous; she just wanted to be herself, to be judged—and she knew by now that people *were* going to judge—on that alone. And that made her extra nervous walking into Dupree on the first day of her senior year, when the only thing on her mind was whether anyone would notice how she'd changed over the summer.

She hadn't told anyone at school but Dwayne about her surgery, but as she entered the front doors of the white stucco Spanish Colonial building, she felt a sudden dampness under her arms. Dupree required every student to wear a uniform, and every morning since she'd arrived in seventh grade, she'd had to worry about ways to conceal her chest. Now here she was, wearing a white Dupree polo without the navy-blue cardigan or sweater on top, as she'd always done to hide the way the fabric stretched across her breasts. What if everyone noticed? What if nobody noticed? She wasn't sure which was worse.

At least Dupree was somewhat of a private space. She didn't have to worry about being ogled or, worse, photographed by someone who recognized her from pictures with her parents or from those websites that had a whole lot of information on celebrities and celebrity-adjacent people, most of it wrong. Everyone knew who Hollis was at Dupree, but she was a small fish in comparison to some of her more famous classmates. And she was okay with that. She wasn't Ardith—she didn't have a career in the business, and she had no interest in being in the spotlight, especially when it was only because of her name. That was why she would never understand the times she'd go out and notice someone staring, or even trying to take a covert photo of her. Most of the time she could move around in the world without being bothered, but when she'd gone in for surgery, her parents had arranged for her to enter and exit the facility through a private entrance and use an alias during her care. It didn't matter what she did, though—whatever it was, some people would always feel entitled to know the details of her life.

Hollis took a deep breath and looked around. Unlike her, most everyone seemed to be returning from the summer refreshed—tanned and rested and sporting a new haircut. She suspected she wasn't the only person who'd undergone a cosmetic procedure that summer, but she might be the only one worried about people noticing.

She started walking, moving from the entryway toward the senior wing—a couple of intersecting hallways with lockers assigned only to the seniors. Hollis had to admit, finally belonging in the space she'd always hurried through felt good, though it was hard to believe it had been three years since she'd first made it to the main building, graduating from the middle school annex off the back. She waved hello to people she knew and cautiously accepted a few hugs along the way, nearly holding her breath as she waited for someone to notice her chest. She was relieved to make it to her first class, AP Lit, without anyone saying anything.

The room was still mostly empty when Hollis walked in, but Reggie, the guy who'd had a locker next to hers last year, was in a seat near the window. The desks were arranged in a circle, and she hesitated, trying to figure out which seat to choose. Reggie looked up from his phone and waved, which she took as a sign that it was okay to sit next to him.

"Blackwood," he said as she settled into her chair. "Your summer good?"

"Not too bad. How about you?"

Reggie ran a hand through his auburn hair, momentarily pushing it out of his eyes. "Boring. My dad makes me go spend a few weeks with my grandparents every year."

"Where do they live?"

"Nantucket," he said, making a face as if he couldn't imagine a worse place to spend the summer.

As she grabbed a notebook out of her bag, Hollis quickly glanced over to see if he was looking at her any differently, or if his eyes were focused on her chest. But he was looking down at his phone, seemingly none the wiser. She exhaled, hoping this was a good sign for the rest of the year.

Lunch at Dupree's upper school was split into two periods, with juniors and seniors taking the second slot. Hollis filled up her water bottle, bought a tofu and spinach salad from the prepared foods refrigerator, and walked outside to the courtyard. It didn't take long to find Dwayne, since he towered above most everyone, even sitting. She didn't know what to expect when she saw him for the first time, but she felt her breath catch in her throat as she watched him. He was laughing with someone sitting across from him whom she couldn't see; she had never noticed how strong his jawline was.

He glanced over then, and their eyes met. A huge smile spread across his face. "Hollis!" he called, waving her over, just as he would have any other day.

She flushed, annoyed at herself. What happened between them had been weeks ago. It was no big deal. This was still just Dwayne Lipscomb. The same Dwayne she'd known almost her whole life.

The Blackwoods and Lipscombs had met when Hollis and Dwayne were toddlers. Dwayne's mom, Libby, had been cast in the first movie Hollis's mother had ever directed. The two of them had "gotten along like a house on fire," as Hollis's mom always said, and after a couple of double dates, their husbands had become fast friends, too—Kenley a big fan of Isaiah's movies, and Isaiah a lifelong fan of the Clippers. Hollis and Dwayne had been slower to come around to the idea of friendship, but once they'd started to get used to being around each other, everything had made sense. They were the same age; they were both part of prominent Black families; and they were both only children. Over the years, their families had taken vacations together, celebrated holidays together, and supported one another through the highs and lows of their very public lives. The Lipscombs had always felt like an extension of her family, in some way. And Dwayne had been Hollis's best friend for years, so these new feelings were . . . surprising, to say the least.

She took a deep breath and began crossing the courtyard toward the lunch table, but her steps slowed as she approached. The person Dwayne was laughing with was Orlando Babineaux. While Hollis wouldn't say she had any *enemies* that she knew of, Orlando would be the closest— and she'd been trying for the past year to figure out why. He was one of the maybe ten Black kids total at Dupree, and they were all friendly enough with one another, understanding the unique position they were in, being small in number and yet so highly visible. Things with Orlando had always been different, though. He was a grade below them, and he and Dwayne had become friends on the basketball team last year, when Orlando was bumped up to varsity. Hollis had always made an effort to be nice to him—because he was friends with Dwayne, but also because things were different for Orlando at Dupree. He was there on scholarship, so she knew his family didn't have the same kind of money as most of her classmates. She figured that might not always be easy for him, so she tried to give him the benefit of the doubt, even though it was clear by now that there was something about Hollis he just didn't like. It had become so obvious that she'd tried to talk to Dwayne about it, but he'd shrugged it off, saying Orlando was just like that with some people and not to take it personally. Dwayne may have been her best friend, but he was also just an oblivious guy sometimes.

Hollis made the mistake of looking at Orlando when she sat down next to her friend, and she could have sworn she saw the realization cross his face that having the same lunch period as Dwayne also meant having to share a lunch table with her for the rest of the year. He fell silent, nodding at her quickly before turning his attention toward his tray.

"I was just telling Lando about all the museums we hit up on our trip," Dwayne said, wiping his mouth. "The Natural History Museum in London was dope, but they have this zoological museum outside the city, in some little town called Tring. One of the top three best museums I've ever been to."

Hollis raised an eyebrow. "Zoological museum?"

"Yeah, taxidermy. I know you don't mess with that shit, but I for sure do."

It was true. Dwayne was the biggest science nerd at Dupree. Biology in particular.

"What did you do this summer, Orlando?" she asked. Even if she didn't really care, there was no harm in trying to start the year off right.

They didn't have to be best friends, but maybe they could at least figure out how to be civil with each other.

He didn't even look up from his food. "Worked."

Or not. "You still at Stella Mae's?"

He nodded before cramming a bite of pasta into his mouth.

Hollis sighed and looked at Dwayne. He shook his head slightly, like she should just let it go, but Hollis wasn't sure how she was supposed to ignore someone hating her for no reason at all.

"Well, I probably had the most boring summer ever," she said, nudging Dwayne with her elbow.

"Hey, I wasn't gone *that* long," Dwayne protested.

"You mean the Blackwoods didn't go on some bougie vacation, too?" Orlando's lips curled up in a smirk.

Hollis opened her salad container with a loud pop. She decided not to take the bait. "My dad was filming. We can really only go on vacation around his and my mom's work schedules."

But when Orlando shook his head, the small gesture was enough for Hollis to sharply ask, "What?"

"I didn't say anything."

"You might as well have. Do you have a problem with my family?"

"It's nothing, Hollis."

"Obviously it's not." Underneath the table, she felt Dwayne gently bump her leg, but she didn't stop. "What, you think we're a bunch of rich assholes who are always on vacation or something?" Hollis was used to ignoring Orlando's digs, but today felt different, and she wasn't going to start off the school year letting him think he could get away with being constantly rude to her. Not if they were going to have to spend every lunch period together.

"Well, you're not just some regular old family, either. People like y'all go on big trips every summer. What's wrong with saying that?"

Hollis paused. She often had to remind herself that their circumstances were different. But that didn't give him the right to be rude. "You mean people like Dwayne's family, too?"

"I mean people who see their last name on a building every day."

His words jabbed into her chest like she'd been hit with a dart. She didn't have to turn around to know exactly what Orlando meant. The new auditorium, a separate building that stood out among the annex and the main school, had been completed and dedicated at the start of her sophomore year. The name on the front, Blackwood Auditorium, was impossible to miss.

Heat rushed up Hollis's neck. She really did try to stay chill most of the time. Her parents had been preparing her for years, telling her all the different ways the world would react to her as a person with such a recognizable last name. She knew most things weren't worth responding to, but when it came to her family being judged by someone who didn't know them at all? Hollis felt a burning hot sensation in her body.

"Hey!" Dwayne said, slicing his hand through the air between them as if he could physically cut the tension. He had seen the look in her eyes, and Dwayne knew Hollis well enough to anticipate what was coming. "Can y'all chill? It's the first day."

Hollis wanted to say that she'd shown up with all intentions of keeping things chill between them—it was Orlando who had decided to start something. And that her great-grandmother, the reason her name was even a name at all, had just died, and it was really fucking gross of him to call out her family like that.

But then Dwayne was rubbing her back—only briefly, but enough to calm her down, to make her rethink shouting at Orlando right there in the courtyard. It made her resentful of and thankful for Dwayne all at once.

By the end of the school day, Hollis was tired. She had been to a few parties with Dwayne right after junior year had ended, but she'd had a lazy, quiet summer overall. Being back in school was a lot. And she was mentally exhausted from replaying what had happened at lunch; the conversation had wormed its way into her brain and wouldn't leave.

She hated that she'd let Orlando get to her like that. Some people were just jerks—she'd known that for as long as she'd known her family was famous. Why couldn't she just ignore him and move on? She was staring into her locker after last period, asking herself that question, when Dwayne strolled up and leaned against the wall next to her.

"What are you doing now?" he asked, angling his body toward Hollis.

She blinked, shaking herself out of her thoughts. "Oh, hey. Going home, I guess."

"You wanna hang?"

She frowned. "You don't have to train?"

"Told the guys I wasn't feeling good."

Hollis raised her eyebrows. "You lied to them?"

Dwayne shrugged. "It's not a lie . . . I don't *feel* like training. Anyway, it's the first day. And it's just preseason. A day off isn't going to kill me."

Hollis knew that wasn't exactly how it worked. It may have only been preseason training, but this year was going to be huge for him. College scouts hadn't been allowed to contact Dwayne until the summer after his sophomore year, but he was on everyone's radar. And they'd all be watching this winter. Hollis knew how long he'd been working for this.

"Uh, okay," she said, swallowing down the urge to ask what was really going on. "You want to come over, or go somewhere?"

"Are your parents home?"

"My mom probably is. She's cooking tonight."

"Let's just walk around Old Town or something. I don't want her telling my dad she saw me when I was supposed to be at the gym."

So, his parents didn't know he was taking the day off. Dwayne avoided her eyes as she processed this, effectively communicating that he absolutely did not want to talk about it. Hollis shuffled the books she didn't need into her locker and closed it, turning to him. "Ready?"

Old Town Pasadena was the hub of the city, where stately old buildings that lined Colorado Boulevard and the surrounding streets housed restaurants, shops, offices, and even some museums. It was the kind of place where you could quickly get lost, only to realize you weren't more than two blocks from where you'd started. It was also a good place to spend money, pass the time, or burn off some energy—and Dwayne appeared to have plenty of extra energy today.

But as soon as they were moving down the crowded sidewalks, blending in among the locals and tourists, Dwayne seemed to visibly relax. His shoulders were no longer hunched up as if he were trying to shrink into himself, and the tense wrinkle across his brow had disappeared. Hollis, on the other hand, couldn't help noticing anytime someone made eye contact with her or gave the two of them a second look. Already six foot five, Dwayne was so tall that people's eyes automatically drifted to him, which made her more visible by simply being with him. She hoped the crowds were thick enough to obscure her and Dwayne from anyone who might recognize them.

"Lunch was kind of awkward," Hollis said as they wandered past a clothing boutique. She paused in front of the shop window, gazing at a dress—long enough for Dwayne to lean in.

"That would look good on you. You should try it on."

"Stop changing the subject," she said, but when she looked over at him, he flashed her a dimpled grin in reply, and Hollis tried to remember when his smile had simply been a smile. Her palms were actually sweating from the quick look he'd just given her. "I'm serious, D. What is his deal?"

Dwayne sighed, pushing the translucent frames of his glasses up the bridge of his broad nose. "Does it matter? You don't even like him."

"I don't like him because he doesn't like me. But I've never done anything to him. And that was pretty shitty, what he said about the auditorium. I didn't ask my family to donate that money."

"I hear you. But . . . I dunno, Holl. Lando's life isn't anything like ours. He really did have to work all summer, just to help out his family."

"Okay, I get all of that." Several students at Dupree received financial assistance, and Orlando wasn't the only Black kid there on scholarship—but it wouldn't have mattered if he were. Nobody made a big deal about it. "But what is his problem with me, specifically? Because we may be different from him, but my family isn't that different from yours."

"I dunno. We're boys," Dwayne said with a shrug. "We play ball together. It *is* different in that way."

"Okay, but I'm your best friend. Shouldn't he try to be cool with me?"

Dwayne's voice softened. "Hey. Don't let him get you all worked up. I'll talk to him, okay?"

"You will?"

"I won't make it into a whole thing. I just want to eat lunch in peace."

He leaned down, close enough that for a couple of seconds, Hollis wondered if he was going to kiss her, right there on the sidewalk. Her throat went dry. He couldn't. Not here. What if someone saw, recognized them, took a picture? And then what if someone examined that picture, like people did, and made comparisons to previous pictures of her—specifically her chest? Not to mention the fact that if people saw her and Dwayne together that way, she'd have to explain something she wasn't even sure of herself at the moment.

But he hadn't been leaning in for a kiss. Instead, he touched his forehead to the top of hers and asked, "You going to try on that dress or what?"

Dwayne pulled back in to the Dupree parking lot a couple of hours later. It was late enough that the guys on the team would have finished working out, but there was still enough time for Hollis to make it home before dinner. She touched the door handle of his Range Rover but didn't make a move to open it.

There was so much she wanted to ask Dwayne, she felt like she might burst. But she couldn't work up the nerve to talk about all of it right now, so she decided to go with a less scary option. "Are you going to tell me why you skipped training? You're obviously feeling fine."

Dwayne stared at the steering wheel where his long fingers tapped out a rhythm she couldn't place. He was silent for so long that she wondered if he was going to answer her at all. Finally, he said, in a low voice, "I don't want to play ball."

"What, like, your last year at Dupree?"

"No, like, ever again. I don't want to play now. I don't want to play in college. I don't want to go pro. None of it."

Hollis's eyes widened. "What happened?" she asked slowly.

Dwayne exhaled. "I don't know. I just don't love it anymore. I'm not sure I ever did. Not like I'm supposed to, you know? Not like my dad does. I'm good at it . . . but I want to go to college to study biology—not just put in my year, go in the draft, and try to come back to science once my knees are shot."

"Shit, D. I didn't know any of this."

He looked at her. "I haven't told anyone."

"I won't say anything," she promised.

"I know. Right now, I'm just trying to figure out how the hell I'm gonna tell Coach. And my dad. He's gonna fucking kill me, and I'd like to live to see graduation."

"You'll figure it out." She paused. "*We'll* figure it out."

Dwayne reached out to tuck a stray loc behind her ear, his fingers lingering on the small patch of skin below her lobe. "Thanks, Holl."

And then—there it was. The look in his eyes, the same one she'd first seen that summer. The one that meant he was going to kiss her. And even though they were alone now, and Hollis's body was sure she wanted that kiss, her mind wasn't so certain. If she kissed Dwayne again, she feared she might not be able to stop. And if they made it a habit, their friendship would have to change. She wasn't ready for that . . . was she?

Her fingers accidentally pressed into the door handle then, sending the passenger door flying open. The warm outside air that rushed in seemed to break the spell, and Dwayne's hand drifted back to the steering wheel. She gave him a quick hug before she got out of the car, but her hand shook as she tried to click the key fob to unlock her own, and she knew for sure that it wasn't a spell. She *liked* Dwayne—more than she'd ever liked anyone.

And she wondered if she'd ever be brave enough to tell him.

Just a Man
1945

Florence Blackwood was born in Doling, Mississippi, in January 1895, the eighth and final child of sharecroppers Bertha and Walter Blackwood. Both Bertha and Walter were born enslaved, and freed as children after Emancipation. Little Flossie grew up working in the cotton fields with her siblings and parents, who rented land from a white planter in exchange for a percentage of the crops they harvested.

Blossom knew that Mama didn't like to talk about her childhood; when she did, her voice changed. It went deeper and the words came slower, as if it were physically painful to recall the hardships back in the South. "We was loved," she'd told her girls once, when Blossom was young. "No shortage of that going around. But love didn't make it easier when that nasty old planter cheated my daddy out of money he'd earned. That we'd all earned. It was real hard work, and it was the only way we knew to survive back then.

"But we was proud people," she'd continued. "My daddy grown up with the name of their master, but he felt ashamed about it. Didn't want the stink of that white man on him. So he changed it when he got old enough. Thought the name Blackwood seemed real nice. Regal. We may have been out there picking cotton till our fingers bled, but we never forgot our daddy thought of us as royalty."

Despite the love of her family, Flossie wanted out of Mississippi.

She was tired of having to work in the blazing-hot fields, tired of having sore fingers that were often shredded from the thorny edges of the cotton bolls, tired of having to watch her daddy and the other colored folks in town being treated like second-class citizens by the white folks they interacted with. But nobody ever left her tiny town; they didn't have anywhere else to go, with little in the way of education and no real skills beyond tending to crops. By the time she was eighteen, Flossie had resigned herself to the idea of staying in Doling for the rest of her life, settling down just as her older siblings had—until one night that changed everything.

Flossie convinced her friend Lola to sneak down to the local juke joint with her so they could meet a couple of boys they knew from around town. Flossie knew her mama and daddy wouldn't want her going down to the little shack in the woods where people in her community gathered to drink and dance and listen to music. But as soon as the girls arrived, Flossie forgot all about Robert, the boy she'd come to meet. She forgot about everything around her except the woman singing at the front of the room that was hot and thick with sweat. She wore a plain black dress, and her hair wasn't fashioned into any fancy style, but Flossie was mesmerized by the way the woman confidently gripped the smooth silver microphone as she belted out songs with ease and stamped her feet to the rhythm of the musicians behind her. A couple of times Robert asked Flossie to dance, but she declined, instead sipping on the cup of beer he'd brought her as she swayed her hips to the music.

"What's wrong?" Lola asked after a while. "You don't like Robert no more?"

"What?" Flossie turned to her friend, surprised to see her standing there.

"You been ignoring him—all of us—all night." Lola glanced toward the makeshift stage. "You know that woman or something?"

"No, but . . ." Flossie paused, finally tearing her eyes away from the performance. "Don't you just want to be her?"

Lola wrinkled her nose. "I don't know. She's not so pretty, is she?"

"Her voice, Lola! The way she's just up there, singing without a care in the world." The woman looked happy. She looked free in a way Flossie had never known all her years in Doling. And Flossie wanted to know her secret.

Afterward, when the band was packing up and everyone had begun to trickle outside, their clothing damp with sweat, Flossie slowly approached the front of the room. The woman was laughing with the banjo player, so she didn't see Flossie until the man nodded toward her. She turned around, the trace of a smile lingering at the corners of her lips.

"Hello there, young lady," she said, wiping the perspiration from her brow with a handkerchief.

"Hello," Flossie nearly whispered.

After a few moments of silence, the woman raised an eyebrow. "Can I help ya?"

"I . . . I really liked that. Your singing and . . . all of this." Flossie swept her hand around the space.

"Thank you, sugar. You ever been here? Ain't seen you around before."

"No, ma'am."

"Well, I'm Annie." She paused as Flossie just stared at her. "You got a name?"

"Mm-hmm. It's Flossie, ma'am. Flossie Blackwood."

"Nice to meet you, Flossie Blackwood."

Flossie paused, then blurted, "I want to be like you."

Annie threw her head back and laughed. When Flossie looked over Annie's shoulder, she saw the banjo player was smiling real big, too. She wished she could disappear into the scuffed wood floor. But then Annie put her hand on Flossie's arm and leaned in.

"Sorry, sugar. It's just I ain't never heard that in my whole life." She cocked her head to the side. "What you mean, though? You sing?"

Flossie nodded. Only at home, or when she was trying to pass the

71

time in the fields, but she'd been told before that she had a nice voice. Nice enough to make people want to stop and listen. But more than that—

"I want to get out of here. Out of Doling," she said quickly. "And I thought maybe—well, where are you from?"

"Georgia," Annie said evenly. "How old are you?"

"Eighteen, ma'am."

"You got a husband? Children?"

"No, ma'am."

"Can you dance?"

"Yes, ma'am."

Annie nodded slowly, and Flossie held her breath.

"All right, then. Listen, I'm staying with a family called the Dillards while we in the area performing. You know them?"

Flossie did. She knew everyone in Doling, which probably meant someone would eventually tell her mama and daddy that she'd been here tonight. But she wasn't worried about any of that as she said yes.

"Why don't you come by tomorrow? After noon, 'cause I'm a real beast if you catch me too early in the day. You can show me what you know."

"Do you mean I could be part of your act?"

Annie laughed again, but this time Flossie could feel the kindness beneath it. "Not ours, but I know of this act that's looking for a new chorus girl. Vaudeville. We supposed to meet up with them in Jackson next week. No promises, sugar, but if you got what they looking for, they just might take you on the road with them."

Flossie was beaming when she finally walked outside to meet Lola, who was standing impatiently against the front of the building, arms crossed in front of her. "The boys left," she said. "You didn't even dance with Robert once."

"Oh, Lola, who cares about all that?" She grabbed her friend by the hand and pulled her off the porch. "I'm gonna be far away from here soon, anyway."

Flossie was nervous as she sang and danced for Annie the next day. She was even more nervous to tell her parents she was good enough that Annie had agreed to take her along to Jackson with the band a few days later, where she would meet the lead performers of the colored vaudeville act Annie had mentioned. Mama and Daddy didn't like the idea of her leaving home, but she was eighteen—old enough to get married and have babies, if she'd wanted. Besides, colored folks had been moving away from the South for a few years now, heading up North for better opportunities and ways of life; Flossie didn't even want to leave the South just yet, but she was aching to see more than what Doling had to offer. So she left anyway, knowing she might never get another chance like this one and hoping her parents would one day forgive her.

After an impromptu audition, Flossie was informed she would be the vaudeville act's newest chorus girl, traveling and performing with their show around the Southern states. While she was told the pay was less than what white chorus girls on the vaudeville circuit took home each week, it was still more than Flossie had ever seen in her entire life. And promising to send money home while she was on the road was the only way she was able to convince Mama and Daddy she wasn't making a mistake, leaving Doling with a group of people she hardly knew.

Work on the road was difficult. Flossie endured long days of rehearsal and late nights performing; fending off audience members and theater owners who tried to get too close; and weeks where she sent so much money home that she barely had enough to eat. But despite all the challenges of her new life, Flossie felt freer than she ever had in Doling. She got to see parts of the country she'd never thought she would visit, and she met all sorts of people she would never have come across back home.

That included Winnie and Frankie Feldman, two sisters who were eleven months apart and worked with Flossie in the chorus. The three spent most of their free time together, and the sisters' warm, welcoming personalities helped Flossie adapt to the unexpected homesickness that rushed in so quickly sometimes, her heart actually ached. They grew so close that one night, after a particularly demanding performance in a little town outside Atlanta, Winnie suggested they split off on their own to form a trio.

"And what exactly would we do?" asked Frankie, the more practical of the two, whose thick eyebrows had instantly risen at her sister's proposition.

"Exactly what we been doing," Winnie replied. "A little bit of dance, a little bit of song, some jokes, and—"

"I ain't painting my face," Flossie said quickly. Their group didn't perform in blackface, but she knew plenty of colored performers would do so for a coveted venue or fee.

"That's my point," Winnie said, her voice breathless with excitement. "If we have our own act, we can do—or not do—whatever we want. We'll be in charge of everything."

It didn't take Winnie long to persuade the other two, and within a few months, they had saved and planned enough to strike out on their own. Flossie didn't mind that they called the act the Feldman Sisters; she was so close to Winnie and Frankie by this point that they felt like family.

And no matter who she performed with or where they traveled to, she would never forget she was Flossie Blackwood from Doling, Mississippi.

Flossie had never really shared much with Blossom about the years between her leaving the act and starting her family. All Blossom knew was that her mother had grown so tired of the segregation and prejudice in the South that she decided to head West, to California. She'd met a man shortly thereafter, and Marla was born in 1924. Three years later, Blossom came into the world.

Once, when Blossom was about four years old, she had asked her mother why they didn't have a daddy like the other children in the neighborhood.

"Y'all don't need one," Flossie had said simply. "I'm the mama and the daddy around here."

But that hadn't been good enough for Blossom at the time. "We *have* a daddy, though, don't we?" she'd asked. "Marla said Sue Adams said everybody has a daddy."

"Everyone do have a daddy, but not all of them is around. Y'all's daddy ain't around. And remember this, Blossom: You don't ever need no man, all right? You enough, all by yourself. And ain't nobody allowed to tell you how to be you." Flossie had paused as if she might have more to say, then abruptly nodded toward the kitchen and said, "Go on and help Marla shell them peas."

Since then, Blossom had thought twice before bringing up her father or anything to do with men in general when she was talking to her mother. Flossie must have known her girls had started to become interested in boys, but her rule was the law, and normally, Blossom knew better than to break it.

But Michael was her weakness. And now he wanted her to tell her mother about them.

"I'm anxious, Michael," she said, closing her eyes. She was leaning against a big, broad eucalyptus tree with Michael facing her, his hands pressed to the trunk on either side of her shoulders.

"Come on, Blossom. It's time."

She inhaled as deeply as she could, the earthy, calming scent of the eucalyptus filling her nose. She was eighteen now—a woman by anyone's standards and the same age Flossie had been when she'd left home. Blossom was supposed to be allowed to do what she wanted. And she'd tried to be so good for so long. But most important, Michael was right. They had been going steady for nearly three years now. They would graduate from Jefferson High in just a few months. It was time to tell Mama about them, whether she'd like it or not.

Michael stepped closer to her so that their hips were touching. This was their favorite tree, one they'd discovered on their walk home sometime during sophomore year. It was large enough to hide them from the view of anyone on the street, and, in a stroke of luck, the owners of the house that it faced were never home after school. They stopped here to steal a few minutes alone, away from the prying eyes of their classmates and before they had to return home to their families. It was a safe place to sneak kisses, to let their hands linger on each other without drawing attention. A few of their friends knew they were a couple, but they'd both decided it was better to keep their relationship largely a secret. Many of their friends' parents knew one another, and Blossom and Michael didn't want it getting back to their mothers that way. Michael's mother would have likely been fine with their courtship, but not Flossie.

"What if we waited until—" she began, but Michael shook his head.

"We should get it over with. Imagine being able to enjoy the last few months of school, with nothing to hide." He only had to dip his head a few inches for their mouths to meet. He gently kissed Blossom, letting his lips brush her chin before he pulled away. "Imagine being able to do that without worrying about who can see us. Without this dang tree being our cover."

"Don't you be mean to Tree." Blossom smiled for the first time since they'd begun this discussion. "It's been good to us."

"I'll be right there next to you," he said, taking her hand in his. "She can't get that upset at you if I'm there."

That might've been the case with anyone else's mother, but Blossom knew Flossie Blackwood.

Blossom walked next to Michael in silence, her stomach beginning to ache as soon as they passed the corner where they usually split up and went their separate ways. Today, Michael kept walking with her, toward the little white cottage on Reed Street. This wasn't the first time Michael had visited her home, but it was the first time she'd felt positively sick about it.

She took another long, deep breath as they walked up the steps of the front porch. It was a warm March day, and the door was open, allowing the jasmine-scented breeze to float through the screen door into the house. Blossom placed her fingers on the door handle and turned back to look at Michael once more. He gave her arm a reassuring squeeze. They'd chosen today because Wednesday was Flossie's day off from her housekeeping job at the Dunbar Hotel. Every other day except Sunday, she didn't return home until well after six o'clock, exhausted and generally uninterested in conversation.

The first thing to catch Blossom's attention was the darkness. The hand-sewn curtains hanging from the two front windows were drawn, the only light coming from the few sunrays that spilled through the screen door. When her eyes adjusted, she saw Flossie across the room, settled in her worn green velvet wingback chair. Next to her, the radio on the end table was playing, but the volume was so low that Blossom couldn't make out which show her mother was listening to. Flossie's hands were in her lap, carefully rolling a cigarette, pinching tobacco from a small tin and dropping the dried leaves onto a long, thin paper.

"Hi, Mama," she said, tentatively stepping into her own home like she was entering the house of a stranger. She wondered if Michael felt the heavy cloud that seemed to hang over the room or if that was simply her nerves at work.

Michael was right behind her, as promised, pulling the screen door closed quietly behind them. "Good afternoon, Miss Flossie. How you been?"

Flossie only grunted in response, not looking at either one of them. Did Mama somehow know already? Blossom's chest tightened as she thought about her sisters. Had Sybil finally betrayed her secret? Or had Marla let something slip when she'd stopped by one day?

Slowly, Flossie picked up a small, heavy glass from beside the radio. It was filled with a dark brown liquid that Blossom rarely saw in the house, let alone at this time of day. She looked at Michael before turning back to her mother.

"Mama?"

"Your daddy died."

Blossom exhaled. "Ma'am?"

"I said your daddy died." Flossie took a long drink from the glass. "He's gone. Heart attack."

"I . . . I didn't know you still talked to him."

Flossie grunted again. "Not much. Had been a while. Years and years. His friend Joe wrote. Said he thought I'd want to know."

"Mama . . . who was he?"

Flossie finally looked at her, and Blossom wished she hadn't. She didn't recognize her mother's eyes. "He was just a man, Blossom. His name was Marlon. Only good thing he ever did was give me you three girls."

Marlon. It sounded like her big sister's name. Had Marla been named after him? If so, that was the only name of his they'd been given. Blossom knew from the look on her mother's face, from those dull, lifeless eyes, that she shouldn't press her for more information. Certainly not now, but perhaps never.

He was just a man.

Michael cleared his throat, reminding Blossom that he was standing behind her. She swallowed and turned to him. She hoped he understood they wouldn't be able to confess their relationship today. Maybe not for some time. She asked in a shaky voice, "Would you like a glass of water?"

"Uh, I'll just get going now," he said, looking back and forth from Blossom to her mother. "I'll see you tomorrow, Blossom. I'm sorry." He quickly rubbed his hand up and down her back. Then, directing his words across the room, "Nice to see you, Miss Flossie. And, uh, I'm real sorry for your loss."

Flossie didn't bother to respond. She returned the near-empty glass to the table and went back to rolling her cigarette.

Blossom watched Michael disappear down the front path and then down the street and, finally, out of sight. She'd missed him as soon as he stepped out the door. She had never seen her mother like this before.

"Do Sybil and Marla know?"

"Sybil ain't home yet. I'll tell Marla on Sunday."

Marla had gotten married and moved out a few months after her own high school graduation three years ago. The apartment she shared with her husband, Harold, was only a few blocks away, so they came over for supper each Sunday. That was Flossie's other day off, but she never complained about the cooking; in fact, she seemed to delight in being in the kitchen on Sundays, preparing a big meal for her daughters and son-in-law.

"Mama, do you need anything? Can I . . . ?" Blossom trailed off, unsure how to finish her sentence.

"Girl, I'm all right." Flossie finished rolling the cigarette and placed it on the table, picking up the glass of liquor again.

"You sure, Mama?"

"I said I'm all right. You go on and do your schoolwork now."

Blossom nodded and went to her room. But she couldn't concentrate on her textbooks; she kept looking out the tiny window between her and Sybil's beds, replaying Mama's words. The only thing she could think about was her father. *Marlon*. Who had he been? Had he lived around here? Of course, she knew she and her sisters hadn't been delivered to Reed Street by a stork, but she had never known Flossie to be romantically involved with a man or even speak of one in a way that indicated she desired companionship. Blossom wondered about the type of man her mother was attracted to. Had their father been serious and studious, like Marla? An outgoing performer, like herself? Thoughtful and kind, like Sybil?

Whoever he had been, it was clear her mother cared enough about him to feel something over his death, and strangely, this disturbed Blossom. Flossie had always taught her girls that they didn't need a man to be complete, yet clearly a part of her heart had been reserved for their father. And now it was broken because he was gone. Blossom had only briefly thought about her mother and father being together and how that had looked, but for the first time, she tried to truly imagine their relationship. Had they been seeing each other regularly—secretively—over the years? Did he ever ask about them?

Sybil arrived home an hour later, after a visit to her friend's house. Flossie was still sitting in the living room, and Blossom stood at the doorway to their bedroom, waiting to see what her mother would say. Nothing, apparently. The radio was turned up then, most likely for the noise; it was some silly show that Flossie would normally never listen to. She heard Sybil greet their mother, pause as she noticed the mood in the room, and then slowly head toward the bedroom, where Sybil practically ran right into Blossom, still stationed in the doorway.

"What's going on?" she whispered before Blossom yanked her into the bedroom and shut the door.

"Our daddy died," Blossom whispered back.

Sybil dropped down onto her bed with a thud. "What?"

"She said his name was Marlon. One of his friends wrote to tell her."

Sybil was five years younger than Blossom; she'd be moving on to Jefferson High in the fall, a few months after Blossom had graduated. But Blossom had noticed more and more how mature Sybil seemed—much more mature than she had been at that age. Her sister had a certain poise that made Blossom believe she could remain cool as a cucumber, no matter the situation.

"Were they still talking?" Sybil asked after a few moments.

"Not for a few years."

"Did you know anything about him?"

"Not until today," Blossom said. "You?"

Sybil shook her head. "Of course not."

A wave of guilt rushed through Blossom then; she should never have doubted that Sybil would have told Mama about her and Michael. Sybil was loyal, and Blossom knew she would have told her if she'd known anything about their father.

"I don't think Marla knew, either."

"I feel a bit sad," Sybil said, twisting her fingers together over her skirt. "Isn't that peculiar? We never even saw him."

"Maybe we did when we were really little and we just don't remember," Blossom said faintly. "Maybe it's a memory you've buried deep."

"I don't think so," Sybil said, her voice breaking.

Blossom sat down and wrapped herself around her baby sister. Sybil burrowed her head into Blossom's neck. She didn't cry, but she remained in Blossom's arms for a while. And the whole time Blossom comforted her, she wondered why she didn't feel the same. She wasn't sad about the death of this man she'd never known, even if he was her father. If anything, she was angry. He had chosen not to be in their lives, and now here he was, wounding both her mother and sister, even in his death. Flossie had said it herself: he was just a man. They hadn't needed him before. Blossom wouldn't let him upset her now.

A few weeks later, Blossom again found herself with Michael on her front porch. Only this time, they were sitting on the steps, their knees and shoulders touching. Sybil was at orchestra practice, and Flossie was working at the hotel; the neighbors could still see them and mention it to her mother, but Blossom cared a lot less about it than she had before Flossie told her about their father. She felt as if all of them—she, Sybil, and Marla—had grown up a bit after receiving that news. For Blossom, it had shown her that Mama wasn't as tough as she seemed, that she had vulnerabilities just like anyone else. The only time Flossie had moved from the wingback chair that night was to use the restroom and refill her glass. Around dinnertime, Blossom had found her nodded off with an unlit cigarette on her lap, *The Lone Ranger* blaring from the radio next to her.

"I want to show you something," Blossom said, her voice hesitant. She wasn't sure how Michael was going to respond to it, and that made her anxious.

"All right." He leaned back on his elbows, giving her a lazy smile. As much time as they'd spent together over the past few years, sometimes Blossom was still struck by how handsome he was. She knew he was aware of how all the girls looked at him, but it never seemed to go to his head.

Blossom slowly pulled a small square of folded newsprint from the pocket of her skirt. She'd been carrying it around for a week now, ever since she'd seen the announcement and clipped it from the *California Eagle*. She unfolded and smoothed it out before she placed it on Michael's leg.

He sat up and read it aloud under his breath. Blossom listened, even though she knew the text by heart. "'The Beatrice van der Kolk Dance Company is seeking new talent. Dancers will have the opportunity to audition for the group on April 7 from nine a.m. to five p.m. at Music Town on Jefferson and Normandie. Company director Beatrice van der Kolk has informed that the auditions are colorblind. Open to all talented individuals.'"

Michael was quiet for a moment, then read it again. At last, he carefully refolded the clipping into a neat square and handed it back to her without a word.

"Isn't this exciting?" she said, slipping it into her pocket for safekeeping. "'Open to all talented individuals.' They're interested in Negro dancers, too. I can audition!"

"So, you want to do this?" Michael asked, his eyebrows pinching together.

"Of course I do! Beatrice van der Kolk is a respected dancer. She studied with Ruth St. Denis!"

Michael gave her a puzzled look.

"Ruth St. Denis trained Martha Graham." When that didn't register with him, either, Blossom pursed her lips. "Martha Graham? She's one of the most famous dancers and choreographers of all time!"

"How famous could she be if I've never heard of her?" Michael said, a smirk crossing his lips. Blossom got the idea he was half joking, but she wasn't in the mood right now.

"She performed for the Roosevelts a few years ago—at the *White House*." She shook her head. "But never mind all that. *I* get to audition for Beatrice van der Kolk, and she doesn't even mind that I'm Negro."

"What about the Negro dance companies? They not good enough?"

Blossom scoffed. "*What* Negro companies? There's Katherine Dunham and her group, but they're in New York City. I'd have to move across the country if I made it, and . . . I'm not ready for that. Yet."

Michael's eyes narrowed. "You planning on moving back East?"

"Not anytime soon. Listen, Michael, this is a real good opportunity for me. They'll be looking at my dancing, not the color of my skin. If they choose me, I can learn everything I need to know right here in Los Angeles. This could be my ticket into dancing or acting professionally."

Michael was quiet again as he considered this. "If you audition for this van der lady and get the gig, you'll stay right here?"

Blossom shifted uncomfortably on the steps. What did Michael want her to say? Los Angeles would always be home. But she knew from Flossie's experience how difficult it was to succeed in show business. Actors, singers, and dancers had to follow the work, which was why Flossie herself had traveled to places she'd never wanted to visit back when she was with the Feldman Sisters. And why Negro entertainers often performed in venues that made them use the service entrances and wouldn't even allow them to sit in the audience among the white people enjoying their shows. There was a reason so many Negroes moved to New York City; she didn't presume her story would be any different one day.

But she knew Michael wouldn't respond well to that. So all she said was, "I want to dance. And perform. And if I can do it here, that's even better."

"Good." Michael pressed his hands to his thighs as he looked at her. "Because I want you right here, Blossom. With me."

Michael was smiling. He didn't agree with what she wanted to do, but as long as she was still with him, he wouldn't complain. He probably thought he was being generous. But to Blossom, those words felt as if they were wrapping themselves around her, binding her in a cage.

She had never been happier to see her little sister walking up the front path. Sybil waved awkwardly at them with the arm holding her books, her other fingers gripping the handle of her violin case. Blossom jumped up to help her, dismayed at how much easier it was to breathe when she was no longer sitting next to Michael.

"How was your day?" she asked, relieving Sybil of the instrument case.

Sybil gave her a strange look, her eyes shifting to Michael for a second before she said, "It was all right. What are you two doing?"

"Talking." Blossom cleared her throat and turned back to Michael. "But you should probably get on home soon. We'll need to start supper so it's ready by the time Mama is back."

Michael nodded and stood up, stretching his legs, and bent down to gather his schoolbooks. It was too early to begin cooking, and they all knew it, but he didn't argue, and for that, Blossom was thankful.

That day, she wasn't so sad to see him leaving.

Blossom arrived an hour before the auditions were set to start, lining up outside the building behind the other women who'd gotten there early. She pulled her wool coat tight around her; it wasn't cold enough for it, but she'd been self-conscious about the tights and tunic she wore underneath, feeling exposed. She wondered if she might see someone from school, but none of the girls looked familiar. She also noticed that, even with what the newspaper had stated, all of them appeared to be white. Blossom tried not to think about the way their eyes roamed over her, how some of them whispered behind their hands as they glanced her way in line.

She had been practicing since the moment she read about the audition, performing her choreography for Sybil whenever she had the chance; her sister was always happy to give her honest opinion. And the evening before, she'd stayed awake to listen to Blossom fret about all the things that could go wrong today.

"What if I forget everything I know as soon as I'm in front of them?" Blossom had asked, not knowing exactly who *them* would be. She assumed Beatrice van der Kolk, but would there be others as well? How many people would she be performing for?

"You won't," Sybil had assured her, looking up at the ceiling.

"But what if I do?"

Sybil had sighed. "Then you'll try again next year, Blossom."

"You say that as if it's so simple," Blossom had said, frowning.

"That's what you'll do, though, isn't it? Audition again if they don't take you this time?"

"But what if I'm not meant for this? What if I'm supposed to do something else instead?" Blossom's mind had drifted to Michael, to how relieved she knew he would be if she didn't earn a spot in the company. The thought had made her feel itchy. But maybe, if she didn't do well at this audition . . . perhaps it was a sign that Michael had the right idea. That she should put her focus into building a life with him after graduation, just as Marla had done with Harold.

Sybil had turned to face Blossom, settling onto her side. "That's not you. You've known you want to be on a stage for as long as I can remember. You won't just give up because of one audition. You can't."

"Michael doesn't like the idea of it."

85

"Since when does Michael make the rules?" Sybil had scoffed. She'd tucked the quilt tightly under her arms. "Do you ever wonder if Mama maybe stopped performing because of our daddy?"

Blossom had been silent for a moment. "Not until now, I didn't. But—no. She had us, that's why she didn't keep at it. How was she supposed to find the time to go on auditions? Or what if she'd gotten a big job where she was needed on set every day?"

"Maybe she could have kept doing those things if our daddy had helped out. Actors, dancers, they have wives and husbands. Children, too, sometimes. Dorothy Dandridge does."

"Well, what man do you know who would want to take care of children while his wife works? And I'm no Dorothy Dandridge, Sybil."

"But you could be." Sybil reached over to turn off the lamp on the little nightstand between their beds. "If you work hard and you want it enough. You're talented, Blossom. You don't have to give up if you don't make it this time. If you want it, you have to keep trying. That's what my orchestra teacher always says when we're playing for first chair violin."

Her sister's words echoed in her mind as the front door to the building opened and Blossom filed in with the first group of girls auditioning. A young woman with a clipboard was giving them instructions about properly stretching before they began, and how the auditions would work, from the group portion, which would narrow down the dancers, to the next part, where the remaining girls would dance individually for Mrs. van der Kolk.

The girl with the clipboard gestured to the corner, where an older woman was quietly watching them. Blossom tried not to stare at her too long, but she couldn't keep herself from glancing over while she found a spot to drop her coat and start warming up.

Some of the girls seemed to already know one another and sat together as they stretched. Others dropped down next to strangers and introduced themselves, chatting about how nervous they were. No one approached Blossom or even sat next to her, and she tried not to dwell on it. She wasn't here to become friends with anyone; she only wanted to dance. Once the girls had all warmed up their muscles at the barre, they took turns doing different types of leaps and turns across the floor as Beatrice van der Kolk and another woman and man observed them. The small group conferred with one another after everyone had taken two turns; Blossom held her breath as they called out the numbers of those they wanted to stay, letting it out in one big rush when she heard them say hers. To her right, a girl who evidently hadn't been chosen glared as a wide smile spread across Blossom's face.

As the morning went on and she awaited her turn to dance alone in front of Mrs. van der Kolk and her colleagues, Blossom could feel a tension filling the space around her. Outside, she had seen one light-skinned colored girl get into line about a dozen or so people behind her, but when she'd tried to catch the girl's eye, hoping for a friendly response, the girl had scowled and looked away. It had taken Blossom a few moments to understand the girl was passing; she didn't want anyone at the auditions to know she was colored. The girl hadn't come inside with Blossom's group, and Blossom wondered if she would have felt so alone if the girl had been in there with her—even if no one else knew she was colored. The looks and whispers from the girls around Blossom hadn't stopped as they made it to the second round; if anything, they were even more conspicuous.

Blossom thought of her conversation with Sybil, of how hard it must have been for Dorothy Dandridge when she'd just been starting out. Maybe Sybil was right. Maybe she *could* be like Dorothy one day. So Blossom held her head high, ignoring the girls around her, and when it was her turn to dance alone, she performed with more grace and strength than she ever had before. She imagined she was onstage, part of the company already, performing for an audience enraptured by her talent and confidence.

When she had finished, her chest rising and falling with her breath, she looked at Mrs. van der Kolk, who was murmuring to the man beside her. Blossom focused on the company director's silver-streaked chignon as she waited for them to address her. Finally, Mrs. van der Kolk looked up and gave Blossom a curt nod. "Thank you, Miss Blackwood. The company list will be posted Monday afternoon."

"Oh, yes, of course," Blossom said, deflating slightly. Did she really have to wait until Monday to find out? "Thank you, ma'am—er, Mrs. van der Kolk. Thank you all for your time."

Blossom heard snickers from the remaining dancers as she exited the room; she didn't know if they were laughing at her performance or the good Southern manners Flossie had instilled in her. As she pushed through the door of the building and back into the sunshine, she decided she didn't care. She'd made it to the second round and danced her very best. She had shown any naysayers why colored dancers should be part of the company, and if Mrs. van der Kolk and her colleagues didn't agree, then she supposed Sybil was right. She would simply have to keep trying. Because the way she'd felt in there—the way nothing else had mattered when she was in the center of the room, that the only person in control of what she was doing was Blossom herself—well, she'd never known anything like it. And Blossom wasn't going to give up so easily on that feeling.

Two days later, Blossom persuaded Michael to take the Yellow Car with her after school to see the cast list. She'd been able to think about little else all day, but as they stepped into the streetcar, she had the urge to turn right back around and walk home. What if her name wasn't on the list? She remembered the way Mrs. van der Kolk had thanked her after her audition, without the slightest bit of emotion. Blossom hesitated on the step so long that Michael, who had just paid their fare, turned to look at her.

"What's wrong?"

Blossom took in a breath. "I . . ."

"What is it?"

"I, er . . . I'm . . ."

The driver craned his neck around Michael, eyebrows raised. "Y'all getting on? Need to move this thing along."

"We don't have to do this," he said. "If you don't wanna go, we won't go, Blossom."

Blossom looked at Michael's face. She saw mostly concern in his expression, but then—there it was. Just the tiniest glimmer in his eyes, the same look he'd had back on her front steps, when she had told him she wanted to audition. The idea that he would be happy if she decided not to go was enough for her to square her shoulders, step all the way into the Yellow Car, and say, "I was only wondering if we were on the right line."

Michael didn't say anything as they found seats together up front across from an older white woman. He didn't speak at all for the entire ride, which was just fine with Blossom. She enjoyed not having to make conversation as she thought of how her life could completely change this very afternoon.

The Yellow Car let them off a couple of blocks away, and Blossom began walking so fast that Michael, whose legs had always seemed twice as long as hers, asked her to slow down.

When they reached the building, she eagerly pulled the door handle. It was locked. Blossom jerked the handle back and forth a few times, but the heavy door didn't budge. "What in the world? It's not even five o'clock yet. How are we supposed to—?"

"There it is," Michael said, his voice flat as he nodded to a piece of paper taped to the inside of the window next to the door.

There it was. Blossom's heart skipped a beat as she stepped closer, holding her hand against her forehead to block the sun's glare. Her eyes ran down the list carefully; she felt like she might get sick right there on the sidewalk in front of Michael. She might not have been the best, but she had done a very good job at her audition. She knew she'd been better than lots of the girls, maybe even some on this list. But perhaps Beatrice van der Kolk hadn't really wanted colored girls in her company, after all. Perhaps she—

"Congratulations."

Michael's voice was quiet, but it roared into Blossom's thoughts like a freight train. She glanced over her shoulder at him, her lips parting in confusion.

"Look." His index finger pointed to the very bottom of the list. To her name in typewritten black letters, just inches from the end of the page: Blossom Blackwood. "That's you, ain't it?"

"Oh my . . . Oh, Michael . . . That *is* me! It is!" Blossom threw her arms around his neck. She was so elated she would have hugged Beatrice van der Kolk herself, had she been there instead.

Michael slowly wrapped his arms around her and squeezed her tight. Into her shoulder, he said, "I'm proud of you."

But his voice was so muffled Blossom wasn't sure she'd heard him correctly. She pulled back, her arms still holding on to him as she asked, "What did you say?"

He looked down at the sidewalk. "I said, I'm proud of you. My mama is, too."

Blossom planted her hands on her hips. "Did Miss Rose tell you to say that?"

"No. Well, yes." He sighed. "But I *am* proud of you, Blossom. I always knew you were a star; now everyone else is going to know it, too. I just . . . I don't wanna lose you."

"You're not going to lose me, Michael." She embraced him again, resting her head on his chest, but the words had hardly left Blossom's lips before she knew it was a promise she couldn't keep. She would never be able to forget the look in his eyes earlier. The look that said he would have been perfectly happy if this moment hadn't arrived for her at all.

The weekend of Blossom's high school graduation, Flossie cooked a big Sunday supper, as usual. But when Blossom went to set the table shortly before the meal was ready, her mother told her to lay out plates for two more people.

"You mean, besides Marla and Harold?"

Flossie nodded, and sure enough, two extra chairs had already been pushed up to the round oak table for a total of seven. She looked at her mother, the question of who they were for poised on her lips. But when it was clear her mother wasn't going to stop humming and turn around from the stove to answer, Blossom began setting out the dishes and silverware.

She had just finished changing into one of her favorite dresses—the lemon-yellow one with puffed sleeves and mother-of-pearl buttons lining the front—when the doorbell rang. Marla never used the bell when she and Harold came over, so it had to be the mystery guests. Blossom waited to see if her mother or Sybil would open the door, but when it was apparent they weren't going to, she hurried out to the living room to greet their visitors herself.

"Oh my goodness!" she said when the door opened to reveal Michael and his mother standing on the other side. They were both dressed in their Sunday best; Michael was even wearing a tie. "What . . . ?"

"Surprise," he said. He was beaming.

She took a deep breath as she opened the screen door to let them in, and said, "It's so nice to see you, Miss Rose." Blossom kissed her cheek, and Michael's mother squeezed her arm warmly in return.

"You're even more beautiful than the last time I saw you, Blossom."

Flossie came out from the kitchen then, wiping her hands on the linen apron tied around her waist as she said hello to their guests. Blossom took the opportunity to whisper to Michael, "What are you doing here?"

Michael shrugged. "Your mama invited us. Told mine she wanted us to celebrate our graduations together." Blossom searched his big hazel eyes, but she didn't think he was hiding anything. Michael grinned at her and leaned down to whisper, "What, you ain't happy to see me?"

She gave a quick shake of her head. "Of course I am."

"Then we should tell them tonight," he murmured. "What better time than now? We've graduated. We're officially adults."

Michael had dropped the subject for a few weeks, but he'd been pushing again recently to tell Flossie about them. Each time, she'd invented a reason they couldn't do so, but she was running out of them. And now it didn't make sense to keep the secret any longer. They were done with high school. It had been two months since Blossom had become one of the newest members of the dance company, and in that time, Michael had secured a job working at the same aircraft factory as his uncle. Blossom had also been hired as a part-time waitress at the Dunbar Grill, the restaurant in the hotel where her mother worked. She'd only started a few weeks ago, just as school was winding down. She wasn't the best waitress the Dunbar had ever seen, but there were few jobs that provided flexibility to work with the company, and Flossie hadn't wanted her to clean rooms or houses. So, Blossom did her best to keep the customers satisfied while also keeping her eyes peeled for any of the established and up-and-coming entertainers who frequented the hotel.

It made sense, them finally telling her mother. But why did she have that feeling again that she'd had on the front porch months ago—the sinking sensation of being trapped?

She looked at Michael, unsure what to say. Luckily, she was saved by the footsteps walking up to the door: Marla and Harold. She held up her index finger to Michael as if to say *one moment*, though she hoped he'd forget all about their conversation as soon as she turned away. She greeted her sister and brother-in-law; then, when Michael was busy saying hello to them, she slipped out of the room and back to the kitchen to join Sybil.

"Did you know Michael and his mother were coming?" she asked just loud enough for Sybil to hear. Even with the commotion in the front room, Blossom was aware the bungalow wasn't that large. When she and her sisters hadn't wanted Flossie to hear them talking at night, they would curl up next to each other in bed and whisper directly into one another's ears, their hands protectively cupped around their mouths.

The guilt showed on Sybil's face immediately. "Mama only told me this morning, I swear. She wanted it to be a surprise." She cocked her head to the side, watching Blossom as she slowly stirred the greens. "Why do you look upset?"

"I'm not upset. I . . ." But Blossom couldn't lie. Her sister knew her too well. She sighed. "He wants us to tell Mama tonight."

Sybil's eyes slid back to the heavy pot of collards in front of her.

Blossom's hands went straight to her hips. "What?"

"Well, isn't it time you did already? What are you waiting for? You've been going steady as long as Marla has been married."

"I know. . ."

Sybil rested the wooden spoon across the top of the pot. "Don't you love him?"

Love. That was one thing Blossom was sure of. Her heart belonged to Michael. She still enjoyed sitting quietly with him or talking about anything and everything they could think of—their families, the happenings at school, the gossip floating around the neighborhood. Whenever she looked at him, whenever they touched, she felt something she never felt with anyone else. She still admired the way he was so focused—on his studies, and now on the new job he'd be starting the week after next. But she couldn't ignore the part of him that refused to take her ambitions seriously. She always had to bring up the dance company first; he never asked about her rehearsals or the other people she danced with. He hadn't seemed all that happy when she'd excitedly told him Mrs. van der Kolk was considering Blossom for a soloist part in the new show she was choreographing. And if he was this uninterested in her career now,

Blossom worried about her future. How could she truly love someone who would never respect her dreams, or support her pursuing them?

But what she said to Sybil was, "I do." She nodded firmly. "Yes, I do."

A few minutes later, they heard Flossie declare it was time to eat, so Blossom and Sybil stationed themselves by the stove while their guests seated themselves around the table. They fixed plates for everyone, including Flossie, and served themselves last. It was a tight fit around the table, elbows touching, but everyone looked happy to be there.

Flossie had spent all day in the kitchen, and it showed: along with the greens, they had meat loaf, macaroni and cheese, cornbread, and onion pie, as well as a gorgeous banana pudding for dessert. Before they began eating, Michael's mother asked if she could say grace. Flossie politely agreed, and they all linked hands, bowing their heads. But as soon as Miss Rose began to bless the food, Blossom, Marla, and Sybil exchanged looks from beneath their half-closed eyes. They weren't a religious family besides the occasional Easter Sunday and Christmas Eve services; this was the first time grace had ever been said at their table. Sybil squeezed Blossom's hand as if to say, *What is happening?* On the other side of Blossom, Michael was gently rubbing his thumb across her palm; it reminded her of the day he'd asked her to go steady, how she couldn't imagine saying no to being with him, even when she wasn't allowed to.

Once Miss Rose had closed out the prayer and they'd all said "amen" and lifted their heads, Flossie stood up from her seat and turned her attention to Blossom, clearing her throat.

Blossom immediately tensed. Mama didn't give speeches unless she had something to say.

"I was real proud to see my Blossom walking up onstage to get her diploma Friday. Can't believe I got two girls who been through school now. I'm getting to be an old woman," she said, laughing. The rest of the table politely tittered. "And now my little girl all grown up . . . So grown

94

up she got herself a steady boyfriend."

Every sound in the room stopped. It was so quiet that Blossom was sure her sharp intake of breath could be heard out on the street. Next to her, Michael stiffened, but Blossom didn't dare look at him. She wasn't sure *where* to look; her eyes slid uncomfortably around her lap, her plate, and the rest of the table before she gained the courage to look up and meet her mother's eyes.

To her utter surprise, Flossie was smiling. "Y'all thought we didn't know?"

On Michael's other side, Miss Rose was smiling, too. Had this been the plan from the beginning? To bring them together under the guise of celebrating their graduations only to announce they already knew what had been going on this whole time? Blossom looked at Marla, who gave a slight shrug, just as bewildered as she was.

"Well? You ain't got nothing to say for yourselves?" Flossie asked, still standing.

Michael cleared his throat. "Ah, we, uh . . . well, ma'am . . ."

Blossom set down her fork. "Mama, how did you know?"

"You really think we didn't notice how close you two been getting over the years? How much time y'all spend together? Can't imagine Michael been walking you home all these years for your protection."

"Mama!" Blossom said, her face going hot. She looked down at her plate, but her head shot right back up when Harold let loose a snicker from across the table. Then Sybil giggled, followed by Marla's loud, unfiltered cackle, and pretty soon the whole table was laughing, Blossom and Michael included. Flossie finally sat down, which put Blossom a bit more at ease. But then Michael, who seemed to have found his words, stood up.

"Miss Flossie, Mama . . . we been wanting to tell you both. For some time now. But we was afraid you'd make us stop seeing each other if we did. So we thought it was best to just keep things quiet until . . .

well, now." He cleared his throat again, looking down at Blossom, whose skin hadn't yet returned to a normal temperature. "I want y'all to know—everyone here to know—that I sure do care about Blossom. A whole lot. I . . . I love her."

Blossom swallowed hard. She couldn't believe this was happening.

Miss Rose patted her son's arm, smiling big at both of them. "Look at how the Lord works, Flossie. We done known each other all this time, since they was babies, and God brought them together like this. We real lucky, ain't we?"

Flossie nodded, but she was still looking at Michael, who slowly took his seat after his impromptu speech. "You really love my girl?"

"Yes, ma'am. I really do. Never met no one like her."

Flossie turned her gaze to Blossom. "You love him, too?"

Blossom usually adored having all eyes on her, that delicious feeling of being in control of a room, but she felt as if she were enduring the weight of a thousand stares as the six other people around the table looked at her. How she wished she were on a stage, delivering someone else's lines, rather than being put on the spot. Having to articulate her feelings about Michael to not only her mother, but *his* mother, Harold, and her sisters, too.

"I care very much about Michael," she said, her gaze drifting between Flossie and Miss Rose. "He's . . . well, he's the most important person in my life besides you, Marla, and Sybil."

"But do you love him?" Flossie's eyes were focused on her so intently, it was as if they were the only two people in the room. Her mother was trying to communicate something, but Blossom wasn't sure what exactly that might be. Was Flossie thinking about what she'd had—or hadn't had—with their father all those years? And she wasn't sure why Flossie had chosen to do this in front of everyone when she could have saved the interrogation for later. Was this her way of punishing Blossom for sneaking around with Michael behind her back?

"I . . . Yes, of course, Mama. Yes, I love him." Blossom looked at Michael with a quick smile; he briefly placed his hand over hers under the table, his face content.

"Hallelujah," Miss Rose crooned, one palm pressed to her bosom as she raised the other to the ceiling.

"Now that's out of the way, we should eat before this food gets cold," Flossie said, but before she took her first bite of meat loaf, she looked at Sybil from the corner of her eye. "And don't you go getting no ideas from this now, girl."

Sybil giggled again. Then Harold informed the table that his cousin, who'd been deployed overseas, would be coming home soon. Discussion quickly turned to the war, how the Germans had surrendered last month and the fighting was officially over in Europe. Blossom had never been more relieved for the focus to not be on her.

Later that evening, when their guests had left and Blossom and Sybil had finished cleaning up, Blossom found her mother sitting in the wingback chair, her feet up on the ottoman, Jack Benny's program playing softly on the radio. She hovered in the doorway, waiting for her mother to say something. When she didn't, Blossom finally said, "Thank you for supper, Mama."

"Y'all helped."

"I know, but . . . thank you anyway. It was nice."

Flossie toyed with the tin of tobacco on the table next to her. "If you too afraid to say you love him in front of people, I reckon it ain't real love."

Blossom stared at her. "Ma'am?"

Her mother sighed. "You took too long to say you love him back. What you think that means?"

"I . . . I wasn't expecting to have to discuss it in front of everyone, I suppose. I felt as if we were on display."

"Girl, you ain't never met an audience you didn't love," Flossie scoffed. She paused before adding, "Caring about someone and loving someone isn't always the same thing."

"Did you care about our daddy? Or did you love him?"

Flossie exhaled sharply, and for a moment, Blossom worried she'd said the wrong thing. She hadn't asked about him since she was a little girl, all those years ago, and she didn't want to upset Mama. But he had been her father. She was half him, and if she would never know who he was, she at least deserved to know how her mother had felt about him.

"Things with me and your daddy was complicated."

"But did you love him anyway?" Normally Blossom wouldn't dare question Flossie like this, but it seemed as if something had shifted between her and her mother. There was the fact that her relationship with Michael was now out in the open, but she was also working two jobs now and had graduated from senior high school. She was no longer the little girl who knew nothing of the world besides her family and the street outside their little bungalow.

When Flossie spoke again, she didn't look at Blossom. Her voice was so low, Blossom had to step forward a bit to hear her. "I loved your daddy so much, sometimes I thought he'd put a spell on me. And I'll always be grateful to him for giving me you girls. But—it wasn't right, the way I let him treat me." She looked up then, directly into Blossom's eyes. "I don't want you to make the same mistakes I did. You smarter than that. And you doing so good already, getting a dancing job straight outta school. I want you to be sure about him."

"Mama—"

"You don't got to love him," Flossie cut her off. "But you do got to be true to Blossom. You only doing a disservice to yourself, trying to convince your heart of something that ain't true."

Blossom lingered in the room a bit longer, waiting to see if her mother was going to say anything else. But Flossie only dug into the tin of tobacco with one hand, turning up the radio with the other, and Blossom knew that meant the conversation was done.

"Good night, Mama," she said, turning to walk the short distance to her and Sybil's bedroom.

Truth be told, she was glad Flossie hadn't had anything more to tell her. She'd already said enough. Perhaps too much, as far as Blossom was concerned.

Ardith

Ardith never knew what people wanted to hear when they asked why she'd gone into the business. Especially interviewers, who were really the only people who ever pretended to care about that type of stuff. There was the easy answer: When she was two years old, her mother had had to bring her to an audition, since no one in the family could watch her at the time, and one of the casting directors had suggested Kimberly take Ardith to a commercial audition one of her friends was working on, looking for young children. Ardith had started doing commercials, which turned into small roles in television series, and then, when she was eight years old, she'd been cast as Tinsley, one of the main child actors on *You Can Say That Again*.

But that wasn't often the answer people were looking for these days; they could find most of that online. They were really curious what it was Ardith loved so much about acting that she'd given up her childhood and teenage years to do it. And that, she didn't really have a good answer for. She'd always enjoyed watching her family perform. She loved that they all had a different role to which they gravitated, based on the qualities that defined them: Mommy was bubbly with a sharp wit but an ever-present sweetness underneath; Uncle Isaiah was the guy who played by his own rules but won everyone over with his charisma; Grandpa Abe was warm and sensible; and Bebe had moved through each scene, as she did in life, with impeccable grace.

Ardith, though, wasn't sure how to align the person she was with the roles she played. Onscreen, she most often portrayed characters with big personalities who loved having the attention on them, who made bold choices and statements that she'd never be comfortable with in real life— and as soon as the director called cut, she felt as if she were shedding a layer of clothing, changing into something that felt more like her. It thrilled her, getting to experience what it was like to be people so different from her, but even so, Ardith didn't understand why some actors seemed to court as much attention offscreen as they did when they were on camera.

Matty Cohen was one of those actors. He was only seventeen, like Ardith, but he'd already won his first Emmy, for a limited series he'd done when he was twelve in which he played a tween addicted to pills. Ardith hadn't known what to expect when they first met for the chemis- try read of *Suite 252*, but he was a generous acting partner—he was more concerned with finding the heart of his scenes with Ardith's character than he was about making sure the focus was on him. Some actors twice his age still hadn't learned that lesson.

Both Matty and Ardith had mostly worked on sets where they were the only kid or one of a few, rather than growing up on one of the shows created by entertainment studios built specifically for children's and teen programming. That meant they'd had more control over their careers in some ways; they didn't have to worry about strict morality clauses or being told what to wear or being strongly encouraged to pursue a music career on the side. But it also meant that sometimes it was harder to get noticed without the continual support of a strong studio behind them.

So far, Ardith enjoyed working on *Suite 252*, which was about a net- work of therapists from all different backgrounds, primarily focused on their personal lives. When Ardith's agent, Daphna, had sent over the log line and the sides for the audition, Ardith had burst out laughing. The role was for the daughter of a therapist—she'd practically been training for this her whole life. She may not have had a parent who worked as a therapist, but she'd been regularly seeing one since she was nine, and Dr. York's office sometimes felt more like home than her own house did.

Today was the table read for the sixth episode of the season they were currently filming, in which Ardith's and Matty's characters were going to kiss for the first time. She hadn't worried too much about it when she'd first read the script, but now that she was sitting around the L-shaped tables with the director, a few of the writers, a couple of producers, the department heads, and the rest of the cast, Ardith felt her throat go dry. She'd done kissing scenes before, and she and Matty wouldn't be acting it out today, but as she paged through the script, she still felt her nerves getting the best of her.

The rest of the room seemed unsettled as well, but for a different reason: Matty was late. Caitlin, the showrunner, kept checking her phone to look at the time; everyone else, especially the producers, kept eyeing the empty seat next to Ardith every few minutes.

As Ardith finished skimming their scene for the second time, Matty strolled into the room.

"Fucking finally," a voice muttered beside her. It was Bryce Fletcher, who played the primary therapist in the practice.

"Sorry, Cait," Matty said with an apologetic smile to the showrunner.

Bryce snorted. "Don't you think you should be apologizing to the rest of us? We've all been sitting here, too."

Ardith took a sip from her water bottle just as Matty slid into the seat next to hers.

"Really, Bryce?" he said with a grin. "Didn't you leave us waiting for, what, an hour last week? Twice?"

Ardith nearly choked on her water. Bryce was a veteran actor from the same generation as Hollis's dad, with film roles stretching back to before Ardith and Matty were even born. He'd only started doing television in recent years, but Bryce was the show's main star power. It was true that he was often late to set, which affected nearly everyone else's schedule since he was at the top of the call sheet; it was rude and entitled behavior, but no one ever called him on it because he was so respected in the business.

But then, so was Matty.

Bryce pursed his lips, and Ardith could see he was trying very hard not to let Matty get to him as he coolly responded, "I hope whatever you were up to last night was worth keeping us waiting. Page Six had a lot to say about it."

"Hey, it's good to hear you're such a fan. I know you haven't seen the inside of a club in about forty years, but let me know if you want to come with next time."

Bryce's face dropped. He looked to Caitlin to see if she was going to say anything to Matty, but she just shook her head and said, "Guys, we don't have time for this. Everyone's here now. Let's get going."

Bryce shot Matty a nasty look and mumbled something Ardith couldn't hear; Matty put on a neutral expression and opened the script like nothing had even happened. Ardith wondered if he and Bryce would have gone back and forth like that if any studio execs had been sitting in on the read that day.

There was no denying Matty Cohen was cute. When Ardith's cousin Prentice had first found out she'd be working with him, he'd fallen to the floor in an exaggerated swoon; he'd had a crush on Matty for years. Matty was mixed, with a Black mom and a white dad; slight in frame with dark, floppy curls; and, on days he wasn't filming, wore nail polish and loads of jewelry, from armfuls of bracelets to dangly earrings. Anyone who paid attention had heard the stories and seen pictures of Matty partying, but, in Ardith's experience, he'd been a real professional on the job. This was the first time he'd ever been late that she could remember, and—until a moment ago—she'd only seen him treat everyone, from his co-stars to the many members of the crew, with respect. None of this surprised her, though—despite Matty's reputation in the tabloids, she'd never heard anyone say he was a nightmare to work with. She knew enough about Bryce, however, to not be surprised by the continually rude things he said and did.

Caitlin started the read immediately. And as they worked their way through the first act, Ardith started to relax. Reading the script alone was always such a different experience than being at the table read. When she was by herself, she was focused on her own lines—trying to memorize them, understanding the different beats in the scene and how her character fit into the episode overall. But when she was at the table, she got to hear the writing and dialogue come alive, and she felt as if she was actually in the scene rather than looking down at it.

Early in the second act, just before Ardith and Matty's scene together, they reached the part where Bryce's character received the news that his mother had passed away. While he was being comforted by another therapist at his practice, played by an actor named Paul, Ardith found herself leaning forward over the table as they read together.

Toward the end of the scene, when Paul offered to call Bryce's character a car to take him home, Bryce's response came out hollow. Haunted, almost. "I've heard clients say this before—that it was like a piece of them died when their loved one did. And I understand now. There's always going to be a part of me that's missing now that she's not here."

In that moment, Ardith let out an anguished gasp. A fat tear splattered onto her script; she touched her fingers to her face and found more of them streaming down her cheeks and dripping down her neck.

"You all right?" Matty whispered, leaning in.

But there was no need to whisper. The whole room had stopped and looked up when she'd made that sound, and now they were staring as she tried to surreptitiously wipe away the tears flooding her face.

"Ardith? Everything okay?" Caitlin asked gently.

"I'm—yes. No, I—" she stammered. "I'm so sorry. I just need a minute, please." Ardith kept her head down as she scraped her chair back from the table and bolted from the room.

She'd barely made it through the restroom door before more loud, choked sobs escaped. What was wrong with her? One emotional scene—right before her big one, no less—and she'd broken down like this? And in front of everyone. Ardith covered her eyes with her palms, but still, the tears wouldn't stop.

There was a light knock on the door. "Ardith? Are you okay?"

Matty.

"Uh-huh," she said, trying desperately to stifle a burst of fresh sobs.

"That didn't sound too convincing," he said. "I'm coming in, all right?"

The door creaked open, and through her wet lashes, Ardith saw Matty poke his head in. "Hey."

She opened her mouth a few times, trying to speak, but she couldn't get anything out.

Matty walked over so he was standing next to her at the sink and put his arm loosely around her shoulder. She stiffened, instinctually, at him touching her. They didn't know each other that well. But when he spoke, his voice was gentle. "Try to breathe. It'll help. In and then out. In and out. In . . ."

Ardith followed his direction, closing her eyes so she could focus, and slowly, her sobs lessened and then stopped altogether. Matty's arm was still around her shoulder, and after a moment, she relaxed, allowed herself to lean into him.

"I can't believe that just happened," she said, sniffling. She was still too embarrassed to look him in the eyes.

"You mean someone finally telling Bryce he's the piece of shit that he is? Not gonna lie, I'm pretty proud of that."

Ardith let out a gasping laugh. "I can't believe that, either. You're kind of my hero."

"Probably didn't score me any points in there, but maybe he'll think twice before he talks to people like that again. I'd already texted Caitlin to let her know my mom got called into the hospital unexpectedly, so I had to take my little sister to school at the last minute. And I'm sure as hell not obligated to defend myself to Bryce—he's gonna think the worst about me no matter what I say." Then his tone softened. "But seriously, that scene was tough. It kinda got to me, too. I believe it's what we call a *tearjerker*, Ms. Blackwood. You were just responding to the work. Which probably feeds Bryce's fucking ego, but let's chalk it up to good writing instead." Ardith laughed again, a little. Matty grabbed some paper towels from the dispenser and handed them to her. "This have anything to do with your great-grandma?"

Ardith wet the towels with cool water and began patting at her face. "I guess? I mean, I still get upset when I think about her, and I think about her almost all the time, but . . . I wasn't during that scene. I was just following along and then all of a sudden, I'm bawling like a little kid." She shook her head. "It's mortifying."

"She hasn't been gone that long," Matty said, hopping up onto the counter as if he planned to stay there awhile. "It's totally normal to still be upset."

"Not in front of all those people, it's not."

"That's not how grief works. You don't get a choice in how or when it comes. It just does."

His words sounded a lot like something Dr. York would say. She looked at him then and saw something stormy in his own eyes. But he didn't elaborate, so she kept talking because talking was the only thing keeping her from crying.

"It's extra embarrassing because my great-grandma always told me

I had to work harder and be more professional than anyone else in the room. As a woman . . . and especially as a Black woman." She leaned her hip against the edge of the counter. "She said I couldn't afford to make the same mistakes as white actors if I want to be taken seriously, and now I just interrupted a table read crying over her. Nobody's going to look at me the same after this."

"Well, nobody's going to look at me the same, either. I just picked a fight with a *Hollywood legend*."

Ardith smiled, but the two situations weren't the same, and she knew it. Being late was frowned upon, but Matty was Matty. He was a guy, so his actions would never be scrutinized in the same way as hers; in fact, all the photos of him out partying only seemed to create more press for the projects he was in. Plus, he didn't have as much to prove since he'd already won a huge award. The pressure Ardith felt of being a Blackwood lingered constantly in her mind—not to mention being Kimberly Arnold's daughter. If she was photographed out wearing shoes from last season—well, she could already see the headlines. Matty was being so sweet, though. She didn't want to get into it. Not now, when she'd finally managed to stop crying.

He gave her a playful nudge. "You feeling better?"

She nodded. Not great, but better. And that would have to be good enough for now. She had to get back to work. "Thanks, Matty."

He left so she could have a moment to get herself together. Ardith splashed water over her face; there was nothing she could do about her puffy eyes, but at least they had dried up for the time being. She would go back in there and do her job, just as Bebe had told her to do when she had a bad day at work. Ardith probably couldn't even imagine some of the things her great-grandmother had dealt with back then.

Matty was standing across the hallway when she opened the bathroom door a few minutes later.

"You didn't have to wait for me."

"Yeah, I did," he said simply, and then tossed his arm around her again as they headed back to the conference room.

There was nothing remotely romantic about it—Matty wasn't her type, and she got the feeling she wasn't exactly his, either. But his arm on her shoulder was comforting, and after a moment, she realized a little part of her hoped that maybe they could become friends. She wasn't used to making friends her age, and especially not friends like Matty Cohen, who just a couple months ago had been photographed lying half-naked on top of a bar in Mexico City with a bunch of influencer-types pouring liquor into his bellybutton. But in the short time they'd been working together, he'd already shown her that there was more to him than that. And to Ardith, that was what mattered.

Grandpa Abe and Taffy went up to Big Sur for a short getaway the next weekend, which meant no Saturday Breakfast—which meant Ardith was free to volunteer at the Swanson Avenue Baptist rummage sale. She'd sent an invitation to the family group text, but everyone had politely declined, aside from Prentice and her father, neither of whom had bothered to respond. Ardith hadn't expected any of them to come—no one was as fascinated by rummage sales as she and Bebe had been. Sometimes, on the way home from church, they would drive through random neighborhoods and follow any signs they saw for garage sales; other times, Bebe would research sales nearby and plan a whole day for the two of them after Saturday Breakfast, mapping out the best routes and times to hit up each one. Occasionally they visited estate sales—like the one they'd eventually have for Bebe's things, once Grandpa Abe and Taffy had finished going through them—but Bebe most enjoyed browsing through regular old yard sales. She said they often had the best stuff.

Ardith headed straight down to the church basement, where all of the volunteers were gathered. In the main room, where they had lunches and dinners and served holiday meals to the community, a small table had been set up with boxes of doughnuts and pastries, jugs of juices and bottles of water, and a little coffee bar. She had just helped herself to a paper cup of coffee when Lexie Arrington walked up next to her.

"You got roped into this, too?" Lexie said, giving her a shy smile as she perused the picked-over box of doughnuts.

"I actually love these things," Ardith said. "Is that weird?"

Lexie shrugged. "I like going grocery shopping with my mom—who am I to judge?" She used a napkin to grab a bear claw, then poured a cup of orange juice. "It is cool that you show up to stuff like this, though."

Ardith blinked at her. "Why wouldn't I?"

Lexie's eyes went wide. "Oh, I just mean that it's so normal! Boring, even. And you're, like, working on a show with Matty Cohen."

Ardith smiled. "Yeah. I guess sometimes I crave the boring stuff."

"Right. But, like, Matty Cohen," Lexie said, bear claw poised at her lips as if she were too excited by the thought of him to take her first bite.

Ardith laughed. "He's a good guy."

"Good and *fine*," Lexie said, which made Ardith snort.

Two hard, loud claps sounded from the front of the room, and they looked up to see Sister Robinson trying to get everyone's attention, travel mug in hand. "Good morning, everyone. We're so pleased you've showed up to help with the annual church rummage sale, which, as a reminder, raises money for the Swanson Avenue building fund. We're going to divide you into different groups, but if you find yourself with nothing to do and see someone needs help, please don't hesitate to make yourself available. In a few minutes, we're going to start transferring the donations onto the tables, so please finish up your breakfast or grab something to eat or some coffee if you haven't already. We're going to need you *energized* and ready to greet our guests!"

"How much coffee do you think she's had?" Lexie whispered.

Ardith tried to hide her smile behind her hand. She hadn't known

Lexie had a sense of humor. Maybe it only came out when she wasn't around her mother. Ardith hadn't talked to Lexie much without Sister Arrington hovering nearby.

Ardith usually brought something to events like this to hide a bit, so she wouldn't draw too much attention. They were staying indoors today, so she'd opted for a baseball cap with a low brim. It was a habit she'd picked up from Bebe, who would usually wear a sun hat and big sunglasses when they went out to garage sales.

About an hour into Ardith's shift at the jewelry table, a small, dark-skinned girl slowly approached her. She was adorable, with a gorgeous crown of cornrows braided in a concentric pattern. She looked up at Ardith with a bashful expression that nearly melted her heart. "Excuse me, are you Tinsley?"

Ardith met her question with a big smile. "Well, hi, there. My name is Ardith, but I *was* Tinsley, on television. Did you like that show?"

"I *love* that show!" the little girl said, her soft voice growing more confident as she spoke. "*You Can Say That Again* is my favorite show in the whole wide world."

"That makes me so happy. What's your name?"

"Kendra," the little girl said, looking down at her shoes, shy again.

"It's very nice to meet you—"

"*Kendra!* What are you doing over here? You can't just run off like that!" A young woman with equally beautiful cornrows jogged up to the table, bending down so she was at eye level with the child. "Do you understand? You scare Mommy when you don't stay with her."

Kendra nodded, but she was pointing to Ardith at the same time, saying, "But it's Tinsley."

"I don't care who—" The woman stopped as she looked at Ardith, her eyes growing wide as she recognized her. "Oh. Oh my . . . Are you that Blackwood girl?"

"Ardith," she said evenly. "What's your name?"

110

"Jaleesa."

"Nice to meet you, Jaleesa."

"Wow, it's so nice to meet *you*. I swear, you're in my house just about every day. This little girl can't get enough of *You Can Say That Again*. She begs me to put on episodes every day. What are you doing here?"

"Helping out. All money goes to the building fund."

Jaleesa raised her eyebrows. "No, but do you go here? To this church?"

"Since I was Kendra's age."

"Well, damn. I can't believe you've been over here this whole time and we didn't even know. Huh. Might have to start coming here ourselves," she said, her eyes scanning the basement.

"Mommy, don't curse," Kendra stage-whispered to her mother.

"Swanson Avenue Baptist is a great place to worship. Come any Sunday," Ardith said, flashing a smile again.

"All right, then. Maybe we will." Jaleesa took Kendra's hand and started to pull her along, but Kendra wouldn't budge. She wanted a picture with Ardith.

Jaleesa snapped a quick photo with her phone, and thanked Ardith. But she hesitated before walking away. "I, uh, want to tell you that I really loved your mom's movies, growing up. She was only a few years older than me, and my big sister and I used to watch her all the time. Wanted to be her." Jaleesa squeezed Kendra tight to her side. "My sister got all messed up—on drugs—but when she saw what happened to your mom . . . Well, it finally convinced her to get some help. This was years ago, and she's had a few slipups since then, but she's mostly stayed sober and . . . I don't know why I'm telling you this. I guess I wanted to say I know what it's like to love someone who's struggling like that, and I'm sorry."

Ardith swallowed hard. "Thank you. I appreciate that. I'm glad your sister is doing better and—"

"Hello, there!" trilled a voice suddenly, startling Ardith. She turned to see Sister Robinson behind her, beaming. She hadn't even heard the first lady walk up, but her attention was turned to Jaleesa. "Thank you so much for supporting the church today. Your daughter is just the sweetest. Have you seen the table of children's books we have over here? There are some real wonderful finds that I just can't let you get away without seeing. Let me show you . . ."

And then Sister Robinson was whisking Jaleesa and Kendra away before Ardith knew what had happened. Kendra turned to wave at her as she skipped off, still holding her mother's hand. Ardith waved back and watched them until they were out of sight.

A few moments later, Sister Robinson returned, sliding into the empty chair next to Ardith.

"If that wasn't the cutest thing I've ever seen," she said, shaking her head wistfully. "You made that little girl's day."

"It was no big deal," Ardith said. "She was a sweet kid. Her mom was really nice, too."

"Oh, of course. I hope you don't mind me steering them away, though. It sounded as if she was starting to get a little personal with you, and I didn't want you to have to manage that."

Ardith started to tell her it wasn't a problem, but Sister Robinson kept talking.

"We are so grateful to you for helping out at events like this. The pastor and I know how busy you are, and that you have to contend with a lot of attention anytime you leave your home. We so appreciate your devotion, so it's important for us to continue making you feel as safe as possible when you're at church functions."

"I like being here, Sister Robinson," Ardith said. "It's not a chore."

"Well, we thank you. Are you doing okay? Do you need a break?"

Ardith shook her head. "I'm fine, thanks."

"Okay, then. Well, it looks like—oh, yes, there's Sister Jenkins waving at me. I'd better go see what the issue is." Sister Jenkins, one of the deacons' wives, was monitoring the table of cookware; in front of her, a man was standing with a cast-iron skillet in hand, looking utterly peeved.

"Be right there, Sister Jenkins!" the pastor's wife called with a wave and a smile. She turned back to Ardith. "We'll see you tomorrow, yes?"

"Yes, of course."

"I hope you'll accept our invitation to come to brunch again. We so enjoyed having you with us last time."

"That would be nice. Thank you."

"Perfect. If I don't get the chance to speak with you again, have a wonderful rest of your day, Sister Ardith."

As Ardith sat there, arranging the costume jewelry, she couldn't stop thinking about Jaleesa. It wasn't often that she heard from people who were both supportive about her mother and also unafraid to talk about her, and hearing that she'd meant so much to Jaleesa and her sister had made Ardith . . . Well, *proud* was the best word, she supposed. She looked around the crowded basement but she didn't see Jaleesa—and anyway, the moment was gone.

It was thoughtful of Sister Robinson to look out for her, but Ardith had been doing this a long time. She didn't need a bodyguard. Sometimes she just needed to feel like a normal person.

Hollis

"I'm going to tell my dad tonight," Dwayne said, looking at Hollis from the corner of his eye.

It was Saturday night, and they were relaxing on the long sectional in Dwayne's family room, Dwayne sitting up and Hollis lying on her side. The giant wall-mounted flatscreen TV was tuned to a documentary about the ocean, the type of show Dwayne watched when he wanted to relax. Nature documentaries always made Hollis feel slightly anxious, worried something bad was going to happen to the animals.

But tonight, Dwayne looked even more anxious than she did.

"Wait . . . you mean about basketball?" She propped herself up on her elbow. The camera panned in on a manatee floating calmly through the water.

"Yeah."

"Tonight? With all of us here?"

"Exactly. This way, when he gets pissed, he'll have your parents here to keep him in check."

"You think that'll work?"

Dwayne shrugged. "I figure it's worth a shot. Your parents are basically family."

Hollis wrinkled her nose. "Does that mean I'm basically family, too?"

"You are, but . . . it's different," he said, gently squeezing her ankle through her jeans. Letting his hand rest there. Hollis liked the weight of it.

"Are you nervous?" she asked.

"Yeah. But it's better that you're here."

Hollis smiled. "Good."

"Well, don't y'all look cozy."

Hollis nearly fell off the couch at the sight of Dwayne's dad, Kenley, standing in the doorway. For such a big guy, he was light on his feet. Hollis had always enjoyed being around Kenley. He was charming, liked to joke around. Still, his quick temper was legendary. She used to watch his games with Dwayne sometimes, and if there was drama on the court, there was a pretty good chance Kenley was involved. He'd been a notorious hothead and shit-talker, which had gotten him into trouble both on and off the court more than a few times.

"We're learning about the ocean." Hollis pointed to the television.

"Mm-hmm," Kenley said, eyebrow raised. "Well, dinner is ready if you can manage to tear yourself away from the manatees."

The dining room table was beautifully set, with two bouquets of ivory-colored flowers and long white candles resting in silver holders. Hollis sat next to Dwayne and across from her parents, with Libby and Kenley at either end of the table.

"Everything looks so gorgeous, Libby," said Hollis's mother, spreading her napkin across her lap.

"Hey!" Kenley puffed up his chest in mock indignation. "How do you know I didn't put all this together?"

Mom shook her head. "You could never."

"Thank you, honey," Libby said, ignoring her husband. "Do the dishes look familiar?"

Dad squinted at them. "Did we get these for you?"

"Yes! The Hermès set, for our tenth anniversary. So sweet of you."

Isaiah held his hands up as if to say, *You know how we do.* "We had to show out since we didn't know you when you got married."

Libby laughed. "I'm pretty sure we were still eating off paper plates back then."

As they continued to make light conversation, Dwayne's knee kept bouncing up and down next to Hollis's. She put her hand on his leg for a moment; when he glanced over, she looked at him, told him silently that it was going to be okay. He nodded and briefly placed his hand over hers before he took the platter of roast chicken from Hollis's dad.

"Rhonda, how is that project going?" Kenley asked, adding a heaping spoonful of sautéed mushrooms to his plate. "Libby said you were still thinking it over?"

Mom sighed. "I definitely would have signed on by now if they'd hired me first, but stepping in for another director who's already laid out their vision . . . I don't know. And I've heard from just about everyone that Wiley Macklin is a nightmare."

"He is," Libby mumbled, picking up her glass of white wine.

"I keep telling her she has to think about the end result," Dad said. "I know from asshole actors, but she doesn't need to be his best friend. All she has to do is get a good performance out of him. And he *is* a good actor."

"And I keep telling *him*," Mom said, gently nudging her husband, "that sometimes a good performance is still nothing but a headache. So what if we do get a great movie out of it? Then I have to go on the awards circuit with someone like that and watch him talk about how much he gave to the role? Act like it was such a wonderful experience? I don't know if it's worth it."

"It might be, if it gets your work out to millions of people who haven't seen it before," he countered.

Hollis knew her parents had differing views of the industry. Her father had acted in films helmed by some of the best Black directors in Hollywood—Ava DuVernay, Spike Lee, John Singleton, Barry Jenkins— and had signed on to a fair number of smaller projects just to work with

Black indie film directors he held in high regard. But he often spoke of the two Hollywoods: Black Hollywood, where many Black actors were household names, and mainstream Hollywood, where a lot of those same actors would never even be considered for lead roles. Isaiah thought it was good to have a foot in both worlds—to continue to act in movies that were made for, by, and about Black people, but to also make a point to seek out mainstream roles, even if it meant taking smaller parts and paychecks. Her mother, on the other hand, was firmly entrenched in Black indie film, and had always been wary of crossing over into bigger-budget Hollywood for fear of her vision being compromised.

She nodded. "I just wish I didn't have to make these kinds of decisions. Say yes to the project where I don't get final say in the casting and potentially have a horrible shoot? Or say no and wait years for another big studio to offer me something?"

"See, this is why y'all should've gotten into sports instead," Kenley said.

Libby rolled her eyes. "Right, because pro sports leagues definitely don't have any issues to address."

"Come on, baby. I'm just saying, we gonna be an NBA family in a few years once our boy gets drafted."

Dwayne's knee started bouncing again.

Libby made a face. "We'll still be one-third Hollywood. And anyway, there are more theatrics on those courts than any film set I've ever been on. Did you forget how you used to act out there?"

Kenley lifted his chin at her. "That was then. I'm Zen now, baby." He looked around at the rest of the table. "I've been doing yoga, meditation. I'm a different person than I used to be."

Hollis's dad snorted, which made the whole table burst out laughing, Kenley included.

Mom turned to Dwayne then. "You've been quiet, sweetie. How is everything? School? Basketball?"

"Everything's fine," Dwayne said before he shoveled in a huge bite of chicken.

"He's gonna have to start making some big decisions soon," Kenley said, waving his fork toward Dwayne. "Senior year. Less than five hundred points from the Dupree all-time scoring record. College scouts practically knocking down our door. It's all happening."

The table was silent as everyone waited for Dwayne to speak, but he just kept cramming in food as if he hadn't eaten in days, staring down at his plate.

"You got any top choices for schools, D?" Dad asked.

Hollis felt Dwayne tense up next to her. She felt bad for him, being put on the spot like this. It reminded her of when her parents' friends and colleagues would ask her when she was going to go into the business, as if it were a foregone conclusion.

"Mm." Dwayne finished chewing, took a drink of water, and wiped his mouth. "Uh, not really."

"He will," Kenley said. "He's just overwhelmed by all the interest. We'll narrow it down soon."

"Actually, Dad . . . that's not it," Dwayne said, his voice quiet.

Libby looked at him. "What do you mean?"

Dwayne cleared his throat. "There's something I need to tell you. Both of you. All of you. I mean, Hollis knows, but . . . um."

Kenley was frowning now. He set his fork down, his gaze latched on to Dwayne. "Knows what?"

"I . . . I don't know if I want to play ball anymore."

Kenley let out his thunderous laugh, overpowering the room, which was otherwise silent. "Man, you almost got me." He shook his head, continuing to chuckle as he picked up his glass of wine. "Talking about you don't want to play ball . . ."

Hollis found Dwayne's hand beneath the table; she slipped her fingers through his and squeezed. He squeezed back, but even through his tight grip she could feel him shaking.

"What's next? You gonna tell me you want to get into acting?" Kenley was still laughing, so loudly that he didn't notice he was the only one doing so.

Libby looked at Dwayne. "Honey, are you serious?"

Dwayne took a deep breath, glancing around the table at everyone. He exchanged a long, meaningful look with his father, whose eyes were boring into him like lasers. Hollis felt Dwayne slowly deflate next to her.

"Nah, I'm just being stupid," he said with a feeble attempt at a laugh himself. "Just wanted to see what you would say."

"See? I knew it." Kenley eyed his son, and, slowly, the smile left his face. "'Cause you'd have some explaining to do to a whole lot of people besides me if you just up and quit now. You know how much of our lives we've invested in this? You'd have to be real dumb to throw all that in the trash. And we all know you ain't dumb, Dwayne."

Dwayne nodded, then stared down at his plate. Under the table, he let go of Hollis's hand.

He didn't speak another word for the rest of dinner.

Hollis wasn't really a fan of parties. She preferred one-on-one hangs, or even the occasional small gathering with a few of Dwayne's other friends. Parties were too big, too loud, and honestly kind of disgusting with all the beer that inevitably got spilled and food that always ended up between couch cushions. She was even less a fan of the fact that she was giving up her Saturday night to go to a party thrown by Orlando. And worst of all, it was at the beach.

"We are not beach people," Hollis announced from the passenger seat of Dwayne's Range Rover.

They had just finished dinner with their families; Hollis had been hoping to skip out on the party, but after the way Dwayne's attempt to be honest with his dad had spectacularly failed, she couldn't say no to him.

"I am absolutely a beach person," Dwayne said, steering them through the heavy traffic on the 110. "You're the one who hates it, so I just never go with *you*."

"Whatever. It's going to be freezing. And we don't exactly live close to Dockweiler. We've been driving forever."

"Tell me about it," Dwayne muttered from the seat next to her. But when she glanced over, he smiled. She was glad to see it, the first one since dinner. "Thanks for coming with me."

She bit the corner of her lip. "Yeah, that was tough back there. I figured you might need someone to do you a favor."

"Then do me another favor? Please be cool to Orlando tonight."

"I'm always cool to Orlando!" He side-eyed her, eliciting a groan. "Look, it's obvious that we just don't vibe. If I don't talk to him, we don't fight."

That was what she'd been telling herself since the first day of school. They had one class together, AP Government, where they sat as far away from each other as possible, so the only time she really had to talk to him was at lunch. They still sat at the same table, but they had agreed to some sort of silent truce. She could tell Dwayne didn't like it, but he couldn't force them to be friends, and it was better than them fighting.

"That's fair," Dwayne said, easily merging into the carpool lane for the last leg of their trip. "But he didn't really have anything bad to say about you when I talked to him."

"What do you mean, 'didn't really'? He did say something?"

Dwayne sighed. "He just said sometimes you come across a little standoffish."

Hollis opened her mouth to argue, but it wasn't the first time she'd been told that, and maybe it was a little true. Still, she had her reasons.

She was always aware that, as a Blackwood, most people put their expectations on her without taking the time to get to know her, and how was she supposed to live up to that? "Okay, fine. But you have to admit he has a huge chip on his shoulder."

"Think about what it must be like for him at Dupree," Dwayne said, his voice a bit tight. "I just think you could give him a break sometimes. Not everyone has it like us."

Hollis didn't want to irritate Dwayne more when he was already upset about what had happened at dinner, so she kept her mouth shut. And she was actually happy when they arrived at the beach so she could escape the tension in the car. Dwayne walked around to the back, popped the trunk, and pulled out a couple of thick blankets, a cooler, a grocery store bag.

He carried the cooler, balancing the blankets on top, and Hollis picked up the paper bag, peeking inside. "Marshmallows?"

"For s'mores," Dwayne said.

Hollis raised her eyebrows. S'mores were so wholesome, and Dupree parties were known for their high quantities of alcohol above anything else. But they'd left his house before Libby served dessert, and something about being around a fire always made Hollis crave s'mores.

They headed down to the sand and didn't have to walk far before they found Orlando. The party was still pretty small at that point, mostly guys he and Dwayne played ball with, a few of their girlfriends, and some guys from Leimert Park, where Orlando lived. The fire pit was already going, and Orlando stood in front of it next to a bag of charcoal and a container of lighter fluid, warming his hands over the flames.

"What up, Lando?" Dwayne dumped the cooler a few feet away so he could dap up his friend.

"Aww, hell. Look what the tide dragged in," Orlando replied, slapping Dwayne on the back as if they hadn't just seen each other a day ago. He spotted Hollis over Dwayne's shoulder. "Wow. Hollis Blackwood gracing us with her presence tonight?"

"I never miss a beach party," she said, pasting on a smile. She remembered Bebe recounting some of the horrible things people used to say to her back in the day, when her only defense was to kill them with kindness if she didn't want to end up on some producer's blacklist—or worse. If Bebe could handle that, she could handle Orlando. "Thanks for having me."

He gave her a look, but didn't say anything. He just reached into his pocket, extracting a fat joint. "Was just about to light this up. Anyone want to help me start it?"

Dwayne declined since he was driving, and Hollis shook her head. She'd been high a few times, but weed mostly made her sleepy, and she wouldn't ever smoke in front of people she didn't trust. She was always paranoid that she'd get too baked and say something she regretted—or worse, that someone would catch those regrettable words on video and blast it out to everyone, embarrassing her and making things harder for her family.

"Man, y'all ain't no fun. I'll be back," Orlando said, sparking up the joint before he went off in search of someone to help him smoke it.

"Yeah, I'm the one who's standoffish," Hollis mumbled loud enough for Dwayne to hear.

"Be nice," he said, but he pulled her to him in a small hug and squeezed, and Hollis took a moment to savor the warmth that shot through her in that moment.

More people arrived, and pretty soon the party had grown so large that Hollis couldn't keep track of who all was there. The beach patrol was never far away, though, so everyone knew to keep their alcohol in soda bottles and In-N-Out cups. Dwayne wasn't partaking in anything, but he'd brought provisions in the cooler, and as the crowd grew larger, Hollis decided she wanted a drink. Just something to take the edge off being somewhere she wasn't quite comfortable. She noticed a few of Orlando's friends looking her way, and she wondered if they recognized her, or if

Orlando had said something to them about her. She'd slipped on a hoodie over her top, but that didn't stop her from wondering if anyone noticed that her chest was smaller.

Dwayne handed her a bottle of Cherry Coke. Hollis took it and lifted it to her nose, sniffing. "What's in it?"

"Rum. You'll like it."

She took a tentative sip that turned into a confident swig because Dwayne was right—it was delicious. They made their way along the sand, weaving through the small groups and occasionally stopping so Dwayne could say hi to people he knew. Hollis felt the booze moving through her, and maybe the drink was too strong, but she wasn't complaining. She didn't often drink, but some nights she really wanted that loose, light feeling. Tonight was one of them.

When they circled back to the fire, two of the guys Hollis had seen looking at her before came up to Dwayne to say hi. He introduced them as Bryan and Amari. "They grew up with Orlando," he explained.

"Shit, we still growing up," said Bryan, taking a long drink from a soda bottle. "Lando just decided to leave us during the week for that fancy school."

"You go there, too?" Amari asked, his eyes moving to Hollis. She nodded, and he looked like he wanted to say something, but he just nodded back and looked down at the sand.

"Hey, D—Lando said you talking crazy," Bryan said, squinting at him. "Huh?"

"He said you talking like you don't want to keep playing ball." Bryan appraised him. "That true?"

Dwayne shrugged. "Man, I dunno. I don't really fuck with ball like that anymore, but I tried to tell my dad tonight, and, uh, it didn't work out."

"He give you hell?"

"No, I . . . He thought I was joking, and so I just pretended I was." Hollis could feel the embarrassment radiating from him, and she had to stop herself from reaching for his hand. "Y'all already know he got a mean-ass temper, and he also got his eyes set on the league for me. Keeps saying we gonna be an NBA family."

"I get it," said Bryan. "You and Lando carrying that team, easy."

"Thanks, man. It's not my thing, though."

"What's not your thing?" Orlando asked, coming up next to them.

"Ball."

Orlando sucked his teeth. "Whatever, man. You are *not* abandoning me our last year together."

"But he shouldn't play if he hates it," Hollis blurted, and immediately wished she hadn't said anything.

Orlando turned his gaze on her, took a step forward. "Do you even get what it's like to be as good at something as D is at basketball?"

"Hey, chill, man," Dwayne said carefully. "She's just looking out."

"Of course I do," Hollis said, feeling heat beginning to rise in her chest. "I've seen him play."

"Yeah, but what are *you* good at? Never seen you play any sports, or care about anything, really. So I don't see how you can get it. But I guess you don't have to care when your last name's Blackwood." Orlando looked her square in the eye as he smirked. "Your family being famous don't mean shit, you know. You're just another nepo baby."

"And what has your family done?" It was out of her mouth before she realized it, but this time, Hollis didn't regret her words. Maybe it was the alcohol, or maybe she just wasn't in the mood for Orlando's attitude that evening, but she raised her eyebrow and stared straight back at him, waiting for his next move.

His eyes reflected the light from the fire pit. He glared at her so long and hard, looking like he truly wanted to beat her ass, that Hollis wondered if he was going to lunge. But he finally broke her gaze, turned his scowl on Dwayne, and said, "Leave your girl at home next time."

He stalked away as best as someone could in the sand, Bryan and

Amari following slowly with wide eyes and nervous smiles. Hollis was so angry she thought she might squeeze the bottle of Cherry Coke in her hand until it popped.

Dwayne laced his fingers behind his head and closed his eyes. "Holl, what the hell? You call that being nice?"

"He has no right to come for me," she said firmly. "Or my family. Of course I'm gonna defend us. I was defending *you*."

"You could've done all that without insulting his people."

"He called me a nepo baby. That's you, too, you know."

"Like that really means anything. Half of L.A. are nepotism babies. It's just words, Holl."

"And words *mean* something."

Dwayne sighed and started walking back to where they had set down their things. "Let's just go."

"Already?" Hollis couldn't believe she was the one making an argument to stay, especially after what had just happened. But when she'd seen those heavy blankets Dwayne pulled from the trunk, she had envisioned spreading one out on the sand as the party started to die down, sitting close to him, and . . . She wasn't sure what she even wanted to happen after that. But she'd wanted the chance to see.

"Yeah, well, I don't feel like sticking around after all that."

Hollis waited for him to change his mind or crack a joke or . . . something. But when he didn't stop walking or turn around or say anything more to her, there was nothing else to do but follow him.

Once they were on the 110 freeway again, nearing the exits for Pasadena, Dwayne, who had been quiet for nearly the entire ride, turned down the music and said, "You hungry?"

Hollis let out a small sigh of relief. She'd been worried for the last half hour that he was mad at her, and this didn't mean he wasn't—but at least he wasn't so mad that he wanted to call it an early night.

"God, yes," she said. "We left before I got my s'mores, you know."

Dwayne shook his head, but he was smiling now, and that made Hollis smile, too.

They ended up at the diner near Dupree Academy where students sometimes met up after school for greasy burgers and surprisingly excellent tacos. Dwayne chose a booth next to the window, and they were both quiet as they looked at the menu, though they got the same thing every time. Hollis looked around after they'd ordered. The diner was empty except for their server, the cook, and an older man wearing a ratty beret at a back table, reading a thick paperback and eating pie.

"I'm sorry I got into it with Orlando," Hollis began, "but I'm not sorry for what I said."

"What happened?" Dwayne asked, stirring sugar into his coffee. "Were you drunk or something?"

"I'm not drunk. Maybe a little buzzed at the time." If that interaction with Orlando hadn't sobered her up, the car ride back certainly had. "I don't understand why you always defend him. Did you see the way he was looking at me?"

"Yeah, I'm gonna talk to him again. That shit wasn't cool." Dwayne paused. "But why get involved, anyway? He's actually really upset that I'm thinking of quitting. He's still a junior, and I'm his closest friend on the team. The guys used to give him shit until I made them stop. I get why he's upset. It's already hard enough for him at school."

Hollis frowned. "Isn't it hard for all of us? Think about when we got to Dupree. There weren't even as many of us there then as there are now."

"Of course, but you know it's harder for Orlando."

"Because of where he's from? Okay, it's definitely easier to grow up with money, but . . ." She trailed off, not sure she even wanted to get into it. Maybe she should just enjoy being with Dwayne.

He took a slow sip of coffee. "Just say it."

"Don't you think sometimes he makes things harder on himself?" Hollis said, poking at her placemat. "Like, he's *always* mouthing off and starting shit and giving people a hard time. And then he gets mad when people don't just take it. Why exactly are we supposed to like him?"

"Getting into Dupree was a big deal for Orlando. It changed how things might have ended up for him. I don't think we should give him shit just because he's not interested in giving a bunch of rich kids the benefit of the doubt."

Hollis sighed. Dwayne was one of those rich kids, too, after all. And how was she considered a "nepo baby" when she wasn't interested in the entertainment business? She didn't even like to be photographed with her parents on the red carpet. There were plenty of kids to pick on at school who had signed modeling deals or were headed for a fancy job at their parent's talent agency after graduation only because of their name. Hollis was just trying to exist, and Orlando didn't seem to accept that. She couldn't help the family she was born into any more than he could. But when Hollis opened her mouth to articulate this, she saw the look on Dwayne's face had changed. His expression was softer, more open.

He cleared his throat, and his eyes didn't quite make it to hers as he said, "I think about this summer—that night—a lot. About us."

"Oh." She blinked. She knew it must have been on his mind, the same as it had been on hers, but now here it was, right in front of them. "I . . . I do, too."

Dwayne reached across the table to take her hands in his. He gently rubbed her knuckles, his touch sending little shivers through her entire body. "What's up? Can't really get a read on how you've been feeling. Did you want it to be a one-time thing or . . . ?"

Hollis exhaled. "I don't know, I . . ."

"I'm not trying to pressure you. It's cool if you're not into it. But . . . I had fun. And I think about you all the time and . . . well, I guess I just had to let you know."

Hollis's face was on fire. So were her hands, which Dwayne was still holding. She didn't know why it was so hard to say what she was feeling. This was Dwayne. He knew more about her than anyone did, maybe even Ardith.

She took a deep breath before she spoke. "I think about you, too. Like, constantly. I don't want to ruin anything between us . . . but I don't want to miss out on anything, either."

"Yeah." Dwayne nodded. "I feel the same way."

Their server arrived with their food: a cheeseburger and fries for Dwayne and a grilled cheese with tomato soup for Hollis. They ate mostly in silence, but their eyes occasionally met across the table and each time, Hollis felt a rush that made her grateful she was sitting down.

Dwayne insisted on paying, and as they headed back to the car, they walked close enough that their arms touched. Once they were inside, he started the ignition, but didn't put the car in gear.

When Hollis looked at him, the tenderness in his eyes nearly took her breath away. They leaned in at the same time, and then Dwayne's hands were cupping her face and seconds later, his lips were on hers. His glasses were a little bit in the way, but neither of them bothered to remove them. Dwayne's lips were softer than she remembered—so, so soft—and when he gently tugged at her bottom lip with his teeth, she nearly melted into the passenger seat. He brushed his lips across her cheeks and trailed them down her neck and by the time his mouth met hers again, Hollis's hands were sliding up under his shirt, moving across the smooth skin of his muscled back.

"So," Dwayne said, and he pulled away an inch or two, but only his lips. His hands were still carefully holding Hollis's face. "Should we just see where things go?"

"Mm-hmm," Hollis breathed, seconds before she went in for another kiss. "We should definitely do that."

A Woman, Not a Child

1948

The first time Blossom glimpsed Marvin Finney, he was sitting in front of the mirrored wall of the rehearsal room, settled into a metal folding chair near the corner. He was a tall, thin white man with hair the color of wheat that was starting to gray at the temples. He wore a navy-blue suit with a dark red tie, and he sat far back in the chair, his legs casually crossed at the ankles. But as her gaze quickly swept over him, trying to understand what he was doing here, it was his eyes that Blossom lingered on. They were blue, like the Pacific, piercing—and they were locked on her like everyone else in the room had faded away.

Blossom smiled politely and quickly moved to the back of the room to stretch with the rest of the company. "Who is that?" she quietly asked, parking herself on the floor next to Amelia, a dancer who had been with the company awhile.

But just then, Mrs. van der Kolk swept into the room, her silver hair pulled up into a chignon, as usual, and her eyeglasses hanging from a chain around her neck. When Blossom had first started dancing with her three years ago, she'd barely been able to look the choreographer in the eye. Now, at the age of twenty-one, well . . . Blossom had to admit she was still a little intimidated by her, but she was much more aware of her talents and comfortable with how she fit into the company.

"Hello, girls," Mrs. van der Kolk said, standing up front. "As you can see, we have a visitor. I'd like to introduce you to Marvin Finney. He's a motion picture producer, and he'll be sitting in on today's rehearsal."

Blossom's heart skipped. A Hollywood producer? Right here in the rehearsal room as they finalized the dances for their upcoming autumn performance?

Mr. Finney stood briefly and smiled out at them. "Thank you for letting me watch you girls practice. I'm looking forward to it."

Mrs. van der Kolk perched on the empty chair next to him, and they began speaking quietly as the company members whispered among themselves. Blossom looked at Amelia, whose left leg was stretched out long to the side, her right foot tucked against her left thigh. She lifted her arm above in an arc and bent over her leg, turning her face from the front of the room as she murmured to Blossom. "It's a good opportunity for the company. Movies need dancers all the time, and Mrs. van der Kolk probably wants him to think of us the next time he makes one that does."

"But I've been here three years now, and I don't remember her ever inviting a producer to come see us rehearse."

Amelia gave her a long look. "Are you sure you want to hear this?"

"Why wouldn't I?"

Amelia sat up straight, looking at the floor as she spoke. "Producers stopped reaching out when she let colored dancers into the company. Apparently, some of the men said they didn't want to have to look at them when they were watching us because it was distracting. And they weren't going to cast them in their films anyway."

"Oh," Blossom said.

Amelia's eyes briefly met Blossom's. "Sorry."

Blossom had heard worse. She knew plenty of people felt that way. Although Mrs. van der Kolk had accepted dancers who weren't white since Blossom had joined the company, there weren't many of them. Blossom's first year, it had been only herself and a girl of Mexican descent. The next year, another Negro girl had made the cut, but she hadn't returned for another season. This year, Blossom was the only one. But hearing Amelia say so openly that producers had stayed away because of dancers like her was still upsetting, even if it wasn't a surprise.

Amelia didn't say any more, but Blossom felt from the way she pursed her lips that perhaps she wanted to. When Blossom allowed herself to look at Marvin Finney, his eyes were trained on her again. She felt herself go warm, and even more so when she noticed Amelia looking back and forth between them.

Rehearsal went smoothly, to Blossom's relief; while she was anxious during the warm-up, her nerves slowly melted away as she lost herself in the familiar moves. Afterward, Marvin Finney stood with Mrs. van der Kolk as the girls finished their post-class stretches and began filing out of the room. Blossom was nearly out the door when she heard, "Excuse me."

She paused, glancing over her shoulder to see if Marvin Finney was speaking to someone else. But no, it was her he wanted.

"Hello," he said with a smile, stepping closer to her and away from Mrs. van der Kolk. "You're Blossom Blackwood."

It wasn't a question, and Blossom wondered if he'd seen her perform before—but no, most likely he'd asked Mrs. van der Kolk who she was. That thought made her feel funny, that a man like Marvin Finney would be asking about her. Though she was the only Negro dancer in the company; she supposed she stood out for that alone.

"I am," she said, looking at him curiously.

"You're very talented," he said.

"Thank you, Mr. Finney." Blossom dabbed at her forehead with the back of her wrist, discreetly trying to wipe sweat from her brow. She'd have preferred time to freshen up before speaking with him, but he didn't seem to mind that she was winded from rehearsal or that her pressed hair had wilted from the exertion, thick curls starting to form near her temples.

His eyes roamed over her face with such intensity that Blossom felt her skin heating up all over again, as if she were still practicing her leaps across the floor. "As Beatrice said, I'm a film producer. Have you ever considered acting?"

Blossom tilted her head to the side, unsure how to respond, but Mr. Finney must have seen the affirmation in her eyes, because he continued. "It's just that—well, you're a wonderful dancer, but I see something else in you. Something that makes me think you'd be absolutely luminous on camera."

Blossom's eyebrows shot right up. As often as she'd daydreamed about a moment like this, she couldn't fathom that it was actually happening. "I—" Her voice came out in an embarrassing croak. She briefly looked down at her bare feet, clearing her throat. "I've always wanted to act."

"This was a lucky meeting, then," he said softly. "Well, don't let me keep you any longer. Lovely to make your acquaintance, Miss Blackwood."

"It's so nice to meet you, Mr. Finney." Blossom nodded shyly at him before she exited the room and walked down the hallway on legs that seemed to be made entirely of jelly.

Mr. Finney attended several more rehearsals after that first one. A few weeks later, on the night of their first performance that season, he watched them dance from the wings. She'd expected that would make her nervous, seeing him standing off to the side backstage in his expensive suit, but, to the contrary, it boosted her confidence. Blossom had received attention from white men before. She'd seen how some of them looked at her when they were visiting the nightclub at the Dunbar Hotel, where she still worked, how some of them stared so hard she'd wondered if they had the ability to see beneath her clothes. But this was new. This was attention from an accomplished, sophisticated man who knew talent—and who also held a unique sort of power.

Later, after an exhilarating performance, Mrs. van der Kolk met them all in the dressing room, as usual. "Nice work tonight, girls. There were some areas that need finessing, but this was a beautiful start to our autumn performances." She looked at Blossom. "A word, Miss Blackwood?"

A low murmur traveled throughout the small room. Blossom slowly followed her to the corridor outside the door, trying to recall if she had made any errors during their performance. But when they were alone, Mrs. van der Kolk smiled.

"Lovely job this evening, Miss Blackwood."

"Thank you, ma'am."

"I wasn't the only one impressed." Her voice lowered as she said, "Marvin Finney has taken notice of you."

"Oh. I mean, yes."

"Though I don't work in the movie business, I do fancy myself a bit of a liaison between our two worlds. I've heard of your aspirations to enter the film industry, and I do believe Mr. Finney could be an immense help to you. I am sure I don't have to tell you that opportunities for Negro girls are few and far between."

"Yes, Mrs. van der Kolk." Blossom felt as if there were something unspoken hanging between them; she waited for the company director to continue.

But all she said was, "Well, then. Mr. Finney would like to see you now."

She disappeared around the corner and a few moments later, Mr. Finney appeared in her place, holding a huge bouquet of roses. They were a deep, dark ruby red, and already the scent from the velvety petals had begun to permeate the narrow hallway in which they stood. Briefly, Blossom thought of Pretty Michael presenting her with a single poppy by the school steps years ago, how back then she'd never have been able to imagine holding an armful of roses like this.

"You were just magnificent out there," Marvin Finney said, eyes crinkling as he smiled and handed off the fragrant blooms. "Brava."

"This is incredibly kind of you," she replied, her tongue thick in her mouth. "Thank you."

"The pleasure is all mine, Miss Blackwood. Blossoms for Blossom," he said, bowing slightly from the waist before he touched the brim of his hat, turned, and walked back the way he'd come.

The girls in the company looked up when she returned to the dressing room, and Blossom saw the way their eyes moved over the roses and then her, trying to make sense of her holding such an impressive bouquet. She was relieved when none of them said anything, and she carefully set them down as she sat in the open chair next to Amelia.

"Looks as if someone has an admirer," Amelia murmured from her seat in front of the mirror. She was slathering cold cream into her skin to remove her makeup.

"He's just a friend."

Amelia paused in rubbing cream on her forehead for a moment, meeting Blossom's eyes in the mirror. "Marvin Finney doesn't only want to be friends."

"What do you mean?" Blossom asked, beginning to towel off the back of her neck.

"Precisely what I said. Trust me." Amelia looked pointedly at the roses before she turned away.

Blossom hadn't had much experience with men besides her relationship with Michael, which had ended two years ago. Still, she wasn't naive. She knew that men didn't simply do nice things because they wanted to. She understood that Marvin Finney likely found her attractive. But was it such a crime that she enjoyed the attention? She hadn't acted in a way that would make him believe her interest in him was anything other than strictly professional. And didn't it mean something that, evidently unlike others in his line of work, he wasn't afraid to search for talent in an integrated company, that he thought Negro women were just as capable and worthy of working in Hollywood? He hadn't brought up his position again since that first day, and she hadn't mentioned it either. He mostly watched her—*admired* her—from afar. And that was fine with Blossom.

And yet, two performances later, in that same corridor outside the dressing room, Marvin Finney asked if he could take Blossom out to dinner. Some part of her must have known this invitation was coming, as she'd instinctively packed one of her best dresses to change into after the show.

Amelia stared at her as Blossom slipped into it and began to fix her hair. Blossom returned her gaze for a moment, providing Amelia with the chance to say what she wanted. But Amelia kept quiet. Blossom could feel her judgment; perhaps Amelia was jealous of the attention Marvin Finney had been showering on her since they'd met, especially considering she was one of the few dancers who'd been with the company longer than Blossom.

As Blossom finished freshening up, she tried to slow the beating of her heart. Shortly, she'd be sitting across a table from a successful movie producer. A man who admired her *and* could make her dreams come true.

On her way out of the dressing room, she saw Mrs. van der Kolk standing at the end of the hallway, smoking a cigarette. "Miss Blackwood," she said when she looked up and saw her approaching. "Just the girl I wanted to see. Mr. Finney says you are having dinner together."

"Yes, ma'am."

Mrs. van der Kolk's eyes took in Blossom's outfit. "You look nice."

"Thank you, ma'am."

"I am sure you are aware that things operate a bit differently in Hollywood, yes?" She didn't wait for Blossom to respond before she continued. "Mr. Finney has only ever been a gentleman around me, but . . . I am not the type of woman he desires. He is a powerful man, and sometimes powerful men like to test the waters. Do you understand?"

Blossom swallowed around the lump that had suddenly appeared in her throat. "Er . . . yes, Mrs. van der Kolk."

"You are a beautiful young woman, and it is your decision how you choose to use your beauty." She took a long drag from her cigarette, exhaling the plume of smoke away from Blossom. "Have a nice evening, Miss Blackwood."

As Blossom slowly walked toward the front of the theater, she wondered if she should pretend to be ill and tell Mr. Finney they would have to have dinner another time. She knew the stories about what went on behind closed doors in Hollywood . . . but the thought of canceling their evening made her feel as if she actually *were* ill. This was her chance, and she wasn't going to squander it.

She checked her hair in the reflection of one of the framed posters on the wall, and headed out to meet him.

Marvin Finney took her to Musso & Frank Grill—which he simply called Musso's. Blossom noted this, as well as the ease with which Marvin Finney generally moved through the world, equally at home wearing a suit at a dance studio as in this restaurant with a dark wood bar and red booths, where Charlie Chaplin once regularly dined. She felt herself trembling as they stepped inside, and perhaps Mr. Finney sensed it, because he gently placed his hand on the small of her back. But that didn't quell her nerves. Wouldn't the host turn them away because she was Negro? It was 1948, but different forms of bigotry existed in Los Angeles, just as they did around the rest of the country—always lurking, always dangerous. She wasn't in the habit of showing up at places where she didn't know if she would be welcome. Mr. Finney may have believed she would one day be an adored actress, but at the moment, she was only a fledgling dancer and part-time waitress who still lived with her mother.

To Blossom's relief, the host greeted them with a smile and immediately led them to a corner booth that Mr. Finney said used to be Chaplin's favorite. Blossom looked around at the other diners, who were digging into steaks and puffing on cigars and swilling red wine. Blossom couldn't imagine they ever questioned if they belonged here. They didn't even seem to notice she was there, either.

"You know what's so special about this booth?" Mr. Finney asked.

"Besides the fact that Charlie Chaplin used to sit here?"

"It's the only seat in the house with a view," he said, pointing to the window behind them. "They say Chaplin used to come here with Mary Pickford and Douglas Fairbanks. He and Fairbanks would race their horses down the boulevard, and whoever lost would have to pay for lunch."

Blossom beamed at this bit of trivia, at the fact that she was sitting in such an esteemed seat.

Before she knew it, a bottle of champagne had arrived at the table. Once the waiter had carefully filled two crystal flutes with the bubbly liquid, Mr. Finney lifted his glass, and she did the same. "To another beautiful performance," he said, "and to the biggest star of the Beatrice van der Kolk Dance Company."

Blossom nodded demurely as they clinked glasses—but she took her first sip too quickly and the bubbles tickled the roof of her mouth. She sneezed.

"Gesundheit," Mr. Finney said with a small smile. "Have you ever had champagne before?"

"Only the cheap kind," Blossom admitted, thinking back to the neighborhood New Year's Eve parties where she and her sisters had sneaked glasses when the adults weren't looking. Truthfully, she wasn't sure she could taste the difference between the cheap kind and what she was drinking now.

Blossom began to peruse the menu, but Mr. Finney sat back in the booth and said, "There's no rush. We can take our time."

"Well, thank you. For all of this," she said.

"You don't have to thank me. It's special to get to spend time with you this way." He paused. "Blossom, where do you see yourself fitting into show business?"

She took another sip of champagne, more slowly this time, and set the flute back onto the table. He was the first person she'd ever met who was anybody in Hollywood, and she didn't want to say the wrong thing. "I haven't quite narrowed that down. I've always wanted to act, but I'm honestly not yet sure what to hope for beyond that."

He leaned forward, his eyes meeting hers with the same intensity as the first day she'd seen him at rehearsal. "Well, what is your wildest dream?"

"I suppose to sign a studio contract, like Lena Horne. Or to put on my own variety show, like Ethel Waters. And I'd like to win an Academy Award, like Hattie McDaniel."

The way Mr. Finney's mouth curved up into a smile, she was worried she'd sounded silly, naive about the business. But when he spoke, he seemed as serious as she was. "You want to do it all, don't you?"

"I do," Blossom said, sitting up straight. The burst of confidence had come as a surprise, but she was grateful for it. She'd become a bit wary of confessing her dreams after the way Michael had responded to them. But this wasn't Michael. This was someone who knew how much this sort of work mattered.

"So, you know what you want." Mr. Finney nodded slowly. "What does being an entertainer *mean* to you?"

"Oh, it means everything," she said, nearly breathless. "I love dancing and singing, because they allow me to express myself in a way that speaking simply can't. But I've always felt like I was supposed to be something . . . *bigger* than just one of the Blackwood girls from Reed Street. My mama was an actress, too, but she gave it all up for us, and so I guess part of me wants to continue where she left off. But also, I've only ever lived in the same home, gone to school with the same people all my life, and lived around them, too. I want to meet new people, and experience new things, become a different version of myself. I think that's part of why acting is . . . Never mind."

Mr. Finney took another sip of champagne, and raised an eyebrow. "Please, do go on."

"It's silly."

"It's not silly if you believe it, Miss Blackwood."

Blossom stared down at the dark wood table. "Acting is magic. I get to step into a new life and become someone else entirely—and for those few minutes, if I'm doing my job, other people *believe* it. Entertainers make it all look so easy, but it's difficult work. If I were able to be part of a real project and experience trying on a new version of myself every day . . . I would feel as if I were doing exactly what I'm meant to be doing. It would be the most extraordinary thing in the world."

She looked at Mr. Finney from beneath her lashes as he leaned forward, tenting his fingers together over the table. "We need more girls like you, Blossom Blackwood. Those who truly understand what makes this art form so special. Who feel it in their bones. Who were born to do it."

When the waiter returned, Blossom asked for the chicken à la king, but Mr. Finney interrupted, informing him she'd be having the filet mignon, same as him. Blossom's neck grew hot at the way he was taking charge—and spoiling her—but she didn't protest. She'd wanted the filet mignon, after all. By the time they finished their meal, Blossom had grown slightly more comfortable around Mr. Finney. She felt in control, even as she noticed he had slowly inched closer to her throughout the course of the evening. His leg was nearly touching hers now.

"Blossom," he said, angling his body so he was entirely facing her, "I've enjoyed getting to know you more this evening."

"I've enjoyed it, as well, Mr. Finney."

He shook his head, blue eyes twinkling. "Please. Call me Marvin. We're friends now, aren't we?"

"Yes, of course," she said.

Then, out of the shadows, their waiter arrived, but instead of a dessert menu, he presented a serving tray with a small jewelry box placed on top. Blossom looked from the box to Mr. Finney—her upbringing wouldn't allow her to call him by his first name even in her mind, despite what he'd said. "Go ahead." He nodded at the box. As she took it, the waiter retreated. "Open it."

Blossom held her breath as she pried open the black velvet box, wanting to savor every moment of this experience. She'd never been given jewelry before; she'd only ever seen these types of boxes in movies and magazines, in storefront windows from a distance.

She gasped at what was inside: a stunning pair of diamond earrings. Small, round, brilliant circles that gleamed under the soft light in the booth.

"Diamonds for a diamond," Mr. Finney said softly. "Do you like them?"

"I love them," she breathed. "But I can't—I—I mean, I can't accept—"

"You deserve them. Mrs. van der Kolk tells me how hard you work, and I see it when you're onstage. They're yours."

Blossom wondered if Mr. Finney had noticed the small holes in her lobes that Mama had pierced with a sewing needle when she was a baby; she didn't wear jewelry when she was rehearsing or performing. As she painstakingly fastened the earrings, she felt brighter. More important. Worthier of sitting in Charlie Chaplin's booth with this successful film producer who'd said she was going to be a star.

But as big as she felt with the diamonds attached to her ears, she began to shrink inside as Mr. Finney's hand clamped down on her knee. Her stomach started to coil and twist as his fingers moved up her thigh.

"How about we continue this discussion with a nightcap at my place?" he murmured in her ear, so close she wondered, for a moment, if his breath was fogging up the diamond. "I want to talk to you about a movie you would be perfect for. I'm going to make you famous, Blossom Blackwood."

Blossom felt frozen in time as she collected her thoughts. About what she would gain if she said yes, let him take her home—and what she would lose if she didn't. She had known from the way he first looked at her that there was some attraction beneath his interest. But he had seemed to understand there was a line that shouldn't be crossed—until this very moment. And perhaps if Blossom had been a bit more experienced, she wouldn't have been so taken aback by the invitation to his home. She'd expected a little flirting, or that he might try to kiss her good night in the car. But the only boy whose home she'd ever been to was Michael's. And, as Mr. Finney began to gently massage her thigh, Blossom had never been more aware that this was *not* a boy.

She remembered Mrs. van der Kolk's words, that it was her choice how she used her beauty. But whatever she decided, her choice would have consequences—either personally or professionally.

"I, um, I have an early morning, Mr. Finney," she said, primly wiping her mouth with her napkin. "At the restaurant. In fact, I should head home now. My mother is expecting me."

"Give her a ring," he said, his hand still moving insistently on her leg. "The waiter will let you use their telephone. Explain that you'll be late."

"I—"

"You're a woman, not a child. The role I want to discuss with you is for a woman. One who knows herself."

The implication was clear. Giving in could mean a role in a Hollywood picture. One that could be seen by anyone who had a couple of quarters to spend at a movie house. People from her own neighborhood. Old classmates and teachers.

But what would she be giving up for it?

Blossom jerked her leg free from his busy hand and scooted to the end of the booth, where she stood. "Thank you for dinner, Mr. Finney. And for the gift. I appreciate your generosity, but I—I won't be able to join you. I'm sorry."

Mr. Finney's face turned a slow shade of red, the color creeping down his neck until it disappeared into the crisp collar of his shirt. His lips pursed, and for a moment, Blossom wondered what she would do if he lost his temper.

But then, just as quickly as he'd filled with fury, his entire body seemed to deflate. He shook his head, muttering under his breath, but when she tentatively sat down again in the booth, he didn't try to touch her. In fact, he barely looked at her the rest of the evening—not as he hastily paid the check, nor when they collected their jackets at the front. As she looked around at the people still enjoying their meals, Blossom couldn't help thinking the restaurant had lost some of its luster; the famed booth she'd sat in no longer seemed so magical.

Once they were standing outside, facing Hollywood Boulevard, Blossom cleared her throat and said, "Thank you again for dinner. I suppose I should head on home now."

Mr. Finney looked down at her, his face twisted into a scowl. "How will you get there? Buses aren't running this late, last I checked."

Was that true? Blossom wasn't usually out this late unless she was working, and she wasn't familiar with this side of town. She wasn't sure how she'd make it home if the buses weren't still running over here. Amelia and Mrs. van der Kolk had clearly had some insight into Marvin Finney's character, but had they known he was the type of man who would leave her stranded in the middle of Hollywood after dark?

"My legs are still functioning." She raised her chin as she drew herself up to her full height of five feet three inches. "Good night, Mr. Finney."

He sighed. "No need for the theatrics. I'll drive you."

Blossom stared at him, hesitating before she asked, "A drive home?"

"Yes, *home*," he snapped. "Come along."

"But why would you do that for me? After . . ." She couldn't bring herself to put into words what had happened back in that booth.

"Perhaps I'm not the cad you think I am," he said before stalking off toward his automobile.

He didn't speak for the entire drive. Blossom's voice was the only sound cutting through the silence as she gave him directions to her house. She sat rigid in the passenger seat, hands clasped in her lap, until they reached Central Avenue and, a few moments later, Reed Street.

She let out a long breath, grateful that he'd done as he'd said and driven her straight home. "You can stop here," she said when the car was a few houses down from hers. She didn't want Mama or Sybil to hover at the front window, looking out at them. And a part of her didn't want Mr. Finney to know where she lived. She wasn't sure why, exactly, and a wave of shame came over her at the thought.

"You grew up over here?" he asked, his voice flat.

"I did."

"And you don't have aspirations to move someplace . . . nicer? Perhaps Sugar Hill? Hattie McDaniel and Louise Beavers seem to have taken a liking to the area."

"Of course I do." She paused. "Negroes can live anywhere in Los Angeles now that the court struck down those rules discriminating against us. Nat King Cole just moved his family into a home in Hancock Park."

"Yes, though not without the help of the former first lady," Mr. Finney scoffed. "You are not Nat King Cole, Miss Blackwood. You are a Negro woman with a hint of talent, and you will not succeed in this business without the help of someone like me. Do you want to keep living in a run-down little house like this, or would one of those homes in Sugar Hill or Hancock Park be more your taste?"

Blossom didn't wait for him to come around and open her door; he hadn't given her the courtesy when they'd set off, and she was certain he wouldn't be doing so now. She exited the car, closed the door, and leaned back in, looking directly into his cold blue eyes.

"They are my taste, yes. But I won't compromise who I am to get there."

He shook his head again, laughing this time. "Then good luck to you, Miss Blackwood. I do believe you'll need it."

He started to put the car in gear when Blossom remembered. She reached up, touching one of the diamonds in her ears.

"Wait! Mr. Finney."

He glanced over at the open window, his expression pinched.

Blossom cleared her throat. "You'll want your earrings, I expect?"

He laughed again, harsher and louder than before. "You think I'd take those back? After they've been all snug up in a nigger's ears? Who'll want them now, girl?"

And then he drove away, leaving Blossom reeling on the street, replaying that word in her head over and over again. She heard it with each step she took, all the way to the front porch of the little white bungalow. This wasn't the first time she'd been called that, of course, but it was the first time it had been directed at her by someone she'd gotten to know, as she had Mr. Finney.

Blossom paused on the front steps, catching her breath. She quickly removed the earrings and dropped them into her pocketbook before she stepped into the house.

Her mother had fallen asleep in her chair, though Blossom had told her not to wait up when she'd called earlier, after the performance. Flossie was as protective as she was gruff at times.

"Good night, Mama," Blossom whispered as she covered her mother with a blanket and turned down the radio dial. She kissed her cheek and switched off the table lamp before she left the room.

Sybil was still awake in bed, the quilt pulled up under her arms, her nose buried in a copy of *The Street*. She looked up and sniffed as Blossom entered the room. "You smell like a restaurant. A different one than normal."

"Well, it seems your nose is working."

"Where'd you go in all that finery?" Sybil asked, her lips quirking. "Mama said you were having supper with a friend."

"I did." Blossom stepped out of her black pumps—the only pair of nice shoes she owned—and placed them neatly along the wall. She toyed with the strap of her pocketbook as she leaned against the door. "If I show you something, do you promise not to raise a fuss?"

"I promise," Sybil said immediately, sitting up and moving her book to the side. Blossom sat on the edge of her bed, just a couple of feet away. Her sister's eyes widened when Blossom plucked the diamond earrings from the bottom of her pocketbook, holding them out in her palm. "Oh, my . . . Blossom! Are these real?"

"Shhh." Blossom put her finger to her lips, though Mama could sleep through a parade marching down Reed Street if she was tired enough. "Yes, they are."

"Where did you get them?"

"At supper."

"What kind of friends do you have?" Sybil said as Blossom held them out for her to hold, briefly.

"I don't think we're friends anymore." She looked anxiously toward the closed door and then motioned for Sybil to move over so she could lie down on the bed beside her. Blossom curled her body up next to her sister's and moved her hand to Sybil's ear, explaining everything in a series of whispers.

"He called you that?" Sybil asked when she was done. Her face crumpled, and Blossom wished she hadn't mentioned that last part. Sybil was only sixteen, and though she seemed to have "been here before," as Mama said when she was acting particularly mature for her age, she was still just a girl.

"It's all right. He didn't hurt me."

"But that *is* hurtful, Blossom. It's not right." Sybil's eyes moved down to the gems Blossom clutched in one hand. "What are you going to do with them? I wouldn't want them anywhere near me after what he said."

Blossom had been pondering this very question since she'd walked in the door. She could sell them. They weren't the largest diamonds—she'd seen bigger ones in the window of LeRoy's downtown on Broadway—but they were real; she could likely get good money for them from a pawnbroker. Money she, Sybil, and Mama could use. But as she rolled the diamonds around in her palm, watching them glitter against her skin, Blossom realized she didn't feel the same way Sybil did, at all.

Marvin Finney had been right about one thing that evening—she deserved these. So, Blossom was going to do something that contradicted everything Mama had taught her about men, and how things were earned: she was going to keep them. They would be a reminder of the way a successful Hollywood producer had tried to manipulate her, to use them as a tool that would persuade her to submit to his advances.

Blossom's decision at the restaurant was evidence that she knew she was enough, that she didn't need a man's help to make her way in life, as Mama had told her when she was a little girl. The earrings were a reward—for making it intact through an evening intended to strip her of her dignity, and for refusing to take the bait from a man who'd assumed he could control Blossom Blackwood with a little bit of sparkle.

Ardith

"What's on your mind?"

Ardith realized only when Dr. York spoke that she'd been staring out the window of the office, silent, for who knows how long. She turned her attention back to her therapist. "Honestly? That being here now feels like being on set."

"How so?"

Ardith had been seeing Dr. Melanie York for the past eight years, and her Los Feliz office was one of the places she felt most comfortable. Dr. York was a Black woman with long box braids, a love of tea, and extensive experience in working with children and artists—something that had been apparent as soon as Ardith began talking to her. Dr. York was familiar with the way that, as a child actor, Ardith had forever felt like she straddled the experiences of being a kid and being an adult. She never made Ardith feel bad for complaining about what Ardith called "champagne problems," the issues unique to someone at her level of fame and success. But Ardith especially appreciated that Dr. York was never afraid to question her assumptions, never let her get away with anything. Sometimes she was still surprised by what Dr. York managed to drag out of her subconscious.

Ardith shrugged. "Well, it's a show about therapists."

"How does that feel? Being around that every day?"

"It's not *exactly* like being here." The cast was so talented that Ardith had no trouble getting lost in the scenes when she watched them filming, but it never took long to remember she was on a television set, with cameras and boom mics surrounding the actors. "But I guess the feel of it—the writing, the direction, the acting . . . There's something . . . *gentle* about it. It feels safe."

"That's nice to hear. I know you haven't always felt that way with your work. What makes this set different?"

"The showrunner, Caitlin. She's great. She, um, made sure I was okay when I had a little breakdown the other day."

Dr. York shifted in her armchair. "Want to tell me what happened?"

Ardith was still embarrassed as she recounted the incident at the table read, but each day it was a little easier to arrive on set and greet everyone without feeling like she wanted to die. A couple of other people had pulled her aside afterward to say they understood getting overwhelmed in a situation like that, and that it was no big deal and that she could talk to them if she ever needed anything. She appreciated the support; some adult actors didn't treat children and teen actors with much respect, and she'd worked on a few sets where it was clear her presence was only being tolerated at best. But she'd never found it easy to trust people, and the unpredictable nature of acting work meant she was never sure if the people she was working closely with on a project would be in her life for years or only a few months.

Which was why the comfort she felt in being around Matty Cohen was so unsettling.

"Is this a romantic development?" her therapist asked.

"No, not at all. That's the thing—Matty is a party guy. He doesn't hang out with people like me."

The hint of a smile tugged at the corner of Dr. York's lips. "Don't you like to go to parties? To have a good time?"

"Not *that* kind of good time," Ardith said, laughing. "But it's not like that, anyway. He's an easy person to be around. The other day he came into my trailer just because. To hang out."

"How did that make you feel?"

"Weird. A little . . ." Ardith paused, searching for the right words. "I guess it made me suspicious?"

"Do you think he wants something from you?"

"No . . . not really. I mean, I don't know. Like I said, we don't like each other like that, and we already work with our set teacher through the day. So . . . I guess it's just weird that he wants to hang out apart from everything else."

"Is that unusual?" Dr. York asked, writing something in the notebook on her lap.

"It depends on the project. And the actors. Most people just want to be left alone, to relax or save their energy for upcoming scenes. Some of them are superstitious about not talking to anyone before they shoot—they think it'll distract them or throw them off."

"Do you have that rule?"

"Not officially," Ardith said slowly. "I guess I haven't ever wanted to spend that much time with anyone. It's almost always just me and a bunch of other adults, or sometimes kids younger than me."

"So, what do you think Matty could want from you? You say he's not looking to date you, and he's on a similar path as you, in terms of career success."

"He won an Emmy five years ago."

"I see."

Ardith took a deep breath. "I keep thinking about my mom."

"How so?"

"I guess . . . I just miss her. Since Bebe died, people are starting to talk about how she never said who my grandpa's dad is. It makes me angry, what they say about her now that she's gone. Like she owed them something, when they didn't even know her. And that makes me think of my mom. How people didn't know the real her—just the person the media reported on."

Dr. York nodded, still writing. "Let me ask you this: how would you feel if Matty didn't have such a party-boy reputation?"

"What do you mean?"

"Do you think it would be easier if he were more like you—kept his head down, wasn't photographed out at clubs and such? Is a part of you worried that if you spend time with him, his reputation might affect yours?"

Ardith frowned. "I don't get what you're asking."

Dr. York set her pen down. "People thought of your mother a certain way, toward the end of her life. They judged her because of her addiction, some of them choosing to ignore the rest of her—what made her a whole person. You, on the other hand, are what many would consider a model teen actor. You've stayed away from drinking and drugs, you go to church regularly and volunteer at their events. You're focused on your craft, you don't court superstardom or engage in what we now consider to be celebrity culture, beyond your volunteer work. Is it that you're worried about making a new friend and letting him in, or are you concerned that doing so might leave you open to the same criticisms that had such an effect on your mother?"

Ardith looked down at her knees, pressing her hands against them. "I don't know. It's like . . . I expected him to be one way, but then a part of him seems different. And then I feel guilty for making assumptions. For thinking we wouldn't get along because of that."

"What were your expectations based on?"

"Social media, blogs . . . He's been super famous since we were, like, twelve. It's kind of hard to avoid him. And I know you're not supposed to assume things about people just because of how they're talked about in the media—of course I know that—but I did. And he's different than that."

"So, is there some part of you that just wants to enjoy this new connection you've made?"

"I guess. But . . ."

Dr. York didn't press her to go on, but Ardith was aware of the heavy silence in the room as they both waited for her to finish her thought. "I haven't had any real friends outside of my family, like . . . ever. Nobody my age. I don't know how to do that. Or why he even wants to be friends with me when I basically only go to work and church."

"But he's showing you that he's interested in getting to know you. You haven't changed since the show started. He's aware of who you are, of what's important to you." Dr. York paused. "I think you should try to stop focusing so much on how people see you, or how you see them, initially. Does he make you feel good when you're around him?"

Ardith nodded.

"Has he given you any reason to distrust him so far?"

Ardith shook her head.

Dr. York stuck her pen behind her ear and set the notebook on the table next to her. She leaned forward. "Then I say let him in. You don't have to jump in headfirst. You can start slow. Maybe invite him over to your trailer, or stop by his one day. Ask if he wants to hit up crafty together. Taking any one of those steps doesn't mean you have to take any others until you're ready. You can see how it feels and go from there. Do you think you can try?"

Ardith hesitated only a moment. "Okay."

"Okay?"

"I'll try."

"Good." Dr. York sat back in her chair. "Where are you at with the exhibit that director wanted to do? The retrospective of your mother's career? Have you decided if you're going to be involved?"

"Not yet. My mom deserves to be celebrated, and the whole thing actually sounds pretty cool. I'm glad he's doing it, but . . . honestly? I'm worried about what it will do to my dad."

"What do you mean?"

Ardith took a deep breath. "We still don't really talk about her. Not unless we have to, like with this exhibit coming up. It's like he thinks it's better if we sort of pretend she didn't exist."

"Does he talk about her with anyone else?"

She shrugged. "I don't know for sure, but I think he's pretty closed off to everyone, even my uncles. They bring her up more than he does."

"Have you ever asked him why he doesn't talk about her?"

"No. I mean, it's pretty obvious, right? The love of his life died."

"Under very public, very scrutinized circumstances." Dr. York took a moment before she spoke again. "Your father experienced trauma, same as you. But his was different. He lost his wife *and* the mother of his child. And, even if he knows better, there's likely a part of him that blames himself for what happened."

"It wasn't Daddy's fault," Ardith said vehemently.

Dr. York nodded. "I know that. And so do you, but you were a child when she died. Too young to really understand what was happening. He was an adult, her partner—and he was trying his best to keep her alive. If he still hasn't spoken to anyone about that . . . well, even mentioning your mother is probably quite painful for him."

"So . . . should I not participate in the opening? I don't want to make Daddy more upset."

"There is no correct answer here, Ardith. I think what's most important is that you do what's right for you."

The day Ardith and Matty were set to rehearse their first kissing scene, she spent the morning alone in her trailer running her lines, only taking short breaks to work with the set teacher, Grace. SAG, the actors union she had belonged to since a national cereal commercial she filmed back when she was four years old, required her to complete three hours of school each day she was shooting. Grace broke up those three hours to work around her scenes, meeting with her for twenty-minute blocks throughout the day. It wasn't ideal, but most of the time, she and Matty were able to work together. That morning, Matty had an earlier call time than her, so she'd be meeting with Grace on her own—which was, honestly, a relief. She didn't know why, exactly, but she couldn't stop thinking about Dr. York's suggestion, that she let her friendship with Matty go where it may.

But now it was finally time to rehearse, and Ardith had real jitters. Perhaps even more than before her first-ever kissing scene a couple years ago. And again, it was unclear why; this was a private rehearsal, with just the two of them, the director, and the DP. They'd both met separately and together with the intimacy coordinator to make sure everyone was on the same page about what would be happening in the scene. And this was Matty. The person Dr. York said wanted to be her friend.

"Ready for the big snog?" Matty said in a British accent as he sidled up to her.

"Snog sounds dirty," she replied, wrinkling her nose.

"I personally prefer canoodle."

"Well, I'm ready. I even used mouthwash for you," Ardith said. If she acted like she wasn't anxious, maybe her nerves wouldn't show.

"Oh yeah? I've been chewing on a handful of garlic I stole from crafty," he said, and that made Ardith laugh and, finally, begin to relax.

They found their marks, and the director, Toni, called action.

"I've been thinking," Matty said, in character.

"About what?"

"About us." Matty stepped closer to her, his eyes tender.

Ardith looked down and then up at him, swallowing hard. "What about your dad?"

"I don't care what he thinks. I know what happened was an accident, and . . . I know what's important to me. That's you."

They both moved closer then, only inches away from one another, and Ardith's heart was beating so rapidly she worried Toni could see it through her shirt. Matty gently stroked her cheekbone and chin, then they leaned in at the same time, their lips connecting. Ardith didn't have a lot to compare him to, but Matty was a good kisser. He'd somehow mastered the art of making it seem as if he were totally into her while not at all making her uncomfortable. For a moment, Ardith forgot she'd been so nervous.

A journalist had once asked her what it felt like to be in the middle of a scene, and she'd struggled to find the appropriate words. She often felt like she blacked out when she was acting, like some inner force took charge of her body, and she, Ardith Blackwood, was no longer in the room at all. She supposed that was what it meant to fully sink into your character, but sometimes it felt pretentious to describe it that way.

Toni called cut, and Matty pulled away from her. "That was great," the director said. Her friendly eyes moved between them. "How do you two feel about it?"

"Fine," Ardith said quickly, self-conscious again now that the scene was over. She peeked at Matty from the corner of her eye.

"Only fine?" He scoffed. "Come on, Blackwood. We were fantastic."

Toni laughed. "My sentiments exactly. You're both pros. But I'd love to run through it again, just to make sure we're hitting the right beats before the kiss."

Ardith and Matty returned to their marks and performed another take with a slight revision. Toni dismissed them, and Ardith let out a long, relieved breath. While it wouldn't be the last kissing scene for the two of them, at least the next time wouldn't be the first time.

"I'm gonna grab a water," Matty said. "You want anything?"

Ardith paused. Normally she would politely decline and head back to her trailer alone. But she remembered Dr. York's advice, about letting herself give Matty a chance. And besides, she wanted to see if crafty had any more of those pumpkin bars she was obsessed with. "I'll go with you," she said, and they headed together over to craft services.

As they perused the tables, Ardith felt her heart beating fast again. Before she could stop herself, she said, "What are you doing now?"

"Probably gonna play some Mario Kart and take a nap. What about you?"

"Nothing, really. You want to hang out?"

"Hell, yeah. I thought you'd never ask." Matty grinned.

"My trailer?" Ardith asked.

Matty nodded. "Yours has better vibes."

Ardith gave him a look. "They're identical trailers."

"Doesn't mean the vibes are the same, Blackwood."

As soon as they entered, he dropped into the chair by her desk. "You seem a little jumpy today. I didn't make you feel awkward, did I?"

"Not at all," Ardith said with a smile. She sat down across from him on the small couch, which could pull out into a bed. She'd never used it, but when he'd been in here before, Matty told her he took naps on his all the time.

"Good. I really can't believe how well that went."

She blinked. "You don't have to sound so surprised."

He threw his head back and laughed, a sound that always made Ardith want to laugh, too. "Not surprised, just . . . Okay, maybe I was a little surprised."

"Why?" She wasn't sure she actually wanted to know the answer, but she couldn't keep herself from asking.

"Don't take this the wrong way, but you don't seem like someone who's kissed a lot of people."

Ardith's mouth dropped open. "Um, how am I supposed to take that?"

"I mean, I dunno. The church stuff? And I've never seen you with anyone, or heard you talk about anyone, so . . ."

"So, you think I'm a nun. Great."

She'd tried to keep her tone lighthearted, but it came out heavier than she'd intended, and she could tell Matty heard it, too. "Hey, hey. Sorry. I don't think you're a nun. I guess I'm still trying to figure you out. You're not exactly like most of the people our age in the business."

Ardith hesitated, unsure if she should say what she was thinking.

"You can tell me if I'm being an asshole," he continued. "My mom says sometimes my mouth moves faster than my brain."

"That's not what I was going to say. Honestly, I agree. We're so different. It's weird that we get along."

"Why is it weird?"

Ardith saw him eyeing one of her pumpkin bars. After a moment, she slid it over to him; Matty immediately polished off half of it.

"Okay, well . . . If I tell you something, do you promise not to judge me?"

He took a drink of water, and crossed his fingers over his heart. "I swear."

"I haven't kissed a lot of guys, but . . . the ones I have, it's all been on set."

Matty clapped his hands together, sitting up straight. "You're shitting me."

"That sounds like judgment," she said, shrinking back into the couch.

"Sorry," he said again. "But . . . you're Ardith Blackwood. You're gorgeous and smart and funny, and it's just hard to believe."

She shrugged. "I don't really know a lot of people our age, and I've been working since I was a kid, same as you."

"Yeah, and I've still somehow managed to hook up with people I wasn't working with." His voice was playful, but when she looked up, his expression was serious. "Does that bother you? Like, do you feel sheltered?"

"I feel . . ." She paused. She wanted to trust Matty, she really did. She thought of the table read, when they'd talked in the bathroom. "I feel like maybe it's different for me. My family has been in the business for decades. We're, like, ridiculously visible. My mom was under a huge amount of pressure, and . . . I get that it's impossible to know why what happened to her happened, but I can't help thinking that was a big part of it. I'm worried about how anything I do might be criticized by the same people who wouldn't leave my mom alone, how my actions might affect my family. All the stuff that comes along with being famous, I'm just not interested in it, you know?"

She let out a deep breath as she stared down at the floor. It was so quiet, she worried Matty actually was judging her now. But when she looked up, his expression was open. "Damn, Blackwood. I didn't realize you . . . I mean, that's a lot."

"Yeah, well. Champagne problems."

"Doesn't mean they're not still problems." He chewed on his bottom lip. "You must think I'm a heathen."

She shook her head. "No, but . . . I'm sort of jealous of you."

Matty put his hand to his chest. "Moi?"

"Maybe you're doing it right. Not caring what people think about you. And you're so good at the work that nobody actually cares what you do off set."

"Eh, that's not really true. My parents care, a lot. So do my reps, but they also know the bad boy–ish image works. People want to see what this little asshole with all the jewelry can do onscreen."

"A lot, it turns out," Ardith said with a grin.

"Aw, shucks, Blackwood." Matty paused. "There's this fundraiser I'm going to in a couple weeks, to benefit LGBTQ youth in the arts. Some chill people will be there, and we'll probably go out afterward. You should come."

Ardith knew the fundraiser he was talking about. "I think my cousin Prentice is going, actually. One of my uncles is on the board of that foundation."

"Perfect. Then you should totally come."

Ardith didn't say anything.

"Come on, it's for a good cause."

"No, it's not that. We would . . . go together?"

"I mean, only if you want." He shrugged. "I could meet you there if that's better."

"No, it's just, I probably won't know anyone else there besides my family."

"That's okay. You'll know me. I'll introduce you to people. Or we can ignore everyone and do our own thing."

"You won't go off with your friends and leave me?" Ardith had never hung out with him off set, but she'd seen pictures of him with his friends, and Matty was the kind of person people were always hanging on to, wanting his attention. She couldn't imagine he'd have any left for her once they arrived.

"I promise. And I'll make you a deal: you come to this event, and I'll go to church with you sometime."

Ardith raised an eyebrow. "Really?"

"I'm not a *total* heathen. I mean, I'm not Christian. I'm Jewish, but more, like, culturally. I haven't been to a synagogue since my bar mitzvah." Matty shrugged. "And I want to see what you're into. You go to a Black church, right? They always look like fun."

"It's a long service," Ardith warned. "Longer than what you probably think is long."

Matty lifted his chin. "I can handle it."

"All right. Then it's a deal." She felt a rush as she pulled her phone out of her bag to put the date in her calendar. She'd been so anxious about Matty. Embarrassed, even. But it was simple, just like Dr. York had said it would be. Maybe he did actually want to be friends with her. "You better not flake on me."

"Me? I'm worried about *you*."

Ardith grinned. As she closed out of the calendar, her phone buzzed. Texts, from her cousin. Prentice, not Hollis.

She opened up the texts to see them in full. There was a link, followed by:

You see this?
Can Uncle A help?

Matty had pulled out his phone as well, and Ardith looked up when he groaned and said, "Ohhh, shit."

Ardith tapped the link, waiting for it to load. "What is it?"

"You need to see this, Blackwood. It's not good."

Hollis

Hollis had been dreading AP Government since she'd walked into Dupree that morning. Or since Saturday evening, if she was being truthful. It was the one class she had with Orlando. But when she walked in just before the bell for third period, it turned out all of her fretting was for nothing: Orlando's seat was empty. Still, Hollis didn't really breathe until their teacher resumed their lesson on the intro to the US Constitution.

She had just started to calm down when she felt her phone buzzing in the bag by her leg. She quickly reached down to see who was calling before she silenced it.

Ardith?

She frowned. Her cousin would be on set right now. Must be a butt dial. The phone vibrated again a few moments later, this time with a text. She ignored it. If Ardith needed something, she'd call back during lunch.

Hollis was so relieved to have avoided another potential confrontation with Orlando that she was halfway to her locker to switch out her books before she realized people were staring at her. At first, she thought she might be imagining it, but it was everywhere she looked: eyes meeting hers before they immediately shifted away. Some people were smirking, while others appeared to be in shock; a few people were laughing, but the most unsettling looks were the sympathetic ones.

Just as Hollis was about to pull someone to the side and ask them what was going on, she saw Dwayne's head bobbing above the crowd, coming from the opposite direction. A little thrill moved through her when she spotted him, and she flushed, thinking about Saturday for the hundredth time since he'd dropped her off: when they had kissed in his car outside the diner, then held hands all the way home, then kissed good night for a while as his car idled at the end of her driveway.

Now Dwayne was pushing through the throng of students, and when she saw his face, her smile dropped. Something was definitely wrong. He stopped in front of her, right at the intersection of the senior and junior wings, his body blocking Hollis's path.

"What the hell is going on?" she asked.

"We need to talk," he said, breathless, and that was when she noticed he was clenching and unclenching his hands into fists.

"Okay. Maybe you can explain why everyone's staring at me like . . ." Like they knew she'd gotten a breast reduction. "Do people know?"

Dwayne didn't respond.

Hollis sighed, looking up at him. "Who did you tell?"

"What?" He wasn't even looking at her. His eyes were on everyone else—and *they* were looking at her.

"Did you tell someone?" she murmured impatiently. "About what I had done this summer?"

"Holl, let's go—"

"I mean, I wish you'd told me you let it slip, but it's not like it's a huge deal. I've seen at least two new nose jobs in the last week."

Dwayne shook his head. "It's not that."

She frowned. "Then . . . what?"

"Come on." He took her hand in his and pulled her along with him down the corridor. It was hard to keep up, with Dwayne's long legs working overtime, but they eventually made it out the doors to the courtyard. It was mostly empty, between classes.

He perched on top of one of the tables, his feet parked on the bench below. "I have to tell you something."

Hollis remained standing. The bell was going to ring any minute now, and she still needed to go to her locker, but she couldn't ignore the knots growing in her stomach at the look on his face. "Why are we here?"

"It's about the pictures." He let out a long breath.

Hollis blinked. "What pictures?"

"The ones I took." His voice was so low she had to lean in to hear him. "Of you. One of them . . . got out."

Then the knots were gone because the bottom completely fell out of Hollis's stomach. "No. You said you deleted them, Dwayne. *No*. What the *fuck*? That's why everyone's staring at me? They . . . ?"

Dwayne slowly lifted his head, his eyes taking their time to get to hers. When they did, he looked terrified. "I thought I did, for real, but maybe I didn't, because—god, I'm sorry, Hollis. I'm so, so fucking sorry."

Hollis swallowed and swallowed. Closed her eyes. Opened them again. She was still standing in the courtyard with Dwayne as he told her that people had seen one of her nudes.

This wasn't supposed to be happening. Not to her. The Blackwood nobody cared about.

"Just one?" she finally managed to ask.

"Huh?"

"You said *one* of them got out," Hollis snapped. "Just one?"

Which one?

"Yeah. I mean, I only saw one." He was still clenching and unclenching his hands, and it was pissing her off. She was the one whose breasts were being ogled by—

"What do you mean you only saw one? How?"

"Someone texted it to me."

"Who?"

Dwayne bit his lip. "I . . . It doesn't really matter, does it? I don't want you to flip out on someone who didn't do anything—"

"*Didn't do anything?* Do you hear yourself right now? Someone sent you a nude picture of me. I'm pretty sure there were no good intentions behind that, Dwayne."

Dwayne rubbed his lips together. "Right. But, the thing is . . . it's probably gotten out to quite a few people now, so I'm not sure it matters who—"

"It *matters* because whoever sent that to you knows we're best friends. And if we figure out how it got around, maybe we can trace it back to whoever—" She paused, trying to clear her mind, to think over the screaming in her head. "I don't get it. Were you hacked?"

"Must've been." He looked down at his hands then, and when he spoke, he answered the question she was about to ask next. "I promise you, I didn't send any of the photos to *anybody*, Holl. I swear."

Hollis thought of the stares she'd gotten in the hallway. Now that she knew what they were about, the smirks were definitely worse than the sympathetic looks. God. This would get around to everyone at Dupree by lunchtime, no question. She stuffed her hands in her pockets so she wouldn't be tempted to punch Dwayne.

"Fuck. *Fuck.* This is—" The bell rang then, cutting her off. She didn't know what she was going to say, so she kicked the base of the bench instead. Over and over again until her toes began to throb inside her sneakers. Until she was panting, just a little bit. Until she was no longer tempted to hurt Dwayne, who was sitting still as a statue just inches from her.

The door they'd come out of opened and Ms. Kreitz, Hollis's freshman year biology teacher, appeared. "Hollis, Dwayne. Everything all right?"

Hollis stared at her, trying to discern her expression. Did Ms. Kreitz know? Was she genuinely oblivious, or was she trying to hide the fact that the photo had made it around the faculty, too?

"Sorry, Ms. Kreitz," Dwayne mumbled, peeling himself off the table. "We were just . . ." He trailed off.

Hollis wouldn't go back into that school. She couldn't. The attention had been bad enough when she wasn't even sure what was happening, but now that she knew all those people—people she had to sit next to in class, at lunch—had seen her naked? No way.

"I have an appointment," Hollis said. She'd get in trouble later for lying, and for not signing out before she left, but that was the last thing she cared about now.

She didn't bother to look at either of them or reassure Ms. Kreitz that the front office was aware she was leaving. She ignored Dwayne as he called out her name. She walked through the quiet campus alone, passing by Blackwood Auditorium as she made her way to the student parking lot. Her breathing had grown heavy, erratic; her skin turned clammy, and she just wanted to sit down right where she was and catch her breath, but she had to keep going. She had to get out of there.

Finally, she reached her car. Her hands were shaking so badly, she had to click the key fob a few times just to open the door. She eventually managed to unlock it, then slid into the driver's seat, seized the steering wheel with both hands, and screamed at the top of her lungs.

Hollis tried to recall her parents' schedules as she drove the few blocks home, but her brain felt like scrambled eggs. Was this the day Dad had meetings across town, or was that Mom? Not to mention her phone kept going off, pinging with texts and phone calls until she came to a stop at a red light and reached over to shut it off.

That was when she remembered Ardith's call and text from earlier, and her hands went sticky against the steering wheel. She must have already known. And if her cousin, who was nowhere near Dupree Academy, already knew, that meant the picture had made its way well past her school.

Fuck.

Her stomach dropped again. No reputable news site would publish a nude photo of her, but trashy gossip blogs didn't have the same ethics, and of course there were bigger sites that would report on the leak even if they wouldn't feature the photo. She had always been proud of keeping a low profile with such a high-profile name, but none of that mattered now. People she didn't even know would be looking at her in one of her most intimate moments.

She closed her eyes, wondering if the news had made it to her parents. Home was the safest place to be now, but even the thought of hiding out in her house didn't feel like a comfort.

A car honked loudly behind her, and Hollis's eyes flew open. The light was green.

She threw her G-Wagon into park behind her mother's BMW in the circle drive; that had seemed like the longest trip of her life. She let herself inside, hands still shaking, and planned to go straight up to her room, telling her mother she'd gotten sick and come home. But Mom peeked over the railing from upstairs to see who had opened the door, and as soon as Hollis saw her mother's face, she dropped her backpack at her feet and burst into tears.

"Honey?" Mom rushed down the stairs and immediately swept her into her arms. She held Hollis for a couple of minutes, rubbing her back as Hollis sobbed against her. Then she gently pulled away and led her to the couch in the family room. "Honey, what's wrong? Are you hurt?"

Hollis shook her head, but she couldn't stop crying. Her mother briefly disappeared, returning with a large glass of water and a box of tissues. "Drink this," she said, and Hollis drained the glass in two long gulps.

When she had finished, Mom touched her arm and asked, "Can you tell me what happened?"

Hollis kicked off her shoes and brought her knees up to her chest, hugging her legs tight. Her toe was sore from kicking the bench, proof that it hadn't all been a horrible dream. "Something really bad happened."

Her mother cocked her head to the side. "Okay . . . Are you in trouble?"

"No, not like that. It's nothing I did. It's something that happened to me."

"Sweetie, the suspense is killing me," Mom said.

"I'm nervous to tell you."

"You don't have to be nervous. It's just me."

"I don't want you to judge me."

"I'm your mom. It's my job to listen, not judge. Hollis, what happened?"

She cleared her throat and took a deep breath before she began, keeping her eyes on the floor-to-ceiling bookshelves across the room. "This summer, I asked Dwayne to take some pictures of me before my surgery . . . without my bra. He sent them to me and said he deleted the photos, but someone apparently got ahold of at least one, and now it's going around school and everybody knows. And . . . it must be outside of school, too, because Ardith called, and I think she was trying to warn me."

Hollis took another long breath and looked everywhere but at her mother. Because Mom knew exactly what this meant. She was a Blackwood, which meant this wasn't just devastatingly embarrassing for her—this was *news*. Hollis could already imagine the op-eds that were being written, about the degradation of celebrity morality, the death of the "class" and "grace" of Hollywood families, the danger of raising your kids in a place like L.A. This wasn't just her problem; this was her family's problem. There were people whose reputations never recovered from things like this.

"Oh, baby," Mom finally said.

"I'm so sorry," Hollis whispered, holding back more sobs. "I never thought this could happen—"

"No, no, I don't want you apologizing. *I'm* sorry someone did this to you." She lifted Hollis's chin with her finger until Hollis finally looked into her eyes. "You didn't do anything wrong by celebrating your body. And I'm proud to have a daughter who is proud of the way she looks."

"But no one else was ever supposed to see them. And now that picture is going to be everywhere, and assholes on the internet are going to be saying stuff about you and Dad and Grandpa Abe and Ardith and . . ." Hollis dropped her head, resting it on her bent knees. Maybe she could just live here in this cocoon on the couch forever.

"One of us could buy the wrong coffee creamer at Whole Foods, and someone would try to make a story of it," her mother said. "Honey, if that's what you're worried about, this is nothing new, I promise you. And one good part about everything being online now is that news moves fast. People will forget about this in a couple of days, and something else will take its—" The ding of her mother's cell phone interrupted. She glanced at the screen. "Shit."

Her mother didn't often curse in front of her, so Hollis knew without asking what it was. "Can I see?"

"I don't think—"

"If it's about me, I want to see it."

Mom reluctantly handed over the phone; Hollis stared at the display through bleary eyes. It was the sort of site where the font and the ads that popped up on the sides and bottom of the screen made it tough to understand what she was looking at. But then she slowly began to make out the title of the blog—*Glitz & Gossip*—and the headline after that:

BLOSSOM BLACKWOOD'S GREAT-GRANDDAUGHTER BARES ALL JUST WEEKS AFTER HOLLYWOOD STAR'S DEATH

Hollis's stomach dropped for the hundredth time. She'd known it would be trashy, but mentioning Bebe in connection with this was beyond what she'd expected. She didn't even have a name or a life of her own; she was just "Blossom Blackwood's great-granddaughter."

And then, there it was. Or there *she* was. A shadowy photo of her nude from the waist up. The blog was attempting to present some semblance of decency, so her breasts were obscured by a thick black bar. But only her breasts. Hollis stared at herself: big, round eyes and high cheekbones on display, her mouth glossy and pouty. She hadn't looked at the pictures in a while.

Hollis had barely comprehended what the post even said—something about her suddenly being a sex symbol, wondering what it meant for her future, and some bad puns—before her mother took the phone away. "That's enough. This site is garbage. Nobody who's anybody looks at this."

"We had never looked at it before today, either," Hollis said.

Mom sighed, turning the phone over. "This came from your uncle August. He's already on it, okay? The photo will be taken down soon."

"But the damage is done. Everyone has seen it." And the one going around at school would not have the black band over her chest . . .

"Honey, I'm sorry. But if there's anything I can promise you, it's that this *will* blow over. Online, and at school. Unfortunately, the only thing that will ensure it does is time." Her mother paused. "Do you want me to make you something to eat?"

Hollis shook her head. "I just want to go lie down."

"That's a good idea. I'll get you some more water," her mother said as she stood. "Let me know if you need anything else. Oh, and Hollis?"

She looked up.

"Leave your phone with me," Mom said. Hollis started to argue, but her mother held up her hand. "You'll drive yourself insane looking at everything that's out there. I don't want you doing that to yourself right now. Go on up, and I'll bring some chamomile tea, too."

Hollis was exhausted, and she tried lying down after finishing her tea, but she felt almost itchy for her phone. Her mother had taken her laptop and tablet, too, leaving her no way to connect to the outside world. When she finally realized the best way to quiet her mind was to actually sleep, she tried to practice the same peace of mind she felt during savasana in yoga class. It worked. She woke a few hours later to a light knock at her door; the sun had set, and her room was completely dark. For a moment, she forgot why she'd been sleeping in the middle of the day.

Then it all came crashing back to her.

Hollis switched on her bedside lamp as her mom slipped in with more water—and what looked like a page of newspaper folded under her arm. "How'd you sleep?"

"Okay, I guess." Hollis yawned, tucking a pillow behind her back so she could sit up.

Mom perched on the edge of the bed, handed the glass to Hollis, and spread the paper out on her lap. It was deeply creased and yellowed with age.

"What's that?"

"This, my dear, is a good old-fashioned print copy of the *New York Post*. Page Six, to be precise."

Hollis looked at the headline and gasped:

ISAIAH BLACKWOOD CAUGHT OUT ON THE TOWN
WITH HOT NEW THING 1 WEEK BEFORE WEDDING

"Mom!"

"I know," her mother said, and Hollis was surprised to see a tiny smile on her face. "Clearly it wasn't true, but we were finalizing plans for a *New York Times* wedding announcement interview, and here comes this thing saying your father was cheating on me with a young actor who had a small role in his new film. Friends, family, strangers—it seemed like everyone was trying to call me, to see if I knew about it."

"What did you do?" Hollis asked.

"We ignored it. And got married the next week." Mom smiled and shrugged. "I had no reason to distrust your father."

"This is . . . gross. I can't believe you and Dad aren't still mad about it." Hollis touched the paper with her pinkie.

"Oh, I spent plenty of time being mad. *Furious*. Trust me." Mom paused. "But the anger will eat you up if you let it. That's why I've kept this all these years. To remind me that with these sorts of things, you have to just let it go and move on. Other people will. There'll be something new to distract them tomorrow."

"You obviously don't go to Dupree Academy."

"I know it's tough, baby. But you have a lot of people in your corner. Ardith, Prentice, and Dwayne all called me when they couldn't get ahold of you, just to make sure you're okay. They all wanted to come over, too, but I told them it was probably best to give you space tonight."

Hollis nodded. She was still too embarrassed to see anyone. Even her cousins. And—"Dwayne called?"

"He was the first one," her mother said carefully. "How do you feel about that?"

"I don't know . . ."

"You don't know if you can trust him?"

Hollis hung her head. She didn't want to feel that way about Dwayne, but she couldn't ignore the part of her that wondered if he might have shared the photo with someone. It had to have started somewhere, and she wasn't totally convinced Dwayne didn't know how it had gotten out.

But how could he be so cruel—to do that, and then keep it from her, too? He knew what it felt like to have his and his family's life scrutinized by everyone. Even if he was being honest, that he didn't show anyone or intentionally let it get out, it must have come from his phone, somehow. She didn't understand how he could be so careless.

"Do you want me to have Libby ask him?"

"Mom, no. You can't."

"Okay. I won't." Her mother reached out to tuck a stray loc back into Hollis's sleep bonnet. "You're going to get through this, honey. You're a Blackwood. It's what we do."

Hollis managed to eat a bit of dinner with her parents. She was mortified to see her father, but he only gave her a big hug and a kiss—and assured her he wouldn't look at the picture. Despite how cool her parents were being about the whole thing, Hollis couldn't help wondering if a part of them was disappointed in her. It wasn't the kind of press anyone wanted.

"I don't want to embarrass you guys," she said sadly, as her father began clearing the dishes from the table.

Dad stopped, halfway to the dishwasher. "You're not embarrassing us, Hollis. Things happen. Would it have been better if the picture had never gotten out? Sure. But it did, and we're dealing with it."

"How can you be so chill about it? Mom showed me that tabloid that came out before your wedding. They've been doing this to us forever. It's not fair."

He looked to her mother, who shrugged and said, "You know I like to save things for posterity. It was funny."

Dad set the dishes on the kitchen island and rejoined the two of them at the table. "Want to know a secret?" he said. "Your mother has a lot thicker skin than I do."

Hollis tilted her head to the side. "You think that's a secret?"

"Very funny." He shook his head with a wry smile. "I can kind of see the humor in that gossip column now, but it took me a long time to get over it. Some actors said I should wear it like a badge of honor, that it meant I'd really made it if Page Six was writing about me. But, honestly, it bothered me even more that it had to have been someone on set who fed them that story."

"Did you figure out who it was?" Hollis asked.

"No. But it did make me realize I couldn't trust anyone outside the family, except a very small circle."

Hollis exhaled. "But how did you know who to stop trusting if you didn't have proof?"

Dad shrugged. "I guess I just had to believe in my gut instinct. It wasn't easy at first, but the older I got, the more I learned who to let in." He leaned forward, a soft look in his eyes. "Maybe you'll laugh about this someday, maybe you won't. But you're not an embarrassment, Hollis. Never."

After dinner, Hollis showered and went back to bed, missing her phone but ultimately glad her mother was still holding it hostage. She didn't need to see what people were saying about the photo. She didn't need to see the photo, either.

The photo. She'd looked at the pictures a couple of times since the summer, happy that she'd taken them, but the pride she'd felt was ruined now. And how could she ever think about that night with Dwayne again without feeling it was tainted, as well?

He had come over to help her calm down the evening before her surgery. She'd been anxious about the breast reduction, though she knew it would be better in the long run—for her back, and her self-esteem. She was tired of people staring at her chest, even when she knew they didn't mean to. And if there was anyone she could talk to about it without wanting to burst into flames, it was Dwayne.

Sure enough, he was so chill that she'd soon felt the anxiety melting away. "What are you most worried about?" he'd asked, his long body draped across the love seat in her bedroom. "Going under the knife? The anesthesia?"

"Both," she said from the bed, where she was sitting cross-legged.

"Surgery sucks, no doubt. But the surgeon is one of the best. It'll be all good, Holl."

She cleared her throat. "I guess . . . I guess I'm also worried I'm not really going to be me after this, you know?"

Dwayne propped himself up on one elbow to look at her. "What do you mean?"

"I'll look different, but it's not just that." She paused as she tried to figure out how to say this to Dwayne. This was something she had been thinking about ever since she and her mother had gone in for her consultation, but the closer she got to the surgery, the more it had pushed itself to the front of her mind. "These have always been a part of me, you know?"

"Yeah, and you're . . . adjusting them." Dwayne shrugged. "They're not really going anywhere."

"What if I don't like how they look? What if I *am* making a mistake?"

"You don't have to go through with it if you don't want to," he said. "But you *are* doing the right thing."

Hollis hesitated, then said, "They're going to take before and after pictures of me, so I can compare them. And they said I should take some of my own at home, too, if I want."

Dwayne mulled this over. "That's a pretty good idea, actually. So if you ever miss them . . ." He trailed off with a sheepish smile.

Hollis had never thought of it that way. When the surgeon had mentioned they'd be taking photos at the medical center, it had sounded clinical. But would photographing herself at home feel like she was taking nudes? Hollis had never taken nudes before, for herself or anyone else. She guessed she'd never felt like she had a reason to. She had kissed a couple of guys at Dupree at random parties, but she didn't have much of a history with dating; she hadn't ever had a boyfriend. Part of it was because no guy had interested her enough, but the other part, the one that loomed large over anything she did, was her parents had always cautioned her about getting close to people. They'd encouraged her to be kind, but to be aware of how people approached her, to make the distinction between those who wanted to know her, Hollis, and the ones who wanted to say they knew her because of her last name.

She looked at Dwayne, who was staring at the floor as he absently chewed on his thumbnail. She felt a real warmth for him in that moment. The truth was, Dwayne was her only real friend. She was friendly with some people at school, but when it came to confiding in someone, in sharing her deepest insecurities and fears, Dwayne was the person she turned to outside of her family.

"Have you ever taken pictures of yourself?" she asked.

"Uh . . . yeah," he replied slowly.

"Really? Have you sent them to anyone?"

She was being nosy, but suddenly she needed to know. She'd heard plenty of people at school talking about trading nudes with hookups, boyfriends, girlfriends. She knew she wasn't the only person who hadn't, but she felt an itch now. To try something she hadn't considered before.

"Just to one girl, a couple years ago," Dwayne said. Hollis thought back to the girls he was talking to sophomore year, one of them a senior she'd never liked, but he interrupted her thoughts, lobbing the question right back at her. "Have you?"

"No, I've never even taken any."

"For real?"

She gave him a look. "You're surprised?"

The corners of his mouth turned up. "I mean, if I looked like *you*? Just saying . . ."

His words had hung between them as her neck, cheeks, and forehead turned warm. When she peeked at Dwayne, he looked the way she was feeling. Embarrassed but buzzing with something—something that was just beginning to bloom. She guessed that something was what made her say it:

"Maybe you could take them. Pictures of me."

Dwayne's brown eyes were so soft as they connected with hers. He bit his lip, looked down and then back at her with an even softer smile. "If you want me to, Hollis. Yeah. I could do that."

Mistletoe and Black-Eyed Peas
1955

"Blossom, Michael's here!" Sybil called from the front room, just as Blossom had smoothed her hand gently over the baby's head, relieved he had finally fallen asleep.

Before she could run to the hallway to shush her sister, a shadow appeared in the doorway. Michael crossed the small room in a few quick steps, standing next to her at the wooden crib.

He peered down at the baby, frowning. "What is he wearing?"

"Michael, hush," she whispered. "You're as bad as Sybil. I just got him to sleep."

"Sorry," he said, lowering his voice, too. He pulled the blanket back a bit to look closer. "But what is this?"

"It's a set Mama made him. Now, come on," she said, tugging his arm until they were outside of the room. She left the door open a crack so they could hear Abe if he cried.

"Why is it yellow?"

"What?" Blossom was exhausted, and his questions were wearing on her patience.

"That thing he's got on. Why is it yellow?"

"Because Mama had perfectly good fabric to use up. You don't like yellow now?"

Michael huffed. "I don't like it on my boy. That's a girl's color, you know."

"Stop being silly. Yellow is for everyone." Blossom started walking toward the kitchen. "Are you hungry? I was just about to make some corn-bread and heat up some black-eyed peas."

"You know I can always eat, girl."

Before she could reach the refrigerator, Michael caught her by the waist and wrapped his arms around her, pulling Blossom close. She pretended to protest as he kissed her neck, but not for long. Blossom was glad Mama wasn't home; she relished these rare moments in which they were able to openly show their affection. They had made a whole child together, but every time Flossie caught them doing more than holding hands in the house, she had something to say about it.

Michael sat at the table, telling her about the early shift he'd just finished. He'd moved on a couple of years ago from working at the factory and had secured a job with the city as a welder. Michael liked the job well enough, but he was focused on a promotion, determined to make his way to the top of the public works department. Blossom appreciated his drive, but she didn't understand how he could talk endlessly about his job when he was barely able to listen to her stories about her own work, which usually varied by day. Blossom stirred the batter for the cornbread, dutifully nodding as he spoke.

"You know, Johnny was saying he about ready to propose to his girl," Michael said, cupping his hands around the glass of water Blossom had put in front of him.

"Oh? That's lovely. She seems nice." Blossom greased the cast-iron skillet with shortening, then poured the batter inside and slipped it into the oven.

"He asked me what we was thinking."

Blossom pulled the pot of peas from the refrigerator. "About?"

"Blossom. Come on now."

She turned to look at him. "What?"

"When we thinking about getting married."

"Oh, Michael. We've been over this. I don't think now is the right time."

He frowned. "When will it be the right time, Blossom? We already got a baby to show for our trouble."

She pursed her lips at him and exhaled. "Can't we keep things as they are? It's been working out just fine, hasn't it?"

"Maybe for you."

"And for you, too—aren't I still cooking for you?" Blossom pointed to the oven where the cornbread was baking. "Letting you come over whenever you want to see the baby, and bringing him to see Miss Rose when she wants to, also? Giving you—" She stopped, her neck flushing hot with the unspoken words. "We agreed to try this out for a while, and it's working. Johnny getting married has nothing to do with you and me."

Blossom banged the pot onto the stove, then remembered—Abe. She held her breath, praying he didn't wake again, only letting it out when the back room remained silent.

"Aw, Blossom. Don't be like that. I was just telling you something," he said, coming to stand next to her at the stove.

"Well, tell me something else." She lit the flame beneath the burner. "I don't want to be badgered."

"You know what them peas make me think of?" Michael's voice was low, and Blossom's skin warmed again. She knew exactly what he was talking about.

Though they had broken up shortly after Michael's nineteenth birthday, they had remained in touch. They'd both still lived in the homes they'd grown up in, so sometimes they would see each other when they were coming to and from work or visiting a friend; they would stop to say hello, or when they were both in a good mood, they would stand on the sidewalk to catch up for a few minutes.

Then Michael's mother and uncle hosted a party to ring in the new year of 1954. Michael had a load of aunts and uncles and cousins, and anytime they had a birthday or some other type of celebration, the house was stuffed to the gills with family and friends. The Blackwoods had all been invited: Blossom, Sybil, Flossie, and Marla and Harold.

Mistletoe hung in various parts of Michael's house, left over from Christmas the week before, but Blossom didn't notice until Michael caught her under it, his hand resting on her waist as he pointed it out above. "You know it's bad luck if you don't kiss me," he'd said with a slow smile. Blossom knew she should refuse, but he'd looked so handsome that evening, recalling the boy she'd known when they first began going steady. So she had obliged, allowing him to peck her on the lips.

Sybil had seen it, of course, because Sybil never missed anything, and Blossom spent most of the evening fending off her sister's relentless teasing. But the truth was, she'd liked the kiss. And as the guests began preparing for the countdown to midnight, one of Michael's aunts weaving through the party with bottles of cheap champagne to fill empty glasses, Blossom looked to see where Michael might be. When she couldn't find him, she stood next to the stove, watching the black-eyed peas that were simmering to usher in the new year. She'd been disappointed, then felt foolish about it. This was Michael. The same old Michael she'd always known. And they were no longer together. What had she been expecting?

But then—there he was, rounding the corner into the kitchen two minutes before midnight. His eyes lit up when he found her, and Blossom took his hand without a word, following him out into the cool, clear night. He held her close as the party inside counted down the seconds to 1954, and when they got to *one*, Michael leaned down and gave her a real kiss. Long and deep and full of passion she'd never felt before.

And, later, Blossom went to bed with him, not thinking about what this meant for them but only how good it felt, how natural it was to be with Michael in that way. She hadn't known what to expect after that evening, but she wasn't interested in anything serious again. Michael was still handsome, still charming—and still as old-fashioned as he'd been when they were together. They saw each other casually over the next few weeks, taking advantage of the privacy of their houses when no one else was home.

Then Blossom realized her monthly cycle was late. Soon after, the morning sickness began.

She told Sybil first, only because her sister caught her getting sick two days in a row. The second morning, Blossom had emerged from the bathroom to find her waiting by the door.

"What's wrong?" Sybil asked, eyebrows furrowed.

"I'm . . . not feeling well," Blossom said, trying to move past her. "Must be a stomach bug."

But Sybil didn't budge. "Are you expecting?"

Blossom laughed, though it was hollow. "Why would you even say something like that?"

"Because you and Michael ain't as clever as you think, sneaking around like you been."

Blossom's shoulders dropped. She hesitated for a moment, then confessed, "My cycle is late. And I've been feeling just terrible when I wake up."

"So you are," Sybil said softly.

She looked at her sister with scared eyes. "Syb, what am I going to do? Michael and I aren't even together."

"Mama won't care about that. She'll just be happy you're having her first grandbaby. Now maybe she'll give Marla a break." Sybil touched her fingers to Blossom's still-flat stomach, smiling. "And I'm going to be an auntie."

Blossom told Michael two weeks later, when her cycle still hadn't come. He'd been thrilled, had scooped her up in his arms and swung her around in a circle, saying how much he hoped it was a boy. And Sybil had been right—Mama was also overjoyed and immediately began talking about the sewing patterns she needed to purchase for Blossom's maternity dresses and the baby's clothes. She and Miss Rose began spending more time together, discussing all the things they needed to do before the baby arrived. But Blossom . . . Well, she might have been the only one who wasn't excited. It wasn't that she didn't want a baby; she just didn't feel that it was the right time. And she didn't know if Michael was the right man.

She had been working as a background actor since she'd quit the dance company in 1950; after five years dancing with Beatrice van der Kolk, she'd only been able to perform solos in two shows, though she'd been one of the best dancers and the most senior among them. And while Mrs. van der Kolk had always treated her kindly, Blossom had wondered sometimes about the strength of her commitment to having an integrated company, as just two other Negro dancers were hired during Blossom's time with the group. Shortly after, she'd gone down to the Hollywood Western Building to register with Central Casting, which had a division specifically devoted to finding Negroes and other minorities work. Blossom called in every day to see if there were any roles for her; sometimes there weren't, and then, increasingly often, there were. These were background parts: no lines, essentially part of the set dressing. But Blossom was proud of every film she'd ever been cast in, even the ones where one could only catch a glimpse of the back of her head.

Supporting and leading roles for Negro actors were not nearly as plentiful as those available for white actors, and the few that were written for Negro actresses usually went to the same small group of established stars. Blossom had begun to think she'd never find real work when one of her fellow background actresses told her she should try her luck on the East Coast, where she'd heard Negro actors were starting to book consistent work in theater. She had been saving up her money from Central Casting, picking up extra shifts at the restaurant where she worked. And she had been just about ready to give New York a try when she'd learned she was going to be a mother.

She and Michael had dozens of conversations about marriage before the baby was born, but they always circled back to the same impasse: Michael wanted to marry her, and he would work while she stayed home with the baby; Blossom didn't want to be married if that meant giving up on professional acting. She suggested a compromise, that they could raise the baby together, whether they officially rekindled their romance or not. But Michael thought it was too modern—and besides, he was determined to be the father he hadn't had.

But as Blossom's belly grew and her ankles swelled and she became more and more tired, he soon realized she wasn't going to give in to his rigid idea of what being a family meant. And he stopped pestering her about marriage. He began dropping by every evening to check on her, and he was there the night her water broke, an early evening in September. Blossom thought, after their beautiful baby, Abraham Eugene, was born, that things would remain harmonious. Michael was a present father, and he was sweet to her, often bringing her small gifts from the drugstore when he'd come to see the baby.

One day, after she'd finished nursing Abe, who was fourteen weeks, Blossom mentioned that she wanted to start looking for acting work again. And just like that, the magical spell was broken. Michael told her it was impractical and selfish, that she should want to be home with her baby, not trying to break into Hollywood. Blossom had told him exactly what he could do with that attitude—and ever since then, the stalemate remained. Abe was six months old now, and they still lived separately; Michael visited often, helping out with the baby whenever he wasn't at work or sleeping. Blossom and Michael's relationship was inconsistent, fluctuating between weeks they couldn't keep their hands off each other and days when they argued so much the very sight of him infuriated Blossom. She sometimes wondered if he thought he could wear her down about marriage, that he could talk her out of her lifelong dreams, the ones she was still pursuing.

Now she shooed him away from her as she tended to the peas, and Michael went to peek in on the baby, wash up, and chat briefly with Sybil. Blossom set out plates and silverware, and by the time he had returned, the food was ready. Michael dug in right away, and Blossom watched him, thinking this might be the best time to share her news. He was always happier when he was eating.

"I have an audition next week," she began carefully, taking a sip of water.

"Another background job?" he asked without looking up.

"No, a real audition. For a part in a play."

"A play, huh? Thought you said there weren't a lot of those around here."

"Well, it's—it's in New York City."

Michael paused, holding a piece of cornbread in midair. "New York?"

"Yes, it's Off-Off Broadway, but it would be an actual role. A speaking part."

He finished chewing and sat back in his seat. "Why you going all the way out there to audition for a part you can't take?"

"Well, if I get the part, I *would* take it. No one auditions for fun."

"Blossom, why you talking crazy?" Michael laughed. "You can't run off to New York and take a job. We got a baby."

Blossom set down her forkful of peas. She hadn't eaten a bite yet. "Yes, but I have a sister and a mother who are more than happy to help care for him while I'm gone. And I'm sure Miss Rose would love some extra time with Abe."

"You can't go."

Blossom blinked. "Excuse me?"

"You're not just gonna go out to New York and leave our baby on a whim. I won't allow it."

The rage in Blossom flared up so hot she could hardly see straight, but her voice was even and strong as she said, "Michael Babineaux, you do not own me."

Michael smirked, but his eyes were steely. "Maybe not, but I'm half of that baby in there. And he deserves a mother who won't just up and run off across the country for some piddly little acting job. How many lines is it, anyway?"

Blossom squeezed her hands around her knees. She was afraid what she would do with them otherwise. "And I'm half of him, too. What Abe deserves is a mother who loves him unconditionally, and he has that in me. You weren't the one up with him all night, trying to get him to eat or stop crying in those first couple of months. You change a diaper a few times a week while I do it what seems like fifty times a day! You don't wash his clothes or bathe him or—"

"Marry me, and I will!" Michael shouted, shooting up from the table. "How am I supposed to be a proper father when you won't just do the right thing and be my wife?"

Blossom stood up, too. "The *right* thing?"

"You know how people look at us? Having a baby out of wedlock but still carrying on like we do? You want Abe to grow up knowing people don't respect his mama and daddy because they wouldn't go down to city hall?"

"Respect has nothing to do with a piece of paper, Michael. My mama never married. Do people not respect her?"

"They didn't respect how she let your daddy treat her."

Blossom's eyes narrowed. "What did you say?"

"Nothing," he muttered, slowly sinking back down into his seat.

"No," Blossom said, her voice beginning to shake. "Say it again."

"Blossom—"

"I want to know what you meant by that, too," Sybil said softly from the doorway.

A wave of guilt washed over Blossom at Sybil's words. She'd forgotten her sister was here. And by the troubled look on her face, she'd apparently heard everything. "Sybil, no—"

"He was my daddy, too. I got a right to know." Sybil turned her attention to Michael. "What did you know about him?"

Michael was still staring down at the black-eyed peas and cornbread growing cold on his plate. "My uncle knew him. He didn't live too far from here, and—he had another family. A wife, and two boys and a girl."

Behind them, Sybil let out a small, strangled cry.

Blossom dropped into her chair with a thud. She could hardly swallow around the thick lump that had risen in her throat. "How long have you known this?"

"It don't matter, Blossom. I'm sorry I said anything. I got caught up in the heat of the moment—"

"You've known? All this time? When you came home from school with me that day, and Mama told me—" Blossom choked on her words. "You knew."

Michael reached for her, but Blossom slapped his hand away. He shrank back in his seat, eyes wide. "I'm sorry. I just don't want people to look at us that way. To think we coulda done better for our boy. Marry me, Blossom. Please. We could be so happy, just you and me and Abe. We could have a real nice house someday, and maybe some more kids, too. I love you. But you need to put away these childish dreams and act like the mama Abe needs. I can't make you my wife when you still out here chasing something that ain't gonna happen."

Blossom was silent for a few moments. She didn't allow herself to look at Michael as she gathered her thoughts. And when she spoke, her voice was low, like her mother's when she really meant business. "I will never marry you, Michael Babineaux."

"I know you mad at me right now, but don't go saying things you don't—"

"*Never.*"

Michael's jaw shifted a few times. He crossed his arms. "Fine. You won't ever marry me, then you can be like your mama and raise that baby alone. I'm gone."

"Don't you threaten me," Blossom warned, her voice still quiet. "I will take you at your word."

"You should. I can't play these games with you no more."

"Then leave us be, Michael."

He shoved his chair up to the table, the legs scraping loudly against the linoleum. "There's something wrong with you Blackwood women. Thinking you don't need no men in your lives. Too bad it'll be too late when you change your mind."

"She said leave." Sybil's voice had returned.

Michael looked between the two of them, then he stalked silently toward the front of the house. Blossom hurried after him, ready to stand between him and the baby's room in case he tried to take Abe with him. But he didn't even bother to peek in on his son. He simply breezed through the front door, slamming it so hard she was surprised it didn't crack off the hinges.

In the back bedroom, Abe began to wail.

Michael didn't return the next day, or the day after, or the day after that. Though this was what he had promised, a part of Blossom had believed he was only calling her bluff, trying to force her hand in the matter. But when Mama told her to go to New York for the audition, despite how they'd left things, Blossom wavered.

"Maybe he was right, Mama," she said, bouncing Abe on her knee as they sat together in the front room. "Abe needs me here. Look how happy he is."

"You don't see how happy he is when you gone, do you?" Flossie said. As if to prove his grandmother's point, Abe grinned widely at her, drool dripping down his chin. "See? He good."

"Traitor," Blossom whispered as she leaned forward to pepper his fat cheeks with kisses. She looked at her mother again. "Mama, you really think it's all right that I go?"

"I think if you let that Babineaux boy get in your head like that, you'll never do anything you want to do. And that's what he hoping for. Girl, go on to that audition. Get that part. Sybil and I got Abe."

Blossom didn't get the part. But while she was there, she was recommended for an audition for a role in another play. The director there told her she was close, but not exactly what they were looking for. He told her to keep working on her craft, to keep auditioning—that he knew he'd see her onstage one day. Blossom returned home simultaneously disappointed and heartened, and the sight of Abe was exactly what she needed. He had just woken up from his midday nap and squealed when he saw her.

"You missed me, sweet Abe? I sure did miss you," she said, taking him from Sybil so she could nuzzle the soft curls at the base of his neck. She paused before she looked at her sister and asked, "Any word?"

"None. And Mama is real mad."

"What happened?"

Flossie still worked a few shifts a week, cleaning homes for white families that paid good wages. Blossom and Sybil had asked if she'd planned to slow down, but Mama said her body would tell her when it was ready. That day, Blossom was happy Mama wasn't home so her sister could prepare her.

"She said she heard Miss Rose is talking real bad about you. Saying you not a fit mama, and that you drove Michael away because of it."

Blossom's mouth dropped. "Sybil, no."

"Yes. She's so mad I had to stop her from going over there and giving Miss Rose a piece of her mind."

"Maybe you should've let her." Blossom had always liked Miss Rose, but the thought of her spreading such lies about her was enough to make her want to march over and tell Michael's mama off herself.

Sybil shrugged. "Mama's been real quiet since then."

That evening, after they had finished cleaning up from supper, Mama asked Blossom to sit down with her at the kitchen table. "Sybil told you about what Rose Babineaux been out here saying?"

Blossom nodded.

"I ain't gonna allow her to drag our name through the mud. You don't deserve that, Blossom. You a good mother."

Blossom blinked. Mama must have been truly upset. She wasn't usually so sentimental.

"You remember Lillian Williams? Her daughter works in a lawyer's office now, typing up his papers. Lillian said she heard about your situation, and we got to talking and . . . Her daughter looked into it and she told me about something we can do," Mama continued. "If you want."

"What is it, Mama?"

"Michael said he was done, didn't he? If he don't come around or give you money to care for Abe for a whole year, the courts call it abandonment."

"What does that all mean?"

"It would mean he give up his rights to be Abe's daddy. Legally."

"Oh." Blossom looked down at the table.

"But we'd have to go to court and . . . well, there's another option." Her mother paused. "We could have a lawyer draw up some papers asking him to sign away his rights."

"He could do that?"

Mama folded her hands in front of her. "Only if you had someone else in place to be a second guardian. And you got me. I'll take care of Abe when you gone, and Sybil will help out when I can't."

"Really, Mama?"

"This ain't good for you, girl. You don't need to worry about nothing but that baby and your work. I don't want him coming up in my house messing with your head. It ain't good for none of us. Especially Abe."

Blossom worried at her bottom lip. She was furious with Michael—but this seemed . . . extreme. She hadn't really considered the possibility that he might never return. Michael was always saying things in anger and apologizing later. It had only been two weeks since he'd stormed out. He could still come back. But then . . . what if he didn't? Could she really raise Abe without him? Mama and Sybil were here to help now, but Blossom knew better than anyone how quickly one's life could change. What if Mama got sick or Sybil met someone? Then Blossom would be alone, and her career would be done, just like that.

And even if they did go through with it, would Michael ever agree to this? She didn't believe so, despite what he had promised. No matter how angry they were with each other, beneath it all there was still love.

"I think we should wait him out, Mama. See if he tries to come back."

"Okay, girl. It's up to you. But I'm telling you, Rose Babineaux better not show her face around here anytime soon, 'cause I sure can't promise things will be cordial."

Blossom spent the next six months taking on as many waitressing shifts as she could in hopes that one day, she would be able to save enough money for acting classes. The classes were expensive, and they would take up a lot of her time, but she had never forgotten the kindness of the director who had told her how close she was to getting cast—that she only needed to spend time working on her craft. Sybil practiced reading lines with her sometimes from old copies of plays she had lying around, and she gave suggestions, but Blossom knew there was only so much she could do on her own.

And the more shifts she took on, the less time she had to think about Michael. In the first few weeks, Blossom had counted the days he'd been gone, her mother's proposition never far from her mind. But she, Mama, and Sybil had a good system going; she tried not to take advantage of their generosity, but they encouraged her to seek out auditions, to still take on background roles when she wanted. And, eventually, she began to forget about Michael. Only for small stretches at first, and then she would go whole days without thinking about him or wondering if he would return. When she did think about him, she felt anxious. Because the longer he was absent, the closer they were to the one-year mark. And though Mama wasn't pressuring her, Blossom didn't know if she could go through with their plan. She supposed she needed one more sign from Michael, something that would let her know for sure she didn't want him in their lives ever again.

One day, Blossom walked out the front door, on her way to catch the bus, only to find Michael standing on the bottom step of the porch, his hands behind his back. She nearly dropped her pocketbook, sure she had seen a ghost. He appeared just as surprised to see her, as if he hadn't been standing outside of her house, watching the door.

Michael looked the same, which Blossom almost found insulting. How could he just look as if nothing had changed when he'd said all those awful things and left them to fend for themselves for months? What had he been doing this whole time?

"I'd like to see my boy, please," he said.

There were dozens of things Blossom wanted to say to him, to shout at him, in that moment. But when she opened her mouth, her words were quiet. Controlled. "His birthday was last week."

"I know. I . . . I got a present for him." He held out his hands, revealing a small, stuffed poodle. "I'd like to give it to him."

Blossom eyed the toy. He hadn't even bothered to wrap it. "It's been *six months*, Michael."

"I was angry," he said, his voice measured.

"But you don't get to just run off and stop being a father because you're angry. You don't get to do that to me—and you especially don't get to do that to Abe. What about when he's older? Old enough to remember when his father gets upset and disappears?"

"I'm here now."

She shook her head. "I don't want you in his life anymore."

Michael's arms fell slack to his side. "Blossom—"

"We are never going to make it work between us, Michael. And you've shown you don't care enough about him to put aside your frustrations with me and be a good father. You've had your mama out here calling us all kinds of names when *you* are the one who stayed away. You think I'm eager to let you see him now?"

"Please. I miss him. And you. I do love you, Blossom. I needed some time away, to clear my head. To—"

"You were so sure I'd come crawling back to you—that *you* would be the one to reject *me*."

"I made a mistake. I'm not like my daddy. I came back."

"You don't get to make those kinds of mistakes when a child is involved. And I may not have known my father, but at least I didn't have him coming in and out of my life." Blossom exhaled. "Do you really love me?"

Michael stepped forward. "I do. I know you think we can't make it work, but I do."

"If you love me, you won't come around again."

He shrank back at her words. "Blossom?"

"If I let you see him today, let you give him that gift . . . I don't want you to come around again," Blossom said, speaking slowly to make sure her words were understood. "And then, after a year, your parental rights will be terminated. And you will no longer have custody of Abe or be able to visit him again."

Michael's face fell. "What?"

"I won't ask you for money. I don't need anything from you. What I need is someone who doesn't threaten me and run when they don't get their way. Someone who can accept me and the life I've built for our son."

"Come on, now, girl. You can't be serious."

"It will be easier this way. He won't know you or remember you. And he won't grow up with two unhappy parents who are no good for each other."

Michael scoffed, kicking at the porch step. "You just gonna let me go like that?"

"You've already let your son go."

At least a minute passed before Michael spoke again. "Fine. If that's what you really want, I won't bother you no more." He pushed the toy into her arms and turned on his heel.

"Where are you going?"

He twisted back around to face her. "You want me gone, I'm gone."

"Don't you want to see Abe?"

Michael shook his head. "Like you said, it'll be easier for everyone if I leave now. You want to terminate me being his daddy, I ain't gonna stop you. It just ain't worth the trouble with you, Blossom."

She stood on the porch, shaking, as she watched Michael Babineaux walk down her front path for the last time. When he was no longer visible, Blossom let herself back into the house, clutched the toy poodle to her chest, and wept.

Darling Abe

The mood at the first Saturday Breakfast after Blossom Blackwood's passing was somber. Typically, the Hancock Park house was bursting with life and light on the mornings they all convened. Today, though, Hollis and her parents arrived with bags of gourmet coffee beans and jugs of cold-pressed orange juice to find the house silent, the kitchen empty, the stove and oven cold.

"Huh," Rhonda said, popping her head out the front door to make sure that Abe's Mercedes had, in fact, been parked in the driveway. She returned to the kitchen and looked at her husband. "Where're your parents?"

Isaiah peered out the kitchen window to find Abe and Taffy sitting out on the patio, in the middle of what appeared to be a rather intense conversation. "They're out here, babe," he said, tapping on the window to get their attention. His mother and father looked up; Taffy offered a weak smile and a wave that meant they'd be inside momentarily.

Hollis hadn't wanted to come. She'd wanted to stay home, where she'd been since the photo got out, but her embarrassment wasn't a valid reason to skip Saturday Breakfast. "It's family," her mother had said. "You'll be safe with them." Hollis had thrown on a pair of roomy lavender sweats with a matching hoodie, retreating into the sort of outfit she'd been most comfortable in presurgery. Maybe if she completely hid her body, no one would be reminded of the photo and the online chatter surrounding it.

Twenty minutes later, the house was filled with Blackwoods. Even August made an appearance. He and Isaiah hadn't seen one another since their grandmother's celebration of life, but they greeted each other with hearty claps on the shoulder. They'd always had that kind of relationship; they had been close for as long as they could remember, but back in the day, one wrong look could send them straight to the backyard, brawling it out on the grass.

Ardith found Hollis in the kitchen, pouring a glass of orange juice. Hollis pulled down a second glass and poured one for her cousin.

"How are you?" Ardith asked softly. "I've been calling."

"I know, I'm sorry. I'm not really into talking to anyone right now," Hollis said. "And my phone . . . I finally got my mom to give it back to me, and I had so many random messages I had to close my DMs."

"Gross stuff?"

"Just dumb, mostly. My account is private, but . . ."

Ardith hesitated. "We don't have to talk about this if you don't want to, but did Dwayne have something to do with it being leaked?"

Hollis had told Ardith about that night, and she knew her cousin wasn't judging her. Still, it was difficult to look her in the eye. To know that she'd seen the photo, too. They had changed in front of each other probably hundreds of times over the years, but it wasn't what was in the photo that was embarrassing—it was what Ardith might be thinking about the circumstances in which it was taken.

"I don't know," she said. "He swears he didn't, but how else could it have gotten out?"

"Hacking?" Ardith pondered.

"Wouldn't other things have been leaked besides a picture of me?" Hollis sighed. "I want to believe him. He's my best friend. But something about it doesn't make sense."

"I'm sorry, cousin."

"Thanks. I just keep worrying about what everyone is going to think of me now."

"Even us?"

Hollis paused. Then, "Yeah."

"I think most of us know how it feels to have things about us out there that we wish weren't," Ardith said, though the most embarrassing paparazzi photo of her to date was from a couple of years ago, picking a wedgie as she walked into Lamill to grab a coffee. "You're kind of in the perfect family for something like this."

"But that's just it. We don't need this kind of attention. People make shit up about us anyway."

"Honestly, it could be worse," Ardith said thoughtfully. "Remember when they found out Juniper Lacey's publicity team had leaked her own nudes? *That's* embarrassing."

"Can everyone gather in the big room, please?" Abe called out, his voice echoing through the first floor.

The house was in a state of transition; flat boxes had been stacked up against the walls in each room while some had already been assembled and filled with the things from Blossom's life. It made them all feel a bit unsettled—each item in Blossom's house had its rightful place, and removing anything seemed to change everything. But the big room was yet untouched. The family arrived from their various corners, hesitantly—the kitchen was where they all gathered for Saturday Breakfasts. The cousins squeezed onto the love seat in their usual spots, with Prentice and Hollis on either side of Ardith. Being in this room together when it wasn't a holiday or special occasion felt plain wrong; the discomfort made itself known in everyone's tensed shoulders, in their tentative expressions.

Abe stood by the fireplace and looked out over the room. His eyes were a bit dewy, as if he was trying to hold back tears. "I have some news to share with you all." He held a big manila envelope in his hands.

"August brought this over yesterday. It was sealed, so he didn't know what was in it, just that Mama asked him to give it to me after her death. It's a letter and—" His voice broke, and Taffy, who had been perched on the arm of the couch, rushed to his side, softly sliding her hand up and down his arm. Abe cleared his throat again and again and took a sip of water from the glass she handed him.

Hollis, Prentice, and Ardith exchanged looks.

"Is it bad news, Dad?" Isaiah asked, eyebrows creased.

Abe glanced at Taffy, who nodded encouragingly. "Not bad. Just . . . I'm going to read it aloud to you, all right?" He closed his eyes briefly before he began.

Dear Abe,

Sometimes we do things we are not proud of. And sometimes these things are also what we believe to be the best for us and our loved ones. One thing I've learned in all my years on this Earth is how complicated life is—including the decisions we have to make, especially those that affect others. And it was my decision not to tell you who your father is—until now.

Clarence gasped from where he sat on the largest couch. Evan grabbed his husband's hand in his own, squeezing tightly.

Abe continued.

His name is Michael Babineaux. He was my high school sweetheart, my first love. He was a good man; he was also a man who made some mistakes with me. He was never supportive of my dreams of becoming an actress—when it came down to it, he wanted me to only sit at home and be a wife to him and a mother to you. I always wanted to be your mother—I've loved being your mother—but I'm sure you understand when I tell you that I needed to be more than somebody's wife. I knew there were bigger things in my future than being Mrs. Babineaux. Or I at least wanted the opportunity to see if that was true.

Eventually, it became clear that what I needed and what he needed were incompatible. When I told him this, he reacted badly. And so, when you were only a baby, I legally cut him out of our lives. I also officially removed him from your birth certificate so you would never know the difference. Michael died in 1992 from heart disease. He was sixty-five years old.

I struggle now to find words to express everything I am feeling. At the time, I did what I thought was best for both of us; whether it was or not, well, I have my answer, and you will have to find yours. Nevertheless, I have come to realize it was self-serving of me to ever believe keeping this information from you was the right path to take, and for that—for any pain I have caused you by withholding this information—I am sorry.

Your whole life, I've only wanted to do right by you. I also wanted to believe—despite what the world has always told women like me—that I didn't have to choose between doing right by you and doing right by myself. I love you, my darling Abe, always.

Love, Mama

Abe's eyes were full when he looked around the room. He wasn't the only one; the tension from before had transformed into a collective fragility. It was as if each one of them could easily break at any moment.

"My goodness," Rhonda said, sniffling as she rubbed Isaiah's back. "This is a lot."

"Are you okay, Dad?" Clarence asked, blinking fast.

Abe nodded, but he didn't say anything. The whole family was silent then, shaken.

"There's more," Abe finally said, his voice low. "A picture. The only one I've ever seen of my father. Maybe the only one of us together."

He pulled a small photograph from the envelope and carefully passed it to his eldest son. "Wow," Isaiah said, looking it over with his mouth wide open. His wife examined it next, brushing tears from her eyes as she handed it to Hollis.

The picture was black and white and spotted with age, but the faces in it were clear. There was young Blossom, perched on a long floral couch next to an attractive young Black man, and on her lap was a baby, Abe. On the back was written:

Us

February 1955

The family passed the photo around the room, tears flowing freely now; even Prentice and August were knuckling away dampness at the corners of their eyes.

"Oh, Dad," Clarence said. "I'm so sorry."

He crossed the room to give his father a hug. Isaiah walked over and wrapped his arms around them, then Rhonda and Taffy added themselves to the circle. Soon, they were one big mass, and it was hard to tell where one Blackwood ended and another began. It was what they needed, to hold one another close. To know that they were there for one another, always.

They cooked then, to ease the pain. Crispy bacon, frittatas with mushroom and kale, buttermilk biscuits, and fried potatoes, too. When the bacon platter was empty and everyone was quietly picking at the last few bites of their frittata, Abe said, "I'm going to try to track down Michael's family."

"Really?" Isaiah said. Next to him, Rhonda gently placed her hand on his wrist.

"Are you sure that's a good idea, Dad?" Clarence asked slowly, reaching for his coffee mug. "I'm still not entirely sure how I feel about Bebe's letter, but maybe there's a good reason she kept us from meeting them all these years."

August frowned. "Yeah, I don't know if that's something we should step into so soon after her passing. Or before the estate sale."

"The only reason we're not in touch with them is because my mother cut my father's family out of my life," Abe said. "So they have no reason to reach out. But we do."

"What do you think, Mom?" Clarence asked.

Everyone's eyes turned to Taffy, and for the first time anyone could remember, she seemed to have trouble speaking her mind. She fiddled anxiously with her silverware, adjusted her coffee cup, and finally dabbed the corners of her mouth with her napkin. "Well, we've talked about it, and you know I support Abe in everything he does, but this . . . I'm not so sure it's a good idea, either. It's been so long, and this might open up a lot of wounds. Decades-old wounds."

"What's the problem?" Prentice said. "Are we afraid they're going to try to take our money or something?"

"I think it's more complicated than that," his father Evan said carefully from across the table.

"But that's part of it, right?" Prentice continued. "I mean, they're probably not . . . um . . . They're not like us?"

He looked around the table, waiting for someone to answer, but all of the adults were silent. Prentice had hit on something they were all thinking, perhaps, but were too ashamed to say aloud.

Finally, Abe said, "We don't know who they are—if they have money, if they don't—and that's my point. Mama wouldn't have written this letter if she didn't want me to make my own decision about what to do with this information." He wiped his mouth with his napkin and nodded conclusively. "I appreciate your concern, but my mind is made up. I'm going to contact the Babineauxs."

Hollis looked up, frowning.

August said, "Dad, should we call Stephanie first? Maybe try to get ahead of this before the news gets out?" Stephanie was the family's lead publicist, who'd most recently been tasked with announcing Blossom's death to the press.

"How would the news get out?" Abe asked.

"Oh, honey," Taffy said, smoothing her hand over the back of his neck.

"I know you're most concerned with doing the right thing here, but let's be realistic, Dad. The press has been hounding Bebe and the rest of us for years about who your father is," August replied. "We don't know who these Babineauxs are; you could contact them Monday, and they could be telling their story to the *New York Times* by Tuesday. The moment this information goes outside this room, we have to assume it's going to be news. And we should have a plan for that."

"Fine, August." Abe sighed. "We'll call Stephanie. But to be clear, I'm not changing my mind. They may be strangers, but they're still family. And I think they don't live far from us."

"Okay, Dad." Clarence nodded firmly. "Then we support you. Let us know how we can help."

"Wait a minute," Hollis said, looking at her grandfather. "Do you mean they live here in L.A.?"

"South L.A., from what Taffy and I could find online in public records. If they're the same Babineauxs. We'll have to do some more concrete research to be sure, but I think it's them. That's where Mama grew up, after all."

"Oh shit."

"Hollis," Rhonda said. "Language."

"What is it?" Isaiah asked.

"I know someone with the last name Babineaux. Who lives in Leimert Park."

"Really?" Evan said.

"Yeah." Hollis groaned. "He hates me."

"I doubt that's true," Clarence said.

"It is. What if it's the same family? And we're related?"

"Well, you'll just have to learn to get along," Abe said. "I've spent my whole life not knowing who my father was. Now that both my parents are gone, I deserve to know his people. All of us do."

"What if they don't like us?" Ardith asked.

Taffy sniffed. "Who wouldn't like us?"

PART TWO

Spotlight

PART TWO

Spoiled

Meet the Babineauxs

The family didn't often find themselves at Abe and Taffy's home in Baldwin Hills, but when they did, most of the grandchildren felt like they were doing something wrong. When they were little, everyone had gathered at Blossom's house, where she didn't care if they climbed on the furniture or spoke too loudly or spilled juice on the rug. Taffy, on the other hand, was as particular about her décor as she was about her personal appearance. Everything in her home was pristine white, from the couches to the rugs to the kitchen to the sunroom out back. It was a wonder actual human beings were able to live there without staining every single surface.

Today, everyone was a little more dressed up than normal, and a lot more on edge: they were having the Babineaux family over for tea.

The week after Abe had shared the letter with them, he'd spent a lot of time on the phone with both August and Stephanie trying to figure out the best way to approach the Babineauxs. They'd decided that Abe would try to reach out by phone first. "We need to be careful about what we put into writing at this point. There are financial aspects to consider," August had said, aware of how his father's emotions could sometimes override his practicality.

August had also wanted Stephanie to be at the tea with them, to ward off any potential mishaps, but Abe had flat-out refused. "How safe would you feel with a publicist sitting in the room as you meet the family you didn't know was yours?" he'd asked. Neither August nor the family had argued that point.

Abe had let everyone know they would be meeting the Babineauxs the next weekend. Taffy had thought Sunday afternoon tea would be best for a first meeting.

"Tea?" Isaiah had said when Taffy and Abe called Hollis's family to tell them. "When have we ever had *tea*? Why not invite them over for Saturday Breakfast? Then they can see who we really are."

"Tea is less pressure," Taffy had replied. "And we want to put our best foot forward, don't we?"

"I don't know that tea is our best foot," Isaiah had said when they'd hung up. "Tea isn't really our foot at all."

Now that the day was here, it was clear from their apprehensive looks that the rest of the adults felt the same. Still, they left their feelings unspoken, not wanting to upset Abe, who was darting around the house running a dustrag over dustless tables and fluffing already-fluffed pillows. Taffy was fussing around in the kitchen, ensuring her tea service would be as perfect as possible. She usually hired help when she would be hosting this many people; perhaps she wanted to appear more relatable to the Babineauxs, to suggest that she was the kind of woman who didn't need help—or maybe, more important, the kind who didn't believe in spending money on such luxuries. It was a bit late for that, considering her house could double as a museum.

"What can we do to help, Taffy?" Rhonda asked, hovering by the kitchen doorway.

"Stay out of the dining room so you don't mess anything up," Taffy instructed as she bent to retrieve a serving platter. "Stay out of here, too."

"Noted," Rhonda said, slowly backing away.

Once almost all of the Blackwoods had arrived, Abe gathered everyone except for Taffy, who was still putting the finishing touches on her tea service. "Thank you all for coming," he said. "I know this is uncomfortable for some of you, and I appreciate you being here to support me. Please remember, this is our family. Our only job is to get to know them. Make them feel welcome."

After that, he began pacing anxiously back and forth from the living room to the foyer. When he heard someone at the door, he nearly jumped and hurried over faster than any of them had seen him move in some time—but it was just Ardith, apologizing that the church service had run later than usual. A few mintues after that, though, the sound of car doors slamming announced that the Babineauxs had arrived.

The Blackwoods began straightening their clothes and adjusting their hair and checking to see if there was anything in their teeth. By the time the doorbell rang, they were all standing in a line, ready to greet their guests as if it were a formal affair. Hollis was noticeably anxious, wondering if Orlando would be among them. She hadn't returned to school since her photo had leaked, and so she had, mercifully, been able to avoid him. She also hadn't been speaking to Dwayne outside of one-word responses to his texts asking if she was okay, and it wasn't like Orlando had come up in any of those exchanges. But now Hollis wondered if Orlando had told Dwayne about what was happening with their families.

The first person to walk through the door was a man around Abe's age. He had long, salt-and-pepper locs pulled back from his face, bright eyes behind his glasses, and he was leaning on a cane. He and Abe looked at each other for a long moment, taking the other in. Then, without a word, they embraced, slapping one another's backs and murmuring, their voices too low for the rest of the family to hear.

After a moment, they pulled apart, and Abe turned toward his family. "Everyone, this is my brother, Eli Babineaux," he announced.

Taffy rushed over to give him a hug while the rest of the Blackwoods offered waves and polite greetings. After Eli came Abe's half sister, Geena, who looked more than a little like Abe. Her skin was darker, but they had similar mouths and eyes. The two hugged for even longer and it was clear to everyone in the room that Abe was trying his best not to cry. Despite their skepticism about this whole meeting, the sight of the two siblings connecting at long last was enough to make several of the Blackwoods dab at their own eyes.

But the happy reunion wouldn't last long.

Two more couples filed in next; they were introduced as Geena's children and their spouses, who seemed to be around the age of Isaiah and Rhonda, and then three boys after them, all teenagers. Hollis sucked in a breath as Orlando appeared, wearing a button-down shirt and a sullen expression. His eyes slid over to Hollis, who nodded at him before quickly looking away. She remembered the Monday after the beach party, how she'd been dreading seeing him—considering everything that had happened since then, that seemed like such a minor concern now. Orlando had surely seen the photo; Hollis wondered, as she watched the Babineauxs assemble in front of them, if they'd seen her picture as well, if they'd already made their assumptions, as much of the internet had, about what kind of girl she was.

Soon, the two sides of the family were standing across from one another, staring with tentative smiles. The Babineauxs appeared to be just as skeptical as the Blackwoods about this meeting. The question hung between them: What if Blossom had made a different choice all those years ago? What would this family have looked like now?

Whereas everyone else shifted awkwardly, Taffy snapped into hostess mode: offering water before she served the tea, taking jackets, and generally being on her best behavior, which meant that, for once, she wasn't sniping or criticizing or inserting herself into other people's business.

"I can't believe this is real," Abe said, looking at the two sides of his family. "That we have, after so many years of not knowing one another, come together in my home to meet. It makes my heart so happy, y'all. First things first, we should go around and do some proper introductions so we can make sure we have the right name with the right face. And maybe we can figure out how we're all related to everyone by the end of this."

"We already know who y'all are," said one of Geena's children, a man with deep brown skin, a goatee, and a head shaved bald. "You been all over TV and movies and magazines since I can remember. And that one goes to school with my nephew."

He pointed at Hollis, who blinked, not sure how to respond to being called *that one*.

Geena looked at him. "So, why don't you tell them who you are?"

He sighed. "I'm Gabe. Geena's my mother. This is my wife, Maxine, and our kids, Shawn and Jamie."

A brief smile flashed across Maxine's face. Shawn and Jamie raised their hands in half-hearted waves.

"And I'm Corbin, Gabe's brother," said a tall man with close-cropped hair and the same complexion as his brother. "This is my wife, Cindy, and our son, Orlando."

Ardith did a double take when her eyes landed on Orlando, recognizing him instantly as her server at Stella Mae's. The one who'd made it clear what he thought of her.

Eli spoke next. "If Abe can't believe this is real, I sure couldn't believe it when I got a call from him. *Abraham Blackwood.* I thought someone was playing a joke on me at first—I hung up on him! He had to call back. I been watching TV my whole life and didn't even know he was my brother. I don't believe in all those distinctions like 'half' this and 'step' that, but just so y'all know, Michael Babineaux was originally my stepdaddy. Since my own daddy wasn't around, he ended up adopting me as his own, God rest his soul. To tell you the truth, there'd been rumors in the family for a while now that we was related to y'all, but Mama Babineaux—my grandmother—always shut it down as soon as anyone started talking. I don't know if anyone, besides my parents and her, knew there was any truth behind it. But now . . . I'm real glad there is. It's an honor to be here with y'all."

The looks on the faces of his family told the Blackwoods that not all of them felt the same way.

Geena smiled, though. She had a kind face. "Abe is my half brother. My daddy was Michael Babineaux, too, but I have the same mother as Eli. And it is true that there were rumors. I never believed them, especially when Corbin told me Orlando came home his first day of high school and said one of the Blackwoods went there. I just thought there was no way, but here we are. Thank you for welcoming us into your home."

"The pleasure is all ours," Taffy proclaimed. "For those of you who don't know me, I'm Taffeta Ford Blackwood, but you can call me Taffy, if you'd like. Abe and I have been married for almost fifty years, and we are so proud of this beautiful family we've created. I'm looking forward to getting to know all of you, but I must excuse myself to finish setting everything up."

The rest of the Blackwoods introduced themselves. Orlando finally looked at Hollis as she spoke. Only a couple of weeks ago, she would have figured most of the Babineauxs might not know who she was, but she had to assume that was no longer the case since the photo had leaked.

Taffy came back to tell them tea was served and directed everyone to the dining room. Abe gestured for the Babineauxs to go first, and they stepped aside to let Eli lead the way, steadily walking with his cane. Taffy's tea service was exquisite: silver tiered serving trays lined the table, filled with scones, finger sandwiches, tarts, and cookies. A sponge cake sat on a stand off to the side, to be served later. Four gold and white teapots were hot and ready for pouring, with enough matching teacups, saucers, and plates for everyone. Taffy stood by the table, proud of how all her hard work had come together.

Gabe squinted at the food. When he reached for a sandwich, he turned it around in his hand, whispering to his wife, "These are like those little sandwiches your grandma used to make. Didn't think I'd ever have to see those again."

Hollis and Orlando ended up next to each other in the line. Orlando seemed perfectly content to stay silent, but after a couple of minutes, Hollis could no longer stand it. "Were you as surprised as I was?" she asked.

"About what?" he said, turning to her slowly.

"Um, us being related?" What did he think she'd meant?

"Nah. Like they said, people in the family have always kind of known." Orlando shrugged. "Now it's confirmed."

"So, you all just talked about this huge secret all the time . . . ?"

Orlando snorted. "Don't flatter yourself. It was more like a movie or TV show would come on and someone would bring up the rumor and then everyone would go on about their business. It's not like we spent all day wishing we were Blackwoods."

"I never said you did," Hollis snapped.

"Whatever. This is all so dumb, anyway."

"My grandfather calling yours the *minute* we discovered we were related is dumb? Nice."

"That's exactly what I'm talking about—y'all acting like we should be so grateful that the *Blackwoods* decided to acknowledge our existence. Having tea? And these dry-ass rolls?" Orlando said, pointing to one of the trays. "And everyone making all these speeches like it actually means something? Nah."

"They're scones," Hollis said.

Orlando shook his head. "See? You probably couldn't wait to tell my ignorant ass what all this shit is."

"I didn't say you were ignorant—but you are being rude. My grand-parents were nice enough to have you in their home, and you—"

"Hey," Abe said, suddenly standing next to them, the teacup he was clutching looking entirely too small in his hand. "Let's not do that today, all right? Try to remember that we're family."

Hollis was so tired of hearing that word, she thought she might scream. What did her grandfather expect this to be? Yes, biologically, they were family—but his mother had cut out Michael Babineaux for a reason. Hollis understood why her grandfather would want to meet them, but she didn't know why the rest of them had to be part of it.

Orlando turned away from her, taking two egg salad sandwiches before he walked away. Hollis let out a sigh, relieved he hadn't brought up the photo.

Back in the living room, once everyone was seated, Gabe took a sip of tea and stood. "I have a question. For the Blackwoods."

"Gabe," said his brother, Corbin.

He ignored him. "Did y'all really not know about us this whole time?"

"We really did not," Abe replied. "My mama didn't tell me until after her death. In a letter, like I told Eli. It was a surprise to all of us."

"Just find that a bit hard to believe, that's all. You knew you had to come from somewhere. You trying to tell us you never wondered? Never looked for your father?"

Isaiah stood, too. "Hold up, now. You don't need to talk to him like that. He already told you he didn't know. Why are you blaming him for something that wasn't his fault?"

"All I know is if I hadn't known my daddy, I would've been looking for him everywhere," Gabe said firmly.

"I guess that was the beautiful thing about Mama," Abe replied, his voice even. "She always felt like enough for me, so I didn't spend a whole lot of time thinking about who my daddy was."

While the adults were speaking, Ardith sat quietly, hands wrapped around her teacup. Her grandfather's words struck her—even after the shock that her great-grandmother's letter had sent rippling through two families, her grandfather didn't question his mother's decision. He didn't seem to have wondered for even a moment if it had been the correct choice. And Ardith understood. Ever since he had read aloud the letter, Ardith couldn't stop thinking about how her great-grandmother was, perhaps, even stronger than Ardith had known—taking charge of her life, especially in a time when it had been much harder for women to assert themselves. She had always admired her great-grandmother for pursuing her dreams, no matter how many forces seemed to be working against her, in both her public and professional life—and, from what she'd written, it sounded like the father of her only child was one of those forces.

And yet . . . Ardith couldn't help thinking that the choice she'd made—to not only cut Michael Babineaux out of her life, but to keep him a secret for almost seventy years—didn't sound like the woman she knew. Blossom Blackwood was the most generous person she'd ever met, someone who spent every Sunday worshipping with others, who gave her time, her money, and her light to people she'd never met before and would never see again. But, all those years, the family of her son's father was just across the city, living a completely different life than all of them.

"But you have all this money," Gabe pressed. "Couldn't you have hired someone to find out who your daddy was?"

"Man, what are you trying to say?" Isaiah asked.

"I'm saying, it seems real convenient that you never went looking for us. That's all."

August raised an eyebrow. "I'll take the bait. Convenient how?"

"There is no bait. Our house could fit in all of y'all's with room to spare. That fancy school she"—he pointed at Hollis again—"and Orlando go to got a whole building named after y'all. That should be Babineaux Auditorium."

"Point at my kid one more time," Isaiah warned.

"Y'all knock it off," Abe said.

"We are not going to engage in any financial or legal discussions today," August said firmly.

"Then what are we even doing here?" Shawn muttered.

His great-uncle Eli gave him a sharp look. "This is our family, Shawn."

"We don't want your money," Geena said quickly.

"No, but I think it's a fair question," Orlando piped up. "I mean, look at us. Hollis is at Dupree paying full tuition, and I'm on scholarship. We come from the same people."

"Yeah, but if it had been up to Grandpa Abe's dad, Bebe never would have even become an actress," Prentice said around a mouthful of scone. "We probably wouldn't *have* any money if they'd stayed together."

"Prentice!" His father Clarence gave him a stern look.

Gabe sighed. "Why y'all got to act so proper? The young ones got this right. There's nothing wrong with putting things out in the open."

"You have to understand the history we're dealing with here," August said.

"Pretty sure I understand it's the same history as ours," Orlando countered.

"My mother was a good woman," said Abe.

"And my granddaddy was a good man," Gabe countered.

At that, Eli spoke again. "Look, y'all, nobody said this was supposed to be easy, but we didn't come over here to get into a pissing match. Neither of them is still here to defend themselves. We can only go on what they told us before they passed. And we don't know how things would've worked out if they'd stayed together. But we here. Now."

Abe nodded. "What he said. I know we still got a lot to work out, but can we at least be civil to one another for the sake of the family? At the end of the day, we're related by blood, and that's thicker than anything else in my book. We can work out all the rest of the stuff in due time."

Eli quickly agreed. "Amen, brother. We all we got."

The remainder of the afternoon was indeed civil—if mostly uncomfortable, for everyone. But their time together had been true to who they were, and that was, perhaps, the best both the Blackwoods and the Babineauxs could hope for.

Back East
1959

"MAMAAAAAAAA!"

The scream echoed from the back of the house. Blossom stood in the doorway to the sitting room while her mother avoided her eyes, staring instead at the bag by the door.

Blossom knew that look. Mama wasn't even trying to hide how she felt about what Blossom was doing. Not that Flossie Blackwood ever tried to hide her feelings.

"You know I would stay if I could," Blossom said. "But rehearsals start Tuesday. I can't be here right now, Mama. I'm sorry."

Her mother was sitting in the green chair they'd brought over from the house on Reed Street when Blossom had moved them to Watts a couple years ago. The upholstery was threadbare in some spots, but when Blossom had suggested buying a new one, Mama just shook her head, saying, "As long as it still holds me up, this chair ain't going nowhere." Blossom had thought that once she'd started booking small parts in film and theater, making enough money that she didn't have to take regular waitressing shifts, Mama might be a little more open to spending some of it. But Sybil had known better.

"Mama's lived through two world wars and the Great Depression. Did you know I found a *half cent* in her jewelry box a couple years ago?"

Blossom had frowned. "What's a half cent?"

215

"They were discontinued about a hundred years ago; she wasn't even born when it could've been spent. It's just an old, useless coin. But Mama still held on to it."

And so her mother was sitting in that same weary green chair now as Blossom waited for her to respond. Mama didn't glance up from the quilt she was stitching as she said, "Seems to me like they'd let their leading lady have a couple more nights with her son."

Blossom held on to her elbows, cradling herself as she spoke. "Mama, that's the point. I'm the *lead*. They can't just perform it without me. And I can't let the project get started with an understudy in my role—how would that look? You know how important this is to me. To *us*."

The *us* was Blossom; Sybil, now twenty-six; and Mama, same as ever. But it now also included Abraham, who was currently screaming for Blossom, ignoring the consolation of his aunt. When she'd first started getting theater work in New York, it had been easier to leave him. He'd been a baby, and he didn't know when she was coming or going. But now that he was older, now that her career was really, finally starting to take flight, he did understand. And that made it harder, for all of them.

She'd known it would be difficult, raising Abe without his father. She'd seen her mother do it, after all—three times over.

"I know how important it is, girl. But so is he."

Blossom inhaled, gathering herself before she spoke again. Mama was practical; she didn't like it when Blossom, as she would say, became "too emotional." But she couldn't help it. Ever since Abe had entered their lives, Blossom felt as if she cried at everything: the sweet, powdery baby smell that filled her nose every time she'd kiss the top of his head; the pitter-patter of his first steps across the front room; his two little teeth that grew in first; how he loved to be read to by Blossom or his aunt Sybil; the way he smiled. Abe had been the very best thing that had ever happened to her, and yet she felt the constant strain of being pulled in two different directions: wanting to be here with him every moment, and

216

wanting to continue pursuing the dream of the promising acting career that, it appeared, was on its way to being something real.

"Will it ever get easier, Mama?"

Her mother rested the needle and thread on top of the quilt and looked at her. "I said I would help you how I could. And I did. I am. But I never said it would be easy."

Blossom rested her hand against the doorframe. "Did you ever consider trying to do what I'm doing?"

"Girl, things was different then. There weren't hardly any roles for me, even if I'd wanted the ones they was offering us. And the one role I got . . . I didn't mind that I was playing a maid because I thought it was going to be the start of something. But they treated me like I was nothing on that set, and I wasn't looking to do that again anytime soon." Mama shook her head. "I wonder sometimes what it would be like if I'd chose differently, what I could have done if I'd had more time. I could've tried to go back to the shows, maybe get back up with Winnie and Frankie. They was still performing after Marla was born. But I wanted to stay put out here. Even if I didn't make it in the pictures, I sure like living here. I liked your daddy, too, and one thing led to another, then you and Sybil was here."

"But how did you know that was the right choice? To stop performing and raise us?"

"I didn't. I still don't know if it was, but I know I'm happy I got my girls. And I'm happy you got Abe, too. Blossom, being a mama ain't never gonna be easy. Neither is your career. But you got to make a decision and be okay with it. Go on to New York and don't worry about that little boy, 'cause you know he got us. Or stay here and don't worry about that play 'cause there'll be other roles for you."

Blossom frowned. Mama made it sound so simple, but it would never be that easy for her. She would always feel as if she were neglecting someone: either Abe, who deserved a mother who could be here every night to tuck him in—or herself, the part of her that dreamed of performing, of doing what her mother and so many women like her weren't able to, and what no one, anywhere, had truly believed she could achieve, besides Blossom herself. The fact that Mama was still haunted by the choices she had and hadn't made did little to soothe Blossom's anxieties—the ones she had been carrying for years.

"Mama," Blossom said, the words falling from her lips before she could stop them, "do you still believe that I can do this? That I deserve to follow this dream?"

The silence in the room was louder than any words Mama could have spoken. She stared at Blossom for a few moments, and the longer Mama took to answer her, the more Blossom felt that perhaps whatever her mother was going to say wasn't what she wanted to hear. But before Mama could respond, a throat cleared behind her. It was only then that Blossom realized the wailing in the back of the house had stopped. She turned to see Sybil standing there holding Abe on her hip, though, at five, he was a little too big to be carried around like that.

"He's asking for you to read from *Charlotte's Web* before you go." Sybil stroked the back of his curly little head.

"I don't *want* you to go, Mama," Abe said, then promptly lodged his thumb in his mouth. Another habit he should have outgrown by now.

Blossom moved across the room to them, gently removing his thumb. "Oh, baby. I have to go, or I'll miss my train. Mama has to work."

"But I want you to stay home, Mama. With me and Auntie Sybil and Mother." Once he'd begun talking, Flossie said she wanted Abe to call her Mother, a tradition passed on from her own upbringing.

Blossom looked at Sybil, who pressed her lips together into a tight smile, and at her mother, who was still silent. Blossom glanced at the clock on the wall above the sofa. She supposed she could spare some time and still make it to Union Station for her train.

"All right. Mama will read to you before she leaves. But just one chapter, okay?" Blossom scooped him up from Sybil and walked back down the hall with him in her arms, rubbing his back. Sucking his thumb once again, Abe leaned his cheek on her shoulder. Blossom briefly closed her eyes, the guilt settling in as it always did. Earlier, she'd desperately wished for him to fall asleep before she left so she could sneak away without the symphony of his tears sending her off. Now she silently reminded herself that she should be grateful for any moment she was able to spend with Abe; it would be weeks before she'd be able to kiss him good night again or wake to his beaming face in the morning.

They settled onto the bed they shared when she was in Los Angeles, Abe's little body nestled into hers, the copy of *Charlotte's Web* cracked open in her hands. Blossom had wondered before they began reading together if the story would be too grown-up for him. She'd already read the book herself and wept nearly uncontrollably at the sweet friendship of the animals and the poignant ending. But, so far, Abe seemed to love it, shouting, "Wilbur!" when he spotted the young pig.

Blossom blinked when her eyes swept over the title of the next chapter. It was called "Loneliness." She took a deep breath and forged ahead, using different voices as she narrated the story of Wilbur's day. Just as she thought maybe the most difficult parts had escaped Abe, he patted at the illustration of Wilbur peeking through the fence at the lamb and said, "Why is he so sad, Mama?"

She kissed the top of his head. "He's lonely, baby. None of the other animals will play with him, and the weather is too poor for Fern to come outside."

Abe didn't say anything else, just continued to pat at Wilbur. Blossom held back tears when she reached the end of the chapter, when the mysterious voice from the rafters said, "Do you want a friend, Wilbur? I'll be a friend to you."

A few lines later the chapter was done and Abe was breathing deeply, his thumb fallen out of his mouth as he drifted off to sleep. Blossom hissed for Sybil until her sister appeared in the doorway to take the book and help her tuck Abe into bed without waking him. Blossom swallowed around a lump in her throat; Sybil was perhaps even more familiar with the routine than she was now.

"I love you, sweet Abe," she whispered into his ear, softly kissing his cheek. "Mama loves you. I'll see you soon."

In the hallway, Sybil caught her arm before she headed back to the sitting room. "We'll take good care of him, Blossom."

And then, as if her sister's words had released a dam, Blossom's cheeks were soaked with her own tears, arriving as heavy and fast as her son's had been only a half hour earlier. They moved to the bathroom, closing the door so they wouldn't wake him. And so that Mama couldn't hear.

"I hope you know how much I appreciate you and Mama, Sybil. I appreciate you so much—"

Sybil reached into her pocket for a handkerchief, folding it over her fingers to carefully dab away her sister's tears. "I know. You don't have to tell me."

"Mama doesn't know."

"She does."

"I'm only trying to give us a good life. If I could find work out here, I would. I promise I would. But the studios—they don't want me. The work is in New York."

"I know," Sybil reassured her. "You're doing what you're supposed to be doing. And you're a good mother. If you weren't, he wouldn't be so upset when you leave."

Blossom wasn't sure that was true, but Sybil was being so kind that arguing with her would be rude. She let out a shuddery breath. "What if I'm ruining his life, living like this?"

Sybil lowered her voice as she said, "Just because Mama gave up her career for us doesn't mean you have to do the same. That was her choice. This is yours. Abe is a good boy. You'll be back as soon as you can. We all know how hard you worked to get this role."

Blossom hadn't let those first failed auditions in New York discourage her, and she had continued returning to look for work when she could. Two years ago, she had spent three weeks back East, the longest spell she could afford to be away, both emotionally and financially, allowing herself the time and space to seek out parts: on and Off-Broadway; in small, experimental theaters; and even a production that would be taking place in the damp, moldy basement of a restaurant downtown.

Her persistence had paid off; during that trip, she'd been cast in a supporting role in an Off-Off-Broadway play, one that received good reviews, if only a meager audience. From there, she continued to earn roles onstage, returning to Los Angeles between jobs—which sometimes meant she went weeks or even months between stays at home. She'd been cast a few weeks ago as the female lead in *The Johnstons*, a new Off-Broadway play; Blossom had received the news a few days after her audition, hours before she was to return to Los Angeles. When she'd arrived home, she celebrated with Mama, Sybil, and Abe over the strawberry cake Sybil had made for her. She couldn't believe it was already time to go back and start rehearsals.

Now Blossom wrapped her arms around her sister. "Thank you."

Sybil nodded into her shoulder. "Besides," she said, pulling away, "taking care of Abe is good practice for when I . . . I mean, *if* I . . ." She trailed off, looking shyly at her stockinged feet.

"You will." Blossom rubbed her sister's arm.

Sybil sighed, shaking her head. "When? I'm a spinster."

"Sybil, you have plenty of time. You're younger than I am, and look at me." Blossom held up her left hand, showing off her bare ring finger.

Sybil nodded, but Blossom wondered, like she always did when they spoke about these things—marriage, children, family—if her sister pitied her. Because the source of guilt that lived at the pit of her stomach—that Michael was not a part of Abe's life, that she had deprived her son of a father—they didn't discuss that. And it was just as well. Because talking about it only made the guilt grow. Between that and feeling as if she would never be able to balance motherhood and her ambitions, Blossom was sometimes afraid the shame would swallow her whole.

The truth was, the play left something to be desired.

Blossom had decided after a couple of read-throughs—one on her own and one with the other actors—that it suffered from mediocre writing. The playwright, a pink-cheeked young graduate of Harvard University, had written a fictional account of his childhood in a small Georgia town where he had a close relationship with a Negro family named the Johnstons. The play was narrated through his eyes but focused solely on the titular family, and Blossom could see the pride nearly bursting through his skin the day of the official cast read-through. Everyone had given it their best shot. But afterward, Blossom's co-star, Clifton, had leaned close and murmured, "His mama done told him he hung the moon, and he actually believe it," and Blossom was so relieved she laughed long and loud for the first time since she'd left Los Angeles.

Clifton Thompson was the first cast member to make her feel comfortable when she arrived in New York; he was also one of the best Negro theater actors back East. Blossom had been nervous to be cast alongside him; he had so much more stage experience than her. But Clifton treated her as an equal, never taking up too much space in their scenes together and patiently working with her when she had trouble with her cues.

The first week of rehearsal, Clifton asked if she'd like to have lunch with him on their day off, the following Monday. Blossom was conflicted. She'd been planning to explore the city as much as she could that day. She'd been to New York several times by then, but she still didn't feel as if she knew the city well; not like Los Angeles, the only other place she'd lived.

Clifton had touched her arm lightly, said, "You don't have to make a decision now. The invitation is open. If you'd like to have lunch on Monday, meet me at Katy's on 125th." He'd held up his hand in a wave goodbye, smiling easily at her before he walked out of the rehearsal space, and that was the moment Blossom decided she would say yes. He hadn't pressured her or expected anything from her. She got the idea from his relaxed demeanor, the way he didn't excessively flatter her, that what he had said was what she would get: a simple meal shared between two people. It was lunch. She had to eat, after all.

Blossom took her time gathering her belongings in the corner of the rehearsal space, thinking about the notes the director had given her. She'd wanted to ask a question earlier, to get a bit more clarification on an observation he'd made about her reading of a specific line, but everyone was exhausted by that point in the rehearsal, and she hadn't wanted to make them sit through it. Now she and the director were the only ones left.

His name was Archie Melamed; he was a quiet, intense white man with round glasses, curly brown hair, and a serious, square jaw. He was looking over some marked-up pages in his chair by the window, and Blossom hesitated, nervous to interrupt him.

"Can I help you with something, Miss Blackwood?"

"I . . . I had a question about the note you gave me earlier. About how Sara would have reacted to Leon's monologue."

"You'd like to go over it now?"

"Oh, only if you have the time. I didn't want to keep the rest of the cast waiting while I asked about it, but if you need to go—"

He adjusted his glasses. "What is your question, Miss Blackwood?"

"Well." Blossom retraced her steps across the room, working up the courage to make her point. "You said Sara might be a little softer when she's speaking to him. More supportive."

Mr. Melamed nodded.

"I'm not sure I agree. I believe she would be a bit more assertive when they are talking. Sara is a strong woman, and the dialogue indicates she knows what she wants from him. For them. I'm not sure she'd be so demure in this scene."

Mr. Melamed motioned for her to sit in the folding chair that had been occupied earlier by the playwright. Blossom's palms were so damp she had to wipe them on her skirt. Her eyes landed on the pages he'd set on his lap and she wondered, briefly, how many of those scribbled notes were about her performance.

"I suppose I don't see Sara's softness in that scene as a weakness, Miss Blackwood. Because you are correct, that she knows what she wants. And Leon is aware of that, too. But at this moment, he needs someone to nurture him. He's looking for that in his wife, his partner. And Leon . . ."

As he continued talking about the characters and their relationship, Blossom found herself lulled by his soft-spoken conviction. There was a certain skepticism that seeped in when a white man was suggesting to her a more desirable way for a Negro woman to inhabit her character, but as she listened, Blossom felt that he understood the balance she was trying to achieve, despite—or maybe because of—the subpar script. And the way he spoke to her, as if she were a seasoned actress who'd had dozens of such conversations, she also felt he believed she was capable of implementing this balance.

"Oh dear," he said, glancing down at his watch twenty minutes later. "You only had a simple question, and I've kept you for much too long."

"It's quite all right," Blossom responded quickly. "I appreciate the extra time you took to speak with me about it, Mr. Melamed. It . . . well, it means so much to me to be in this play with such accomplished actors and a director like yourself."

"It means so much to all of us that you are in this production, Miss Blackwood. You earned your role," he said. And then he smiled, for the first time that she could remember. They were quiet, both of them, for several seconds, until he cleared his throat and said, "Well, I suppose we are done here for the day, then. I will see you tomorrow, Miss Blackwood."

"Yes, tomorrow. Good night, Mr. Melamed." As Blossom walked to the door, she found her skin inexplicably flushing.

When Blossom stepped into Katy's on Monday, she was overwhelmed with the smells of home. If she closed her eyes, she could believe, for a moment at least, that she was back in her mother's kitchen, watching her pull hot chicken from the skillet while bean stew simmered on the back burner. Blossom stood near the door, looking around until she spotted Clifton sitting at a table in the middle of the small diner. He glanced up at the same time, giving her that easy smile as their eyes met.

"I'm happy you're here," he said, standing as she approached the table.

"I'm happy to be here," she replied, slipping into the seat across from him.

"You been here before?"

"No." Blossom looked down at the menu. "What's good?"

"Anything. *Everything*." He laughed. "I ain't had cooking like this since I left home."

"It smells like my mama's cooking, too," Blossom said, smiling.

"Your folks always been in California?"

"My mama's from Mississippi. I didn't know my daddy. He never came around."

Normally, Blossom avoided the topic of her father. She didn't like to think about what people were really feeling while they blinked at her sympathetically. She could have simply said her father had passed—but, curiously, she felt as if she could trust Clifton with the truth.

"That's a loss for him, ain't it?" he said, taking a long drink from his water glass.

Blossom was grateful for his kindness. "Where are you from?"

"Boley, Oklahoma."

"I've never met anyone from Oklahoma. What's it like?"

"Boley is a Negro town. All folks who look like us."

"Do you miss it?"

"Sometimes. It's real quiet compared to here. And I never saw myself here, not at first. I was supposed to study at Morehouse, years ago. I was all prepared to go, with a scholarship to study education."

"Morehouse! What happened?" Blossom asked.

"This," he said, pointing between the two of them. "Deep down in my bones, I knew the only thing I wanted to do was act."

"Your parents didn't mind?"

"They were furious with me. I don't think they've forgiven me, still."

"Perhaps they'll come around?"

"I think I'd have to win a Tony Award first. And even then . . ." He shook his head. "Do you miss California?"

She nodded. "I have a son back there, so—"

"What can I get y'all today?"

Blossom looked up, surprised to see the waitress standing at their elbows. She hadn't heard her approach, but then, small as Katy's was, it was also filled with the sound of sizzling meat and clinking dishes and the cook calling out to the waitress who was serving them now. Blossom shared a swift look with Clifton before her eyes swept down to the menu. Had he heard her before the waitress interrupted? If not, should she tell him about Abe or pretend she hadn't spoken? As suddenly as the thought entered her mind, shame washed over her for it.

Clifton ordered oxtail soup, and after more than a little internal debate, Blossom chose the fried fish, hush puppies, and mustard greens.

"A woman who can eat," he said after the waitress had left to give their order to the cook. "I can appreciate that."

"That is why we're here," Blossom said with a small shrug. She was hungry, and it was their day off. She supposed she'd picked up Mama's habit of wanting a nice meal when she didn't have to work, even if she didn't cook it herself.

"Your son . . . how old is he?" Clifton asked.

"Five," she said, smiling. At the thought of Abe, whom she missed dearly, but also because Clifton had been listening.

"That's quite an age," he said. "They got a lot of energy and a lot to say."

"You have children?"

"No, no. I'm an uncle. To my sister's boys." He cleared his throat. "Is it difficult? Being away from him?"

"It is," Blossom replied. "He's growing so quickly. I feel as if one day I'll come home and he'll be heading off to senior high school."

"Ah, you still got some time. How are you liking it out here? The East Coast and all?"

"Well, it's no California. But I suppose it's all right," she said with a wry smile. "I like it over here, though. Harlem reminds me of where I grew up."

Blossom had understood as soon as she'd set foot in the neighborhood why Central Avenue had been called the Harlem of the West Coast. This part of Manhattan was rich with Negro culture, from the legacy of Langston Hughes to the Apollo Theater to the political presence of Adam Clayton Powell Jr. Though the people walked and spoke and dressed just a little bit differently from the way they did in Los Angeles, she had been pleased to rent a room in an area that felt, in some ways, so much like home.

"I could show you more of it after we eat," Clifton said. "If you'd like."

Blossom felt as if she had her own personal tour guide as they walked through the city streets, between rows of historic buildings and stately brownstones. Clifton pointed out landmarks like the Harlem Opera House, which was rumored to be demolished soon, and the former site of the original Cotton Club, where several of her favorite entertainers had once performed. While the neighborhood appeared as vibrant as she'd imagined before she arrived in New York, Blossom could sense that it had changed quite a bit, that it was still in flux.

"Where is the Savoy?" she asked, recalling the name from articles she'd read about the great ballrooms and jazz clubs of New York City.

"It was up that way," Clifton said, pointing behind them. "Between 140th and 141st."

"Was?"

"You just missed it. Torn down earlier this year to make way for housing. It's a damn shame. That was a real beautiful ballroom." Clifton looked at her from the corner of his eye. "You like dancing?"

"I do." She refrained from saying that she was a trained dancer, that she'd done so professionally for years. That seemed like lifetimes ago; she wasn't sure she was the same person she'd been back then.

Before Blossom knew it, the afternoon sun, which had been so bright and hot when they had first met that day, was beginning to make its descent below the tops of the trees. She allowed Clifton to escort her to the boardinghouse. She felt shy as they stood at the bottom of the steps. Had this been a date? Or was it simply lunch between colleagues? Blossom wasn't sure, but she did know that she had liked his company more than she'd expected. So many of the people she'd met in New York came off as pretentious; Clifton was affable and wholly unaffected, and if she hadn't already known, she would have been surprised to learn he was an actor.

"Thank you for inviting me to lunch," she said, clutching her pocket-book at her side. "I enjoyed today."

"It was my pleasure. Thank you for spending the day with me, Blossom Blackwood." He briefly squeezed her shoulder before he turned and began walking down the street the way they'd come, whistling a slow, soft tune she couldn't quite place.

Blossom's friendship with Clifton grew during the next few weeks, bringing with it more lunches and walks and, occasionally, a casual supper after a day of rehearsal. Throughout those weeks, she found herself wondering, when they parted, why she didn't feel more for him. He was handsome and talented and kind, all of the qualities she could ever want in a man. It was clear he'd been raised with similar values as her, and that he respected her as not only an actress but a mother, too. The way his eyes landed on her sometimes, she was aware he'd be happy if their friendship became something more. But when Blossom allowed herself to truly think about it—about the prospect of them as a couple—she couldn't help but feel that something was missing: a spark that would lead to a flame. A heat that was supposed to shoot through her veins when he came around, when he smiled at her.

The thing was, Blossom felt a spark. She felt that heat. But it was for the wrong man.

Since that first evening she stayed late to talk with Mr. Melamed, Blossom had found herself alone with him one or two times each week. Sometimes they would both happen to arrive early, getting the chance to chat in the sun-dappled room before everyone else began trickling in. Other times she would stay after the rest of the cast had left and they would discuss all sorts of things, from line readings and emotional connections of the characters to plays he thought she would enjoy reading. He'd most recently sent her home with a copy of the script for *Trouble in Mind*, a fascinating study of race and male chauvinism in the theater written by a Negro woman, Alice Childress.

"How did you like it?" Mr. Melamed asked when Blossom returned the script a few days later.

"I loved it so much I read it twice," she said, eyes shining. "I wish I'd been able to see it performed."

"I recently saw *A Raisin in the Sun* over at the Barrymore," he said. "Hansberry is brilliant, but I remember a few years ago when *Trouble in Mind* was playing in the Village. It was supposed to be the first show put on Broadway by a Negro woman playwright, ahead of *Raisin*."

"What happened?"

"The producers wanted to change the ending before it transferred—they found it too bleak. Childress disagreed, so it never went to Broadway."

"How do you know so much about Negro theater?" Blossom asked, then put her hand over her mouth, afraid she'd spoken out of turn.

Mr. Melamed smiled. "I am interested in all types of contemporary theater, Miss Blackwood. Which is one reason I signed on to this project."

Blossom had seen the ring on his finger, knew that somewhere, a Mrs. Melamed must be wondering why the rehearsals were running so late. But she adored being in his presence. She liked his serious nature, how much of himself he gave to the work even as the production operated on a shoestring budget. She liked that he never raised his voice and how he seemed to consider each one of his words before he spoke. And, most of all, she liked that when she grew brave enough to speak candidly about her acting dreams, he listened and encouraged her to keep pursuing them, praising her natural talent and work ethic.

Their relationship was strictly platonic, as was her friendship with Clifton. But an electric current ran beneath her interactions with Mr. Melamed, so strong that at times Blossom had to stop to take a breath and reorient herself. She was positive he felt it, too. But, of course, they never discussed it, never acted on it—and she was left to consider her feelings, and wonder about his, alone. She didn't speak about it with anyone.

Not until one evening after Sunday supper at Katy's, when Clifton walked her home as he usually did.

They'd said good night and she had almost reached the top of the front stoop when he said, "Blossom, why haven't you let me touch you?"

Her mouth fell open slightly as she turned. "Clifton?"

"Excuse me for being so forward, but—dang, girl." He stuck his hands in the pockets of his slacks. "We been seeing each other for weeks now. Spending all that time together during rehearsal, and outside of it, too. At first, I thought we was starting something . . . that you dug me like I dig you. We grown people, Blossom, but it feels . . ."

Blossom tensed. "What does it feel like?"

"It feels like we back in school."

"I had a steady boyfriend in school," she said.

"That's beside the point." Clifton sighed. "Blossom, I know when a woman wants me to touch her. And when she wants to touch me. You sure never look like you want to."

She stared down at the steps.

"Is it him?"

Her head snapped up. "Who?"

Clifton raised his chin. "It's real clear, the way you look at him during rehearsal . . ." he trailed off. "He's married, you know."

Blossom exhaled. There was no use denying what he had already seen with his own two eyes. It would only insult his intelligence, and she didn't want to hurt him. "Nothing has happened. And nothing will."

"All right."

"You don't believe me."

He shook his head. "I believe you want to believe that. And I believe it's true what they say: it's real hard to get ahead in this business without the help of a white man."

Blossom's whole body shook with rage. She hurried down the steps until she was face-to-face with Clifton again. "How dare you say that to me, to act as if I didn't earn this part based on my talents. Unlike you, I wasn't offered my role straightaway. I had to audition, and then return for two callbacks."

"Well, I heard he's working on getting funding for a film about a Negro girl and a soldier set during the First World War."

231

"And?" Blossom crossed her arms in front of her chest.

"And I hear he's thinking of you for the role." Clifton's voice was even, his posture straight. This man, this version of him, reminded her of the person she'd initially thought he would be: relentlessly poised, even as she stood here seething.

"He hasn't spoken to me about that. I don't know anything about it." She attempted to match the coolness of his tone although inside, she was reeling. "I've done nothing wrong. He's teaching me about the business and helping me become a better actress. Isn't that good for the play? Good for all of us?"

"Guess it would be if we was all getting extra help, huh?"

Blossom's lips tightened at the smugness that registered in Clifton's voice, on his face. "This is all I know, Clifton. I didn't have the privilege of turning down a college scholarship. If I fail, I go back to Los Angeles with egg on my face, an empty pocketbook, and a son to provide for. I don't have the money to take classes right now—I won't apologize for trying to make myself a better performer."

"If that's how you see it . . . all right. Good night, then, Blossom." Clifton strode away with his shoulders back, his head held high, and Blossom knew that it was the last time they would be seeing one another outside of the play.

She did her best to try to forget their conversation the next day, which she spent alone. But no matter how Blossom occupied her time—completing chores around the boardinghouse, tending to the tiny garden plot out back, reading the newest issue of *Sepia* cover to cover—Clifton's words rang through her mind. They followed her to rehearsal Tuesday, and they clung to the air between her and Mr. Melamed when they were alone. She had no reason to stay late this time; though Blossom didn't care to admit it, a part of her wanted to know if Clifton had been correct about the film the director was working to get funded. But she couldn't find a good way to bring it up, and when she looked at him standing next to the grimy window of the rehearsal space, gazing out at the city below, shirtsleeves rolled up to his elbows, all she could think about was the feelings that were becoming increasingly harder to ignore.

Blossom walked to the window, standing beside him, looking out, too. "Do you suppose the others mind how much attention I'm receiving?"

"They are welcome to seek my advice outside of rehearsal, same as you," Mr. Melamed said in the practical tone he always used, with or without other people around. His light brown eyes were busy behind his glasses as he followed the trails of people weaving up and down the sidewalks, the automobiles and taxicabs clogging the streets.

"I'm happy they don't." When he failed to respond, Blossom inhaled deeply, gathering all of her courage to speak again. "Because, well . . . Don't you feel it, too? This . . . thing? Between us?"

He remained quiet for so long that Blossom, embarrassed as she was, wondered if she should repeat herself. But then he turned suddenly, his face displaying a blend of emotions she couldn't identify. "I have a wife."

Blossom swallowed. Nodded as her eyes drifted down to the floor. What had she been thinking? Even if she knew, in her heart, that he felt it, too, people held all sorts of feelings they didn't express, didn't act on.

Mr. Melamed removed his glasses; he carefully folded them and slipped the frames into the front pocket of his shirt. He rubbed the bridge of his nose and briefly closed his eyes. When he opened them and stepped closer to her, Blossom forced herself to meet his gaze.

"I have a wife," he repeated, his tone softer. "I won't be able to see you the way I'd like. I won't be able to take you to all the places I would, otherwise. We'll have to be discreet."

Blossom froze. *Discreet.* Yes, of course that would have to be the compromise. She hadn't thought, before she'd spoken, about the ramifications of being so open with her feelings. Their whole situation was

233

terrifying; she'd never seriously considered being with a white man before, nor with a man who was married. And theirs was a working relationship. He was in charge of the whole production—he could fire her if things turned sour. Then what would she do? Her reputation in New York theater would be sullied, and she'd be forced to return home to waitress and look for background work in an industry that didn't want her. Mama would be disappointed in Blossom, for letting her heart speak for her brain.

Her attraction to him was more than physical; she appreciated the way he valued her work, how he'd never made her feel that she had been cast only because of her looks. He treated her like the working actor that she was, one who could rise to even greater heights the more she improved her craft. He made her feel that all of her sacrifices had been worth it, and Blossom would always be grateful for his belief in her.

The look in his eyes propelled her forward, made her step even closer to him. He swept his thumb gently across her cheekbone. "Of course I feel this. I've felt it the whole time. And it frightens me."

"Do I frighten you?" she whispered, unabashedly leaning into his touch.

"You captivate me, sweet Blossom." His other hand pressed lightly into the small of her back, pulling her toward him. And then, after weeks of silent yearning, Blossom's lips met his in a long-awaited kiss, the heat that had been building between them fused together at last.

Ignited.

Ardith

"What do you think of this shirt?" Matty asked, turning toward Ardith after he'd slipped a light gray T-shirt over his head.

"I think it has holes all over it," she said, squinting.

"Does it make me look like I'm trying too hard?"

Her lips twisted into a smile. "Trying to what?"

"To . . . not look like I paid two hundred dollars for it," Matty said, shrugging.

"You do realize you've taken twice the time to get ready that I did?"

"Never said I wasn't vain."

Ardith let out a laugh and leaned back on the small couch. They were in Matty's trailer; he'd asked her to come help him choose an outfit before they headed to the fundraiser. He hadn't had a shirt on when she came in, though, and she'd hesitated for a moment in the doorway. But once she realized that her being there didn't seem to bother him, she figured maybe it shouldn't bother her, either. And soon, it felt comfortable. Almost like they were friends.

Matty thoroughly examined himself in the full-length mirror on the bathroom door, twisting from left to right, front to back. He ran a hand through his curls, adjusted the faded black jeans slung low over his hips. "Okay, let's do this," he said, hoisting his backpack over his shoulder. "You ready?"

"Sure," Ardith said, but she didn't move. Suddenly she didn't want to leave the trailer.

Matty sat down next to her. "What's up? You nervous? I promise I won't leave you alone with anyone. Unless they're annoying. Then all bets are off."

"It's not that." Ardith shook her head. "There's just some . . . stuff going on with my family."

She hadn't been able to stop thinking about Bebe's letter to Grandpa Abe. And meeting the Babineauxs, seeing the reality of her great-grandmother's secret, didn't do much to ease her anxiety. She supposed she'd always assumed Bebe had kept Grandpa Abe's father's identity a secret because he had run out on her and never returned, or that maybe he was someone Bebe had known casually and hadn't ever had a real relationship with. It had never occurred to Ardith that Bebe could have known him her whole life, long before Grandpa Abe was born—that it had been a difficult decision, choosing her son, herself, and her career over a man whom, it seemed, she had truly loved.

Part of Ardith couldn't help sympathizing with Bebe—that in a time when it was so difficult for her to find acting work, and probably just as difficult to raise a child on her own, Bebe had bet on herself. Ardith wondered if she would have had the courage to do something like that, knowing people might not understand what she'd been through or the choices she'd made, and judge her for them. But then, the other part of her ached for Grandpa Abe, knowing Bebe ultimately regretted never introducing him to his father—and thinking of what the selfless, family-loving woman she'd always admired had been capable of. That she chose to never tell her son the truth to his face, to leave Michael's family in the dark about their relationship and her life-altering decision. Ardith thought again of the look Orlando had given her at Stella Mae's, how she'd had no idea who he was then—but he had known.

"Is it the stuff with Hollis?" Matty asked.

"Oh. No." Ardith couldn't believe she'd nearly forgotten about that. She knew Hollis was still upset—and rightfully so—but she wondered if the meeting with the Babineauxs had managed to get her cousin's mind off her own troubles, at least for a bit. It was all Ardith could think about. "Our family's being decent about it. Most of the media seems to have moved on, and Hollis has been staying away from the sites that haven't."

"Do you want to talk about it? Whatever it is?"

Ardith looked at Matty. He was leaned forward in his seat, eyes sincere. The news still wasn't public yet, much to her father's irritation, and unless one of the Babineauxs decided to take matters into their own hands, it would still be a few days before it was announced. She might be able to trust Matty; he knew what it was like to have his private life publicized, and she didn't think he was the type of person to go telling other people's business.

But still, she was hesitant. The idea of trusting anyone outside of her family . . . she knew what Dr. York would probably tell her to do, but she just wasn't there yet. Besides, she wanted to get her mind off of it before the fundraiser, where there would be photographers and industry people and they would be expected to put on their best faces.

"It's okay, thanks," she said, finally standing, forcing a smile. "Let's go."

The fundraiser was being held at a private home on one of the Bird Streets in the Hollywood Hills, above the Sunset Strip. Like many homes in the Hills, it was somewhat unassuming, if beautiful, from the outside; once you stepped through the front doors, however, it revealed itself to be a sprawling, multistory home with an impossibly perfect view of the city off the back.

They were greeted by a young woman with copper-colored hair and a bright smile. "Welcome, and thank you for coming. We really appreciate your support of LGBTQ youth in the arts. The gathering is on the first-level terrace, straight through to the back. And here's some information about the organization, if you'd like."

She handed them each a glossy brochure with pictures of grinning kids and teens on the front. Her eyes lingered on Matty, and Ardith wondered if he noticed the way people looked at him.

He whistled as they stepped inside, gazing around at the glass-paneled walls lining the open expanse of the first floor. "This is pretty badass," he murmured to Ardith.

"What do you think it's worth?" she asked. "Fifteen million?"

"With that view? Twenty, at least." They continued to marvel at the architecture as they wandered through the bottom level toward the back terrace. In the kitchen, they spotted a gorgeous walk-in refrigerator, a solid marble island, and, at the end of a small hallway, gleaming silver elevator doors, which Ardith figured probably led to a full gym, or a home theater, or a spa.

"Is that a La Cornue stove?" Matty whispered.

Ardith shrugged. "Just looks like a stove to me."

"Are you kidding? Those things can go for half a million."

"Well, I can't think of anything I'd rather spend my money on," she said, tilting her head and narrowing her eyes as she pretended to admire it. Matty grinned. "But seriously, who would even pay that much for a *stove*? Does it actually cook the food any better?"

"I'm pretty sure being this rich makes everything taste better."

Ardith laughed. "How do you know so much about appliances, anyway?"

"My mom's super into real estate, so I've been reading *Architectural Digest* since I was, like, ten. This house is incredible."

She nodded, but really, Ardith wondered how anyone could live here. It looked *too* perfect—she couldn't imagine anyone taking a nap on the crescent-shaped couch in the front room, or eating a quick breakfast standing over that marble island. It must have taken an army of house managers to maintain it, and a team of au pairs to keep any kids the owners had from breaking everything.

When she was little, her mother hadn't wanted to hire anyone to care for Ardith. Though she was often busy working long hours on set or location, she preferred to bring Ardith with her when she could, or have her stay with family. Ardith and her father still lived in the house they had shared with her mother, a home perched in the hills of Silver Lake, above the reservoir. It was comfortable and cute, but it wasn't nearly as big or fancy as some of their neighbors' houses. It was the only home Ardith had ever known, and though she knew she would eventually find a place of her own, she was glad her father hadn't moved them anywhere else—not when so many of her mother's memories were tied to it. And she liked living in a normal house, the kind that didn't interest people enough to want to feature it in *Architectural Digest*.

Before they could make it out back, Matty was accosted by a couple of cute guys Ardith recognized from a dance competition show. They couldn't stop giggling and definitely looked too young for the glasses of champagne they were holding, but Matty was gracious. He let them chat him up a bit and take a couple of selfies before he and Ardith made a smooth exit to the terrace. She paused before they stepped outside, her eyes sweeping over the crowd that was hanging around the infinity pool. Her pulse started to pound at the sight of so many unfamiliar faces, but she took a deep breath and reminded herself that this was just like any other industry event. She would smile, shake hands, maybe pose for a few photos. Plus, this time, she would have Matty at her side—and the thought of that made her feel calmer.

They'd only been outside a couple of minutes when Ardith spotted her uncles and Prentice. "I need to go say hi to my family," she said, gesturing toward them. "I'll be right back."

"You're not getting rid of me that easily, Blackwood," Matty said with a smirk. "Told you I'm not leaving your side."

Her cousin noticed them coming first—a slight nod when he spotted Ardith, his eyebrows arching when his eyes landed on Matty behind her. "You actually came," he said as they approached the high round table.

Ardith didn't bother replying, but she gave him a quick hug and introduced him to Matty. Prentice blinked at him, and though no one else around them would have picked up on it, Ardith could see how hard he was trying—and failing—to keep his cool. While Grandpa Abe, Uncle Isaiah, and Aunt Rhonda worked in film and television like Ardith, Uncle Clarence was a playwright and Uncle Evan was a professor in USC's drama department. Prentice had grown up in the orbit of plenty of famous people, but he wasn't often around celebrities his age—something he mostly blamed Ardith for. He was always begging her to go to more events so she could take him with her.

He extended a tentative hand toward Matty, who scoffed and brought him in for a big hug. Over Matty's shoulder, Ardith watched Prentice's eyes close briefly as they embraced; he looked as if he might actually faint from pure joy.

Her uncles were deep in conversation with a man she didn't recognize, but when Uncle Evan saw her, he smiled warmly. "You're here!" he said in a bright voice. He introduced her to Tom Dremel, who was director of the organization that was raising money that evening. Tom looked happy to meet Ardith, but his eyes positively shone when he saw Matty with her. He gushed over him, suggesting a future meeting with Matty to talk about collaboration opportunities; Matty was polite, saying Tom should call his reps to discuss setting up something. Ardith wondered what it must be like to know everyone you met would instantly fall in love with you. It seemed like a lot of pressure, but if Matty didn't enjoy it, she couldn't tell.

After a few minutes, Matty excused himself, saying he was going to look for something to eat; he asked Ardith if she wanted to come. She told her uncles she'd be back and invited Prentice to walk around with them.

He didn't waste any time saying goodbye to his dads as he clamped his hand onto Ardith's arm, not wanting to lose them in the tightly packed crowd.

"Is he single?" Prentice whispered to her as Matty got stopped by yet another person.

"I don't know, but he's too old for you," she whispered back.

"What? I'm fifteen, and he's your age. That's only two years."

"He's an old seventeen."

Prentice rolled his eyes. "Taffy says I'm an old soul."

"Taffy would tell you anything you wanted to hear," Ardith mumbled, trying to make herself as small as possible as they navigated their way through a large group.

"Hater."

"Just don't be weird with him, okay? We have to work together. And we're kind of . . . becoming friends." It sounded strange to say it aloud, and she hoped Prentice didn't notice.

"Don't worry about me," Prentice said coolly. He smoothed a palm over his two-strand twists.

Matty turned around, holding his phone. "Hey, some of my friends are up on the roof. You wanna go?"

Ardith glanced back to where her uncles were still chatting. "I don't know if—"

"Totally," Prentice responded, flashing a smile as his grip around her arm tightened. Ardith hesitated for a moment, then nodded.

"Let's go," Matty said, already leading them back toward the house. "Should be more chill up there."

They walked quietly to the elevator off the kitchen and took it up to the top floor. Ardith hadn't been comfortable downstairs, but she felt even more awkward wandering off from the party; she didn't even know whose house this was. She held her breath as the doors opened onto the rooftop. Matty led them around the corner of a protruding skylight, breaking out into a grin as he found his friends. He bounded over and fell into the group of people sitting in a circle, sending a wave of squeals and laughs around the roof.

"Oh my god," Prentice said, eyes wide.

After all her years in the business, Ardith rarely found herself starstruck, but even she had to admit this was a remarkable group. There was Deenie Dinella, who had grown up on her family's reality show and had just signed a contract for a spinoff that would follow the start of her modeling career. Next to her were the Park twins, Ginny and Gia, who were competitive surfers and dabbled in modeling themselves. Matty's head was currently resting in the lap of Cooper Bronson, who had been appearing in family-friendly films and television shows since he was a little kid, but these days seemed to spend more time traveling and partying than he did acting. Rounding out the circle was Simone—Ardith's heart skipped when she saw them; she'd listened to Simone's new single on repeat for pretty much her entire workout that morning—and some guy who Ardith didn't know but could swear was wearing the exact same outfit as the cater waiters downstairs.

"It's Ardith Blackwood!" Deenie exclaimed, thrusting a bottle of champagne toward the sky. "Welcome to our lair."

"Yup, and that's her cousin," Matty said, still stretched out.

"Prentice," he said, but his voice was too faint for anyone to hear.

"Oooh, Matty's hot new co-star," said Cooper, gently pulling his fingers through Matty's curls. "I thought you, like, never went anywhere but church."

Matty looked up at him. "Don't be a dick."

"Well, he's not wrong," Ardith said, slowly making her way toward them, Prentice close behind.

"He's still a dick," said Simone. They scooted over and beckoned for Ardith and Prentice to sit down next to them. "I'm Simone."

"I know," Ardith said. "I love your music."

"Really? That's so sweet. Thank you." They paused. "I used to *love* that show you were on. The one where you played Tinsley? It was, like, so heteronormative, but I could not get enough of that shit."

"Oh my god, I still watch it sometimes," said one of the twins. Ardith never had been able to tell them apart; they were identical, with the same sunny, open faces and thick black hair down to the small of their backs. "I love falling asleep to it. It's so cozy."

"Do you want something to drink?" Deenie asked, gesturing with the champagne to the guy in the white shirt and black pants. "This is our new friend Jason. He hooked us up with some bottles and a shitload of apps."

"Nice," Prentice said, heading over to check out the trays sitting on the edge of the circle.

Jason nodded, holding a vape pen in one hand and his phone in the other. Ardith wondered if this sort of thing happened to him all the time at functions like this.

She leaned back on her palms next to Simone, politely declining the plastic cup of champagne Deenie held out toward her. Prentice took it, though, returning to sit on the other side of Ardith with a napkin full of bite-size snacks. Ardith eyed him, but he'd gulped down most of the cup before she could say a word.

"So, what's it like working with Matty?" Cooper asked. Matty had sat up a bit so that he was now positioned between Cooper's legs, his head leaning against Cooper's chest. "Is he a total nightmare?"

"Not at all. He's a dream," Ardith said without thinking, and immediately wished she hadn't when Cooper burst out laughing.

"A *dream*," he mimicked, throwing the back of his hand across his forehead. "Do you practice being so adorable?"

"Cooper, seriously fuck off," Simone said. They tossed a balled-up napkin at his face, then turned to Ardith. "Don't listen to him. He's this terrible to everyone, unfortunately. That's what happens when you spend years being controlled by a corporation that doesn't give a fuck about you except for how much money you can make them."

"Yeah, like you're the model for anticapitalism," Cooper shot back. "Remind me, how much is the VIP package going for on your tour? Isn't it over a thousand?"

Simone threw up a middle finger.

"Well, Ardith is the real dream," Matty said, smiling at her. "She's one of the best actors I've ever worked with. And she comes from Hollywood royalty."

"That's right!" Simone snapped their fingers. "Your grandma was Blossom Blackwood."

"Great-grandma," Prentice said in between bites of mini toasts. "Our grandma was actually a model back in the day."

"Like me!" Deenie said with a grin.

Ardith tried to hide a smile of her own. Taffy had been one of the most successful Black print models in the seventies and eighties, gracing the covers of *Essence*, *Ebony*, *Jet*, and nearly every fashion magazine that would feature Black women back then. She could just imagine what Taffy would say if she heard Deenie comparing her career to Taffy's decades of work.

"Were you close with her? Your great-grandma?" Simone asked.

"We were best friends," Ardith said, feeling the weight of the past tense as it rolled off her tongue.

"Gosh, I'm sorry," said Simone.

"What was your favorite movie of hers?" asked one of the twins.

"Um, probably, I . . ." she stammered, then fell silent. Ardith had never had trouble talking about Bebe before, but in that moment, she couldn't get the look on Grandpa Abe's face out of her mind. The hurt and betrayal that had descended over the house like a thick cloud as he'd shown them the picture of him with his father.

"Ardith's mom was an actor, too," Prentice said, saving her. "They're going to do an exhibit at the Academy Museum celebrating her career.

You guys should all come to the opening."

Ardith gave him a hard look, but either he didn't see or was pretending he hadn't.

"What kind of exhibit?" Matty asked, looking at her.

Ardith felt her palms begin to sweat as she spoke. "It's just a thing one of her old directors is putting together. Barton Lerner. It's the twentieth anniversary of *Riviera Sunset*, and they're going to exhibit a collection of her things, honoring her work."

"Barton Lerner?" Cooper actually sounded impressed. "He's kind of a big deal."

"So was Kimberly Arnold," said Simone. "Your mom was amazing. *Riviera Sunset* is iconic."

Ardith felt as if she should say something profound about her mother or her career, but she was worried that if she offered anything at all, they'd only ask more questions. And Ardith knew by now that when it came to Mommy, it was better to keep quiet. As nice as most of them were being, she didn't feel comfortable enough to go there with them.

Prentice was staring at her. "What's wrong?"

"Nothing," Ardith said, glancing up to see Simone and the twins were also looking at her, concerned. "I'm just tired."

Matty stood up, ignoring Cooper's groans of protest as he vacated his lap. "We have that early call tomorrow. You want to head out, Blackwood?"

She nodded, cradling her arms in front of her chest.

"Nice meeting you!" called Deenie as they headed back to the elevator door. "DM if you ever want to film with me on my new show!"

When they got off the elevator, Matty walked outside to hand the valet their ticket, and Prentice stepped close to her. "Hey, cuz. Are you okay?"

"Yeah, I just wasn't expecting you to bring up my mom. In front of people."

"I'm sorry. I guess I thought—"

"No, it's fine," she said, shaking her head. "I think it's just . . . the past few weeks have been kind of tough."

"Yeah. I get it." He squeezed her shoulder. "Seriously, though, you should invite Simone to the opening. Did you see how excited they were about Aunt Kimberly?"

"I'll think about it," she said slowly. "Matty and I are gonna go now. Tell your dads I said bye?"

Prentice nodded. "For sure. See you Saturday."

Ardith walked out as the valet was pulling Matty's Porsche up to the curb. Matty tipped him and Ardith had just opened the passenger side door when she heard someone call her name. She turned to see a twenty-something guy striding toward her, cell phone in hand. She stifled a groan; the last thing she wanted right now was to take a picture with a stranger. She smiled, though, and straightened out her shirt.

"Ardith, how's it going?" he said, and she realized too late from his overly friendly tone that this wasn't a fan at all. He was a blogger. "Got a minute?"

"Um," she began, hating that he'd caught her off guard. "I'm actually—"

"No, she doesn't," Matty said loudly, coming over to stand by her side. "And what is with you guys? Do you really get off on trolling charity events?"

"Matty Cohen. Look at you, being all philanthropic." He smirked, looking between them. "Not the kind of party I'd expect to see you at, but I guess there's a little do-gooder in all of us." He turned back to her. "Ardith: Why did your great-grandmother decide to keep her baby daddy a secret? Now that she's dead, are we never going to find out who he was?"

Ardith felt as if her knees were going to buckle beneath her. Matty must have sensed it because he took her by the elbow, turned her around, and helped her into the passenger seat, closing the door firmly behind her. Through the window, she saw him pointing his finger in the guy's face as he spoke to him. The blogger didn't flinch, but he did hold his phone up to Matty, sneering as he showed him he'd been recording the audio the whole time. Matty held up both of his middle fingers and stormed back to the car; he slammed the driver's side door and peeled out before Ardith could speak.

He cut up and down the twisty residential roads, finally pulling over on one of the dead-end streets. "Fuck that guy," he said, putting the car in park. "You okay?"

Ardith nodded, then leaned her head against the window, closing her eyes for a few seconds as she tried to get her breathing back to normal.

"Sorry. I know you can handle yourself, but the way that asshole was coming at you—"

"I appreciate it." Maybe she could have handled herself on a different day, but tonight, she'd needed him.

"What happened up on the roof probably didn't help. Coop likes to pick on new people, but I didn't think he'd try that shit with you."

"It's not that." She paused. "I just . . . I wasn't expecting my mom to come up."

Matty was quiet for a moment, then asked, "Is that all it was, though? You've been kind of out of it all day."

Ardith looked down at her hands. She wished she could simply tell him everything, especially after what had just happened with that blogger. But there was no way. For starters, her father would be furious if the Michael Babineaux story leaked ahead of the press release they were still formulating, and although she was sure Matty would understand the circumstances and consequences, it was a risk she would never take. But it was more than just that. Ardith still wasn't sure how she felt about what Bebe had done, and she didn't need someone else passing judgment on her. Someone she actually liked. She had no idea what Matty might say, and right now, she didn't want to know.

Ardith exhaled. She also didn't want Matty to think she was holding back, so she turned to him and said, "I think I'm just having an off night. I don't go to things like this, and . . . sorry I was weird in front of your friends."

"No complaints here." When she looked at him, Matty was smiling. "Don't be so hard on yourself. We've all known each other for years. I get that it wouldn't be so easy to just come into a group like that."

"Why are you being so nice to me?"

"Because we're friends?" he said softly. "You don't have to be a certain way around me. I like that you don't pretend as if this world we're in isn't completely bizarre. I try to talk to Cooper about it sometimes, but he just acts like it's normal."

"How'd you become friends with him, anyway?"

Matty glanced in the rearview mirror, as if to make sure the blogger hadn't somehow followed them. "We had this friend in common. His name was Eddie. He, um, killed himself a couple years ago."

"Eddie Frees?"

"Yeah." Matty ran a hand over the back of his neck. "We worked on this movie together when we were kids and stayed friends. He knew Coop through the business, too. Cooper and I didn't really hang out until Eddie was gone, though. We met at his funeral and kept checking up on each other, and now I guess we're friends, too . . ."

"I'm sorry about Eddie," Ardith said.

"Me too. I miss him." Matty blinked a couple of times. "And—sometimes I wonder why I'm even still friends with Cooper, you know? But I guess he kind of feels like my last real connection to Eddie. He's the only one I know who knew him like I did, and if we're not friends anymore . . ."

"I get it. When my mom . . ." Ardith paused, but only for a moment. "After my mom died, my dad sort of disappeared, emotionally. And I didn't have any friends I could talk to. I was living this totally sheltered life because of who my family was. I didn't even know another kid whose parent had died. But then her death was so public it was, like, the only thing everyone wanted to talk about. Except nobody cared about how that made us feel, and . . . it was lonely. I missed my mom so much, and then it was just me and my dad, who seemed like he would rather forget about her."

"I'm sorry, Blackwood. Have you ever . . . talked to anyone else about this?"

She shook her head. "Not besides my cousin. And my therapist."

"My parents made me see a therapist after Eddie died. I think they were worried the same thing might happen to me, but—Eddie had different problems than I do. Being in this world was tough for him."

"It was tough for my mom, too. And the older I get, the more I keep thinking people are going to assume I'll turn out like her."

"Do you want to be like her?"

Ardith looked at him sharply. "What do you mean?"

"I mean, she had an addiction, but she was more than that. You loved her and you still love her. And so do a lot of other people." Matty paused. "I guess what I'm trying to say is, I remember reading all these pearl-clutching articles about Eddie and his depression and what brought it on, but he wasn't his depression. He was really fucking funny and he made amazing omelets and he was super dedicated to acting—he kept reminding me that I couldn't coast just because I won an award as a kid and—" Ardith waited for him to go on, but he shook his head, said, "Sorry."

"What?"

"I don't know, sometimes I feel dumb bringing this up."

"Why?"

"Because I feel like I should be over it by now."

Ardith gave him a sad smile. "What was it you told me? That we don't get a choice in how or when grief comes?"

"You know you're wrong, throwing my words back in my face like that," Matty said, but he smiled a little, too. "Hey, you hungry? The food at that party was such a tease."

"I'm starving."

"Tacos?"

"Absolutely."

Matty put the car into gear and stepped on the gas. Ardith let her arm hang out the window to feel the nighttime breeze as they wound down the hills toward Sunset.

Hollis

It had been three weeks since Hollis had last been at Dupree Academy, and she was starting to get restless. The head of school had called her parents to explain they were taking the whole ordeal of the leaked nude quite seriously; they'd held an assembly to talk about cyberbullying and how it was never okay to share compromising photos of people without their consent, that if they found students sharing things like that again, there would be consequences. And that if they found evidence of who had shared Hollis's photo, there would be consequences now, as well.

Hollis woke each day with the intention of putting on a brave face and heading back to Dupree . . . but then she thought of how everyone had looked at her that day in the hallway. The DMs she'd received. The websites that, she knew, were still discussing the photo and what it meant for *the Blackwood legacy*. And the fact that Dwayne still hadn't explained how, exactly, one of the pictures he had taken and promised he'd deleted had gotten out in the first place. Once her mind cycled through all of that, she found it almost impossible to get out of bed.

Today, when she finally did, she found her mother standing in the kitchen, finishing up the last of her coffee, purse and cell phone sitting on the counter in front of her.

"Hi, honey." Mom paused. "No school today?"

Hollis shook her head. "What are you up to?"

"Just getting ready to head out for those meetings."

Hollis pulled a package of English muffins from the bread box and started rummaging in the refrigerator for yogurt and berries. Mom studied her for a while, as if waiting for Hollis to say something. When she didn't, her mother kissed the top of Hollis's head and grabbed her purse and phone from the counter.

"I'm thinking about it," Hollis said. "Going back, I mean."

"I know, honey," she replied. "If you want to talk about it, I'm here."

Then she left, and Hollis was alone.

She ate her breakfast out by the pool, as she'd taken to doing since she'd been home in the mornings. It was peaceful watching the sunlight reflect off the water, flooding her vision with shades of blue. Sometimes she fell back asleep on one of the chaises, waking a minute or an hour or more later, disoriented. Today, she lay back and let her mind wander, as it often did, to the night before her surgery. When Dwayne had agreed to take the pictures.

Her heart had been thumping so violently in her chest that she wondered if Dwayne could hear it from across the room. Had she really just asked him to take topless photos of her? And had he really said yes? She must have looked as unsure as she'd felt because Dwayne had gotten up from the love seat and walked toward her, stopping a few feet away.

"We don't have to do this if you don't want to," he said softly. "It was just a dumb idea."

"I want to, I just . . . Give me a minute."

Hollis went to the bathroom, where she stared at herself in the mirror for a long time. She tried to figure out exactly how she felt in that moment. Something had shifted between them, and she was sure Dwayne felt it, too, but nothing had happened—yet. She knew, though, as soon as she stepped out of the bathroom, everything between them would change. She slowly took off her top and bra. Even if something had shifted, she still wasn't sure she was comfortable undressing in front of Dwayne. She ran her fingers through her locs, took a deep breath, and stepped out of the bathroom clutching her sweatshirt against her chest.

Dwayne froze, phone in hand, when he saw her. His Adam's apple bobbed in his throat as he swallowed. "Uh . . . hi."

"Hi," Hollis said, biting her lip.

After another moment, Dwayne seemed to find himself again. "Okay, so where did you want to take them?"

"I think the light is best over here." *The light is best?* It's not like they were taking senior portraits.

But if Dwayne thought that was corny, he didn't say anything. He framed her up in his phone camera, shyly asking her to move to the left or right until he said it was perfect.

She blinked at him. "I'm nervous."

"Don't be," he'd said easily, even though she could tell by the way he was standing straight as a pin that he was nervous, too. "It's just me. And these are for you, so—"

Hollis let her sweatshirt drop to the floor.

Dwayne's mouth fell open. "I . . . um. I—wow, Holl."

Her whole body immediately flushed, but she forced herself not to cover her chest with her arms. Just barely.

"Sorry. I'm not trying to be a creep." He let out a long breath. "You're just really beautiful. All of you."

She smiled, feeling her nerves start to settle, just a bit. She stood up straight, shoulders back. "Ready?"

Dwayne had taken pictures of her from the front, in profile on both sides, and with her back to him, Hollis looking over her shoulder. About midway through, she'd started to get comfortable. She stopped thinking of how she was half-naked, how it was her old friend holding the camera. She was used to being photographed without her consent by people who wanted proof that they'd been in the same space as her, or paparazzi who wanted to sell the photos. It felt new, almost freeing, being photographed this way; these pictures were about her. For her.

There was no shame about her body as it was, and at the same time, she knew she was also doing the right thing by changing part of it tomorrow.

"How's that?" Dwayne asked after a while, snapping her out of her thoughts.

"Good." Hollis bent down to pick up her sweatshirt. She had no idea how many photos they'd taken. "Thank you, Dwayne," she said, looking up at him.

He turned his phone over in his hand, nodding. "Of course. You're welcome. Anytime."

Hollis laughed, and Dwayne instantly shook his head.

"I mean, not that you're going to do this all the time," he said in a rush. "But if you do, and you need someone"—his lips curled into a soft smile—"I volunteer."

And then, for the second time that evening, Hollis released her shirt.

Dwayne inhaled sharply and swallowed, looking at her with gentle eyes. "Hollis?"

She reached out and touched her fingertips to his, drawing him nearer so there would be no question that she wanted him. Dwayne pressed his thumb against her lips, then leaned down to kiss her there. He softly traced his knuckles down the side of her arm, then his hands slid over her stomach and up her rib cage, stopping on her breasts. His mouth had followed. She'd shivered and said his name, barely louder than a whisper.

"You okay?" he asked, pulling back, and she nodded, smiling sheepishly because as good as it had felt, it was still Dwayne with his lips on her, and she couldn't have imagined it before that evening. Did he feel the same way?

But it wasn't the time for words. They had spent years only talking.

He led her to the bed, where they sat down next to each other, inches apart. Dwayne reached out to trace his finger from her temple to her chin and back up again.

"You have to be up early . . ." he began, but didn't finish the sentence.

"Stay. If you want to, I mean."

"I do, Holl."

They'd had plenty of sleepovers in the past, so neither of their parents would think twice about him being there. Even as they'd gotten older, it had been normal to find Dwayne sleeping on her bedroom floor or the pullout mattress from her love seat in the morning.

Hollis scooted back on the bed as Dwayne removed his shirt and undershirt, tossing them to the rug, and carefully placed his glasses on the nightstand. They slid under the covers together, bare skin to bare skin. She hadn't known what to expect, but it was perfect. No sex. But she'd never felt closer to anyone than she felt to Dwayne that night.

She fell asleep, her naked body pressed against his, and woke a few hours later to Dwayne gently stroking her shoulder. When she opened her eyes, he was smiling. "Hi," he said.

"Hi." The sheet only covered the bottom half of his body, and she tried not to stare, but she couldn't look away, either, watching the way his brown skin glowed in the soft morning light. Was this the last time they'd be together this way?

He held out his phone to her. "The photos. I wanted to show you before I go."

She took it and flipped through what he'd taken. Hollis thought she might be embarrassed, looking at them in front of Dwayne. She still couldn't believe what had happened between them, and these photos would always be a reminder. She loved them. That she had taken these for herself, and that she trusted Dwayne enough to share this moment with her. She trashed her least favorites, then told Dwayne to text her the rest and delete them after. He agreed and slipped out of bed, kissing her on the

255

lips one last time as he smoothed the duvet over her shoulders. He told her he'd check on her after the surgery, and then he was gone.

She hadn't thought she'd need to watch him delete the photos. She hadn't even thought about the fact that they could have used her phone to take them. By that point her mind had been occupied with how close they had been. How the sleeve of Dwayne's shirt had brushed against her bare arm when he'd kissed her before he left. And how she'd wanted, very much, for him to come rushing back into the room, then, to touch her, one more time.

She opened her eyes now, staring out at the pool in front of her, water rippling from the light wind moving through. How could that same guy, who'd been so tender and gentle with her every second of that night, so respectful and kind, betray her trust? It didn't make sense, and although she felt like she still wasn't ready to talk to him now, she needed, so badly, for him to give her another explanation.

Hollis was cleaning up her breakfast dishes when the doorbell rang. She ignored it, since both of her parents were out and they weren't expecting anyone, but then it rang again. And it kept ringing. Hollis sighed. She went into the front room to peek out the window and immediately froze.

Dwayne's Range Rover was parked in the driveway, nose to nose with her G-Wagon.

She considered pretending not to be home, but Dwayne must know she was there. He'd seen her car, and he'd known her long enough to be sure that if she hadn't come back to school yet, this was the only place she would be.

Hollis walked toward the door, but she didn't reach for the knob. She leaned her forehead against the dark wood. "What do you want?"

"Can you open the door, Holl? Please?"

She took a deep breath and twisted the knob. She'd have to see him sometime. She might as well get it over with.

He was standing on the porch in sweats and a hoodie, his hands twisting together in front of him, eyes shifting around behind his glasses. They finally, tentatively, landed on Hollis. "You haven't been texting or calling me back."

Hollis just stared at him. "What are you doing here?"

"I miss you." When she didn't respond, he said, "Can I come in?"

"My mom's home."

"No, she's not. She has meetings today. She hates leaving you alone right now, when you don't seem ready to come back to school, but she couldn't miss them." He shrugged. "You know my mom loves a speaker-phone."

Hollis didn't say anything, but she moved aside, holding the door wide enough for him to come in. Once inside, he stepped closer to her, slowly, and a part of her wanted to tell him to back up, to get away from her, to leave. But there was a part of her that she couldn't deny, that missed him, too. That ached to be wrapped up in one of his big, warm hugs. It was the same part of her that wanted to believe he had nothing to do with that photo getting out.

"I swear I didn't send that picture to anybody, Hollis," he began, as if reading her mind.

"Then how was it leaked?"

"I wouldn't do that to you, I promise. But . . . I did find out what happened."

Hollis leaned against the banister at the bottom of the staircase, arms folded.

"The thing is . . . So, after I texted you the photos, I deleted them. Then I went into our text thread, and deleted them there, too. And then, I went into my deleted folder to delete everything, permanently. And

I did . . . most of them. But, Holl—I was about to delete the last one, and . . . I couldn't."

Hollis stared at him, unmoving.

"It was, like . . . a reminder. Of that night. I'd thought about that happening with us for a while, but I didn't figure it would. And then it did, and it was amazing. But I knew I wouldn't see you again for a while because of the surgery, and I wasn't sure what it would be like when we were together again. I didn't know if you would want to pick up where we left off or if you'd want to go back to being friends. I just kept thinking about all of that, and . . . I didn't get rid of it. I left it in the deleted folder."

Hollis stood as still as possible, doing her best not to react. Inside, she was shattered—thinking about how they'd woken up together, how she hadn't been able to stop looking at the way the light kissed Dwayne's skin. She had felt the same way as Dwayne, not wanting it to end. But that still didn't explain how the photo had leaked.

"Okay," she said, taking slow, even breaths. "So, what happened after that?"

Dwayne's eyes dropped. He played with the strings of his hoodie, pulling them back and forth. "I knew it would eventually delete itself after a month or whatever, and I honestly didn't really look at it again. I just wanted to know I had it. But then, the day it got out, after you left school, I looked in my deleted folder, and it was still there. That's when I realized . . . The day after Orlando's party at the beach, he and some of the guys on the team came over. And, um, we have this thing where we go through each others' photos, to find any embarrassing ones—like, if we take a bunch of selfies in a row and half of them look stupid, that sort of thing—and text them to each other. I guess I figured it had automatically deleted by then, and I usually never let the guys touch my phone anyway. But they must have, at some point. When I wasn't looking."

Hollis gripped the banister so hard she thought it might crack in half. There it was. The explanation she had wanted. It was exactly what she'd asked for, and also terribly anticlimactic. Dwayne had been careless, someone had taken advantage of that, and she'd gotten caught in the middle. But it also confirmed her greatest fear—that the photo *had* gotten out because of Dwayne, even if it wasn't purposely.

And, she realized in that moment, he'd known all this since the day she left school, but he was only telling her now.

"Who was it?"

"I'm sorry, Hollis. I'm really, really sorry. It's completely my bad and . . . I don't know how to make it up to you, but I'm going to spend forever trying to do that." Dwayne sighed, so heavy she felt it, too. "That night . . . it was amazing. One of the best nights of my life. I would never do anything to mess that up."

Hollis's heart skipped and for a moment, she wished she could ignore everything else, focus only on the feelings they shared about that night. But no matter what she felt, his words weren't good enough. "You didn't answer my question. You know who you were hanging out with that day. Who was there?"

Dwayne just looked at her, his eyes begging her not to keep asking.

Hollis slowly shook her head. "You're really going to choose them over me?" *Isn't that what you've been doing all this time?*

"Holl, it's not like that. I just . . . I don't want you to get pissed and do something you'll regret."

"Something *I'll* regret? Like what? Call an asshole an asshole? Hold someone accountable for what they did?"

"I just wonder, if you told your uncle, he might want to take legal action . . ."

She paced across the foyer, stopping by the doorway to the living room. "Jesus Christ, Dwayne. You know Uncle August. You think he just sits around all day waiting to sue somebody?"

He threw his hands in the air. "This is L.A. Everybody sues everybody."

"*I'm not everybody*. And I'm definitely not interested in suing any of the stupid guys on the team. But I deserve to know who did it." She paused. The photo had gotten out before Grandpa Abe had read them Bebe's letter, before they'd made contact with the Babineauxs or even known they existed. "Was it Orlando?"

"No. He was there, but I know it wasn't him."

"Come on, Dwayne. He hates me."

"It wasn't him, Holl."

"Fine, then, who was it?"

He looked down at his shoes as he spoke. "It had to be either Danny, Jase, or Patrick."

The other guys who trained with him and Orlando in the off season. "And you haven't asked which one of them did it?"

"Of course I have!" he said. "Nobody's owning up to it. You think I'm not as pissed about this as you are?"

"That's *exactly* what I think. It took you *weeks* to tell me what actually happened when you've known it was one of them the whole time!" Hollis crossed the foyer again, standing closer to him than she'd been since he'd entered the house. "How can I trust you, Dwayne? You're supposed to be my best friend, but you don't even care enough about me to tell those guys to fuck off?"

"I feel like shit about all of this. I hate that I have to see those assholes at school every day. That we're still on the team together, still supposed to be friends." Dwayne cleared his throat. "I'm sorry. If I'd known any of this would happen, I never would have taken those photos for you. I—"

"I didn't do anything I didn't want to," Hollis cut him off. "I just didn't want the whole fucking world to see."

Dwayne chewed on his fingernail. She watched him, wondering what she was supposed to do now. She believed it had been an honest mistake, that he'd never meant for anyone else to see that photo. But how could she trust him again when he had been thoughtless enough to get her into this situation? When it had taken him weeks to tell her the truth?

"How can you still hang out with them?" she asked. "How can you be around people who did something like that to me?"

"It's different now," he said. "I don't talk to any of them except Orlando. Unless one of them has to spot me in the weight room or something. We're just sharing space."

"Oh, well, of course you needing someone to help you lift weights is more important than sticking up for me, isn't it?"

"Come on, Holl, you know what I—"

"Whatever. But what about when the season starts?" Hollis felt like the tips of her ears might burst into flames. "All that's going to change, isn't it? You'll have to talk all the time. Be a *team*. Unless you quit—but you're not brave enough to do that either, are you?"

"I still want to, but—"

"This is the perfect chance. Your dad would absolutely understand that you can't be on the team after this."

"The only way he would understand me quitting is if I were in a full body cast," Dwayne said. "Even then, he'd be trying to get me into PT the second I was out of the hospital. His mind doesn't work like ours. He would say I need to ignore them and keep my focus on the game."

"So you're not even going to try talking to him."

Dwayne stepped toward her. "You know you're more important to me than those guys or basketball or any of this. I . . . I love you, Hollis."

Those words took her breath away—but only for a moment. She set her gaze on his. "Then show me, Dwayne."

She watched as the hope in his eyes slipped away, and she knew the conversation was over.

Before any of this had happened, Hollis was sure Dwayne would only ever be honest with her. Now, her faith in him was cracked—if not shattered, then shook.

She thought of Bebe again, how she had decided she and Grandpa

Abe were better off without his father. Bebe and Michael Babineaux had known each other for such a long time—loved one another—but then something had changed so deeply, so irrevocably. Hollis didn't want things to be different with her and Dwayne, but the truth was, they already were. And she wasn't sure if they could ever go back.

Could she love someone and also not completely trust them?

A Beautiful Wreck

1961

"Billy, I simply can't." Blossom cast her eyes low before tilting her chin and gazing up, meeting the intensity of his stare. "My apologies, but my heart belongs to Freddie, and . . . I'm going to wait for him. He'll be coming home soon."

"Cut!" the director called, and Blossom waited a moment before she let herself fall out of character. She glanced at the director's chair just in time to see him step down and exit the soundstage.

She then looked at her co-star, Lawrence, who was fanning himself with his hand. He raised his eyebrows. "What do you think that means?"

"Well, he didn't ask for another take."

Lawrence laughed. "You are always looking on the bright side, Blossom."

She grinned at him, but the smile slid down her face as she turned to find Ricky, the first assistant director, at her elbow.

If Blossom sought to be a positive force on set, it seemed as if Ricky was put there to balance that. He had a strong work ethic, which Blossom appreciated; it was the same one Mama had instilled in her and her sisters. But, somewhere along the way, Ricky had forgotten he was in the business of making movies—a job that was supposed to be enjoyable, exhilarating even. Blossom had learned after a few days that the permanent scowl on his face had nothing to do with her, but after weeks of shooting, his energy was starting to wear—on her and everyone else.

Anytime Blossom found herself becoming irritated by an incident on set, though, she took a moment to remind herself that this was it: she was living her lifelong dream. She was the lead in a Hollywood studio movie. Gertie, in *Love, Gertie*. Her name, first on the call sheet.

"Mr. Melamed would like to see you," Ricky said in his clipped tone.

"Is this about the last scene?"

"As I said, he'd like to see you now. In his office." Ricky looked down at his clipboard, but before Blossom started to walk away, he said, "You didn't ask, but in my opinion, the scene was just fine."

Blossom had worked with him long enough to know that was high praise.

She left the soundstage, winding her way through the sunny studio lot to the building where the offices of the producers and executives were located. As she walked, Blossom thought, as she often did, about how her dreams were actually, finally coming true. Just two years ago, *The Johnstons* had premiered Off-Broadway to middling reviews that praised the casting and direction of the play, but criticized the story for being banal and, at times, reductive. Archie had arrived at her apartment early the morning their review was printed in the *Village Voice*; they'd sat together at her tiny kitchen table over coffee and bagels, each of them reading the review aloud. "'Blossom Blackwood is particularly fetching as Sara; her natural charisma and grace shine . . .'" Archie repeated, leaning over to kiss her. "They love you, darling." Blossom beamed at the words—both at their meaning and hearing Archie read them to her—but she couldn't help finishing the rest of the paragraph in her head: *. . . next to Clifton Thompson, who is strong and dignified as her husband, Leon. The pair's chemistry is undeniable.*

Clifton's declaration had never left her mind all these years—that without Archie's help, she would still be floundering in her career. After

The Johnstons, she had won leading roles in three more Off-Broadway plays, one helmed by Archie and the other two by directors he was friendly with. Shortly after, Archie had secured funding for *Love, Gertie*, for which she'd had to audition. He'd explained that if it were up to him, she would have gotten the part without any sort of discussion, but the studio believed she was too green to hire without a screen test. Blossom didn't mind; deep down, she knew Archie believed in her talent and always had, but she would never want anyone to think she'd been cast for any reason other than her skill and hard work. The hours were long, but she treasured living in Los Angeles full-time with her family—getting to kiss Abe good night every evening and being back with Mama and Sybil. Archie had been over for supper a few times, and though Blossom had never confessed the true nature of their relationship to Mama, she suspected her mother understood what was happening. Flossie never mentioned it; she wasn't particularly warm or cold to Archie—she was just Mama. She seemed to be content that Blossom was happy and working on projects that fulfilled her.

Blossom arrived at Archie's office to find his secretary away from her desk, which was odd; it wasn't yet lunchtime. But when she spied the heavy doors to his office were slightly ajar, she understood that perhaps she had been sent away.

Blossom smoothed her palms down the sides of her costume dress and knocked, lightly.

"Come in."

She stepped inside and shut the doors behind her with a soft click. Archie was sitting behind his large mahogany desk, furiously scribbling on a sheet of paper, just as he used to during their play rehearsals and performances back in New York. He didn't like to be interrupted when he was writing, so Blossom strode silently across the room, perching on one of the chairs facing him. As she waited, she glanced around the office. She hadn't spent a lot of time in here; to tell the truth, she found it a bit intimidating. The furniture was dark and heavy. A large bronze statue sat in the corner, unfamiliar to Blossom the first time she'd seen it; he had informed her that it was Buddha, an ancient philosopher whose spiritual teachings he had begun to study. She stared at the peaceful expression on the statue, only looking away when the director cleared his throat, setting down his pen.

"Ricky said you wanted to see me," Blossom said.

"Yes. I have some notes from your scenes this morning that I'd like to—"

"When will you stop doing this, Archie?"

He frowned, pressing lightly on the rim of his round glasses. "Excuse me?"

"Summoning me to some private location for notes when you're perfectly capable of giving them to me on set as you do the others."

"You're my leading lady. The attention is warranted."

"I don't want to spend our time alone discussing my performance," Blossom said. "Besides, I'm a fast learner. I know what I'm doing now on camera."

"You do," he agreed. "But there's always room for improvement."

"All right, Archie." She leaned forward, looking down at the page, trying to read his chicken scratch upside down.

But instead of relaying the notes to her, he removed his glasses, setting them on top of the paper. "How was Abe's birthday?"

Her eyes slowly rose to meet his. "It was nice. I made his favorite, yellow cake with chocolate frosting. He can hardly put down his new Etch A Sketch. I can't believe he's seven years old."

"They grow so quickly." Archie pushed his leather chair back and bent down, retrieving a wrapped rectangular box from beneath the desk. He placed it on top, pushing it toward Blossom. "I got him something."

"Oh. You didn't have to do that."

"It's nothing extravagant. A Mr. Mercury robot toy. It has a remote control. I can't promise you won't be thoroughly irritated by it." He gave her a rare smile. "But I thought Abe would like it. I'm sorry I couldn't be there to celebrate him."

"Thank you, Archie. He'll love it." She ran her hands over the gift wrapping. She couldn't help wondering if his conveniently absent secretary had been the one to buy it, or if Archie himself had visited a department store, just for Abe. "And it was probably better that you weren't there. I would have loved to have you, but he's older now. He knows you're a friend, but . . . children are perceptive. I don't want to confuse him."

"That's fair." He paused. "You are doing a lovely job on set, Blossom. You have improved, so much, since you began acting on film. You were born to do this. And I want to ensure your performance in this project guarantees you another one."

"Do you have another part in mind for me already?" She wished her voice weren't so hopeful, but she knew that Archie had fought hard for *Love, Gertie*—for his role as director of his first feature; for her, a relatively unknown stage actress, as the lead; and for a film about Negroes in the first place.

"Blossom." Her heart sank. His voice was hesitant. Archie was never reluctant to speak to her. He tented his fingers on the desk in front of him. "Marian is unhappy."

From what she'd heard of Archie's wife, that wasn't so unusual, but Blossom remained quiet, waiting for him to continue.

"She suspects you and I have grown closer during filming. And . . . I assume you haven't forgotten her suspicions during our time in New York."

Blossom inhaled. "What does this all mean?"

"She has forbidden me to cast you in any of my future projects, or to direct any film in which you are appearing."

"*Forbidden* you? What, as if she's your mother?"

"Blossom, please try to understand. I admire you in so many ways. What we have is special. I love you."

Those three words still took her breath away, but she had heard them from Archie before. The first time, they had been accompanied by a gold Cartier bracelet, gifted to her after *The Johnstons* had come to the end of its short run. She wore it when they were alone together—the only time she wasn't afraid of the questions that would follow if someone noticed it glinting on her wrist.

"But you don't love me enough to leave her. For us to finally make what we have public."

Archie shook his head. "Think of all the trouble that would cause. People simply aren't ready for a man like me and a woman like you to be together."

Blossom's blood turned hot. "A woman like me?"

"Blossom, you are the most beautiful woman I've ever had the privilege of being acquainted with. Your talent is unmatched, and your resilience in pursuing a career so many have tried to deny you inspires me each day. But we've spoken about this. We wouldn't be able to have what we have out in the world. Even your mother doesn't trust me."

"Mama's from Mississippi. She has no reason to trust white people. And perhaps the reason we keep discussing this is because nothing has changed. It's been two years, Archie. When will being honest about our love become more important than whatever we fear in revealing it?"

Archie briefly closed his eyes before he spoke again. "If this were a different time . . . if we were different people . . . perhaps this could work. But my children are growing older, too. Old enough to notice that something is strained between me and their mother. I owe them a normal childhood. Just as you owe one to Abe."

"Don't talk to me about how I raise my son." Blossom was well aware what many people believed about how she was bringing up Abe— her often being absent from his life, his growing up without a father. Michael's warnings, about what people would think of them and their son if they didn't get married, were in her thoughts each time she returned home from a job, and each time she prepared to leave again. She didn't need the reminder from Archie.

"Blossom, please. If it were up to me, we would be together."

She stood abruptly, looking down at him. "It is up to you, Archie. *You* are allowed to do whatever you want. It's *me* who is scrutinized at every turn, made to feel I have something to prove for simply existing. Whose opportunities are bound by what makes others comfortable, what they are prepared to accept. I can't help that I fell in love with you. Or that you feel the same way. But please do not pretend that you are powerless in this situation. You hold *all* the power. We could be together if you chose to. And you could cast me in your films if you really believed in me."

He swallowed. "I have only ever believed in you, Blossom. I believe in you enough to know you deserve someone better than me. Someone who can give you everything you want."

"You are a coward," Blossom said, refusing to break eye contact until he did. Then she marched across the room and out the doors before he could say another word.

Later, Blossom retired to her bungalow to gather herself before she drove home. She'd been astonished when production started to find her dressing room was one of the private bungalows on the lot, which were usually reserved for the most esteemed actors or the performers who held contracts with the studio. She was certain most Negro actors and actresses weren't afforded this luxury, whether or not they were a lead. Even Dorothy Dandridge hadn't had a dressing room like this when she'd starred in *Carmen Jones* for 20th Century Fox. Blossom understood it was Archie's doing—one of the few discreet ways in which he could show how he felt about her. But she would have traded this dressing room for more time with him in a heartbeat.

269

Blossom decided to draw a bath, but she stood in the front room for several minutes, unmoving. Archie's news had left her dumbfounded— at the fact that things could change so quickly, but also that she didn't know what this meant for her career. The issue wasn't her talent or her willingness to persevere . . . It was in the realization that she had worked for nearly two decades to reach this point and now everything she had built was leading to an uncertain future. There was always the chance that *Love, Gertie* wouldn't do well at the box office, but everyone on set seemed aware that they had something special on their hands. It was one of those rare projects where everything, from the studio to the film crew to the talent, had seamlessly aligned. And now the man who had the most faith in her—whose faith had never wavered—was severing their ties.

Why had she allowed herself to fall for him? Archie had been right. She did deserve someone who would fully give himself to her, who would be devoted and unafraid of what others said about their love. Sometimes Blossom wondered if she was being punished for how things had ended with Michael. Though he had been out of their lives for years now, she would never be able to fully remove him from her memories. Or stop wondering what her and Abe's lives would look like if she'd decided to stay with him. She wished, at times, that she could meld the two men into one perfect partner; he would have Michael's handsome looks and confident way of moving through the world, and Archie's gentleness, his passionate, ambitious nature.

But what she wanted most of all was something neither of them had: the ability to accept her for who she was—every single part of her.

Blossom was perched on the edge of the clawfoot tub in her bungalow, adding drops of bath oil to the running water, when she heard a knock at the door. She was still for a moment; she wasn't expecting anyone. But it was likely Ricky with changes to the script for the next day's filming. Blossom turned off the faucets, tied her silk robe tight around her waist, and hurried to the front room. She pulled the robe close to her throat as she cracked the door open a few inches and looked out.

Archie was standing on the small porch. He never came by her dressing room. His suit jacket was hung over his arm, the wrapped gift from earlier tucked in his hands.

"You forgot this," he said, holding it out. Before she could speak, he added, "Please take it. I want Abe to have it. If you'd rather he didn't know it's from me, say you bought it."

Blossom didn't accept the package, but she opened the door wider and stepped aside to let him in. She looked outside before she shut the door, wondering if anyone on the lot had seen him.

"I'm sorry about how I spoke to you earlier," Archie said, carefully placing the gift by the door. "I only wanted to be honest with you."

"I've just run a bath, and I don't want it to grow cold. You're welcome to sit with me if you'd like." Blossom turned and loosened the ties of her robe, letting it slip halfway down her back before she headed to the rear of the bungalow.

Archie followed. He leaned against the sink, watching as she shed her robe completely and slipped into the steaming tub. She sank down until the water crested her shoulders, then turned her head to look at him. The room was warm, humid; Archie unbuttoned his shirtsleeves and rolled them up to his elbows.

"I *am* a coward," he said, his voice quiet. "And I *am* in love with you. Both of those things can be true."

"What's also true is you've shut me out of future opportunities for a reason that has nothing to do with the work," Blossom retorted.

"Not all opportunities. Just those that involve me." He paused. "And I've only done so to save my marriage."

"What is there to save when you're in love with another woman? Marian deserves better, too."

Archie relaxed the knot in his tie. "I know how many people have tried to tell you what you can and cannot do, Blossom. I never meant to be one of them, making it even harder for you to succeed in this business, as a Negro and a woman. It's more difficult now than ever."

Blossom frowned. "What do you mean?"

"Well, there is so much going on these days . . . with the boycotts and the sit-ins and the Freedom Rides down South."

"It has always been difficult for us," Blossom said. "It's just that now, the world is watching."

"Yes, of course. I do believe there are significant changes on the horizon. I see all the ways people are coming together, working to make things right. And I'm trying to do my part, in the best ways I can. But even if I could leave Marian . . . I don't know how safe it is for us to be together. We would be stared at everywhere we went. Judged and discriminated against. Violence worries me, too—if we were to travel. We could be married here in California, but our union would be illegal in several other states."

"I don't need a lesson on our bigoted country," Blossom snapped. "Do you think I wanted to fall in love with a white man, of all people?"

Archie's face fell. Blossom felt guilty for her harsh tone, but not enough to apologize. He crouched down in front of the tub. Her eyes roamed over the familiar lines of his face, the indents his glasses left on his skin.

"You are a true talent. You've become one of the finest actors I've ever worked with, and beyond that, the camera doesn't lie—you are an absolute vision onscreen. Once other people see this film, they are going to understand all that you can do, and the roles will come. I will recommend you to producers and casting directors whenever I can—but you don't need me, Blossom Blackwood. You were determined to succeed before we began working together, and your determination will be rewarded afterward, too.

"But still, I'm sorry. I am sorry I can't be more for you, sweet Blossom, when that is what you deserve."

She had never seen Archie cry. Not even the time she'd tried to break things off between them—a year ago, after their second play together had ended and before *Love, Gertie* had begun. Now he bowed his head, but that couldn't hide his shallow breaths, the tears that fell silently onto his trousers.

Blossom wanted to see it—to experience every emotion of his before they had to separate for good. She reached her hand out from the tub to lift his face, dripping water onto him, but he didn't seem to care. He gazed up at her openly, honestly, with red-rimmed eyes.

"Look at what you do to me," he said, laughing through his tears. "I'm a wreck."

"You are my wreck, Archie Melamed. My beautiful wreck." Blossom leaned her forehead against his, tenderly kissing him on the lips.

After her bath, Blossom moisturized with the floral body cream that matched the scent of her bath oil, then slipped on her robe and the Cartier bracelet. In the living room, Archie was standing next to the record player; he'd put on her favorite Sam Cooke album. They met on the sofa, where Archie stretched his legs and laid his head in her lap.

"Did you ever know a man named Marvin Finney?" Blossom asked just as Sam's soulful voice began belting out "Wonderful World."

"I don't recall the name," Archie replied. "Why?"

Blossom hesitated. She hadn't ever spoken to anyone about Marvin Finney besides Sybil. The longer she'd gone without speaking of it, the easier it was to forget her encounters with him had actually happened. "He was a producer I met years ago, back when I was dancing. He wooed me with flowers and jewelry and a fancy supper, and when I wouldn't go to bed with him . . . Well, he called me out of my name and told me I'd never make it in Hollywood and I . . ."

"What is it?"

"I've always wondered if he did, in fact, try to sabotage my career. If that's why it has taken so long to break into the business." She sighed. "Though perhaps I simply wasn't good enough during my auditions. Or perhaps it was always going to take this long because I'm a Negro woman in a business that doesn't care about us or our stories."

"Well, when he sees *Love, Gertie*, he'll realize he was a fool for underestimating you, won't he?"

Blossom gently ran her hand over Archie's curls. So many times over the years, despite how well she felt she knew him, she had questioned whether she could truly believe Archie when he told her how talented she was, that she could make it as an actress. She had been but a child when she'd first admitted her ambitions to Michael, and all these years later, Blossom wondered if she would ever be able to fully trust anyone when they praised her merits.

"I want you to know, it had never crossed my mind that being with you might benefit my career."

His eyes met hers. "I know that, Blossom."

"I will miss working with you," she said quietly.

"This isn't goodbye. Not yet."

"Then why does it feel as if it is?"

"We still have weeks left on our film," he said, and with that, he released the loose knot of her robe, exposing her bare skin. He brought his nose to her stomach, inhaling the floral scent.

"You'll smell like me," she warned as he began to stroke the small of her back.

Archie responded by softly pressing his lips to her navel. Blossom closed her eyes, allowing everything else in the world to disappear.

Ardith

The press release went live on a Thursday morning.

Daddy had told her to expect it but still, Ardith's heart began to race when he dropped the link in the family group chat:

ABRAHAM BLACKWOOD BREAKS SILENCE ON
IDENTITY OF FATHER, LOCAL SOUTH L.A. MAN

The statement was short, simple, and heartfelt, just as Grandpa Abe had wanted. Their publicist had written that although he appreciated his mother's need for privacy all those years, the Blackwoods were in the unique position of living their lives in the spotlight, which meant that sometimes news needed to be shared. And that, with the agreement of the Babineauxs, they were happy to share this news in particular as they celebrated the two families coming together. Then the release quoted Grandpa Abe, as well as his brother, Eli Babineaux, and ended with a request to respect both families' wishes for privacy at this time.

A part of Ardith was relieved the news was finally public, but the other part of her dreaded what was to come: a myriad of op-eds, endless questions from both strangers and people they knew, and assumptions about why the news had been private for so long. And she didn't want to talk about Bebe when she was still trying to process what was happening.

Matty saw it on her face when she entered the trailer they used for school. Ardith said hello to their teacher, Grace, then plopped down in the empty chair.

"I heard the news," Matty said carefully. "You want to talk about it?"

Was it only a few days ago that Matty had saved her from yet another "reporter" bombarding her with questions about Grandpa Abe's father? He was being extraordinarily human, asking her so gently. But Ardith just shook her head.

"Got it." He paused. "Want to go out tonight?"

She raised her eyebrows.

"Okay, I know. But what if I told you some of my friends from the other night want to celebrate me getting the cover of *GQ*?" he said sheepishly.

Ardith smiled for the first time that day. She couldn't remember ever seeing him be self-conscious about anything. It was cute. "Matty! That's amazing. Congratulations."

"I get that it's not great timing, but I'd love for you to be there if you want to come. We're going to Luster. Ever been?"

She pursed her lips. "Do I look like I've ever been to Luster?"

Matty grinned. "I don't know the kind of stuff you get up to when you're off the clock, Blackwood. You could have this whole secret life I know nothing about." He inhaled sharply. "Shit, sorry. I didn't mean it like that. I—"

"It's okay." Ardith glanced over at Grace, who was tapping away on her laptop, doing her best not to involve herself in their conversation. "But that's exactly why I can't go. The press release *just* went out. They'll never leave me alone."

"Okay, but hear me out," Matty said. "You're going to have to go out sometime, right? And like with that blogger the other night, the questions aren't going to go away. What, are you gonna stay inside forever? You can't let them control you like that. They don't get to decide what you do and where you go. That's letting them win."

She knew he was right, but Ardith thought of how she hadn't even been able to stutter through a practiced response that evening before Matty had to save her. What if that happened again?

As if Matty were privy to her thoughts, he said, "I'll be with you the whole time. And you know I have no problem telling someone to fuck off."

Ardith had to laugh at that. And though she still felt uneasy, she did want to celebrate Matty. Besides, going out with him and his friends might help get her mind off everything that was going on. She'd never had this option when she was upset about something before. Maybe being around other people would actually help.

"Okay," she said. "I'll be there."

It had been a while since Ardith had found herself under the lens of the paparazzi. They usually caught her doing something tragically normal, like popping into Walgreens to pick up contact lens solution or waiting to cross the street to go to a doctor's appointment at Cedars-Sinai. Now, as the black SUV that had driven her pulled up in front of Luster, a newish club downtown that had suddenly turned into an L.A. hotspot, she felt the dread creeping in—the distinct feeling that no matter how much she tried to blend into the background, someone would be watching.

But for now, all their attention was on Matty, who was standing out front waiting for her.

Ardith would have been drowning in flop sweat, but he looked relaxed as ever, coolly leaning against the brick wall as he chatted with the doorman. Ardith thanked her driver and quietly closed the door behind her before she attempted to make her way, without being noticed, through the crowd of photographers, bloggers, and people waiting to get in.

Matty saw her coming and bounded past the line to get her, scooping her into a side hug and rushing her past the velvet ropes before anyone recognized her. "I'm so glad you came. If you'd told me six months ago I'd have Ardith Blackwood out at a club . . ."

"Uh, same. This is . . . really something," she said, holding on to Matty's arm as he walked her up to the door, keeping her face turned away from the paps. She heard a couple of people calling out to her and Matty, but they weren't close enough for her to hear their questions.

"It's all good," Matty said. "We'll be in VIP, and it's mostly the people you met last time."

Ahead of them, a large group of young women flanked by two guys were let in; as the door opened, Ardith could hear dance music thumping. Matty squeezed their way up to the doorman, ignoring all the people who had been waiting as he told him Ardith's name and said she needed a VIP wristband. The doorman looked her up and down a few times, and she was sure he was going to ask for ID or turn her away. But then he laughed and started shaking his finger in the air. *"You Can Say That Again!"*

Ardith blinked.

"Your show! Tinsley! Right?"

"Oh, right. Yeah, that was me."

"Dang, I loved that show." He shook his head, still grinning. "Here's your wristband. Y'all let me know if you need anything the rest of the night, 'kay?"

"Appreciate you, man," Matty said, throwing up peace fingers. He helped Ardith attach the wristband and then the door was open, the bass was shaking her body, and they were inside Luster.

Ardith felt as if all of her senses were exploding. The club itself was dark, shot through with multicolored lights that were centered on the busy dance floor. The room smelled like liquor, dueling colognes, and faintly of weed. She could feel the sweat in the air, and the music was guiding the energy, setting the mood. It was unlike anywhere she'd ever been before, and Ardith could only stare, taking everything in.

"What do you think?" Matty asked. He had to shout to be heard, even standing right next to her.

"You do this all the time?" she yelled back.

"Not all the time. Just enough so it still feels exciting when I'm out." He pointed to a section in the corner, accessible by a small set of stairs with gold railing around the exterior. A bouncer stood by the stairs, eyes on everyone. "We're up there."

The VIP section did look a bit like that night on the roof; there were Simone, Ginny and Gia, and Deenie, all packed onto a midnight blue velvet couch. A couple of people Ardith didn't know were perched on the arms, talking to them. The table at the center was filled with buckets of ice, bottles of champagne and liquor, and several half-drunk glasses sweating with condensation.

Simone looked up as they approached and jumped up to give Ardith a hug. "So good to see you again," they said warmly.

The twins and Deenie smiled and waved as they shouted hello, and Matty introduced her to the two people she didn't know, beauty brand influencers who were apparently friends with Deenie. Matty had saved a love seat for them, which was a little bit away from everyone else but still close enough to hear everything that was going on in VIP and see everything out in the rest of the club.

"You want a drink?" he asked as he crouched in front of the table.

"Just water," Ardith said, wondering if that was a thing here.

"We're not so good about hydrating. I'll have the server grab you some when she comes back." Matty quickly topped off a drink on the edge of the table, then joined her on the love seat.

"Is anyone up here twenty-one?" she asked, incredulously. They were surrounded by alcohol, and Deenie had just pulled out a vape pen, despite the NO VAPING sign hanging a few feet from her head.

"I don't think anyone's even eighteen," Matty said, swirling the straw in his glass. "Nobody cares about anything as long as we don't get photographed with drinks in our hands. So we keep the drinking up here."

Just then, Cooper bounced up the steps to the VIP. "Hey, church girl!" he greeted her with a grin.

"Hazing's over, Coop," Matty said, giving him a look.

Cooper squeezed his way into the middle of the love seat that was too small for the three of them. "Chill, Cohen. She can take it. Can't you, church girl?"

Ardith scooted over so that as little as possible of her was touching him. "Of course I can, ferret boy."

His mouth dropped open. "Et tu, Ardith Blackwood?"

Years ago, Cooper had played the lead in a movie where his co-star was a CGI ferret, and at the end, when the ferret had died, Cooper had given what online lists called one of the most iconic crying performances of all time. The movie had recently been released on streaming, and a cut of Cooper's scene, snot running down his face, had gone viral earlier that year, earning him the new nickname.

"Guess she can take it." Matty smirked.

"You're braver than I am, coming out tonight," Cooper said to her, sipping his drink. "That news about your family is everywhere."

Ardith tried her best to look as if she hadn't been thinking about it for nearly every second of the day. "Well, I couldn't miss this. *GQ* is a big deal."

"Eddie would be proud of you, man." Cooper nodded toward Matty. Suddenly serious.

Matty pulled hard at his straw; Ardith watched the drink he'd just poured disappear in seconds. "I don't remember him being much of a *GQ* guy."

"No, but he was really fucking happy whenever anything good happened to you. He used to talk to me about all the shit you were doing when you and I didn't even know each other."

"He was a good friend."

"He was just, like, so invested in how your career was going. Dude was practically your manager. He wasn't even that much older than us."

Matty set his glass on the table, turned to Cooper. "And? Are you jealous or something?"

Ardith looked away as Cooper flinched. The pain on his face was so raw, so unexpected.

"Dude, what the fuck? Of your friendship with our dead friend?" He shook his head. "I'm just talking."

Ardith inhaled.

"And maybe I don't want to talk about him literally every time we hang out. I know he would be proud of me. I know how much he cared about how I was doing. Honestly, all this shit only makes me feel guilty for not knowing how bad things were with him until it was too late."

"Cohen—"

"I'm gonna grab you that water," Matty said to Ardith, shooting up from his seat. He was down the steps, disappearing into the crowd before they could stop him.

"Fuck," Cooper said, putting his head in his hands. "I wasn't trying to piss him off."

Ardith believed him. She'd felt it in his words. "I don't think he's mad at you. More like . . . sad."

Cooper groaned, but he stood up, too, said, "I'm gonna go check on him."

Ardith nodded. She had never seen Matty like this. And she hadn't known he'd felt that way about Eddie—guilty for something that wasn't his fault. It reminded her of what Dr. York had said about her father, how a part of him probably still unfairly blamed himself for her mother's death.

A shadow fell over Ardith. She looked up to find Simone standing above her. "Want some company?"

Ardith looked at the velvet couch that Simone had fled; Deenie, her influencer friends, and Ginny and Gia were piled on top of one another, posing and pouting as they filmed themselves on Deenie's phone.

"Sure," Ardith said, smiling.

Simone sank down gratefully, taking a small sip from the champagne flute in their hand. "What happened with Matty and Cooper? Looked kind of dramatic." They paused. "Not that that's anything new."

"Cooper brought up Eddie, and Matty got upset."

Simone rolled their eyes. "Cooper really can't help himself."

"What do you mean?"

"Anytime something good happens for Matty, Coop tries to get in his head. When Matty got *Suite 252*, Cooper threw a party for him, but it just *happened* to be on Eddie's birthday, and by the end of the night, Matty was crying in the bathroom."

"Wow."

"I'm not even sure if he knows he's doing it, but it's fucking annoying." Simone absentmindedly ran a hand through their hair, which was styled in a perfect twist-out. "They never really made sense as friends, but the Eddie stuff adds a weird layer to it all." They shrugged. "Anyway, how are you?"

"Honestly? Kind of happy to be dealing with other people's drama so I don't have to worry about my own," Ardith said with a wry smile.

"Right." Simone nodded slowly. "Did you know that release was coming out today?"

"Yeah, but it's still strange that it's out there. It was this big question for so long, and now . . . everybody just knows."

"That must feel good, though, right? That it's not something people can keep asking about now?"

"Oh, they'll still ask about it. But I know what you mean. I think it would feel better if my great-grandma was still here to talk to about it."

Simone sat back on the love seat. "I DMed you after we met, you know."

"Oh!" Ardith gave them an apologetic look. "I'm sorry—my publicist's assistant is usually the one running my accounts. I'm hardly ever online."

"I just hoped we didn't scare you off," they said, sincere. "I know we can be a lot, but you seem cool. Different than most of the people in our group. In a good way." Simone paused. "And Matty . . . he hasn't gotten close to anyone since Eddie died, but I can tell he really likes you."

Ardith felt warm inside at this confirmation from someone in his inner circle.

Simone tipped back their glass, finishing the champagne, then pulled their phone from their pocket. "I have to get going. Early dance rehearsal tomorrow." They held out the phone. "If you don't check your DMs, would you want to put your number in? My European tour starts next week, but me and you and Matty should hang when I get back."

Ardith smiled. "For sure." She keyed her number into Simone's phone and wished them a good tour. She was disappointed that they'd had to leave just as Ardith was starting to get comfortable with them, but she was also freaking out a little bit. She had just exchanged numbers with *Simone*.

As Ardith stood and looked out over the club, wondering where Matty and Cooper were, she realized, with growing anxiety, that she had to pee. She glanced over to the couch, where the other girls were still making videos, now singing along to the old Britney song pulsating through Luster. The nape of her neck started to sweat before she reminded herself that she was Ardith freaking Blackwood. She could manage a public restroom by herself.

However, that meant she had to brave the dance floor. Which was packed from corner to corner with people grinding, bodies writhing and gyrating with pure freedom. Ardith took a deep breath and waded in, maneuvering around people with a deftness she hadn't known she possessed. She occasionally got boxed in between people, or accidentally bumped against the chest of a guy who took that as interest and tried to grab her to dance, but eventually, she made it to the other side, breathing a grateful sigh when she found the restrooms.

Ardith nodded at the attendant stationed by the door with her table of gum, perfume, and lotions, and headed to the farthest stall. After she'd peed, she sat on the toilet for a while, her head in her hands. She wanted to go home, but she felt bad that she'd barely spent any time with Matty. She looked up as she saw two sets of heavily spray-tanned legs enter the stall next to her. The girls were bumping around and laughing loudly and shushing each other—over and over again. Ardith finally flushed, and when she went out to wash her hands, the attendant was eyeing her. The girls from the stall next to hers came out a couple of seconds later, eyes darting around the room; one of them rubbed her finger across the gums of her top teeth.

"Oops, think I forgot something," the other one said, tugging her friend back toward the stall. "Help me look for it?"

"No!" the bathroom attendant said, hopping off her stool. She pointed toward the restroom door. "Out."

"But we—" one of the girls began to complain.

"Now!"

They stumbled over each other, trying to be the first one out the door.

Ardith had just turned off the faucet, wondering what was going on, when the attendant glared at her. "You, too. Don't come back in my bathroom."

She blinked. "Excuse me?"

"You little girls come in here every night, thinking you can do whatever you want just because you've got some money. I am not going to lose my job because you want to play around with club drugs."

Ardith's eyes widened as she looked after the girls, then back to the attendant. "You think I was doing drugs? I don't even know them. I'm—"

"Out!" the woman barked, then muttered, "Not in my bathroom. Uh-uh. Not tonight."

Ardith stepped back out to the main room, dazed. Why would that woman assume she'd been doing drugs with them? She didn't even know the difference between club drugs and regular drugs. Had the woman known who she was, or did she look like the kind of person who would be into that? Ardith leaned against the wall, suddenly worn out. She just wanted to be home, and the thought of having to make her way back across the dance floor, touching all those random, sweaty bodies, made her want to lie down. Plus, she couldn't get the restroom attendant's voice out of her head—so accusatory, so judgmental, so sure of who Ardith was without knowing her.

She glanced to her right and saw two guys kissing. She looked away, wanting to give them what little privacy they could carve out back here. Except—was that the same blue shirt Matty had been wearing? And did the guy tangled up with him have the same haircut as Cooper?

Matty and Cooper were making out next to her.

Ardith started to walk away, but just as she'd stepped back into the crowd, she heard her name, felt a hand on her arm. She turned to find Matty, looking guilty.

"Hey, sorry. I meant to come back with that water. You good?"

"Yeah, but I'm heading out now. It's been kind of a weird night."

"Sorry," he said again.

"No, it's not you, it's just—I'll tell you later." She paused, looking over his shoulder. "I didn't know you and Cooper were . . ."

"We're not. I mean, sometimes we . . . I don't know. It's complicated. But I'm sorry you're leaving. I wanted to hang out more."

"Don't apologize. This is your night. I'll see you tomorrow."

"Let me at least walk you out," he said, turning around to motion to Cooper that he'd be back.

Ardith wasn't going to turn down help getting through that dance floor again, and she was glad to have him by her side as she texted her driver to come pick her up. "Five minutes," she said, tucking her phone back into her clutch. They were standing in an alcove off to the side of the entrance.

"If you had to rate this night on a scale of one to ten," Matty said. "Ten being best . . ."

Ardith looked at him, thoughtful. "Ten for the company, and maybe a negative one for the ambience?"

Matty laughed. "Clubs aren't your thing. Noted."

"I tried," she said, shrugging.

"Well, I haven't forgotten about my end of the deal. When can I come to church with you?"

"Whenever you feel like it. Open invitation."

Ardith's phone vibrated, confirming her driver would be pulling up in a couple of minutes. She turned to give Matty a hug, but he shook his head and took her by the arm again, leading her outside. "This is the worst part about going out," he said quietly. "You think I'm going to make you do it alone?"

The throng of people outside Luster started buzzing as soon as they emerged from the building.

"Is that Matty Cohen?" a girl in sky-high platform heels shouted.

"And Ardith Blackwood!" the girl next to her shrieked. She held up her phone to snap a photo. "Oh my god, we love you guys! We love *Suite 252*!"

Matty flashed them a heart-melting smile, but he was focused on the line of black cars and SUVs out by the curb. "Do you know which one is yours?"

"Um, let me check the license plate," Ardith said, opening her texts. "Okay, it's—"

But she stopped as Matty's grip tightened. She looked up, past the line of clubgoers, to see at least a half dozen people with cameras and phones pointed in their direction, all shouting at the same time. Words jumped out at her, overlapping so quickly she couldn't make out any of the sentences. She tried to swallow, but her throat felt like sandpaper. She closed her eyes, but that was a mistake because then, the words began to make sense:

"Matty, are you and Ardith dating?"

"Have you two made it official?"

"Is it true that Bryce Fletcher is an ass on set?"

"Ardith, what do you have to say about your family's announcement?"

Matty was still trying to pull them through, and just when Ardith thought they would make it to her waiting car without an actual incident, a voice stood out among all the rest. Loud, mocking, and snide.

"You gonna bring any of your new cousins out to the club? Or are they too 'South L.A.' for that?"

"Just ignore them," Matty said through gritted teeth. "Keep your head down."

Ardith knew to do all of this but she was overwhelmed and exhausted.

The voice continued.

"What made you give up the church for the club, Ardith? Did it get boring over there in Jesusland, or are you finally starting to follow in Mommy's footsteps? Because we all know the apple doesn't really fall far from the tree—"

Ardith whirled around, coming face-to-face with a guy in a polo shirt, holding his phone in front of him as he recorded.

"What did you say?"

He laughed. "Come on, now, you're out at a club drinking, doing drugs. Partying with Matty Cohen. But by all means, get behind the wheel of a car, Kimber—I mean, Ardith." He smirked.

Ardith's mind went blank and then, suddenly, all she saw was red.

Matty tried to pull her away, but she jerked out of his grasp, lunging forward.

"I wasn't even drinking, asshole!" she shouted, trying to shove the phone away.

He dodged her hand and held it right back in her face, still smirking. "I know this is exactly the way your mom would act when she also *hadn't been drinking,*" he said.

"Fuck you!" Ardith screamed, her hands curling into fists. "I'm nothing like her! You don't even fucking know me! *Go to hell!* And leave me and my family alone, you disgusting sack of—"

Matty's arms wrapped around Ardith's waist from behind, and she felt herself being dragged away, still sputtering. A few moments later, she was being shoved into the back of an SUV. Matty jumped in beside her and slammed the door, breathing hard.

The driver turned around, staring at them with wide eyes as he quickly shrugged back into his suit jacket. "Uh, sir, I don't think you're in the right—"

"Drive," Matty said.

"But—"

"I will pay you five hundred dollars if you get us the fuck out of here."

"Sir? I—"

"Dude, can't you see we're in a fucking crisis? *Go!*"

Ardith couldn't stop shaking.

Matty squeezed her tight against him, softly stroking her hair as the car pulled away from the curb. "You're fine," he said in a low voice. "It's gonna be okay."

But even as they drove away from Luster, Ardith knew that wasn't true. What had just come out of her mouth? She had never spoken to anyone that way. And she couldn't take it back or pretend it hadn't happened. The guy had recorded the whole thing; it would probably be online in a matter of minutes.

"Matty," she said, her voice hollow in the silent car. "What did I do?"

Hollis

By the time Hollis joined her father at the breakfast table Friday morning, she had already watched the video of her cousin three times. She felt guilty for giving it additional views, but she couldn't quite believe that was Ardith screaming—*cursing*—on camera.

Ardith had texted her the night before, a cryptic message that only said *I really messed up*. When she hadn't responded to Hollis's replies, Hollis had called her, but the phone went straight to voicemail. So had Uncle August's. But it had been clear, once she'd woken up and checked her phone, exactly what her cousin meant.

The video had been picked up by all the big gossip sites and reposted hundreds of thousands of times on social media. Some people were speculating that Ardith had flipped out because of the news about the Babineauxs. That would have been bad enough, but others were suggesting she was looking for attention and going the way of so many child actors—not to mention her mother.

"Morning," Hollis said to her father, who was sitting at the kitchen table, drinking coffee and scrolling on his tablet.

"Good morning to you." He slid the tablet aside as he looked up at her. "I'm sure you saw the latest news?"

Hollis nodded as she sat down across from him, placing her phone on the table. "I just texted Ardith, but I think her phone is still turned off." She paused. "She was right, though—what she said in the video. Why won't they just leave us alone? Everything has been so shitty since Bebe died."

"Language," Dad said, but he didn't sound as if his heart was in it. "It seems that way, doesn't it? Though if bad things happen in threes, looks like we're done here for now."

"I mean, Grandpa Abe finding out about the Babineauxs wasn't a *bad* thing, right?"

Her father winked. "That's exactly why I didn't count it."

"Oh." Hollis bit her lip. For the first time since the day her photo had leaked, she'd almost forgotten about her own brush with the blogs. There had been so much to consider, from learning about Bebe's complicated relationship with Grandpa Abe's father to finding out she was related to Orlando. And now, Ardith's very public rant.

"You look worried," Dad said.

"Just thinking . . . Did you ever wonder why Bebe never got married after she broke things off with Grandpa Abe's dad?"

He nodded. "It crossed my mind a few times. She was so beautiful and talented, I guess I thought she must have chosen to be alone."

"But she loved love."

"Yes, she did. She was really happy when all of us grandkids found our people and settled down. I'm sure she had her pick of men over the years."

Hollis hesitated. "But . . . what if she was so hurt by what happened with Michael Babineaux that she could never let herself get close to anyone again?"

Her father looked at her carefully. "Bebe and Michael split up when Grandpa Abe was a baby. She lived a long life and met a lot of people after him. I think it's pretty obvious now that there was plenty about her we didn't know. You can never know everything about anyone."

"So, you think she had other relationships?"

"Maybe. The point is, she eventually healed from what went down with her and Grandpa Abe's dad. It was messy and difficult, but she did what was best for her." He took another sip of coffee. "Any reason this is on your mind?"

"I guess I just think she was pretty brave. For trusting herself more than anyone else."

"Sometimes I think we won't ever know just how fearless she had to be to get to where she was. To get *us* to where we are."

Hollis's phone buzzed; she did a double take as she looked at the screen.

Hey, it's Orlando. You got some time to talk later?

She stared at the text. Was he pissed about the press release? She thought it had been fair and inclusive, but Hollis knew, maybe more than anyone, how easy it was to piss off Orlando. Before she could overthink it, she texted back:

Want to come over after school?

He was already going to be on her side of town, and the news was still fresh—it probably wasn't the best day to be a Blackwood and a Babineaux seen talking in public. Still, she wondered if he was going to think she was trying to show off, send a message by inviting him into her home. But he wrote back right away:

Send me your address. I'll text when I'm on my way

Hollis looked up. "Uh, I hope it's okay that I invited Orlando over later?"

Dad squinted as he rolled the name over in his head. "Orlando. Why does that sound familiar?"

"He's one of the Babineauxs. You know, the one who's friends with Dwayne and pretty much hates me?"

"Right. And he's coming here?"

Hollis shrugged. "We'll see if he actually shows."

Orlando showed.

"I was going to wait until you came back to school," he said when she opened the door. He was still wearing his Dupree Academy uniform. "But it started to seem like that was never going to happen."

"Good afternoon to you, too," Hollis said flatly. He stepped inside and she shut the door behind him. "We could have texted, you know."

"I hate texting. It's easier to talk to people in person. That way the meaning doesn't get lost." Orlando spun around slowly as he walked through the foyer. "Of course you have one of those big-ass staircases."

"Do you want something to eat?"

"I've seen what y'all call snacks," he said, holding his hands up. "I'm good on that. Could take some water, though."

He followed her to the kitchen and wandered over to the glass doors, looking out back. "How often you use that?"

She glanced over her shoulder. "The pool? Maybe once a week or so? More in the summer. It's expensive to heat up."

Orlando scoffed as she handed him the glass of water. "Don't tell me y'all worry about that kind of stuff?"

"Money is still money," she said. "You don't just stop thinking about it because you have it."

"I'm just saying, with a house like this, doesn't seem like you'd need to worry about much."

Hollis took a deep breath, trying to stay calm. She didn't want a repeat of, well, nearly all of their previous interactions. "What did you want to talk about? The press release? I didn't write it."

He took a long drink, then set the glass gently on the island, as if he was afraid of breaking it. "That's not why I'm here. Dwayne's a mess."

"Okay." Hollis crossed her arms. "What does that have to do with me?"

Orlando rolled his eyes. "Pretty sure you know it has everything to do with you."

She gave him a long look. "Do you know everything that happened?"

"Yeah. Listen, those guys have always been assholes. That's part of the reason I never wanted Dwayne to quit the team. I'd lose my shit if I had to deal with them on my own." He paused. "But after he told me what happened . . . Man, if it were me, I don't think I could still train with those guys."

"But you were there, right? The day they found the picture?"

"I was, but I swear I didn't see what they were looking at. As soon as they took his phone, I walked away." He sighed. "Those guys are idiots, but even I didn't think they'd go that low They knew exactly how bad this would be for you. It's fucked up. Cruel. You didn't deserve that, Hollis."

She stared at him. She didn't think anything could surprise her after the month she'd just been through, but Orlando taking her side left her speechless.

"And I know Dwayne was stupid about how he handled the whole thing. Like, really stupid. But I've never seen him like this."

"Like what?" she asked slowly.

"Basically, he can't talk or think about anything else. He's always checking for messages from you, talking about you. He's been skipping out on training. He's not even eating like he usually does."

"So, only one Tommy's burger instead of two?"

"Hollis, I'm being serious. He's taking this pretty hard."

"Well, whose fault is that? I didn't tell him to keep a photo he should have deleted."

"He feels like shit about it. Like, top regret of all time." Orlando took in a breath, then loudly exhaled. "Look, I should probably let him tell you this, but you're the most important person to him outside of his family. He really fucking cares about you, and it's eating him up that he hurt you, knowing you're so mad."

Hollis's heart squeezed. She'd known Dwayne felt that way, and he was her most important person, too. But she'd never expected him to admit it to Orlando.

"I'm not mad. I mean, not anymore . . . I don't think." She paused. "He just really let me down. He didn't care enough about my feelings to tell me what was going on for, like, weeks. To know he was hiding that from me the whole time . . ."

"I get it. And I'm not trying to make you forgive him before you're ready. But I just thought you should know. Since we're *family* and all."

She refilled his glass from the dispenser on the refrigerator and slid it back over. "I can't believe you're here right now."

"I'm tired of seeing Dwayne mope around. It's not cute." He shrugged. "Plus, Great-Uncle Eli won't stop going on about how we're related to the *Blackwoods* and that we need to stick together."

Hollis leaned against the counter. "So, I guess everyone at school is talking about the press release?"

The media outlets certainly were. Since the release had gone out, countless articles and think pieces had dissected the families' news—all within the last day. But despite how many people were discussing it, they were all trying to connect the same story: What it meant that Bebe had never publicly acknowledged her son's family, who were living an undeniably different life than the Blackwoods, with their various avenues of wealth and fame.

Orlando nodded, turning the glass around in his hands. "They keep asking how we're related."

Hollis hadn't thought about how this news might give her yet another reason to be at the forefront of Dupree gossip, but maybe that was a good thing. If people were talking about this, that means they weren't talking about her photo.

"Well, do you know?" she asked Orlando.

"Yeah, second cousins, according to my parents." He paused and closed his eyes, as if he were doing equations. "Geena is my grandma, and she's your grandpa's sister. Half, because they have the same dad but not mom. Anyway, that makes your grandpa my great-uncle. So, we're second cousins. Technically half second cousins."

"Wow. You told everyone that?"

"Mostly I told them to mind their own fucking business." He cleared his throat. "I know it's public, but I didn't know how you wanted to, uh, talk about it. Or if you did at all."

Hollis looked at him. "You think I'm embarrassed or something?"

"I mean, I dunno." For the first time since she'd known him, Orlando appeared to be truly uncomfortable. "That day your grandparents had us all over wasn't what I'd call a happy little family reunion."

"Not at all, but . . . you thought we were ashamed?"

"There was a pretty clear divide."

"Hey, Gabe was going pretty hard at us."

"I think he was worried y'all were going to judge us. That you thought you were better than us because you have all this," he said, spreading his arms around.

"I promise you, *no one* in my family would think that. And it felt like you were doing your best not to appreciate any of the effort we were making. My grandma is a lot, but I've never seen her be that nice to anyone she didn't think could do something for her. We were all trying really hard because we knew how much it meant to Grandpa Abe."

Orlando nodded. "Great-Uncle Eli was pretty upset about how it turned out. He really likes your grandpa."

"So, this is it? We announce that we're family, but we never get together again?" She sighed. "We don't sit around having fancy tea parties all the time, or judging other people's lives. We're actually pretty normal when you get to know us."

"I think maybe it's harder for us. It's one thing to hear rumors that you might be related to famous people and a totally different thing to be in their house, seeing how they get to live every day."

"But we didn't choose this. Bebe worked really hard, and Grandpa Abe worked really hard, and my parents—"

"You may not have chosen it, but you still get to live this life. Look around at your house, and imagine what mine looks like. It's not a shack or anything—my parents keep it up nice. But it's a small two-bedroom, and our backyard is mostly a patch of dead grass, and we all share a bathroom. I bet you have at least five. Don't you?"

"Seven," she mumbled.

"See?"

"See what?"

"Y'all are rich," he said, laughing.

"I'm pretty sure that was never up for debate with you," Hollis replied coolly. "You remind me of it every chance you get."

"Because you try to brush it off every chance *you* get."

"What do you want me to do, Orlando? Wear a T-shirt that tells everyone my family's net worth?"

"I want you to be honest about the fact that you have a fuckload of money. And stop acting embarrassed by it if it's not such a big deal."

"My *parents* have money. Not me."

Orlando blew out air through his nose. "Why do you always do that?"

"Do what?"

"Every time someone mentions the fact that you guys are loaded, you get all defensive."

Hollis frowned. "I do not."

"Yes, you do. And sure, it's your parents' money, but you benefit directly from it. You have a trust fund and you're going to inherit property and you are always going to be okay, Hollis. I don't have that kind of life and I never will, and it is what it is, but—" He stopped, shaking his head.

"But what?"

"But at least I own it. Y'all keep saying how hard your great-grandma worked to get you where you are today. That means something, same as my great-grandpa working his way up to power plant manager before he died. But when we talk about money, you always try to downplay what y'all have like it's not a big deal, and I dunno, man. It doesn't make you look more down-to-earth, it kinda makes you seem ungrateful."

Hollis didn't know what to say. Dwayne had told her a bit about Orlando's feelings on how he grew up and what it meant to go to Dupree, but it was different to hear it directly from him. Stated so plainly, so matter-of-fact, that she had no choice but to listen.

"I didn't come over here to lecture you, or whatever. But people are gonna be asking questions and—I guess we need to be able to talk to each other about this stuff before we start discussing it with other people."

It wasn't easy to digest what he was saying, but Hollis knew she had to at least try. And that, unfortunately, he might have a point. The Babineaux family added a whole new layer to what it meant to be a Blackwood. She couldn't ignore that forever.

"Where do you keep the movie theater?" Orlando asked, looking around as if it might be hiding in a drawer. "Dwayne's is dope, but he said yours is even better."

"It is. Come on, I think my dad is watching something in there now. Nothing makes him happier than showing off that room," Hollis said, leading him out of the kitchen.

Watts
1965

"Boy, get away from that window."

Abe darted back as soon as his grandmother spoke, the living room curtains fluttering in his wake. Mama was always so calm when she scolded Abe, yet he listened to her right away. Every time. Never mind that Blossom had already told him twice. Abe always seemed to listen to her mother, perhaps because she had been around all the time when he was younger, the one who had disciplined him more.

Mama eased into the faded floral armchair with a heavy sigh. Blossom had tried not to dwell on how her mother was aging, but it was hard not to notice these days. Before, when she'd spent so much time back East, she'd noticed only when Mama had let enough time lapse between dyeing her hair that the silver roots began to show. Now that she was permanently back in Los Angeles, she had more time to pay attention to these things. Like how Mama hadn't picked up a bottle of hair dye in years and now wore her head of silvery-white hair in a thick braid down her back. Or how she moved slower, taking a full minute just to get to the phone in the next room. Blossom supposed it shouldn't have been a surprise— Flossie had turned seventy in January, and she wasn't in the best health. A few years ago, the doctor had diagnosed her with diabetes, and she complained frequently about her swollen, arthritic joints.

But she was still the matriarch, the boss to everyone who lived under her roof. And she was calm as ever in the face of what was happening in the streets—what had been happening for nearly twenty-four hours now, as night fell again in Watts. The news reporters were calling it a riot, but that word didn't seem right. It was hard to parse exactly what had happened, but Blossom knew for sure the police were at the center of it. Which was no surprise—sometimes she wondered if the Los Angeles Police Department had any other job but harassing the community of Watts. And it was no coincidence that the neighborhood was mostly Black. That morning's *Los Angeles Times* said it had all started with a traffic stop, the police department's specialty.

"Can't believe that sister of yours still ain't called nobody," Flossie said as she propped her thick ankles up on the ottoman.

Blossom had stood up when her mother entered the room, hopeful she had news about Sybil. Now she sat back down, perched on the edge of the sofa. "Mama, what if she's not all right?"

"Sybil too smart to get caught up in all that." Mama sounded pragmatic, but when Blossom looked at her, she saw a flicker of worry in her eyes. She blinked, and it was gone. "As long as she stay away from Parker's boys, she'll be all right."

Blossom had never met a Black Angeleno who had anything nice to say about Police Chief Bill Parker, but it was possible Flossie Blackwood hated him the most of anyone. She had been known to throw objects at the television when he appeared onscreen, and she regularly referred to him as "that despicable piece of trash." Blossom could only imagine what Parker would have to say about the current unrest. For now, though, they were worried about Sybil. They hadn't heard from her sister since she'd left the house the previous evening, when she'd taken the bus to meet her friend Elaine at the movies. They'd telephoned Elaine when they woke this morning to find Sybil hadn't come home; Elaine said she hadn't heard from her since they'd parted ways after the film.

Blossom's hands twisted back and forth with anxiety. Sybil may have been her little sister, but she was the reliable one. It wasn't like her to just up and disappear—especially not when something so enormous, so destructive was going on in their own neighborhood.

"I'm going out to look for her, Mama," Blossom said, standing. "I can't take this waiting anymore."

"You sure you want to do that?"

"She's my sister."

"And you got other responsibilities." Flossie didn't have to look at Abe for Blossom to know what she meant. Slowly, she sat back down. "Stop worrying, girl. I called the hospitals. They don't have her. She fine."

POP!

POP!

POP!

Blossom, Abe, and Flossie simultaneously flinched at the ring of gunshots. They were distant, but no less upsetting; Blossom couldn't keep track of how many they'd heard by then. The newspaper had reported that a thousand "rioters" had attacked the police, but with the LAPD's track record, it was hard to believe it wasn't, in fact, the other way around.

Abe leaped to the sofa, scooting close to Blossom. She wrapped her arms around him, rubbing his shoulders as she murmured that it was going to be all right. Just as Mama getting older unnerved her, the fact that Abe would be eleven next month and was nearly as tall as her was difficult to grasp. As was the realization that Blossom herself had, somehow, become thirty-eight years old. It felt as if it were only yesterday that she was cradling her brand-new son in the hospital, or watching him splash around in the bathtub with his rubber ducks, or teaching him to ride a bicycle. It was only a couple of years ago that he'd crawled into bed with her at two in the morning, awakened by a nightmare about *The Birds*. He'd bothered her to go see it at the theater for days after it opened, insisting he was old enough to see an Alfred Hitchcock picture. Now, as then, she didn't like seeing him upset . . . but it felt nice to be needed. After being away from him so much when he was younger, she cherished any chance to be here for him.

"We okay," Mama said, absentmindedly massaging her wrist. "We okay."

Blossom tried to think of anything to distract them from the violence going on just blocks away, from the fact that Sybil was still nowhere to be found. But the only thing that mattered to Blossom was family.

Well, family and work. But there wasn't so much of the latter to concern herself with these days.

"Mama, did you see they're making a jazz film with Sammy Davis Jr. in the lead? The cast is nearly all Black. It's an independent."

"Sammy Davis Jr.," Mama scoffed. "He still running around with all those white men, calling themselves the Clan?"

Blossom ignored her like she always did when Mama began disparaging people in the industry. These were actors she hoped would be her co-stars one day—though she knew that, at her age, the clock was rapidly ticking on her career. She felt it every time her talent agent told her the casting directors were looking for someone younger, or when he suggested she lie about her age if she was called back for a screen test.

"I like Sammy Davis Jr.," Abe said thoughtfully. "He's a good dancer."

"I agree," Blossom said, winking at him. Then, to her mother, "The cast is Easterners, mostly. Ossie Davis, Cicely Tyson. And it's supposed to be a truly musical film. I heard they're going to book Louis Armstrong."

"Mm-hmm."

Blossom didn't know why she attempted to talk to Mama about work anymore. Just as quickly as her career had grown in the late fifties and early sixties, the last couple of years had seen it come to a steady halt. *Love, Gertie* had received fantastic reviews, praising Blossom's screen presence, her dancing and singing, and her shared chemistry with each of her scene partners. Blossom had reveled in this acclaim, sure that it was the start to a burgeoning career in film, despite what had happened with Archie Melamed. Surely casting directors and studio executives were reading the same reviews she was, and even if there weren't many roles for Black actresses, she had to have been on the list for the ones there were. Perhaps someone would even create a role just for her.

But as much as Blossom was unwilling to admit it, her dream, once so vibrant and sure, had faded in the years since. There had been parts after her big role, but nothing like Gertie. Each time she spoke with her agent, he said the same things: that she was a dedicated actress, that her perfor- mance in *Love, Gertie* was exquisite, that one day the right project would come to them. But the studios hadn't called. The casting directors weren't interested. The supporting roles she did book sometimes allowed her a scene or two to shine, but most of them were hardly more substantial than a background actor, with one or two lines to move the plot along. Usually, the parts were so small and dull that she sometimes wondered why she even bothered spending a whole day getting across town to audition for them. She had finally admitted defeat and taken a part-time secretarial job to bring in regular pay, a choice that still embarrassed her each time some- one brought up her film career—or what was left of it.

Lately, she had found herself wondering if Clifton Thompson had been right. His words came back to haunt her often. Especially since, once she'd parted ways with Archie, her career stalled. She had loved Archie, deeply. She would have loved him even if they had not worked together . . . but that was the whole point, wasn't it? That she had fallen for him after seeing how committed he was to the work, how invested in the storytelling of theater and film, in the achievements of his actors. Their collaboration had been stimulating and intense, and she missed that as much as she missed him.

She'd often feared he was the only person to see something special in her, to want to nurture her talent. But deep down inside, she didn't believe that was true. Someone else, maybe more than just someone, must have connected with her performance enough to want to see her onscreen again in a leading role. But if those people were out there, they weren't brave enough to fight for her. Same as Archie.

Flossie reached for her tobacco and rolling papers in the drawer of the side table. "Well, an independent film ain't gonna pay nothing, and it ain't gonna make nothing, either. You can do better."

Mama had a way of making Blossom believe she'd wasted all these years in the business while simultaneously declaring every project, director, and co-star to be beneath her. It was a confusing message, one that made her repeatedly question if she was doing the right thing, continuing to look for work when there was none to be found. None for her, anyway.

"Mama . . ." she began, before trailing off.

"What you got to say, girl?"

Blossom hesitated. Every conversation like this eventually left her with the same question on her lips—the one she'd never wanted to ask aloud, for fear of how her mother might respond.

But perhaps now was the time. With the danger outside, she didn't know how long they would be stuck in here together—nor how much longer she could sit quietly with her thoughts.

"Do you think I should quit? Acting, I mean."

Flossie's hands paused on her rolling papers. Next to Blossom, Abe was silent, looking between the two of them.

"Why you asking me that now?" Mama finally said.

"Because I don't know the answer myself. And you've been where I am. You know how the business works."

Flossie finished rolling her cigarette, licked the edge and sealed it, then stuck it in the corner of her mouth, lighting the end with a match. She inhaled, closing her eyes for a moment, then exhaled a thick stream of smoke. "Blossom, you know I can't tell you what to do with your life no more than my mama could tell me what to do with mine. You a grown woman now."

Blossom didn't always feel like it. She and Abe should have their own home by now instead of still living with Mama and Sybil. With the exception of her time in New York—where she'd first stayed in a boardinghouse, then moved into the apartment Archie had rented for her so she could be comfortable and they would have a place to be together—she had never lived without her mother. At times, this made her feel as if she hadn't actually started living her life, despite the fact that she had a son and a résumé that proved otherwise. But nights like tonight, she was grateful to have Flossie so close. She was the levelheaded, reassuring force they needed when things were so tumultuous outside. And, perhaps this was how it was always supposed to work out—Blossom keeping her family close. Even if she did one day earn enough to purchase a house for her and Abe, there was no question she would take Mama and Sybil with them. They were her anchors in life; they always had been.

"But what would you do if you were in my position?"

"We already been over this. I was in your position. I chose y'all."

Outside, a group was running down the sidewalk, speaking loudly but not loud enough for Blossom to hear what they were saying. She held her breath as their footsteps scuffled on the pavement, silently hoping they would keep moving. What if someone came up to the house? Or shot at it?

"Mother," Abe spoke up, looking at Flossie, "what do you mean, you were in Mama's position?"

"Baby, you know Mother was an entertainer before she had me and your aunts," Blossom said. "Remember how we talked about the old days of Hollywood?"

Abe nodded, but he looked as if he was still turning some questions over in his mind. Throughout the years, he'd shown interest in performing as well, from the parts he'd won in grade school plays to the way he would sit in front of television and movie screens, enraptured, for as long or as often as they would let him. Blossom would never forget the first time he saw her onscreen; he'd gasped so loudly she thought he was choking. His eyes had shone with wonder as he'd looked at his mother, magnified at the front of the theater. He'd whispered, "Mama," and reached out a hand, as if he could touch her all the way from his seat. It had brought tears to her eyes; she'd never be able to make up for all the time she'd spent away from him, but seeing how much he loved watching her act, how special that was to him, had made her believe maybe it was worth it.

Now she wasn't so sure.

"Why didn't you keep working in Old Hollywood, Mother?"

"It was real tough back then. Wasn't no roles for us unless we wanted to play maids, butlers, and drivers to white people. And we had to fight each other for those parts. I didn't want it. Not bad enough to keep working for people who didn't respect me." Flossie's eyes cut over to Blossom. "People in the business respect your mama . . . It's just the ones who making the decisions ain't real smart about who they decide to take a chance on."

Abe considered this, quiet for a few moments before he turned to his mother. "You really gonna quit acting, Mama?"

"I don't know, baby." She paused, looking down at her hands. "What do you think I should do?"

Flossie huffed. Blossom knew Mama disagreed with the way she spoke to Abe sometimes.

"You love acting," he said thoughtfully.

"I do."

"And you're real good at it."

"Thank you, baby."

"Mr. Peters always tells us that if there's something we like doing, we should work at it as hard as we can, until we get real good. But you're already good at acting, so I don't think you should quit," he said with a definitive nod.

Blossom squeezed him to her, kissing the top of his head. How strange it was to hear such encouragement from the boy who was walking around with Michael Babineaux's entire face. It was impossible to ignore how much he looked like him, from the shape of his nose to the dimple in his chin. Blossom had been relieved when they'd decided to move to Watts, as she'd always been worried about running into Michael in the old neighborhood. She feared that Abe might recognize himself in his father if he saw him, but more than that, she didn't want him to hear any of the things people might be whispering about his parents. She'd been spared from learning the identity of her father as a child, but people weren't so proper these days; Abe might not be so lucky.

"Go change into your pajamas," she said. "I'll be there in a few minutes to tuck you in. And stay away from the window."

Once Abe had left the room, Mama looked at her. "Now what?"

"Ma'am?"

"You asked his advice, and he don't want you to quit."

"I wasn't asking his advice. I wanted to know what he thinks."

Her mother shook her head, eyes still on Blossom. "You remember Fredi Washington?"

"Mama, of course. She was my favorite actress when I was little."

"Girl, you ain't got to remind me. You wouldn't talk about nothing but *Imitation of Life* for a month after I took you to see it." Flossie dragged off her cigarette. "You ever wonder what happened to her? Why you didn't see her in much after that picture?"

"I suppose I never thought about it. She was so talented, and absolutely lovely, too."

"Even so, they found a way to keep her out. Said she was too light-skinned to play Negro roles, but they wouldn't cast her in leading parts with white people, either. She left the business 'cause she couldn't find work." Mama stopped for a moment, her gaze holding steady. "What I'm trying to say is, Fredi had her moment. And you had yours with *Gertie*. Maybe this is how it's supposed to be, Blossom. Maybe some little Negro girl seen you up onscreen and that made her want to be an actress. And maybe, because of you, she'll get a little further than you did someday. Just like you got further than me."

Blossom nodded, looking down, trying to blink away the tears before Mama saw them. She had asked, and Mama had answered; even if it wasn't what she'd wanted to hear, perhaps it was what she needed.

A violent crash sounded outside then, no more than a block away. Blossom couldn't identify the noise, and she wondered if the scuffling footsteps from before had anything to do with it. She stood up quickly, said, "I'm going to check on Abe."

He was sitting on his bed in his pajamas, slowly paging through the Spider-Man comic he'd begged her to buy him last week. He looked up as she walked in. "Mama, is Aunt Sybil coming home?"

"Yes," she said with a confidence she wished she felt. "I'm sure she'll be back by the time you wake up."

After Blossom had tucked him under the quilt and kissed him good night, she stood outside his door in the hallway and closed her eyes.

Sybil, come home. Please, please come home.

Blossom wasn't a religious person but she hoped that, wherever she was, Sybil could hear her prayers.

Sybil came home.

At three o'clock in the morning, with disheveled hair and rumpled clothes and a tearstained face that Blossom tenderly took between her hands before she embraced her sister as tight as she could.

"Oh, Syb." Blossom smoothed down Sybil's hair. "Are you hurt?"

Sybil shook her head and began silently crying, her tears soaking the shoulder of Blossom's nightgown. Blossom held her until the sobbing slowed, grateful Mama was sound asleep so she didn't have to see how upset Sybil was. Then she drew her sister a hot bath, made her a cup of warm milk with honey, and perched on the edge of the tub as Sybil explained that she'd been on her way home, walking back from the bus stop the previous evening, when she got caught in the ruckus outside. The police had stopped her for no reason, forced her up against the side of a building with a group of strangers, handcuffed them, and made them stand there for an hour before they took them down to the police station.

Blossom gaped. "Did they arrest you?"

"No, but I was—I didn't know what they were going to do. I told them I was coming from a movie, but they wouldn't hear it. They kept saying . . ." She hugged her knees up to her naked chest, wrapping her arms around them. She looked so small in the tub, and for the second time that night, Blossom held back her own tears, imagining her little sister in handcuffs. The thought made her ill. "They kept calling us *nigger*. Show me your hands, nigger. Get up against the wall, nigger. And accusing us of being prostitutes and dope dealers. It was the—it was the worst thing that's ever happened to me. They wouldn't even let me call you."

Sybil began to cry again, and Blossom didn't know what to do but stroke her hair and tell her it was going to be okay.

"They held us for over a day," Sybil sobbed. "I thought I was going to die there. Or that they'd—"

"Shh, shhhh. It's okay, Syb. You're home now."

Abe and Flossie had their own bedrooms, tiny as they were, and Blossom and Sybil shared a room again, just as they had when they were girls. That night, Blossom crawled into her sister's bed, and as she embraced her from behind, she realized she had no idea what she would have done if Sybil hadn't returned. It frightened her to think of what could have happened to her sister, sickened her that they should consider themselves lucky the police hadn't done worse.

As if she were watching a film reel of her life, Blossom thought of all the times Sybil had been there for her. For so many years now, her baby sister had been a constant, for her and then Abe, allowing Blossom to live the life she had always dreamed of. Perhaps this was all a sign, that Blossom was meant to be home, to give back to her family the way they had given to her. She could still audition for parts, when they were worthwhile, but . . . perhaps Mama was right. Was the decline of her career a sign that she should accept this is where she belonged? Perhaps this persistent rejection from the entertainment industry would be easier to receive if Blossom made peace with it first.

Her sister's breathing slowly steadied, then deepened. And, finally, Sybil fell asleep in Blossom's arms, just as the sun began to rise over Watts.

Later that day, as Sybil slept, Flossie, Blossom, and Abe sat in front of the television, watching the news. The whole program was focused on their neighborhood. Video played of bloodied people being manhandled by the police, running out of stores with their arms full of food and clothing, and, in some cases, being chased by police officers who gripped batons. Blossom closed her eyes as she thought of Sybil, who'd been in the middle of it all.

"What are they doing?" Abe asked, pointing to a couple of young men who were bursting from the front doors of a market as people rushed by them on their way in.

"Looting," Flossie grumbled, shaking her head. "Should be ashamed of themselves, stealing from people like that."

"Or maybe they need the food to feed their families," Blossom said carefully. Sometimes it was best to keep her mouth shut when she disagreed with Flossie about issues like this. She'd assumed things would change the older she got, and yet here she was, close to forty years old, still biting her tongue around her mother. But she didn't want Abe to hear only one side of situations like these. There was always more to the story than what the media reported.

"They need the food, they can work for it like everybody else," Flossie said without missing a beat.

"Where are the jobs, Mama? Do you know Mr. Franklin down the street has been looking for work for the past *year*? He said he'd take anything, but there's nothing out there. They hire up all the white people first, no matter how much experience we have. What's left for us?"

Blossom had found herself growing increasingly frustrated with the state of things in both her community and the world over the past few years; the loss of jobs and increase in poverty, the rampant abuse from police, and the country being in the middle of yet another war had made her feel helpless—and then ashamed for feeling so helpless—until Sybil had intervened one day.

"You can't just keep moaning about all of the problems and expect things to change," she'd said. "You could at least get out in the streets with everyone else."

So, a couple of years ago, Blossom had tagged along with her little sister and her friends to a protest one afternoon. She had found it exhilarating, empowering to march with like-minded people who wanted better conditions for all. Each time she marched, holding up hand-painted signs that advocated for equality, for peace, for jobs, she felt as if she had done her civic duty. Even if her voice was a tiny one among millions, she was proud to add it to the movement.

But when she saw what was happening now, Blossom felt helpless yet again. As she watched her own neighborhood falling apart because of these long-ignored issues, she wondered if the protests would ever result in real progress. It had taken so long for the government to pass the laws against discrimination, and yet here they were, once again watching Black people being mistreated. She felt, at times, that her activism was similar to her career—never knowing when to give up because things could change at any instant.

Flossie started to respond but grimaced instead when Police Chief

Parker came onscreen. Blossom pursed her lips, waiting for him to speak; the sound of his voice made her feel as if bugs were crawling over her skin. The reporters kept calling the unrest a riot, pondering how long it would take the police officers to restore order in the neighborhood.

"In the first place," Parker said, shaking his head, "a great number of those people came from areas in the country where they were further dislocated, much more seriously dislocated than they are here."

Mama narrowed her eyes. *"Those people?"*

"We didn't ask these people to come here," he continued defensively. "Certainly, they want our total community to adjust itself to a small segment that has suddenly come in and taken over a section."

"Someone needs to come get this fool," Mama said, slapping the air as if Parker's face were in front of her. "According to his rules, Los Angeles only for white people. Don't like that some of us didn't stay in the South, so he just hired all the good old boys who come from there to try to keep us in line. We see you, Parker."

Blossom couldn't stand to listen to a minute more of his drivel. She stood up, smoothing her hand down the front of her slacks. "Abe, let's go make some lunch."

He turned to face her from his cross-legged position on the rug in front of the television set. "Aww, come on, Mama. Can't I keep watching?"

Blossom started to say no, but Mama cut her off.

"Let him watch, girl," she said in a low voice. "You want to ask him his opinion all the time, like he's an adult? Well, then he needs to hear what they really think about us."

"Fine." Blossom started to walk out of the room.

"Chief Parker," said a reporter on television, "how did a traffic stop of a Watts resident lead to all this trouble?"

Blossom paused in the doorway as Parker's answer came slicing through their home.

"One person threw a rock," he said, "and then, like monkeys in a zoo, others started throwing rocks."

"*Monkeys?* How do you like this rock, you goddamn piece of—"

THUNK!

Blossom stepped out of the room just as Mama's heavy glass ashtray hit the wall.

Ardith

Ardith had never wanted to stay in bed more than she did on Sunday morning.

She'd had bad days before—bad weeks, even. When her mother had been using and everything felt like it was falling apart; when she was auditioning after *You Can Say That Again* had ended and casting directors couldn't see past her longtime role as the precocious child; when she'd realized Bebe's health was rapidly deteriorating.

But this was different. This was because of something she'd done, something she'd brought on herself. She hadn't even tried to avoid the headlines this time:

GOOD GIRL GONE BAD:
ARDITH BLACKWOOD LOSES CONTROL

TINSLEY LASHES OUT

KIMBERLY ARNOLD'S DAUGHTER INSISTS
SHE IS "NOTHING LIKE HER MOTHER"

She had watched the video, over and over, the morning after the incident. Trying to understand how she had gotten to that point. Wishing more than anything that she could take back her words. She didn't even recognize the girl in that video.

The day after the club, she hadn't been needed on set until the afternoon, and she'd spent every moment of her free time in her trailer, trying to figure out the next steps with her publicity team. Because of the antagonistic way she'd been approached and continually provoked, they'd decided an apology wasn't necessary. But no one could deny it was a bad look, and they'd agreed it was best for her to keep a low profile until it blew over—no more volunteering or charity events or nights out with Matty. She would only go to work, and church if she wanted to. Just like before. Matty had tried to cheer her up, and the crew and other actors hadn't mentioned the incident, but from the soft smiles they gave her, the gentle way they all moved around her, she knew everyone had seen it. Everyone at Swanson Avenue would have seen it, too. Ardith could only imagine what Pastor and Sister Robinson thought of her now.

Swanson Avenue had always been healing, a place she could turn to for solace and compassion—but this was different than needing support after Bebe had died. She'd made a public embarrassment of herself, shouting things she'd never before said in her life. Things she hadn't known she was capable of thinking, let alone saying. Would they still accept her?

Ardith pulled herself out of bed, plodding down the hallway to the kitchen. She startled when she heard her father call her name from the dining room; he often used it as his unofficial office on nights and weekends, but she hadn't known he was home today. She stepped tentatively into the doorway, taking in the file folders and thick stacks of paper spread out around him.

"How are you doing?" Daddy asked, setting down the yellow highlighter he'd been using.

"Not great."

"Yeah, I figured. You're staying home today?"

"No, I should go."

"You don't have to, you know."

"I know. But I think I should." She started to walk toward the kitchen but stopped, slowly turning around. Her father was still looking at her. "Daddy, I'm sorry. For what I said."

This was the first time they'd had a chance to speak about it alone, and she was nervous. Ashamed.

"You don't need to apologize, Ardie. We all lose our temper sometimes."

"But that's exactly what they were trying to get me to do. And I fell for it."

"You're human."

"But what I said about Mommy—"

"Ardie, it's okay." He hesitated, then, "I don't expect you to be perfect. I never have. The pressure you're under, all the time—for not just being you, but being a Blackwood and Kimberly's daughter . . . I know it's a lot."

Ardith swallowed.

"I've tried to make things easier by shielding you from what was going on when your mother was sick, and then sending you to talk to someone after she died . . . but I know it hasn't always been enough. I'm sorry for that, Ardie. And I love you."

Ardith hadn't realized how much she needed to hear all of that until it was out there in the open, sitting between them like the contents of a dam that had just been released. She felt seen, in a way she never had been by her father—in a way that made it seem as if she finally had permission to breathe.

"I love you, too, Daddy."

He nodded, but she couldn't help noticing the faraway look in his eyes. The look that made her wonder if he would ever truly be able to forgive her for the things she'd said.

Ardith entered the vestibule of the church, stopping for a moment to take a couple of deep breaths. So far, she hadn't made eye contact with anyone, but she felt their stares, assumed the low murmurs must be about her. Part of her wanted to turn back around, to get in her car and drive home where she could be alone again. But she was here. People had seen her already, and if she left now, that would only make everyone think they had a right to judge her.

She held her head high, pushed her shoulders back, and walked into the sanctuary as if nothing had happened. Slowly, she let her gaze drift to the other churchgoers, the people who had known her since she was a child, who had never seen her be anything but perfect. Some of them looked away immediately, as if the Ardith from the video might rub off on them if they met her eyes. Others watched her curiously, like they didn't know if or when she might snap again. But others offered up friendly smiles, kind looks. Sister Singer pulled her in for a tight hug, said, "God bless you, baby," in her ear.

Still, as much as Ardith had hoped she would feel better, she only felt worse once the service started. She was in her favorite pew, but as soon as she'd sat down, Sister Arrington had given her the stink-eye and made a big show of turning away when Ardith looked over. Next to her, Lexie gave her a small smile but quickly stared down at her lap. Ardith assumed that when Donnie began playing the opening notes of "Down by the Riverside," it would help lift her spirits, but instead, it only made her feel guilty for being in the presence of such joy. It was one of her favorite gospel songs, one she'd grown up with, but hearing it now reminded her of Bebe, who had especially loved the Mahalia Jackson recording and used to play it on their trips to and from church. What would Bebe have thought about the way she'd acted, the things she'd said? Bebe had worked her whole life to make the Blackwood name upstanding, impenetrable— and in just a few reckless minutes, Ardith had behaved in a way she was sure would have disappointed her.

"Gonna lay down my burden," Ardith sang and clapped along with the choir, "down by the riverside, down by the riverside, down by the riverside!"

But she felt wooden, as if she were only going through the motions. She looked at the members around her, all clapping and singing, too. Up front, Sister Robinson stood tall, the brim of her fuchsia-colored hat swaying along with her; one by one, people began to stand as well, unable to contain their enthusiasm for the Lord. Normally, their happiness would have been infectious, but today, Ardith felt nothing.

By the time Pastor Robinson began the sermon, she couldn't concentrate on anything except what she'd said outside the club. Around her, the entire congregation was engaged: heads nodding, arms waving, frequent shouts of "Tell 'em, pastor!" and "Let the Lord *use* you!" Ardith, however, felt ill at the words cycling through her mind:

I'm nothing like her! Go to hell!

She was still lost in her thoughts when the service ended and the congregation began to make its way out of the sanctuary. She felt a tap on her shoulder and looked up at Lexie, who was standing, Bible tucked under her arm.

"Are you okay?" she asked, her eyebrows bunched together in concern.

Any other time, Ardith would have pasted on a bright smile, put on one of her public faces that made other people more comfortable. But today, she couldn't manage it. She shook her head, said, "Not really."

"I'm sorry," Lexie said. "I saw the video, and they never should have been hassling you like that. It's not—"

"Lexie, it's time to go," Sister Arrington snapped, swinging her purse over her shoulder. She cut a glance at Ardith before she turned to head out the other side of the row.

Sorry, Lexie mouthed, following after her mother.

Ardith waited until most of the congregation had filed out before she stood and began walking toward the doors of the church. The pastor was speaking animatedly with Deacon Miller, but Sister Robinson was standing quietly, hands clasped in front of her.

"Sister Ardith," she said, with the type of bright smile Ardith hadn't been able to conjure earlier. "I was wondering if I might pull you away for a quick chat?"

Oh no.

"I won't keep you long. I'm sure you have a moment."

Ardith didn't, really; she was supposed to meet Hollis after this. But she had a feeling she knew what the first lady was going to say, and she might as well get it over with now.

"Okay, Sister Robinson." She inhaled as they stepped out into the sunshine, feeling momentarily better with the warmth on her face.

"Beautiful day, isn't it?" the first lady said as they walked around the side of the building.

"It is," Ardith replied wanly.

Sister Robinson pulled a small key ring from the pocket of her suit skirt and unlocked a door that led to the administrative hallway. This part of the church was especially quiet on Sundays, and Ardith thought it felt a bit eerie as they walked down the corridor, Sister Robinson's heels clicking methodically against the floor.

She had never been in the first lady's office, but she wasn't surprised to find it was cozy and well-decorated. Sister Robinson's desk was long and cream-colored with curved legs and a matching chair with a powder-blue seat cushion. Across from the desk was an overstuffed couch in the same creamy color with blue and gold throw pillows placed in each corner. The walls were filled with tasteful art prints, mostly abstract renderings of Black women. A large gold cross hung on the wall above her chair. Ardith felt as if she were in one of the fancy tea rooms in Beverly Hills or Pasadena.

Sister Robinson took a seat on the couch and gestured for Ardith to join her. "Would you like some tea?"

"Thank you, but I can't stay long. I'm going to meet my cousin after this," Ardith said.

"Then I suppose I'll get right to it." The first lady cleared her throat. "Sister Ardith, you know how much we appreciate your contributions to Swanson Avenue. Your willingness to volunteer and, of course, your presence each week. However—"

"Sister Robinson," she interrupted. "Respectfully, I don't need a lecture right now. I know that what I said the other night reflects poorly on the church, and I'm sorry. I . . . I never should have come today."

The first lady frowned, and Ardith closed her eyes, composing herself as she waited for the lecture that was sure to come anyway. But then Sister Robinson's hand was on her shoulder, and when Ardith looked at her, she was smiling softly.

"I'm sorry you feel that way. Because the pastor and I sure are glad you came."

Ardith blinked. "Did you see the video?"

She pursed her lips. "I did. And I will admit, I was surprised to hear that from you."

Ardith looked down.

"But I understand it."

"You do?"

"Do you know the verse I keep returning to again and again throughout my life? John 8:7. 'So when they continued asking him, he lifted up himself, and said unto them, *He that is without sin among you, let him first cast a stone at her.*' A classic," she said with a wink. "I love that verse because it reminds me that as easy as it is to get caught up in the pursuit of perfectionism, none of us will reach the heights of our Lord and Savior. We all have our own struggles, but the truth is, some of us have more problems to deal with. And it doesn't behoove us to judge others when they are struggling."

Ardith sat completely still as she listened.

"I've known you since you were a little girl, and you've always been nothing but kind, generous, and loving to everyone around you. I've watched as you've taken on an adult career at such a young age, how you've never once strayed from that kind person as the demands in your life continued to pile up. And then, after your mother passed . . . Well, you've handled each obstacle with grace and class, just like your great-grandmother. All while living your life in the spotlight."

"But that's just it," Ardith said. "My life *isn't* mine. Whatever I do affects everyone around me—my family, the show, the church—"

"Family is there for one another during tough times. And I hope I don't have to remind you that we are your family, too," she said gently. "My dear, you know that your great-grandmother, God rest her soul, came to Swanson Avenue rather late in her life. So while I didn't know her long, I did know her well—well enough to know that all she ever wanted, from the moment I met her, was for you and your family to be happy. To maybe be spared some of the struggles she had in her own life." She smiled and patted Ardith's hand. "That's not to say, of course, that you're not going to have many of your own struggles to overcome. And when you do, we're here."

Ardith inhaled, closing her eyes again. She tried to find that feeling of connection she always experienced at Swanson Avenue—connection to the pastor and first lady, to her fellow congregants, to God. But it wasn't there.

She appreciated Sister Robinson's kind words. But even if she understood that Ardith had made a mistake, even if she really believed the girl on the video was not who Ardith truly was, Ardith knew that everyone had limits—to understanding, to forgiveness. And what if this wasn't just a simple mistake? What if the pressure became too much, if she was tempted to relieve it with a few drinks, or more? What if her anger took over again, in public? Would Sister Robinson still be here for her, so patient, so calm? Or would Ardith's support system start to fall away, start to believe she was the person the media said she was, just like what had happened with her mother?

Would she ever be able to meet the expectations of the people she cared for and also live her own life?

When she opened her eyes, Sister Robinson was still looking at her kindly, but Ardith didn't have the strength to confess her worries. Besides, she didn't want to burden the first lady after she'd been so generous. And so all she said was, "Thank you, Sister Robinson."

When Ardith had asked her father what belongings Barton Lerner had requested for the exhibit honoring her mother, he'd said the email only suggested they pull anything "poignant or memorable or authentically Kimberly." She didn't know what that meant, but she was hoping Hollis could help her figure it out.

"Thanks for doing this with me," she said.

Her cousin was across the storage unit, pushing aside dusty boxes to try to establish some sort of order. "No worries. I needed an excuse to get out of the house."

Ardith opened a box of her mother's old jewelry, digging inside to see if there was anything exhibit-worthy. All she found was a pile of costume jewelry; Mommy's real jewels were locked up at home in a safe. "You haven't gone back to school yet?"

"I think I'm going back tomorrow."

Ardith looked over her shoulder. "That's a good thing, right?"

"Yeah, I think so. It's going to be awkward no matter what, but . . . it's time."

"Have you talked to Dwayne?"

"Not since that day at my house. But you'll never guess who came over to tell me I *should* talk to him."

"Who?"

"Orlando. Our *cousin*."

"He went to your house? And didn't burn it down?"

"Actually, we ended up watching *He Got Game* with my dad, and it was, like, kind of normal?" She sighed. "Anyway, he said Dwayne is all torn up about things, but I don't know how to feel."

Ardith remained silent, letting Hollis gather her thoughts.

"It's just, nothing is simple with Dwayne. Not anymore. I can't imagine my life without him, but I don't want him to think he can get away with treating me like that." Hollis paused. "But also . . . he told me he loves me."

Ardith gasped, whipping around to face her. "And you're just now telling me?"

"I'm still freaked out by it."

"Because you love him, too?"

Hollis nudged a box with her toe. "Because I don't know if I can trust him. If I let him back in after that, what does that say about me? I keep thinking of Bebe, how she cut off Grandpa Abe's dad, even though she loved him. It seems pretty clear that love wasn't enough for her."

"Her letter sounded like maybe part of her regretted it—"

"But not enough to fix it. Not while she was alive, anyway." Hollis shrugged. "We'll never know, I guess."

Ardith paused. "I'm probably not the best person to give advice about this, considering I don't really have any friends besides you . . . and maybe Matty. But what you and Dwayne have . . . it feels like that doesn't always come around. Someone who understands you like he does, who you're comfortable with." Ardith remembered what Sister Robinson had told her earlier that day. "I've been thinking a lot about what Bebe did. And I'm wondering if maybe some of the sacrifices she made, like cutting Michael out of her life, and other things we'll never know about . . . maybe she did it so we wouldn't have to make those same types of sacrifices."

"So what are you saying? You think I should give him another chance?"

"I think maybe you shouldn't cut him off just to feel like you're doing the right thing. It's okay to forgive him if you want. But you have to do it for you, not him. And whatever you decide, it's okay. Because it's your choice, not his."

"It makes me sick how wise you are," Hollis said, making a face. "I'm the older one, you know."

"Yes, didn't you see the headlines? 'Ardith Blackwood makes series of smart decisions after night out at Luster.'"

Hollis gave her a sad smile. "How was church?"

Ardith reached into the box in front of her and pulled out a shopping bag filled with a tangle of giant necklaces, followed by a crinkled sandwich bag of tarnished rings. "Mostly everyone was okay. Especially the first lady. But . . . Holl, I can't stop thinking about what I said."

"Everyone drops an f-bomb sooner or later. It's therapeutic. And, look—I know you wish you could take it back. But you're allowed to be angry. You're always so put together, all the time. Honestly, it kind of made me feel better seeing you lose your shit for once. No one can be perfect all the time, Ardie. It's not fair for anyone to expect that of you."

This was essentially the same thing Sister Robinson had told her and yet somehow, Ardith felt better hearing it from Hollis. But Ardith knew, deep down, her anger wasn't the real issue. "Thank you, Holl. I appreciate it. Really. But what I mean is . . . what I said about my mom."

"Oh, Ardie."

"How could I talk about her like that? My whole life, I've had to put up with people saying horrible things about her and making assumptions and then I did the same thing."

"But you didn't. What you said wasn't bad—you just said you weren't like her."

323

"Why was I so quick to say that, though?" Ardith swallowed hard. "Everyone thinks of her addiction first, and what I said makes them think I do, too. And I don't. She was my mom. If I'm not willing to defend her, who will?"

Hollis shook her head firmly. "Nobody who matters is judging you on what you said about her—not when some dickwad was shoving his phone in your face, trying to piss you off. You got caught in a bad moment. We all know how much you loved Aunt Kimberly. And how good of a person she was and . . . You can't beat yourself up about this, Ardie. Shit happens."

Ardith dumped the bags of jewelry back into the box and stood up, moving to the silver clothing rack in the corner. "You know how Bebe always used to say that if we gave people what we thought they wanted, it would still never be enough? That they would just make up something to fit their narrative?"

Hollis looked up from a banker's box of screenplays. "That's so depressing."

"Well, I wonder if that's why she didn't tell anyone what happened with Grandpa Abe's dad. Maybe she realized people were going to think whatever they wanted, no matter what she told them . . . so it was just best not to say anything at all?"

"I get that," Hollis said slowly.

"Yeah . . . me too. And I keep thinking about Mommy, how Daddy and I don't talk about her, in public *or* private, because we're worried about the things people used to say . . . that they're still saying." Ardith bit her lip. "But that's not fair to her. Or us. If people are going to say whatever they want, why can't we remember her like we want to? Talk about her, celebrate her?"

"See?" Hollis said, grinning. "Wise."

The storage space was quiet for a while, minus the sounds of ripping tape and crinkling bags and sliding hangers. Ardith's mother's dresses were all wrapped in plastic from the dry cleaner, and she lifted the ends of them one by one to get a better look. She remembered where her mother had worn most of the dresses, the magazine features and blog photos coming to mind. The dark purple shift was from her first year at the Emmys, and the white, off-the-shoulder gown adorned with pearls had been worn at the Oscars. There was the pink full-length gown from the time she presented at the Grammys, and the black sleeveless jumpsuit she'd worn for the Spirit Awards. The clothing rack was like a time capsule, and Ardith leaned in close, trying to see if she could still smell Mommy anywhere in it all. Her scent had mostly faded from Ardith's mind, but she would know it if she smelled it: gardenias mixed with coconut oil.

At the end of the rack, pushed all the way in the corner, was the one dress not sheathed in plastic. It appeared to have been shoved almost hastily onto the hanger, and when Ardith pulled it out, she saw why. It was a black minidress with short sleeves and a mock neck, covered in looping patterns of intricate gold beading. Ardith must have made a sound when she touched it, because Hollis looked over right away, then jumped up to come stand next to her.

"This is what she wore the night she died," Ardith said quietly.

Hollis squeezed her arm. "It's beautiful. Just like she was."

"I'm kind of surprised Daddy kept it."

"Why wouldn't he?" Hollis asked.

"Because of all the articles that described it when they wrote about her death. The red carpet photos from that night that *still* pop up when you search for her. And also—she was tiny when she died. Her addiction . . . it had taken almost everything from her by then. This dress is so small compared to her other clothes. I think it reminds him of how sick she was."

"Are you glad you have it?"

"Honestly? I used to wish he had thrown it out," Ardith replied, the guilt burning her ears. "But not because it made me sad. I was embarrassed. Almost like if the dress didn't exist, nobody would remember her that way."

"Do you still feel like that?"

"I thought I would, but . . . I don't know. What am I so embarrassed by? Whatever people say about it, it's still part of her story."

Hollis nodded, still staring at the dress. "Are you going to let them display it?"

Ardith touched the beaded hem, rolling it between her fingers. "I haven't decided. I'm not even sure if I'm going to speak at the opening. Barton Lerner keeps asking, but . . . I don't know."

"Well, whatever you decide, the exhibit is going to be amazing." Hollis wrapped her arms around her cousin from the side, resting her head against Ardith's shoulder.

Ardith closed her eyes and exhaled.

Hollis

I want s'mores

Hollis sent the text to Dwayne when she got home from helping Ardith. Her hand shook as she pressed send on the message, but a second later, a bubble popped up onscreen as Dwayne wrote back to her.

Pick you up in an hour?

Now they were in the car, on the way to the beach, and Hollis wondered if she'd made a mistake. They hadn't spoken much since Dwayne had picked her up; in fact, she couldn't remember them ever being so quiet around each other. Dwayne kept glancing over at her nervously, asking if the music was okay or if she wanted him to turn on the seat warmers, like he was a hired driver or something. But Hollis didn't want to try to talk to him while he was driving, so she said hardly anything on the ride across town.

She couldn't believe she was happy to see the beach. As soon as she stepped out of Dwayne's Range Rover, she breathed in deeply. The smell of saltwater flooded her nose as her ears picked up the soft roar of the ocean beyond them.

"You know we could've just done this in my fire pit, right?" he said as he got the supplies from the back.

"Neutral territory," Hollis replied.

The beach was busier than she'd thought it would be on a Sunday evening, but they were able to find an empty pit. Dwayne worked on making the fire while Hollis set out the ingredients for the s'mores. He used charcoal and lighter fluid to get it going, and soon the fire was blazing hot, flames licking the air in front of them.

Hollis handed Dwayne a skewer with a jumbo marshmallow speared through the top.

"I quit the team," he said, eyes on the skewer as he held it over the fire. "I told Coach first, then I had him set up a meeting with my dad—the three of us. At our house."

She raised her eyebrows. "How did that go?"

"Uh, about as well as you'd think."

"Is your dad still pissed?"

"Oh yeah," Dwayne said, slowly rotating the marshmallow. "It's gonna take him a while to get over this. He really thought me playing ball was a done deal. It's not just that, though. I used to think he was so set on me going into the league because of *his* legacy. Like, he had this dream that the Lipscombs were going to be this NBA dynasty, or whatever, and if I quit ball, I was going to kill that dream. But when we actually talked about it, it was more than that. He didn't grow up with a lot, and basketball was his way to give him and my grandparents a better life. He got so wrapped up in his story, he forgot it's not mine, too. I had to remind him that Dupree wasn't just about basketball for me. I've got options he didn't have."

Hollis nodded. "How do you feel?"

"Relieved. Quitting was the right thing for me, and I couldn't train and play with those assholes anymore. Not after . . ."

Hollis felt him looking at her, but she kept her eyes on the fire. "Your dad will get over it."

They finished toasting the marshmallows, then assembled the s'mores on paper plates. They were sticky and gooey and chocolatey and perfect; Hollis and Dwayne ate them in silence. When they were done, they dipped their fingers in the ocean to wash off the crumbs. Dwayne spread a blanket out on the sand near the water, and Hollis sat next to him but not too close, using the other one to cover her shoulders.

Dwayne stared out at the dark seawater before them.

"I love you, too," Hollis said quietly.

He turned to look at her.

"But what you did really hurt me. I trusted you with those photos, but I also trusted you to be real with me. Always. That night was really special to me, Dwayne."

"It was special to me, too."

She slid the toe of her sneaker across the sand, forming a half circle. "I was already nervous about us, if we were ever going to go back to how we were that night. And then when the photo got out, I didn't even have time to think about it because I was so worried about trying to protect myself, and so confused about how it had happened when the only people who knew about those pictures were you and me."

"I'm so sorry. If I could do over anything in my life—"

"I know. It's just . . . our family has really been going through it, and you're the one person I trust outside of it, and I couldn't even talk to you. We haven't discussed the whole Babineaux thing—that I'm related to freaking *Orlando*. Or how I'm still trying to wrap my brain around what Bebe did—how hard that must have been for her, but how it hurt Grandpa Abe, too. I needed you, but I don't even know if I can trust you now."

"I hated that I couldn't talk to you about it, too. My mom told me about all your family stuff, but you weren't really answering my texts or calls and . . . I'm sorry. I know I keep saying that, but I want you to believe me."

They were quiet for a moment, then Hollis said, "Remember second grade? When you pushed me off that dome thing we used to climb on the playground?"

"Yeah." His voice was sheepish.

"I wanted to kill you when I got back to school."

"You might have if Ms. Paulson hadn't pulled you off me that day. You split my lip."

"And you made me break my arm. I had to wear a cast for two months! You think I wasn't going to find a way to hurt you for that?" She would never forget standing at the sinks in the girls' bathroom, cleaning Dwayne's blood off the purple plaster before her father picked her up that day.

"I deserved it," he said.

"I forgave you for that. But with this . . . it kind of feels like if I forgive you, then I'm betraying myself. And if I don't forgive you, I'm not even allowing myself the possibility of trusting you again, and that doesn't feel right, either. But I don't feel like making that choice right now. Maybe I never will." Hollis pulled the wool blanket tighter around her. "I don't know. I need some time to think about all this before things can go back to normal between us or . . . whatever they'll be."

"Okay. I can live with that, Holl. I just . . . I really need you in my life." He paused, then said, "Do you remember that night when I said you were like family, but different?"

She nodded.

"What I meant is . . . You feel like home to me."

She looked at him. And in that moment, she was reminded of why their bond was so special. She didn't have to say she felt the same way; Dwayne knew as soon as his eyes met hers.

They sat together silently on the blanket, and as Hollis gazed out at the water, she thought maybe she understood why people liked it here so much. There was something about the vastness of the ocean, the waves crashing up to the shore, that made her feel content.

Hopeful.

Building a Legacy

1974

"Ladies and gentlemen . . . *Dick Cavett!*"

Blossom took a deep breath as the horns and percussion from the band launched into the show's cheerful theme song, not far from where she sat in her dressing room. She looked in the mirror, closed her eyes, and opened them again. She was here. After years of watching *The Dick Cavett Show*, she was really here. Just moments from being whisked onto the same stage where he'd interviewed dozens of her fellow actors, comedians, musicians, and politicians.

She had hardly believed her agent when he said a producer wanted her to audition for a new film called *Fields of Crimson*. She'd been even more shocked when they'd asked her to come back in for screen tests after that. It had been so long since she'd auditioned for a leading role of this caliber, a project that truly excited her. But, initially, she'd worried over the subject matter—was it disrespectful to act in a movie about a war in which young men were still fighting, still dying? A war that she personally believed never should have begun, let alone gone on so very long? She'd ultimately decided the positives—shining a light on Black servicemen and portraying strong Black love—outweighed the negatives. A heaviness that had lived within her for so long that she had almost grown used to it finally lifted when she realized this film was her second chance.

The one so many deserving Black actors would never get.

There was a quick rap of knuckles at the dressing room door. "Miss Blackwood? We're ready for you."

Blossom fluffed her Afro, checked to be sure there was no lipstick on her teeth, and straightened the collar of her geometric-print shirtdress. This was as good as it was going to get.

The young man outside the door was wearing a headset and holding a clipboard. He led her down the hall toward the stage, where from the wings they could see Mr. Cavett warming up the audience.

"He'll say a few words about you, then he'll introduce you, and that's your cue to walk out onto the set," the young man reminded her. "Do you have any questions?"

"Yes," she said, sliding her sweaty palms down the front of her dress. "Is it normal to be so nervous?"

The man smiled, which helped relax her a bit. "You'll be great," he said. "My wife and I loved the film, by the way. You and Clifton Thompson are so good together."

Blossom thanked him, then closed her eyes again, trying to get her bearings. She heard Mr. Cavett mentioning some of her past projects and how the audience members might know her more from her activism than her film work these days. Then, finally, he said, "She is, I believe, one of the most underrated actresses of our time, and she's here tonight: Blossom Blackwood."

She exhaled as she walked around the corner and onto the set, her eyes sweeping from the live audience to Mr. Cavett, who was facing her with his easy smile. Blossom waved to the audience, and though she knew Abe was out there somewhere, she couldn't see anything beyond the bright stage lights. It was like being back onstage in New York. She felt as if she were floating as she walked to the carpeted area, where Mr. Cavett greeted her warmly. The audience kept applauding and cheering, even after she'd sat down next to him in the butterscotch leather chair.

"Well, *I* didn't get that kind of reception. I guess we see who they're really here for," Mr. Cavett said to scattered laughter from the audience.

"It's very kind of them," Blossom said.

"I only offered them a small bribe, right, everyone?" This time, they roared.

"Well, my son is in the audience, and I *know* you didn't bribe him."

Mr. Cavett raised an eyebrow. "Your son? You mean that dashingly handsome young man who plays on the soap operas?"

Blossom beamed. "That's him. Abraham Blackwood."

The audience whooed and clapped, and Blossom imagined Abe smiling bashfully under the lights.

"Abraham's father—he's not in your lives, is he?" said Mr. Cavett easily, as if he hadn't just brought up one of the most private parts about her increasingly public life. Blossom remembered the cameras and that Abe himself was sitting there in the audience as she calmly nodded, waiting for him to go on. "That seems a bit . . . well, radical. For such a successful and beautiful woman to choose to be a single mother. How did you come to that decision?"

The audience members were silent, as was Blossom. Though she and her publicist had gone over potential topics, they hadn't prepared for this one. As the seconds ticked by, she was aware they were all waiting for her answer, and so Blossom forged ahead.

"I think sometimes life makes decisions for you," she said carefully. "I will say that I didn't necessarily know, when I had Abe, that I'd be raising him on my own, but we've all seen how he turned out, and I'm so proud of that. Proud of him."

"Indeed. Well, it appears talent just runs rampant in your family," said Mr. Cavett, leaning his arm casually over the arm of his chair. "Is there anyone in there who *can't* act?"

"My sisters aren't in the business."

"Lucky them," he deadpanned to more laughter. He waited for it to die down before he continued. "But I heard about your mother. She just passed recently, is that correct?"

Blossom looked down at her lap. "Yes, a little over two months ago. Just after Christmas."

"I'm so sorry." His voice was solemn. "I know she had a profound influence on your life."

"Thank you. And yes, she did. My mother was the reason I knew I could be an actress. Every once in a while, my sisters and I could get her to talk about her time in show business."

"What types of roles did she play?"

"She started out on the Black vaudeville circuit, and then she tried to break into Hollywood. But there weren't many opportunities for Black actresses then. Even fewer than now. Mostly maids or slaves or, you know, a role like Hattie McDaniel played in *Gone with the Wind*."

"Mammy."

"Yes, Mammy." Blossom paused. "I'm proud of what my mother accomplished. She didn't get to do a lot, but she worked hard at the opportunities she was given."

"And she taught you that you should follow your dreams."

"Yes, she did." Blossom didn't quite believe in the concept of heaven and hell, but lately, since Flossie had been gone, she often wondered if her mother could see her. If she could sense, from wherever she was, that all of her hard work and sacrifices, the guidance and wisdom she'd offered, had finally paid off for Blossom—that it was paying off for her beloved Abe, too.

"Well, we're thankful for her. And she must've been very proud of you," Mr. Cavett said. "Your son, too. You're one of the few Black women who've been nominated for both a Golden Globe and an Academy Award for best actress. The late, great Dorothy Dandridge comes to mind. How does it feel?"

The audience cheered so loudly that Blossom had to wait a few moments before she responded. It was hot under the lights, and her nerves went haywire each time she remembered this was going to play on national television. But then she looked at Mr. Cavett, who nodded encouragingly, and Blossom reminded herself that she was supposed to be here. She had earned this.

"It's incredible, and a little surreal. I remember watching Dorothy Dandridge when I was a girl, wondering what it was like to be her. We were all so proud when she was nominated for *Carmen Jones*. Just like we celebrated Ms. McDaniel when it was her turn."

"What do you think about that, though? That Black women are so often nominated for roles calling for them to play servants or sexy 'vixens'? Is that boxing you in?"

"Well, just last year, Cicely Tyson and Diana Ross were nominated for parts that were neither of those things. So I'd say we are making progress. But sometimes these are the meatiest roles, and so the choice becomes whether you work steadily with what's being offered or if you decide to take a chance and wait for the . . . *right* role to come to you."

"That makes me curious about how you've approached your own career," he said. "Some of our audience may not know you started in New York theater in the late fifties, where you first worked with Clifton Thompson, your costar in the new movie. Then you were in a terrific film about another war, called *Love, Gertie*, back in 1962."

Blossom nodded.

"But that was twelve years ago, and until *Fields of Crimson*, we've only seen you in supporting roles here and there over the past decade. Was this about that selectiveness you just referred to?"

Blossom tilted her head as she considered his question. "To be honest, I've been told time and again that there just weren't roles out there for me. And you're never told why these days, just that you weren't right for the part."

"That must be frustrating." Mr. Cavett paused. "Did it surprise you that you had trouble booking work after *Love, Gertie*?"

"Yes," Blossom said without hesitation. "That film was a joy to make, from beginning to end, and it was also, as you said, terrific. But . . . I was more naive then. I didn't understand that Hollywood is not a meritocracy. Now, don't get me wrong—there are plenty of hardworking people in the industry. But there are also people who must work twice as hard just to get the same opportunities, who don't have the privilege of relying on connections."

He nodded. "This is true, but I'd like to turn that answer back around to you, because I'm curious—now that your son is acting as well, it seems you're starting somewhat of a legacy in the entertainment business. Abraham could have children who want to follow in their father's footsteps, and then their children, and so on."

"Abraham is twenty years old," Blossom said, raising an eyebrow. "Let's not get ahead of ourselves here."

The audience laughed along with Mr. Cavett. "That's fair. But I suppose my question is, how do you feel about the fact that people might say Abraham is getting opportunities based on his name? A name that you established."

Blossom gazed out at the audience, still indistinct shadows under the lights. But she imagined she was looking directly into Abe's eyes as she said, "First, my son is brilliant, and he would have gotten exactly where he is without the help of his name. But I would also say . . . very few Black actors are given the chance to build that sort of legacy. And so, if I could have any part in that, I would be honored."

"Well, anyone who has seen your work knows that you are well on your way to creating just that," he said with a wide smile. He looked straight at the camera then. "We'll be right back after a message from our local station. And when we return, we'll talk about Blossom Blackwood's Academy Award–nominated role in the film *Fields of Crimson*."

The 1974 Academy Awards would come to be known as one of the most memorable shows in history, from the mustachioed streaker who ran naked onstage behind host David Niven to the much-loved Katharine Hepburn making her first-ever appearance at the ceremony, despite having been nominated for the top acting prize eleven times, three of which she'd won. It was not a night to miss, and Blossom was grateful to be there on an evening of such humor and surprises.

But what she would always remember was her time with Abe. Blossom had known from the moment she was nominated that she wanted her son to escort her to the ceremony. He was the most important person in her life, the one who had perhaps sacrificed the most at the expense of her career.

"You want to take *me*, Mama?" he'd asked, his eyes as big as grapefruits. "You sure?"

"You're the best date I could ask for, Abraham Blackwood." And though she wouldn't say it, Blossom thought it would be good for Abe to brush shoulders with the best of the best in Hollywood. You never knew who was scouting for their next movie, and it was true that Abe was starting to turn heads with his television work.

He'd whooped, scooping her up in his arms and spinning her around. "No, *you* the best, Mama."

Little Abe was a grown man now. He had a real presence onscreen, and she didn't think that just because he was her son. She saw it, what everyone else did. That sparkle. And she wanted him to have more opportunities than had ever been available to her. Blossom hadn't given up her career for him, but now that it was finally peaking, she would do whatever she could to help him get his off the ground.

Her hair and makeup people came to the house to get her ready for the ceremony, people she'd worked with on previous jobs and trusted—and some of the few people who knew how to work well with Black hair and dark skin. Sometimes she couldn't believe how lucky she was; Flossie used to tell her how there just wasn't anybody for them back in her day. How the makeup was always the wrong shade, even though it had to be specially mixed, and how sometimes the Black actresses would have to wear the same makeup that had been created to darken the skin of white actresses who took on Black or mixed-race roles. And if there were Black makeup or hair people you wanted to bring in, they would often be turned away because they weren't part of the union.

Once Blossom was all done up, she stood in front of the full-length mirror on the back of the bathroom door. She wondered what Flossie would've thought about her dress, with its strapless, gold-sequined bodice and full, snow-white chiffon skirt. It had been designed by Bill Whitten, who'd created Cicely Tyson's stunning Oscar gown the previous year. Mama probably would've said the light-catching sequins were too flashy, and the top too suggestive, with her arms and shoulders fully bared. It was hard to picture Mama living through the rest of the seventies, with things changing so quickly and her insistence on clinging to modesty. And the feminist movement was making strides, though it was largely concerned with white women and not those who also faced discrimination because of their race.

But she couldn't believe she'd have to live the rest of her life without Flossie. She missed her immensely. She even missed Mama's fussing, and the way she'd criticized Blossom's growing and public activism in her final years. Mama thought it hadn't looked right, women marching and protesting out in the streets with men. Which was pretty rich, coming from a woman who'd insisted—and proven—that she didn't need a man to care for her family. And who had convinced Blossom that she didn't have to give up her career or desire to have her own family, either.

Abe had moved out of their home in Watts the previous year, now sharing an apartment with another up-and-coming actor, and Sybil had met a kindhearted man poised to take over his father's construction business. He treated Sybil like a queen, but Blossom wished, at times, he hadn't persuaded her baby sister to move with him to Santa Barbara. Though it was just under two hours, door to door, she missed seeing Sybil every day. The house was so empty now.

Abe arrived just as she was fastening her earrings. They were going to take a limo downtown to the Dorothy Chandler Pavilion.

"You look beautiful, Mama," he said, handsome in his tux. He gave her a careful hug, trying not to mess up her makeup or meticulously coiffed hair, which she'd had pressed and curled for the occasion. "You ready? The limo pulled up right behind me."

"I'm nervous," she said, looking up at him.

"It don't matter if you win or lose, Mama. You made it this far." Abe smiled. "This is what you been working for your whole life. They can't take none of this away from you."

Blossom didn't win.

The award went to British actress Glenda Jackson for her work in *A Touch of Class*. She had also won the Golden Globe that year. It wasn't lost on Blossom that it seemed like a rather cruel twist of fate, as Jackson had played a woman carrying on with a married man.

Blossom and Abe were seated next to Clifton and his wife, a former dancer with Alvin Ailey's company. She hadn't seen Clifton since their theater days back in New York, and she hadn't known what to expect when she showed up for their *Fields of Crimson* screen test together, before their contracts had been signed. They had been cordial to each other throughout the run of *The Johnstons*, but their friendship had ended the night he'd confronted her about her feelings for Archie Melamed. That seemed like so long ago now, and she'd been relieved that Clifton no longer appeared to be bothered by it, either. That he was happy to see her, to work with her again and re-create their chemistry on film this time. Clifton was still one of the best actors she'd ever worked with, and she was thrilled the Academy had recognized him with a nomination, as well.

Blossom's eyes darted around the room after the ceremony had ended; she was still having trouble believing she was surrounded by some of the biggest and brightest names in Hollywood—that the Academy had decided she belonged here, too.

Clifton turned to her. "Is it better or worse that we're both going home empty-handed this evening? I'd already cleared a space for the award."

"He's not kidding," Sonia, his wife, said over his shoulder.

Blossom laughed. "I think it's better for *me*, because now I don't have to pretend not to be wildly jealous of you."

"Oh, how I've missed your honesty, Blossom," he said, smiling. "I saw you on *Dick Cavett*. You didn't pull any punches there, either."

"I was only answering his . . ." Blossom trailed off.

Behind Clifton and Sonia, Archie Melamed and his wife were walking down the aisle, arm in arm.

She felt, for a moment, as if time had stopped. Archie looked older now—the lines in his face deeply set, his curls thin and graying. But even from here, she could see that he was still the same man with the serious face and warm, curious eyes. He had kept his word to Marian, never working with Blossom again. She had seen his name over the years in different films, as he was producing now, in addition to directing. But anytime her agent asked if she wanted him to try to get her an audition for one of Archie's projects, Blossom found some reason to say no without revealing the real one.

She had thought about him constantly at first after they'd parted ways, and then less and less often. She wondered if he'd kept up with her career before *Fields of Crimson*, if he was aware that, despite what he'd assured her, she hadn't been able to carve out her own space after *Love, Gertie*. And that, if he'd recommended her to industry people, it seemed they hadn't believed in Blossom enough to take a chance on her.

She felt proud now, to be standing here with Clifton, both of them Oscar-nominated, a title that would forever precede their names. And she willed Archie to look over, to meet her gaze, to tell her with the face she used to be able to read so well that he was proud of her, too. That she had finally made it.

But he and Marian walked steadily along, looking straight ahead. And if Archie felt the heat of her stare, he didn't acknowledge it.

Clifton followed her eyes, then slowly turned back to her. "Blast from the past, huh?"

"A lifetime ago," Blossom said quietly.

Suddenly, she was sad. Not because Archie hadn't acknowledged her—not exactly. It was that she realized she was no longer the same woman she had been when she'd known him. That version of Blossom had believed she was on the cusp of stardom, that her new film would open the hearts and minds of moviegoers and Hollywood executives who would see how much talent they were missing out on from Black performers. That she had finally met a man whom she loved, and who loved her, too, in the way she'd wanted to be loved. But the Blossom of today . . . she had experienced enough to understand there was a good chance she and Clifton would never be recognized in the way they deserved. She knew now that this evening might be the biggest highlight of their entire careers, whereas, for many white actors, being nominated was only the beginning.

"You and Abe want to have a drink with us?" Clifton asked as he and Sonia stood.

Abe was giving Clifton a long look, but Blossom didn't notice as she said, "I am officially old enough now to know it's time to call it a night."

"Abe?" Clifton said, his voice friendly.

"Uh, thank you, sir, but I'm actually going to meet up with my girl at a party."

His girl was Taffy Ford, a bubbly young model Blossom had met after the *Dick Cavett Show* taping. She could tell by the way Abe talked about her that he really liked her, but Blossom wasn't sure how she felt about her yet.

"Well, it was certainly nice to meet you, young man." Clifton smiled. "I've heard a lot about you from your mama, and the women in my family are big fans of yours."

A sheepish smile spread across Abe's face as he thanked him.

"It was lovely to see you both," Blossom said, hugging Clifton and Sonia. "Do let me know the next time you're back in Los Angeles?"

"Absolutely," Clifton said. She watched for a moment as they disappeared into the crowd.

"Mama," Abe said, stepping closer to her, "is he my father?"

Abe asked it so plainly, so straightforwardly, as if he were asking for the time of day, that at first, Blossom didn't believe she'd heard what she did. But when his words registered, Blossom shushed him, taking his arm as she led him through the people lingering in the seats around them. Out in the lobby, Blossom could hardly hear the crowd for how loudly her heart was beating.

He chose to ask her this *now*? How long had he been considering this possibility?

Every moment it took for their limo to pull up to the curb felt like an hour to Blossom. Abe was silent beside her. Pensive. Once they were inside the car, Abe gave the chauffeur the address of the party, then Blossom asked the driver to put up the soundproof divider. She turned to her son.

"Why did you ask me that?"

"Because I want to know."

She sighed. "Of course. But why now? And why Clifton? You haven't asked me about your father in years."

"That doesn't mean I haven't been thinking about it," he said.

"And. . . I don't know. You used to act with him back in the day, when I was little. I guess he kind of looks like me, from a certain angle."

He wasn't wrong, but it pained her to realize how deeply he'd been analyzing her co-star, trying to find some piece of him in his features. "Oh, Abe. No, baby. He's not your father. He's only ever been my colleague."

Abe sat back in his seat, thinking. Then, "Did you ever like my daddy?"

Blossom remembered her conversation with Mama so many years ago, how her mother's honesty about her feelings for Blossom's father had shocked her. But it had also made her feel good, that Mama had trusted her enough to be honest with her.

"I loved him. For a long time. But you and I would have very different lives if he'd been around."

"You don't think you would've been happy?"

Blossom hesitated. "I wonder, sometimes. If perhaps I could have been a different kind of happy with him. Or if both of our lives, yours and mine, would have been better with him around and . . . I don't think so, Abe. We wanted such different things, and I was sure at the time that he would never change."

"You never talk to him?"

"Not since you were a baby."

"What did he want?"

"Darling?"

"You said you wanted different things. What was it that he wanted?"

"Not this. He thought being an entertainer was too unstable. That it wasn't something to be proud of." Blossom took a deep breath. "I know that you didn't have the most conventional upbringing, that I was gone for weeks at a time when you were young. And I never wanted you to grow up without a father—especially as a young man. But I had to make difficult decisions back then, and sometimes taking the right job meant

343

leaving you. I wanted to be your mother and I wanted to follow my dream, and while it wasn't easy, I am lucky that I got to do both."

He nodded, his eyes never leaving hers.

"I've worked hard to get where I am, and still, I am always hoping for better projects, for greater success. But when I learned that you wanted to be an actor, too . . . that meant the world to me. It meant I had raised you in a home where you had the freedom to pursue your art without judgment. And everything I had to give up for that, your father included, was worth it."

The car was quiet for a moment, then Abe said, "It doesn't really bother me that I don't know him. I guess I wonder who he might be. If I'd like him if I met him. But then . . . I've never needed him. The way you and Mother and Aunt Sybil were always around for me—I didn't ever need more than y'all. There was enough love in that house for five families."

Tears sprang to Blossom's eyes. "Oh, Abe. Do you really believe that?"

Abe nodded. "I'm proud of you, Mama. You doing the damn thing. How many people can say they mama came *this close* to winning an Academy Award?"

The limo pulled up to the club that was hosting the party. Abe unbuckled his seat belt and Blossom leaned over to kiss his cheek before he exited the car. "Have a nice time. Call me tomorrow. And give Taffy my regards."

"I will." Abe squeezed her into a big hug now that he didn't have to worry about wrinkling her dress for the cameras. He paused. "Mama, what you said to Dick Cavett, about starting a legacy . . . You really think we could be that kind of family? Like the Fondas?"

"We are Blackwoods," she said, smiling softly. "I think that means anything is possible."

As the limo drove through the streets of downtown Los Angeles, Blossom let her mind wander to Michael. It had been so long ago—two full decades. She had worked hard to distance herself from any of their mutual friends and acquaintances, and had no idea what path his life had taken. She had wondered in recent years if Abe would benefit from knowing his father now, if she should consider calling Michael to see if he would be interested in meeting him.

But whenever she thought about Michael, she remembered the anger in his voice the last time they'd spoken, how easily he had agreed to an arrangement that had been so painful for her to propose. How he had never felt comfortable allowing her to be who she was. And because she hadn't let him control her, she had accomplished what few Black actresses had ever achieved, and she had a son whose star was quickly rising—a young man who saw a promising future for himself that she never could have imagined being within grasp at his age. The Michael Babineaux she knew would never believe, no matter how much they succeeded, that her and Abe's dreams, their work, was important.

And so Blossom believed now, as she had then, that they were better off without him.

Ardith

"I didn't know there would be a red carpet," Ardith's father said as they stepped out of the black car on Wilshire, in front of the Academy Museum of Motion Pictures.

"Daddy, you know how these things work," Ardith replied, not unkindly. "We'll just go take a quick picture before we go inside."

"I . . . I'm not prepared for that."

"You're wearing a tux. And you look really nice," Ardith said. "Isn't it a waste not to be photographed in it?"

"Ardie—"

"Daddy, please. For Mommy."

He took a deep breath and looked at her for a long moment, then said, "Okay. But I'm not standing up there all night. Let's get in and out."

Ardith hadn't expected her father to be so open about his anxiety around this event, and she wondered if he'd been like this when he escorted her mother to all those parties and premieres. She'd known it would bring up some old memories, but she was determined to help him push through his nerves. The calmer he was, the more her own nerves would be settled, and she was the one who needed it—she had agreed to give a speech tonight. And though she was trying to be brave for her father, she was also trying to tamp down her own anxiety about being out in public, on a red carpet again, the most visible she'd been since her

346

outburst at Luster—and to celebrate her mother, no less. It was February now, so she had survived the autumn, made it through the relentless coverage about her meltdown, but she'd still felt goose bumps rising on her arms as they pulled up in the car.

They were some of the first people to arrive, and Ardith hoped that made it easier for her father as they walked onto the carpet—to not have dozens of people staring at them as flashbulbs popped in their faces. She knew it was helping her ease into the night with a little less apprehension.

"Come on, August—one little smile?" a photographer coaxed, which made Daddy laugh. Ardith looked over at him when he was mid-grin, hoping the cameras were catching it all.

Barton Lerner had offered to let the two of them have a look at the exhibit before the opening ceremony, but they had declined, wanting to be surprised this evening. And once they stepped inside, Ardith was glad they'd waited, because it was even more wonderful than she could have imagined.

Somehow, all of the things she and Hollis had found in the storage unit looked so much fancier now, more extravagant in this space. The dresses were exhibited in clear, well-lit cases with the event, year, and designer all recorded on white cards at the front of each box. Including the gold-beaded dress, which Ardith had specifically asked to be displayed. Her mother's old screenplays were positioned on a long table, and they'd even devoted a locked glass case to her high school and college play memorabilia, everything from programs and pictures to small props she'd kept.

Ardith wandered silently with Daddy through the exhibit, taking in each piece of her mother's life as if it were the first time she'd seen it.

"What do you think?" she asked, looking over at him as they stopped in front of an enlarged photo. It was one Daddy had snapped of Mommy at home. She was lying across the living room floor, dressed in jeans and an oversize sweatshirt, chewing on the end of a pen as she read the script of *Riviera Sunset*. Ardith remembered seeing this photo when she was younger, but looking at it now, she felt another type of closeness with her mother, seeing how engrossed Mommy was in the script. Ardith knew now how it felt to fall in love with a project, what it meant to connect so deeply with the material. She was happy that her father had been able to capture such a special moment, one that showed a part of her the public never got to see.

"I think . . . it's really great, Ardie." He turned to her, swallowing. "You know I wasn't sure about this. So much that I broke out in hives the other day when I picked up my tux."

"Daddy! Why didn't you tell me?"

"Because I didn't want you to be nervous, too. This is a good thing. I'm happy we're doing it."

"Me too."

He chewed on his lip for a moment, then said, "I used to break out in hives before I'd go to these types of things with your mother. She used to tease me, but it was instantaneous—as soon as I saw a red carpet, I was done."

"Is that why you never posed with her for pictures?"

"Partly. I would have, if she'd wanted me to. But . . . she was so gorgeous on her own, I know nobody really cared if I was up there, including me. It was all eyes on her, all the time," he said, voice wistful.

Barton Lerner swooped over then, his white-blond hair gelled into his signature old-school pompadour, his black sequined suit jacket sparkling under the lights. "August, Ardith," he said, air-kissing them both, "I'm so glad to see you."

"Thank you so much," Ardith said. "For everything. This is amazing."

"Oh, the pleasure is all mine, Ardith. Truly. Your mother deserved so much more than she ever got, especially at the end, and if I can do my part to help rectify that now . . . well, it's an honor."

The room began to fill soon, with dozens of people, some familiar faces and some less so. Every member of the Blackwood family was in attendance. They all gathered in an unofficial circle by the box holding the pearled Oscar gown from 2008.

"This is lovely," Aunt Rhonda said, touching Ardith's arm as she looked at her and August. "You two did such a beautiful job getting her things together. Kimberly would be proud."

"Please, this was all Ardie," Daddy said, rubbing Ardith's back in an unusual show of affection. "I wasn't even sure I wanted to be here, but . . . I'm glad we are."

Ardith's eyes moved over to Hollis, who had arrived separately from her parents, with Dwayne. They had been slowly rebuilding their friendship, and Hollis had confessed that she was becoming comfortable with him again. Ardith knew her cousin was still guarded, but she noticed the way Dwayne's hand rested on the small of Hollis's back, how Hollis didn't seem to mind it.

"We don't mean to interrupt, but we wanted to say hello before you get too busy," said a voice, and Ardith turned to find Grandpa Abe's sister, Geena Babineaux, at her side.

"You're not interrupting at all," she said, smiling as she turned to look at the rest of the Babineaux family. They were all there: Geena, Eli, Orlando and his parents—even Gabe and his family had come out. "Thank you for being here."

The Babineauxs and Blackwoods had seen each other about a month ago, when Grandpa Abe had invited everyone over for a meal of black-eyed peas and greens to kick off the new year. There was still a bit of discomfort in the air, but they were slowly getting to know one another, to accept the differences between the two families—and also celebrate what they had in common. Now that the media attention over the reveal of Bebe's secret had finally begun to die down, they were able to do so without the judgment of others.

Members of the catering staff were weaving through the crowd, passing appetizers and drinks. Ardith had just picked up some sort of puff pastry bite when she saw Matty and Simone walking in from the red carpet. She excused herself and had to keep from running over, she was so happy to see them.

"This is fucking incredible," Matty said, giving her a big hug.

"Yeah, you were talking about it like it was some small thing, but this is huge," said Simone, next in line for a hug. "Look at all your mom's dresses. I'm *obsessed*."

Ardith twisted her hands in front of her. "I'm still not sure what I'm going to say."

"You got this," Simone assured her. "Remember what we talked about the other night? You're not doing this for anyone but your mom. And you. All you have to do is make sure it's from the heart."

Simone made it sound so easy.

Once cocktail hour began winding down, the guests moved into the theater for the screening of *Riviera Sunset*. Ardith was relieved Barton was speaking first. She knew she should have prepared something, but every time she had sat down to try to write, nothing came to her. For as long as she'd been thrust into the spotlight, so much of her public persona was curated, practiced—whether she was reading from a script or responding to interview questions on which she'd been coached by her publicity team. And the last time most people had seen her . . . that hadn't been her choice. This was one of the rare opportunities she could stand in front of others and be herself, the Ardith Blackwood she wanted people to know, who spoke openly and honestly about what her mother had meant to her. This was different from when she'd been antagonized outside of Luster, but what if this went poorly, too? What if people didn't *like* the real Ardith?

Barton took command of the room as people finished settling into their seats. "Thank you to everyone for coming. Kimberly Arnold was— is—a person who means so much to me, personally and professionally. Even so, when I had this idea for an exhibit to celebrate her fine career on the twentieth anniversary of our first film together, I didn't know if it would work. My husband will tell you that I have plenty of ideas that don't work." Gentle laughter traveled around the room and a white man in the front row, decked out in a brocade suit, blew him a kiss. "But I eventually took my little idea to Kimberly's family, and thank god they agreed to be involved, because otherwise all we'd have sitting out there would be a couple of DVD cases and a call sheet."

More laughter.

"I am eternally grateful to August and Ardith Blackwood for being so generous with their memories and mementos from Kimberly's life, including some photos of her that have never before been seen. It is because of them that this commemoration came to fruition. If I may, I would also like to say what an honor it is to have the entire Blackwood family here tonight." He cleared his throat. "The first time I met Kimberly, I was enchanted. She was an ingénue, reminiscent of the magnificent Dorothy Dandridge. She had no formal training, but as soon as she stepped into my audition room, there was no doubt in my mind she was a true thespian. I cast her in the supporting role right there on the spot, but I immediately began telling everyone I could about this dazzling young talent who was fresh on the scene. Not long after that, I directed her first leading role in *The Chronicles of Colette*, and I knew from the first take of her first scene that she was more than just a talented actress—she was going to be a star. The world soon saw what I did, but I felt special, knowing the real Kimberly—the woman who, beneath all the celebrity, was whip-smart and kind, as dedicated to her family as she was to her work. The first time I saw her with her daughter, Ardith . . . I was blown away by the love that radiated between them, fascinated that this woman who the whole world wanted a piece of was also one of the best mothers I'd ever known.

"Years after I met Kimberly, the Criterion Collection released a restored edition of a film called *Love, Gertie*—the debut screen appearance of Kimberly's grandmother-in-law, Blossom Blackwood. Though I already admired Ms. Blackwood from the first time I laid eyes on her in *Fields of Crimson* when I was just a boy, watching her in *Love, Gertie* was a revelation. Ms. Blackwood was more than just a beautiful woman and a wonderful actor—she was someone who created something quite special: a family who loved one another and the art of acting as much as she did; who shared that passion with people they brought into their family, like Kimberly; who passed their skill and respect of the craft down to their children. And she did it all while dealing with challenges I am quite certain none of us has or will ever face."

He looked at Ardith then, his expression soft. "I also saw, throughout the years, how the media has treated this family. I saw it firsthand, as one of Kimberly's lifelong friends, and I saw it from afar, as so many of us have, before and since. How they've been picked apart and put on display when they are simply trying to live their lives. It's an impossible way to live, and I admire each one of them for all that they've endured. Especially Ardith, who has been working in this business since she was a child, and who has carried herself with poise and grace . . . even in the face of someone who pushed her too far."

Ardith looked down at her lap, heart thrumming. Next to her, Hollis took her hand.

"I know what it's like to be goaded into behaving in a way you might not be proud of later—trust me, I haven't forgotten my own incident at the *Vanity Fair* party in 2014," he said, which brought forth more laughs. "But when I saw the video that made the rounds, in which Ardith was assaulted with derogatory comments about Kimberly, things no daughter should ever have to hear about her mother, what struck me wasn't the verbal abuse of the 'reporter' but the beauty in seeing this young woman get to respond the way she did. It reminded me that Ardith's mother and great-grandmother not only paved the way for her to become a successful, working actor but that she was able to thrive in the industry that tried so hard to keep Ms. Blackwood out, that had no compunction about trying to shape the narrative of Kimberly Arnold's life. And that Ardith has been able to build the beginning of her career with a freedom that neither Ms. Blackwood nor Kimberly ever really experienced. A freedom that allows her to tell vulgar gossip site writers exactly where they can go—rightfully so, I might add—without that being the only bit of her story that the world will know."

Ardith let out a shuddery breath; as Barton spoke, she felt a bit of the weight that had been plaguing her for as long as she could remember starting to lift. She had never heard someone put into words what it meant to be part of her particular family—it was as if Barton had seen right into her, understood everything she, her mother, and Bebe had struggled with all these years.

"Well, I've said enough now, but thank you again to the Blackwoods. Kimberly's beloved daughter has kindly agreed to share a few words with us before we begin. Ardith?"

Hollis squeezed her hand before she stood up. "Break a leg," she whispered.

Ardith smoothed down the front of her jumpsuit—the sleeveless black one of her mother's that fit so perfectly she'd had to keep it for herself—and joined Barton at the front of the theater, where he spread his arms wide, handing the room over to her. As she looked out at the dozens of faces staring back at her, she once again regretted not preparing something. But she was here now, and as she closed her eyes for a few seconds to ground herself, she remembered Simone's words: *from the heart*. She took a deep breath, opened her eyes.

"Someone once told me that if you pay attention to your good reviews, you have to pay attention to the bad ones, too," she began. "So I used to wonder if that meant I had to listen to the awful things the press said about my mother late in her life just as I did the praise she received throughout it." The theater was so silent she heard someone clear a tickle in their throat, all the way in the back. "Once my mother's addiction became public, the world took every opportunity to make *that* the story of her life, and that's when I realized some people *don't* listen to everything they hear about someone—and that the piece of the story they choose to believe . . . well, I think we all have an idea what that usually is. Especially for someone like my mother.

"Kimberly Arnold was the most beautiful person I ever knew, but some of the awful things printed about her . . . those were true, too. It was all part of who she was, and those things don't cancel out the beauty she put into this world while she was here. That was all she ever wanted, was to make people smile, whether it was with her movies or a picture or an autograph."

Ardith paused, aware that the weight was lifting even more as she spoke. Her gaze briefly landed on Hollis, who nodded at her, blinking back tears.

"I guess I've learned that people are more than one thing, even if you think you know everything about them. And that sometimes they only reveal what they think are the good parts, because maybe someone has told them the other parts are too shameful, or unacceptable. I don't believe that. I think you have to take the good with the bad, just like reviews. My mother struggled with addiction, and it got worse the more her career grew. But that is nothing to be ashamed of, not now and not then. Her death was tragic, but she was not a tragedy. Mommy was an amazing human who also happened to be one of the most famous people in the world when she was at the top of her career—and that was too much for her. It would be too much for a lot of us. But please, never forget she was more than the dark parts of her life. And in the end, no matter what anyone has said or will continue to say about her, *she* owns her story. The way her work lives on, finding new fans every day, is proof of that. I am proud to be her daughter. I love her, and I miss her, and she would be so happy you all are here to celebrate her career. Thank you, Barton, for being such a good friend to my mother. And thanks to all of you for coming."

Ardith felt as if she'd been holding her breath for hours, and she finally let it out when Barton hugged her. People were still applauding, even after she was sitting down again, next to her father and Hollis.

"You killed it," her cousin said, looking proud.

"Well done, Ardie," her father said, squeezing her to him.

She briefly looked up, hoping her mother and Bebe were proud of her, too. She knew she'd felt their presence, their strength in her as she was speaking. Ardith felt it, always.

But especially tonight.

Hancock Park

1988

Blossom had been in her new home for only a week when her past unexpectedly came crashing into her life again.

She'd had professional movers to handle the furniture, and Abe and Taffy had come by to help set up the house when they could, but it was all the little things that seemed to take up every minute of her day now: hanging pictures, arranging books, figuring out the best room in which to display her fine china. It all took up so much time that she worried she would never be done decorating. The house was so much larger than anyplace she'd imagined she would ever live, for one thing. She still couldn't believe she owned a home with a kitchen large enough to hold a tiled island in the middle of the room, let alone that she had three whole bathrooms to herself now. But then, she never thought she'd be standing here in her own house in her dream neighborhood, the distinguished Hancock Park.

Blossom would never forget the trouble when Nat King Cole and his wife had moved into the area in 1948; she'd been just barely out of her teens. Their move had made the national news, as the neighborhood had been exclusively white back then—by law. Mama had often said how funny it was that the South got such a bad reputation for its segregation when those same types of restrictions existed in every pocket of the country. There had been bribes, threats, and harassment, all because one of the most famous Black men in the world—one of the most famous men, period—had wanted to move into a house he liked on Muirfield Road. The old-money families who lived in this peaceful neighborhood of spacious homes had somehow thought themselves to be above a man they'd happily go see perform at Ciro's when they wanted to be entertained. The Coles had fought hard to keep their home, and they'd persevered. But even forty years after they had integrated the neighborhood, Blossom was one of the few other Black people who had ever lived in the area, and she had to wonder: Would she wake up in the dead of night to a cross burning on her lawn? To firecrackers in her bushes? To signs in the yard calling her a nigger? In her entire career she had seen only a fraction of the fame Nat King Cole had achieved by the time he bought that house—why would she be treated any differently? The restrictive housing covenants had been struck down the same year Nat King Cole and his family moved in, but Blossom knew that the changing of laws didn't necessarily dictate a change in attitudes. She loved her new house, and she hoped that one day she would be able to fully relax in it, feel like it was her *home*.

Abe, Taffy, and the boys were coming over for supper in a few hours, and as much as Blossom wanted to put her feet up until it was time to start cooking, she wanted these last few boxes out of her sight even more. She sat down on the floor in front of one marked MISCELLANEOUS and reached inside. Her hands landed on the worn cover of a book, and slowly, she pulled out Abe's beat-up old copy of *Charlotte's Web*. She must have read it to him at least a dozen times during his childhood. She began flipping through the yellowed pages, running her fingers over the familiar illustrations. When she got to the end, she found something caught in the pages.

A photograph. Blossom lifted it out and inhaled sharply. It was a picture of her and Michael and Abe, when Abe was only six months old. Just weeks before her terrible fight with Michael, when he'd threatened to leave them, and then had. She sat with her back against her new couch, hand over her mouth as she studied the black-and-white photo. She hadn't seen it in years—no, decades. How had it gotten in this book? She was sure Abe hadn't seen it, or he would have said something by now.

Despite Abe's reassurance all those years ago that he hadn't missed having a father, Blossom's decision had begun to haunt her. She wasn't sure why. Abe's career was going well—he had long ago branched out from soaps, and in addition to roles on television movies and dramas, he had already landed parts in several feature films—and he and Taffy had barely spent a day apart since they'd met, eventually getting married and now parents to three boys of their own. He was a wonderful father, patient and kind and doting when it came to his sons.

But the more she watched Abe settle into different stages of father-hood, the more she thought about Michael. What was he doing now? Did he have other children? Had he found a woman who could be the wife that he needed? Blossom sincerely hoped so. And she knew it would be easy enough to find out, but ever since Michael had given up his parental rights, she'd done her best to cut ties with not only the physical presence of the Babineauxs, but anyone who was close with them, as well.

This picture, though. Finding it this way after years of forgetting it even existed—that had to mean something, didn't it?

And before she knew it, Blossom was in the kitchen, hauling her thick copy of the Yellow Pages from the drawer. She opened to the residential listings and ran her finger down the column of names that started with *Ba*, not expecting to find Michael's number among them. Perhaps he had moved away from Los Angeles by now, or had an unlisted number, like herself.

But there it was. Michael Babineaux. Just one listed.

Blossom hesitated for only a second, afraid that she would lose her nerve, wedging the telephone receiver between her shoulder and chin as she dialed the number. It rang once, twice, three times, and then four. She was just about to hang up when someone picked up the line.

"Hello?"

A man's voice. She didn't think she'd recognize it after all these years, but it was him. She was sure of it.

"May I speak to Michael Babineaux, please?"

Her question was met with a fit of coughing; finally, though, she could hear him taking a long drink of water and then he said, "Please excuse me. This is Michael. Who's calling?"

Blossom closed her eyes. What was she doing? She hadn't spoken to him in more than thirty years. They were entirely different people now. Their son was a grown man with children of his own.

"Hello?" he said again. "You still there?"

"Michael, it's Blossom."

The other end of the line was so quiet that Blossom wondered if he had hung up the phone. Then he said, "Say that again?"

"It's Blossom. Blackwood."

He chuckled a bit, a sound so unexpected it sent a whooshing sigh of relief shooting from Blossom's lips. "As if I know any other Blossom."

"Michael, how are you?"

"Besides dealing with this damn cough, I'm trying to figure out why you calling me. It's been a long, long time, Blossom. Never thought I'd hear from you again."

She wrapped the curly phone cord around her index finger until it was tight enough to leave indentations in her skin, to convince her this was real. "I didn't think so, either. But, I found a photograph of us. With Abe. From when he was a baby. And I've been thinking of you, so . . ."

"So you thought you'd just call me out of the blue to shoot the shit?" She could practically see him shaking his head. "What do you want, Blossom?"

"Have you kept up with Abe over the years? Seen how he's been doing? He has a lovely family. Three beautiful boys: Isaiah, August, and Clarence."

"And a model wife, too." Michael coughed again. "Yeah, I seen him around on TV and in magazines and things. I seen you, too. On *China Beach*."

"*St. Elsewhere*," she corrected him, and immediately wished she hadn't.

"Huh?"

"I guest starred on *St. Elsewhere*. *China Beach* is about Vietnam, and I was in a movie about Vietnam back in the seventies, but . . ." She trailed off, embarrassed. Michael didn't care that she'd found success in television at this stage of her career, that she'd won an Emmy for her guest role on the drama three years ago. She could scarcely believe he'd watched something she'd been in on television.

Blossom waited, but Michael was silent, and she supposed since she had initiated the call, it was up to her to speak. To tell him why she'd rung him up.

"Michael, I'm sorry for what Mama and I did. Asking you to stop being Abe's father." She swallowed hard. "It wasn't right to keep you from him, to not give you a chance to be better. I've seen how people can grow now, and—I'm sorry."

With that apology, Blossom felt a mixture of emotions: sadness for how long it had taken her to make this call, regret for the way she had handled things all those years ago, anticipation that just maybe this could be the start to a new chapter in their lives, one in which Abe and Michael could finally forge a relationship.

Michael didn't hesitate before speaking. "I don't need your apology, Blossom. What you said back then was right. We wasn't no good for each other. And it seems like you got it all figured out. You said you didn't need me, and you didn't. You told me all those years ago that you were going to be a big Hollywood actress, and you made it happen. Good for you, Blossom."

Blossom didn't sense any animosity in his voice; he spoke plainly and openly, as Michael always had. But she sensed a peacefulness that hadn't been there back when they had been together, a comfort with who he was.

"But don't you want to meet Abe? And your grandchildren? They really are beautiful, and I was hoping we could put the past behind us, start fresh. We could set up a supper some evening with all of us. Or start small, if that's better. Maybe the two of you could meet for coffee."

There was a long pause on the other end of the line before Michael coughed again. His voice was a bit hoarse as he said, "Blossom, I got my own life now. I'm married, got a son and a daughter of my own. Grandsons of my own, too. He don't need me coming around now at his big age, trying to be his daddy."

"But it's not too late, Michael. I would tell him everything, explain what happened. He wouldn't be upset with you." Blossom's tone was pleading, so desperate she knew Michael must hear it, too.

"It's been thirty-three years since you kicked me out of that boy's life. Now, I know I made some mistakes, too, but what you doing this for?"

"So that you can know one another . . . before it's too late."

"Abe been asking for me?"

Blossom sighed. "Michael—"

"It's a simple question. He been asking for me?"

"Not for a while," she finally said.

"Then he don't need me back in his life. So that makes me think this is about you and not Abe. Or me."

Blossom's eyes filled. Even after all this time, Michael Babineaux was able to bring her to tears of frustration. "This is about doing the right thing, Michael."

"It might be the right thing for you, but we not on the same wavelength with this one. We ain't never been with just about anything except how we felt about each other. And we was such babies then, what did we even know about love?"

Blossom's heart sank at his characterization of their old relationship. Even though she knew he hadn't been the love of her life, she would never deny what she had felt for him.

"Look, I appreciate you calling, but after all this time, I think it's best if we say goodbye now. Take care, Blossom," Michael said, and then the line clicked, and he was gone.

Blossom listened to the dial tone echo in her ear for a full minute before she finally hung up.

For years, every time she picked up the phone, she'd worried that Michael's voice would be on the other end of the line. That he would reach out to her at the worst moment, complicate the secure life she had built for her and Abe. When she'd booked the role of Sara in *The Johnstons*, then the lead in *Love, Gertie*. When she'd been asked to come on talk shows or been photographed marching with civil rights activists. When she was recognized for her acting work on televised programs broadcast from coast to coast. But especially when Abe had made his acting debut, when he was suddenly projected into people's homes all over the country, she had been sure the Pretty Michael from her past would come knocking on her door.

Perhaps Michael was right. Perhaps it would have only caused trouble if she'd brought him back into their lives now. It might have been his pride talking, trying to pay her back for the heartache she'd caused him all those years ago. But if Michael wanted nothing to do with them, there was no point in telling Abe who he was now. She refused to bring even an ounce of pain or confusion into his life just to ease her own conscience.

Blossom had worked hard to make a family on her own terms. And they were thriving. She made a promise to herself then and there: she would tell Abe about Michael—once she was gone. She would write him a letter, seal it an envelope, and tell her attorney to pass it along to him only after both she and Michael had died. Michael had family, too. Maybe, once they were both gone, the Blackwoods and the Babineauxs would be able to come together.

Maybe their children, and their children's children, would be able to heal the wounds she and Michael never could.

Kith and Kin

"Now, *this* is what I'm talking about," Gabe said, rubbing his hands together at the full plate in front of him. He looked across the table at Taffy, who was passing the platter of bacon to Eli, sitting to her right. "Didn't know y'all could throw down like this in the kitchen."

"Oh, I can throw down," Taffy said, raising a perfectly shaped eyebrow. "Our New Year's Day dinner wasn't up to par for you, Gabe?"

"Hard to mess up black-eyed peas," he said with a grin.

Taffy pursed her lips, but the corners of her mouth soon lifted in a smile, too.

Isaiah shook his napkin out over his lap. "Told y'all we should've just had them over for Saturday Breakfast in the first place."

"You were right, you're always right, et cetera," August said, rolling his eyes.

"Ain't that some shit, coming from the lawyer," Isaiah shot back.

Gabe laughed, looking down the table at his brother. "Dang, Corbin, they sound like us."

Corbin just shook his head, but he was smiling like most everyone around the table. The relief was palpable that this fourth try at getting the families together had, so far, been successful. The tension had slowly started to melt with their second meeting, on New Year's Day, and a little more at the opening ceremony for Kimberly Arnold's exhibit. And now it appeared that the families were, perhaps, finally ready to find some common ground.

Hosting them at Blossom's house had been a good start. While the items that would be donated, tossed, or sold in the estate sale had been hauled away or put into storage, most of the bottom level, especially the dining room, kitchen, and big room still looked as it had when Blossom lived there: welcoming, soft, and cozy. The Babineauxs had walked slowly through the downstairs, where Blossom had cooked and relaxed, examining her awards that were on display: the Emmys she'd won for guest stints on *St. Elsewhere* and *The Incumbent*, the National Medal of the Arts that was awarded in 1989, and the Presidential Medal of Freedom in 2012. Blossom had left the Hancock Park house to Abe, who had no plans to sell it; every single Blackwood was relieved the home that had meant so much to Blossom and each one of them would remain in the family for the foreseeable future.

"So, Hollis, do you and Orlando see each other at school much?" Geena asked.

"We do," she said. She glanced at Orlando, then added, "We have lunch together."

"And AP Government," Orlando said.

"But we've been seeing each other outside of school sometimes, now, too," she said. "He's good friends with my best friend."

"*Best friend?* Is that what we're calling him now?" Orlando teased.

Hollis gave him a look as she said, "Dwayne and I have known each other most of our lives. Our parents are friends."

"And Hollis and Dwayne are . . . embarking on a new stage in their relationship," Rhonda offered, breaking off a piece of bacon.

"Mom!"

"He's a nice kid," said Cindy, Orlando's mother. "Always so polite when he comes over."

"Ain't it funny how life works?" Grandpa Abe mused. "All this time, Orlando was right here next to us, and we had no idea."

"With all due respect, my brother, we've all been here next to you," Eli said, slathering his biscuit with a generous pat of butter. "You could stand to get out of your bubble a little bit."

"Man, I live in Baldwin Hills."

Eli laughed long and loud. "You hear yourself? Baldwin Hills, like you just one of us regular folk."

"Did I miss something?" Grandpa Abe laughed a little, too, wiping his mouth with a napkin. "Baldwin Hills ain't Black anymore?"

"It's still bougie," Eli said.

"Well, I may live there now, but don't forget I'm from South L.A., just like you. One day I'll show you the houses I grew up in. Used to live right off Central Avenue, then we moved to Watts with Mother and aunt Sybil. They took care of me when Mama was gone. She was back and forth between here and New York, working."

"Abe just told me the other day that Blackwood was Blossom's maternal name," said Geena.

Corbin looked up. "Really?"

Abe nodded. "My mama didn't know her daddy, either—she didn't even know his last name. Whatever it was, Mother said she wasn't about to give it to her girls."

"I kept my name, too," Geena said proudly. "And I made sure Stuart knew before we got married that our kids were gonna be Babineaux."

Eli shook his head. "I thought she was about to lose that man for sure."

"Stuart was old-fashioned, but he was no fool. He wasn't about to lose *me* over no argument about names."

"But—" Ardith began, then quickly closed her mouth.

Geena smiled at her. "Speak your mind, baby."

"Well, it's just . . . your dad sounded pretty old-fashioned, too. How did he feel about you keeping your name?"

"It wasn't a big discussion or anything, but I think he saw it the way I meant it—as a way to show him respect. I loved our daddy and I love his name, so it wasn't a choice for me. Besides, who wants to be a Jones when you can be a Babineaux instead?"

"I love that," Rhonda said, then looked at her husband. "Is it too late to change Hollis's name?"

"Mom!" Hollis protested again.

"What was Miss Blossom like?" Geena asked. "She was a legend around the neighborhood after she was in that one movie. What was it called? The black-and-white one?"

"Love, Gertie," Prentice offered.

"She loved doing that film," Ardith added. "She said she wished every movie could have been like that one."

"Mama was . . . she was more than beautiful," Abe said. "She was elegant and strong and a great artist and resourceful. I miss her."

"Me too," Ardith said.

Hollis expressed her agreement, along with the rest of the Black-woods. She sneaked a glance at Orlando, letting her gaze travel to each of the Babineauxs. They must have wondered how Blossom's family could continue to admire a woman who had hidden her child's father's identity from him until it was too late for them to know one another. But it was more complicated than that, and if today was any indication, perhaps the two families were ready to slowly start working through those complications, trying to make sense of the errors that had been made on both sides so they could forge a future together. August had been busy at the firm, working out the details of a Babineaux family trust that would be set up with some of the money Blossom had left Abe in her will. All of the adults had agreed it was a good start to what they hoped would be a fair situation for everyone involved.

"I still say y'all need to get out more," Eli said, looking around the table. "How about we have you over to one of our places next time?"

Taffy nodded enthusiastically. "We would love that."

"Now, we proud of our homes, but they ain't nearly as big as this one. Or yours," Eli said.

"We don't care about none of that," Grandpa Abe replied. "We just want to keep getting to know y'all better."

"Hear, hear," said Eli, holding up his glass of orange juice.

"Hear, hear," the Blackwoods and Babineauxs repeated, all raising their glasses, too.

There would be many more meals to be had between the two families, and not all of them would be as agreeable and easy as this one. But they weren't perfect—they were family. And every person at the table knew the significance of that bond.

Author's Note

My love of entertainment began from almost the moment I laid eyes on a television set. I was raised with an appreciation for a wide variety of TV programs, everything from soap operas (we were a *Young and the Restless* household) to sitcoms (*227*, *The Golden Girls*, and *Amen* were family favorites) to reruns of old shows that had been on when my parents were growing up, like *The Flintstones* and *The Brady Bunch*. As soon as Saturday morning cartoons were done, I'd switch over to the culinary shows on PBS, watching Jacques Pepin and the like teach home cooks how to flex their skills in the kitchen. When MTV's *The Real World* began its long run in the early '90s, I was just entering my adolescent years and became instantly hooked, sparking a lifelong infatuation with reality television. As much as I loved reading, I equally relished the opportunity to see stories and talent come to life onscreen.

Nick at Nite debuted when I was a child, and I became obsessed with programs from the 1950s and 1960s, like *The Patty Duke Show*, *Leave It to Beaver*, and *The Donna Reed Show*. By the time I was a teenager, I was sure I knew all of the groundbreaking and popular shows from the past—until I discovered *Julia*.

From 1968 to 1971, Diahann Carroll starred as the titular character of the NBC sitcom, which was the first TV show to feature a Black woman playing a character with a professional career, and the first to star a Black actress since *Beulah* aired in the early 1950s. This was before the advent of streaming television, so while I wasn't able to watch it right away, I eventually caught several episodes during a special airing on Nick at Nite.

Diahann Carroll was a beloved actor who'd costarred in *Paris Blues* with Sidney Poitier and had supporting roles in the celebrated films *Carmen Jones* and *Porgy and Bess*, as well as other film, theater, and modeling work. She would later be nominated for an Academy Award for her starring turn in 1974's *Claudine* (my personal favorite of her filmography) and also play the iconic role of Dominique Deveraux in the original *Dynasty*. So I couldn't stop wondering: Why was *Julia* not considered essential viewing on Nick at Nite, same as the other shows of the time that were in heavy rotation during my childhood?

Years later, I was hired as a copy editor at *Backstage*, a trade publication for the entertainment industry; for nearly a decade, I edited every article featured in the weekly issues, reading hundreds of interviews with actors. I noticed Black actors often brought up the same entertainers from decades past who'd inspired them: Ms. Carroll, Hattie McDaniel, Dorothy Dandridge, Lena Horne, Cicely Tyson, Sidney Poitier, Ruby Dee, and Ossie Davis, among others. I always nodded in agreement, impressed by these pioneers' ability to carve out successful careers when substantial roles for Black actors were rare, not to mention often stereotypical. Still, I was left thinking they all deserved more recognition than they'd received, even when they were considered to be in their prime.

The idea of a Black family with a Hollywood history stretching back to the early twentieth century began to percolate until, finally, I settled on the intersecting stories of the Blackwoods. Blossom Blackwood, who came of age in the 1940s and was inspired by her own mother's stint in vaudeville and Old Hollywood, is not based on any specific actress. Instead, she is my rendering of dozens of talented Black actors whose careers, though often brief, were hard-won and paved the way for the entertainers who came after them.

While *The Blackwoods* is fiction, remaining as historically accurate as possible was vital to the creation of this novel. *Bright Boulevards, Bold Dreams: The Story of Black Hollywood* by Donald Bogle is an engaging nonfiction book that was tremendously helpful during my research, providing a detailed history of the origins of Black Hollywood, dating all the way back to Madame Sul-Te-Wan, who emerged as a film actress in the 1910s. The book is also a love letter to Los Angeles, bringing to life the vibrant world of Central Avenue (the "Harlem of the West Coast") and its significance to the city's Black community throughout the early decades of the twentieth century.

Jefferson High School, where Blossom and Michael earn their diplomas, is the fourth oldest high school in the Los Angeles Unified School District, and it boasts an impressive list of Black alumni, from award-winning dancers Alvin Ailey and Carmen de Lavallade to Nobel Peace Prize winner Ralph Bunche and Grammy winner Barry White. The school was known for its strong music program, in large part due to Samuel Browne, who, as mentioned in this book, was the first Black educator to be hired alongside the all-white faculty in the 1930s, when the student body was predominantly Black.

Influential Black newspaper the *California Eagle*, where Blossom finds the information for the dance company audition, was founded as the *Owl* in 1879 by John James Neimore and renamed by Charlotta Spears Bass when she took over leadership of the publication in 1912 upon Neimore's death. Based in Los Angeles, the paper was heavily focused on activism, fighting against racism in Hollywood and the military, and condemning police brutality and discrimination in the workplace. The modern dance company Blossom belongs to is fictional, but it was loosely inspired by white choreographer Lester Horton, whose eponymous company was staunchly committed to racial integration in the 1940s and 1950s.

Trouble in Mind, the Alice Childress play Archie shares with Blossom, was supposed to be the first production by a Black woman playwright to open on Broadway. It debuted at the American Airlines Theatre in 2021, more than sixty years after Childress refused to water down the script. The limited run on Broadway was staged by the Roundabout Theatre Company, whose performance included Childress's original ending. In 2022, the show was nominated for four Tony Awards, including best revival of a play.

The television interview Blossom, Flossie, and Abe watch in 1965 was created from real quotes taken from interviews with former police chief Bill Parker, who ran the LAPD from 1950 until his death in 1966. Throughout his tenure, he was known for refusing to hire Black police officers, ignoring several dozen documented instances of racial violence spurred by white supremacy, and encouraging his police officers to violently enforce racial segregation in Los Angeles. He was also a close collaborator with the creator of radio-turned-television-show *Dragnet*, playing a strong role in the development and production of the long-running police drama.

Some of my most enjoyable research was reading memoirs of Black Hollywood actors, including Diahann Carroll's *The Legs Are the Last to Go* and *Just as I Am* by Cicely Tyson. I grew up admiring both of their careers, and it was a real gift to read about the struggles and successes that enabled them to become household names in the Black community and, eventually, worldwide.

Like these trailblazers, Blossom Blackwood faced her own share of struggles—sacrifices and hard decisions that allowed her to create and provide for a family on her own terms. Which in turn allowed her great-granddaughters, Ardith and Hollis, to live as young Black women with agency—young women who can make mistakes, both publicly and privately, while still maintaining control over their narratives.

It was an immense joy to write *The Blackwoods*. I don't know if I'll ever be able to summarize all the ways in which I am moved by the power of visual storytelling, but I believe this book is a start. It is my ode to Black Hollywood, and I am honored to share it with you.

—Brandy Colbert

Acknowledgments

The Blackwoods was such an interesting, challenging, and gratifying project for me, and I'm grateful to all the people who have helped turn my dream of writing about a Hollywood family into a book I'm so proud of.

Tina Dubois, thank you for encouraging me to write this story after I first emailed you the vague pitch for it years ago, and for reading every single draft once I was working on it in earnest. Your friendship and belief in me throughout my career has been a gift I will forever treasure. Thank you for everything you've done for me.

Alexandra Machinist, I'm thankful for your expertise and for your excitement about this book. I'm so happy we are working together, and I'm looking forward to everything that lies ahead.

Jordan Brown! Editor extraordinaire, thank you for understanding my vision for the Blackwood family, for caring about them as much as I do, and for helping me get closer with each draft to the story I was trying to tell. There's no doubt in my mind that I've grown as a writer after working on this book, and I'm incredibly grateful for your thoughtful, thorough edits.

I'm indebted to the hardworking team at HarperCollins and Balzer + Bray for your dedication, talent, and enthusiasm: Alessandra Balzer, Donna Bray, Suzanne Murphy, Mark Rifkin, Shona McCarthy, Ana Deboo, Lisa Lester Kelly, Corina Lupp, Alison Donalty, Shannon Cox,

Anna Bernard, Audrey Diestelkamp, Patty Rosati, and Christian Vega. Many thanks also to Poppy Magda for a gorgeous cover that so perfectly captures the essence of my characters.

Thank you to my friend Nina LaCour for reading an earlier version of this book and providing thoughtful, encouraging feedback. I'm also grateful to my friend Margaret Ruling for being an excellent coworker for so many years and for your patient, detailed answers to my questions about acting.

Finally, I'm grateful to my mother and father. I am lucky to have grown up in a home that respected creativity in all forms, where television and film were treated with the same seriousness as books, and in which Black artists, from actors and dancers to writers and musicians, were happily, constantly celebrated.